"Due has become a modern-day O
who stands tall among her horror
King."

"Tananarive Due has one of the more interesting voices in contemporary American fiction."

— *The Washington Post*

More praise for *BLOOD COLONY*

"Beware of spooky plot twists that will have your heart racing as you eagerly turn the page."

— *Essence*

"Due expertly mixes genres and intertwines sociopolitical issues. . . . Like the late, great Octavia Butler, she fearlessly tackles contemporary issues."

— *Baltimore Sun*

"*Blood Colony* will steal your breath on every impossible-to-put-down page. Due is masterful in crafting this thrill-ride of a tale that was truly worth the wait!"

— *New York Times* bestselling author L.A. Banks

"An elegant, scary, richly exciting tale—all that we've come to expect from Tananarive Due."

— *New York Times* bestselling author Greg Bear

This title is also available as an eBook

"I enjoy reading the kind of novel that seduces me right into it and makes me forget about work or sleep. *My Soul to Keep* does that beautifully."

—Octavia Butler

THEN, IN THE CAPTIVATING, AWARD-WINNING SEQUEL, DUE'S UNSTOPPABLE HEROINE BECAME THE UNWITTING TOUCHSTONE IN A SUPERNATURAL BATTLE TO DECIDE THE FATE OF HUMANITY. . . .

THE LIVING BLOOD

Winner of the American Book Award, 2002

***Publishers Weekly* Best Novel of the Year, 2001**

***Los Angeles Times* and *Essence* bestseller**

"Stunning . . . an event of sustained power and energy. . . . This novel should set a standard for supernatural thrillers of the new millennium."

—*Publishers Weekly* (starred review)

"The pantheon of modern horror gods is a small and frighteningly talented group: Stephen King, Anne Rice, Peter Straub, Clive Barker, Dean Koontz—and Tananarive Due. If there is any justice, Due's exciting, powerful, ambitious, scary, and beautifully written supernatural thriller will be the first of a decades-long string of hits that will sell millions."

—Amazon.com

"Smart, soulful, crafty Tananarive Due deserves the attention of everyone interested in contemporary American fiction. In *The Living Blood*, this young writer opens up realms of experience that add to our storehouse of shared reality, and by doing so widens our common vision. She is one of the best and most significant novelists of her generation."

—Peter Straub

For Octavia Estelle Butler,
with love and gratitude

"All that you Touch, you Change."

(1947–2006)

Jesus said, "If you bring forth what is within you, what you bring forth will save you. If you do not bring forth what is within you, what you do not bring forth will destroy you."

—Coptic Gospels, *Gospel of Thomas*

Don't wanna' die for a while.
I think I'll fly for a while . . .

—Phoenix, "Gotta Fly"

Renewal requires that death
precede it so that the weary
may be replaced by the vigorous . . .
To thwart it is the first step
toward thwarting the continuation
of exactly that which we try to preserve,
which is, after all, the order
and system of our universe.

—Sherwin Nuland, *How We Die*

After three days of waiting, Stefan was told he could see his old friend. The wait had not been unexpected, but he was anxious. Stefan had delayed this visit for decades, and he cursed himself when he realized he might be too late. He might never see Lolek again. It was all he could do to restrain himself from running across the polished marble floors.

"You have five minutes," said a white-haired caretaker who met him in the regal hall. The man looked like a mouse, with a hunched posture and eyes and ears too big for his face. Most men were mice, of course, but few looked the part so convincingly.

"Is he awake?"

"Sometimes yes, sometimes no."

He had almost waited too long, then. Now, he had only chance on his side. *Or prayer, perhaps.* That thought made Stefan smile, but sadly. When it came to matters of life and death, he had learned that prayer was chance of the riskiest kind.

Wide marble stairs took him to the apartment, which was surprisingly drab and dark. The palatial halls below were appointed with timeless artwork. Daddi. Raphael. Michaelangelo. Stefan marveled at how changed Lolek's life was now. Lolek had always shied from riches. How had such a modest soul come to live in the bosom of opulence, waited on by an army?

One of the constant attendants sat in a wooden chair two strides from the bed where Lolek lay on a mound of pillows. The attendant's eyes were trained to the book in her lap; always the same one, no doubt. The portly woman hardly took notice of Stefan's entrance, offering neither greeting nor smile.

"I was told we would have time alone," Stefan said.

The woman's face, already severe, hardened. But instead of objecting, she stood and lay her leather-bound black book on her seat. "I must not leave the apartment," she whispered. "But I will move outside the door. You have been told five minutes?"

Stefan nodded. *Ridiculous.* "Yes. Five minutes."

The room was deathly silent except for the sound of the woman's flat soles across the floor and Lolek's heroic struggle to draw one breath, then another. His ventilation tube whistled, a piteous sound. Moving the attendant's well-worn book to the table at Lolek's bedside, Stefan pulled the chair to the edge of the bed.

Lolek might be in a coffin, if not for the tubes attached to his throat. His complexion was so pale that his skin looked powdered, his white bedclothes freshly pressed to match. Lolek's eyes were closed and still, the lids bluish. Stefan had not seen his friend—the poet, playwright and priest—since Lolek's hair had been a thick mat across his scalp, black as midnight. *It was curious how memories remained frozen in youth,* Stefan thought. He did not recognize Lolek in the old man he had become.

Lolek's eyes flinched.

"Lolek? Are you awake?" Stefan said softly. He doubted the faithful attendant would approve, but he rested his hand against Lolek's cool cheek. Only then did he realize how much he missed his friend, how far their paths had diverged since Stefan's innocent respite at the seminary. "It's Stefan. I've finally made good on my threat to visit you."

His voice had an immediate effect. How many years had it been since anyone had addressed Lolek by his playful nickname? Lolek's eyes fluttered, and he made a soft sound, turning his head toward Stefan from his pillow. With brilliant late-afternoon sunlight from the open bay windows bathing his chair, Stefan wondered if Lolek thought he was dreaming. Or did he imagine that the angel sent to usher him to St. Peter had taken a most improbable form?

"We'll go out with our kayaks again, my friend," Stefan said. "I've reserved our cabin. Maybe the old innkeeper is still there, and this time he won't be too drunk to stand."

Lolek smiled. Slowly, he raised a scolding, unsteady finger. It had been more than sixty years since they'd visited the Drweca River together, and the old drunken innkeeper who had cursed at them must be long dead. Still, Lolek's smile as he shared the memory felt like salvation.

"Not today, then. Another," Stefan said and squeezed his hand. Lolek squeezed back. His strength surprised Stefan. But then again, hadn't it always?

Lolek's blue eyes sparkled, a portal to the past. Practically unchanged. Stefan savored the moment—but like everything in life, it vanished right away.

Lolek's unblinking eyes went from jovial to silently disapproving. Stefan recognized the shadow across his friend's face; he had seen it many years ago, when he'd first confessed his discovery. His calling. On that day, their friendship had ended.

Lolek, dear confused soul, believed he could never abide any role in The Cleansing.

"I haven't much time, Lolek. Neither have you," Stefan said, his voice low. "You know what I have, and what I can do for you. The world needs you here with us. Let me give you a few more years, free of suffering. You might gain a decade. Then, when it is time, I'll come to you again with the same chance to live. You'll be immortal. I can do this as a friend, Lolek."

Lolek's gaze, this time, was heartbroken. His mouth fell open as he wheezed, struggling to speak. "So . . . afraid." His speech was nearly impossible to understand, except to a friend.

Stefan squeezed his hand. "Of course you are."

Lolek smiled again, shaking his head. "Not me . . . *you*," he said. "Do not . . . be afraid."

Lolek must have been fooled by Stefan's face, to speak to him like a child. Lolek and his misguided sense of propriety. He should be grateful for such a gift!

"You must think about it, at least—" Stefan begged.

Lolek raised his unsteady hand again. He waved it toward Stefan with weary, ritualistic precision. The sign of the cross. "May God . . . have mercy . . ." A mere wheezing. Lolek gasped the words, air stolen from his last breaths: ". . . on your soul."

God will never have my soul, my friend, Stefan thought. He leaned over the old man his friend had become and kissed his forehead. "I'm not far, at the Hotel Nova Domus. Please ring me there, no matter what the hour, and I will come to you."

Only Lolek's heaving chest and whistling tube answered. His eyes closed again.

Stefan sat in silence at Lolek's bedside, mourning already. The irreversibility of the moment felt devastating. A plan so long laid was shattering before his eyes, but it was worse than that, even: Lolek was a good man, and always had been. Stefan's sins might have been forgiven if Lolek had agreed to accept the Blood. How could any other man deserve an escape from death if dear, gentle Lolek did not?

Stefan heard the attendant's approach to signal that his time had ended. "Good night, Sister," Stefan told the nun, smiling politely despite his tears.

"Grieve not, young man. He goes to God. That brings me great comfort. *Ciao.*"

Stefan planned to leave Rome right away, but he could not make himself go to the airport. He lingered at his hotel for two more days, cloistered in his room while he prayed to be called back to his friend's bedside. From his window, he admired the timeless dome at St. Peter's Basilica. His summoning never came.

He was at the hotel bar when the word came on the television news.

Shutters were drawn across the window of the magnificent apartment he had visited two days before. The tolling bells of the Vatican signaled that the ailing pope had died.

GLOW

Knowledge is wonderful and truth serene
But man in their service bleeds.
—Bhartrihari,
    seventh-century Hindu poet

One

Gramma Bea was the first to rise in the Big House.

Each morning, Fana Wolde found her grandmother in the kitchen with Mahalia Jackson's soaring voice consoling her from the old CD player while Gramma Bea patted balls of dough between her palms, measuring drop biscuits. Gramma Bea cooked with care, hour after hour, as if the fate of the world depended on her getting the ingredients and temperature just right.

Beatrice Jacobs was eighty-four, but she looked youthful in the black silk kimono she sometimes wore all day, when she didn't have the energy to get dressed. By lunchtime, she would be sweating from the heat, but she never left her kitchen. When she wasn't cooking, she was sitting at the kitchen table, either dozing or reading her Bible. Sleeping and praying took up the time left after cooking. She spent more time doing all three since her heart attack.

Like most people, Gramma Bea wore her thoughts like clothing, so Fana didn't have to peek inside her grandmother's head to understand her. Fana could see it plainly: Gramma Bea stored her grief in her baking breads and stewing pots. Cooking was her meditation.

Fana's grandfather had died five years ago, when his car had overturned in a ditch in the woods a half-mile from his kitchen table, during a rainstorm. The accident had happened at three-thirty in the afternoon, snapping Fana out of meditation. Fana, the first to know he was dead, had shared her grandfather's last, startled gasp.

Grandpa Gaines had been dead before anyone had been able to bring blood to him, where a drop might have saved him—or Dad might have been able to perform the Ceremony at the instant his heart had stopped, in the ancient way. It was so unfair: Gramma Bea had lost her first husband to a car accident, too. *And to lose someone here must feel worse,* Fana thought. No one died here. Fana knew why Gramma Bea always kept her grandfather's chair at the breakfast table empty, as if she expected him to come downstairs to eat, too. His absence was inconceivable.

"Don't just stand there, baby," Gramma Bea said. "Start squeezing the juice."

The kitchen smelled like oranges in the mornings because Gramma Bea was from Florida and insisted on squeezing her orange juice fresh. The oranges were already chopped and waiting, so Fana only had to pick up her dripping fruit, hold half an orange in her palm, and scrape off the pulp in the white plastic juicer with the methodical turns of her wrist Gramma Bea had taught her to perfection; one of the few things Fana believed she did well.

Mom had bought a mechanical juicer years ago, but Gramma Bea wasn't interested in technology except to listen to Mahalia and the Mississippi Mass Choir and the other gospel she filled her silences with. Gramma Bea thought machines were a distraction, and the music brought her closer to God. And closer to Grandpa Gaines, of course.

Gramma Bea thought about dying for a long while every day, working her way up to the idea. Sometimes, she didn't mind. Day by day, she minded less. She had begun to think of it as an appointment she had to keep, one she'd put off long enough. Fana wondered what else her grandmother would do with her time if she didn't have to think about dying.

But she doesn't have to die, Fana reminded herself. *She knows she has a choice.*

"You've got some nice little hips now," Gramma Bea said, dropping her dough into neat rows on the cookie sheet. "Nice legs, too. *My* legs." Gramma Bea's kimono was cut high, the way a younger woman would wear it, to show off her legs. Her calves were veined blue, but her smooth shins had resisted wrinkles. "You should wear a dress when you go driving tomorrow."

Fana felt alien enough outside without Gramma Bea's criticisms! Mom and Aunt Alex never wore anything except T-shirts and jeans either. Sometimes it was hard for Fana to believe that Mom and Gramma Bea were the same blood: Mom never had casual conversations with her about going outside, especially not about clothes. Mom only filled Fana's head with warnings.

"Why do I need a dress?" Fana said. "It's just a driving lesson."

"And lunch," Gramma Bea said. "At a nice restaurant."

"Pass. I'll pack some food from home."

Gramma Bea *tsssked,* a click against her teeth. "Go to a restaurant, Fana. Sit with the people for a while. It'll be good for you."

Fana hated restaurants. They always smelled like meat, and the tension was thick behind servers' smiles and the kitchens' closed doors. Restaurants never felt at peace.

"Don't you want to feel more comfortable around people, Pumpkin?" Gramma Bea said.

Fana felt stung. Now Gramma Bea sounded like Mom. "What do you mean?"

"I knew a young man from Midway, Florida, ... a trumpet player," Gramma Bea said, speaking in a story, as she often did, never going forward until she remembered all the details. She wanted to make sure her life's adventures would be remembered, even in passing. "He swore up and down he loved me, but I came to find out he didn't invite me to his sister's wedding. He said he was worried I wouldn't know which fork to use and what-not. So seditty! And I told him, 'Billy Taylor, what kind of love is that?'"

Fana waited. Sooner or later, Gramma Bea always remembered her point again. Gramma Bea went on: "Baby, liking from a distance isn't the same as liking up close. You can't like people if you won't let them close to you."

Fana felt her teeth grind. How many times did she have to tell Gramma Bea that crowds gave her headaches? Her family tried to understand, but they couldn't. Not really. And what good would it do to go out and meet people? She would only lie to them, too.

I care about people in the way that matters, Fana thought. *I heal them.*

"I have friends," Fana said instead. When she wasn't reading or meditating, Fana was posting on ShoutOut, where she had hundreds of friends around the world who knew her as Aliyah Martin, an American student and Phoenix music fan living in Tokyo.

But Gramma Bea was wrong if she thought she spent her days role-playing and gossiping.

Fana never used her webcam, and only three people outside the colony knew her real name. One person alone knew who she *really* was, and Fana hadn't seen her best friend in three years. She and Caitlin saved their real communications for an encrypted site, at least once a week. They deleted and scrubbed each other's messages immediately.

Fana hadn't gotten any messages from Caitlin in two weeks. Something was wrong.

Anxiety nested in Fana's stomach, and she knew that the chewing sensation would follow her until she tried to go to sleep, just like last night. She dreamed in nightmares, and always about Caitlin. Was Caitlin dead, like Maritza? *She can't be,* Fana thought. *I would have felt her die.*

Was Caitlin on the run, then? She had to be. *But where?*

"Typing on a screen isn't the same as talking face-to-face," Gramma Bea said, prying Fana's worries wide open. "Life is something you touch. Typing is easy. Touching is hard."

Gramma Bea was right: Fana needed to see Caitlin in person. But Caitlin couldn't come here, the one place she might be safest. One of the Brothers would know Caitlin's thoughts as soon as she arrived, and Fana couldn't count on masking her. *If I were a normal person, I could just drive out of here and go find Caitlin myself.*

It was the worst quandary of Fana's life, and not talking about it consumed her. Was it time to tell her family the truth?

Fana almost told Gramma Bea everything, right there in the kitchen on Friday morning.

". . . that dress I got you for Easter is casual enough to wear as a tea dress," Gramma Bea was saying, and Fana enjoyed remembering how much her grandmother had loved buying her clothes, even if she'd never worn them. Gramma Bea hadn't been on a shopping trip in a year, and her catalogues were piling up in the coat closet. "You're such a pretty girl, Fana. Why won't you let anyone see you? It's like you want to bury yourself in the ground and disappear."

Did Gramma Bea know? Fana had started trancing again, too.

Sometimes when Fana meditated, she let herself get lost, hiding from herself the way she'd first learned when she was three and the world had gone badly wrong, when she'd stayed lost for years. Life was hard again, and Fana wanted to step out of it.

Fana felt her grandmother's fingers beneath her chin, and the kitchen came into sharp focus: rows of cookbooks, watermelon knickknacks and a polished floor. *Did I trance that fast?*

Gramma Bea looked her in the eye, knowing. "Try to get used to things on this side, too. Not just the universe in your head, Pumpkin," she said patiently. "Start with this."

Gramma Bea held up a tube of lipstick the color of ripe mango pulp.

"It'll do wonders for your smile," she said. "You just put some on and stare at yourself in the mirror. It'll make you feel good. Sit in your skin a while, child. Now, pucker."

Fana pouted her lips, and her grandmother painstakingly guided the tube over them. Fana smelled perspiration, talcum powder and sweet, familiar Giorgio on her skin. Fana would know her grandmother's scent with her eyes closed.

"Look at that!" Gramma Bea said, glowing as if she and Fana shared a face. She held up the shiny aluminum toaster for Fana to see her reflection: blurred brown features and a shimmer of orange-yellow light. "A little color works miracles. See how it brings out your lips? I still feel naked if I go outside without my lipstick, and nobody's noticed my face for years. But, once?"

She laughed, her eyes twinkling with memories both joyful and sad. Gramma Bea rarely saw how beautiful she was; she only noticed what had changed since she was seventeen, too.

"Don't worry, Gramma Bea," Fana said. "Nobody's noticing me either. Ever."

Everyone else who lived at the colony was related to her by blood or marriage, or was just a kid or old enough to be her ancestor. Not to mention that she was also a freak.

"Somebody will notice you when you're driving," Gramma Bea said, certain.

"Like who?"

"You never know who, Pumpkin," she said. "That's the fun part—finding out. Twice in one lifetime I was blessed with a good man. *Twice.* True love is an experience everyone should have, but you can't find anyone when you're hiding."

Gramma Bea was from a generation when girls got married right out of high school, Fana remembered. They couldn't be more different in that way. Fana had known since she was three that she would always be alone.

"Men have the curse of their eyes, Pumpkin," Gramma Bea said. "Their eyes catch onto things first. It never seems right or fair, but it's in their makeup. Until a man sees you with his eyes, it's like he can't see you at all. And if a man's eyes take hold of his heart? He'll move a mountain for you."

"That just sounds shallow," Fana said. "Why would I want anyone like that?"

Gramma Bea shrugged. "We didn't make this world. The Lord did. We just visit here." Fana sighed and picked up the toaster again, adjusting its angles in the light from the window to try to see her face through a stranger's eyes.

"Do you see what I see now?" Gramma Bea said.

Fana nodded, forcing a smile.

The lipstick's color was a promising speck, but Fana still couldn't see her face at all.

Two

Johnny Jamal Wright thought he must be dreaming.

He was too confused by the sight of Ryan LaCroix at his dorm room door to hear what he was saying. Ryan's orange-brown hair was cropped short, marine style, and his two hundred pounds filled the doorway. At the Cotton Bowl, Ryan LaCroix's quarterback sneak at the end of the fourth quarter had made him a folk hero and gotten him on *Saturday Night Live.*

Now he was clasping Johnny's hand in a grip that was too hard.

"What?" Johnny said.

"I said . . . I need some Glow," Ryan said, his grip a bit tighter. When Johnny tried to tug his hand away, Ryan held on. His eyes were blue ice. "Where do I get it, Wright?"

"Uh . . . I don't know," Johnny said. Glow! If Ryan LaCroix had roused him from bed to get drugs, he was a year too late. Caitlin was gone.

Suddenly, the grip wasn't a handshake anymore—Ryan was pinching off Johnny's circulation. Johnny almost told Ryan he was hurting his hand until he realized Ryan wanted to.

Ryan sounded like he was whining. "Who's your supplier? Come on! What's her name?"

"Wh-what the hell, Ryan?" Johnny said. Ryan shoved, and Johnny took two stumbling steps backward, into the room. Ryan kicked the door closed behind him, not letting Johnny's hand go.

One glance at his roommate's bed and Johnny remembered Zach's late-night gig. As usual, Zach hadn't come home. Johnny was alone with a crazed Ryan LaCroix.

And Ryan was about to break his hand.

"You said she's got a pipeline," Ryan said. "She can get Glow any time she wants."

Had he said something that stupid last year? Johnny's elevated pulse made him dizzy. Maybe he'd been trying to pump up his connection to impress a football player and his friends. There had been girls involved. And alcohol. The memory tried to surface, but all Johnny remembered was how much he'd ached to lose his virginity. Johnny had made a lot of unlikely friends freshman year when word had gotten around that he'd known how to find the underground drug called Glow. Football players. Celebrities' kids. Professors, even. Good days.

But the best part had been Caitlin. Those days were gone.

"I was kegged when I said that!" Johnny said. He hoped the lie wasn't plain on his face. "I knew a girl who got lucky and snagged some Glow. That's it."

Caitlin would asphyxiate him for what he had said already. *Never talk about me.* Her number one rule. And he'd given out too much information: Ryan knew she was a girl who'd dropped out of Berkeley in the past year. Someone could find her if Ryan opened his mouth.

Caitlin had hooked Johnny up with Glow only once, and she'd agreed only because he had exaggerated Ryan's better qualities and the depth of their friendship. Johnny had never told her it had only been for Ryan's herpes.

And this wasn't Ryan. The guy standing over him might as well be a desperate junkie.

Suddenly, Johnny saw a hospital in his future.

Johnny hoped the feeling was chickenshit nerves, not the psychic bone Mom was always talking about—but the notion felt real. Johnny had gotten through middle school and four years at Leon County High without a fight. Ryan LaCroix was a bad choice for his first beatdown.

"Just give me her name, Johnny," Ryan said. Now he was almost begging.

"She's gone," Johnny said, his mouth dry. He tried not to sound as scared as he was. "Whatever you've got this time, they'll give you meds at the clinic."

"I don't want it in my medical report," Ryan said. "Coaches see it. Selective Service. My dad and mom, too. I don't want that shit in my blood. I want my test clean, like last time."

Ryan flipped Johnny's wrist into a painful wrist-lock. Johnny's shoulder twisted, his face shoved against his pinewood closet door. "Stop being a dick," Ryan said. "Give me her name."

Was this why Caitlin had left Berkeley? Caitlin had said Johnny was too childish to understand the stakes, and maybe she'd been right. *Especially after what happened to Maritza.*

Johnny felt his stomach constrict into a cold, hard ball of fear. But his outrage won out.

"Get the fuck out of here," Johnny said.

Johnny felt his head snap backward as Ryan yanked a handful of his shoulder-length dreadlocks and slammed his face into the closet door. Hard. Johnny had enough reflexes to turn his head so his nose wouldn't break, but his cheekbone met the door with enough force to hurt. Johnny felt the inside of his lip tear against a tooth.

Blood. He could taste it in his mouth. Johnny was too shocked to move. No one had hurt him before. He had never considered what to do if someone did.

Ryan pulled Johnny's head again, winding up for another throw.

The sound of the room door opening made them both jump. Ryan's claw loosened enough for Johnny to shake himself free and duck to the other side of the room.

Johnny's roommate Zach walked in, bleary-eyed, pushing dyed black hair out of his face.

Until that instant, Johnny had never truly appreciated Zach. They were a random housing assignment practical joke: Johnny was a near-virgin premed who had almost gone to a seminary before deciding to be a doctor. Zach was the lead singer of a crunk-rap band who thought sobriety was a mortal sin and whose major area of study was soulless sex. Zach was a gentle weedhead, but he was big. His chest was a tapestry of tattoos.

Johnny had never been so happy to have a roommate.

"Fresno," Zach said, looking Ryan in the eye.

"What?" Johnny said.

"I heard about Glow in Fresno," Zach told Ryan. "From a chat-room."

All of them were pretending Johnny's lip wasn't bleeding, that things hadn't just gone too far. Johnny was so relieved to avoid a beating that he was afraid he might piss in his briefs. The army wanted *him* to pick up a rifle and fight after college?

He'd better pray he got into a good med school.

"OK," Ryan said. "Give me the site."

Zach burrowed through the clutter on his nightstand, looking for a pen. "Watch what you put in your veins," Zach said. "It's called Blast, Cure or Glow. Whatever you call it, most of the stuff out there is fake, and people get fried shooting up bad shit. There's test strips for sale on the website. The government's putting out fake shit, try-ing to make it look dangerous. If somebody got you the real deal, you were one of the few. Good luck in Fresno."

Ryan snatched the paper from Zach's hands and headed for the door. Zach gave Ryan the finger on his way to the door. "You can't throw deep for shit, LaCroix," Zach mumbled.

The door slammed behind Ryan, and it was a typical day again. Except for the blood.

"You all right, man?" Zach said.

Johnny wasn't all right, and he had a problem far worse than a split lip or bruised feelings.

He would have to tell Caitlin.

How R U? Call me ASAP

Johnny typed the text message to MIDNYTE on his slender sil-ver Wyre phone, which he kept strapped to his forearm. His phone was the pride and joy of his life, the birthday present that brought him in step with the real world: big screen, holographic keyboard option, great sound for movies, GamePort compatible, and plenty of memory for his lab reports and Af-Am lit papers.

Johnny was walking toward the science building for his 10 a.m. quiz, but his mind wasn't on RNA molecules and protein synthesis in sophomore bio. Only Caitlin. Her number only led to a voice mailbox that was always full, so he had to wait for her to text him back. Or, even better, maybe she would call him.

"Yeah, sorry your girlfriend died," Johnny rehearsed aloud as he sidestepped a busty, red-faced faculty member jogging with her black Lab. "Now I feel like a jerk for trying to talk you out of moving in with Maritza. So . . . how ya' been?"

God, he'd been so pathetic.

Johnny had known Caitlin O'Neal since he was twelve, when his father had taken him to the retreat in the woods that had been so secretive he still wasn't sure whether it had been in Oregon or Washington. They had flown to the Portland airport, but they hadn't been able to see a thing outside the blackened windows in the backseat of the Town Car that had met them. It had seemed like an adventure out of a James Bond movie, even though Dad had seemed more nervous than excited.

It had been a scientific research facility. That was all Dad had ever said. He'd heard about it from his scientist friend, the one people called Dr. Voodoo. A government thing, Johnny had figured. But the place had seemed more like a commune; just a few families living in the woods.

While Dad had been in meetings with scientists, Johnny had met Caitlin and Casey O'Neal playing dodgeball outside. The O'Neal girls were two years older, blonde-haired and blue-eyed identical twins. But the twins were nothing alike.

Caitlin had been adventurous, sneaking cigarettes in the woods and grabbing his hand to give him the forbidden tour. She had taken him to the long cedar building called the Council Hall, where she'd said, the children were never invited. She'd dared him to peek into the window, and he had seen his father sitting side by side with Caitlin's at a long table, talking to two black men who'd been wearing only white. The strangers' stern eyes had found them immediately, so they'd run away.

But Johnny had never forgotten that gathering. Those men in white had looked like royalty.

Johnny was sure Glow had something to do with that commune. Johnny's father had never been invited back, as far as he knew, but Johnny had kept in touch with some of the kids he'd met there. Caitlin had pretty much dropped contact with him since Maritza died, but Casey still posted letters to him on ShoutOut every couple of weeks. And Fana wrote too, now and then.

He had missed a message from Fana, Johnny realized as he scrolled on his phone. ALIYATOKYO had posted a note two days ago, and he'd overlooked it. Fana's visual sig was a photo from the 1800s, Harriet Tubman or someone. Intense kid.

> I'm worried about C. Have you heard from her this week? Her heart is traversing territories she doesn't have maps for. -F.

Much shorter than usual for Fana. She was seventeen by now, but Johnny always pictured Fana as the amazingly shy ten-year-old girl who barely met anyone's eyes, his *Lil' Sis*. Fana was the most sheltered person Johnny had ever known. Casey and Caitlin lived in New York, but he didn't think Fana had been anywhere else.

With one eye on the bicyclists navigating toward him on the sidewalk, Johnny wrote back:

> Trying 2 find her too. AWOL for 3 weeks. Call me and I'll tell u about my weird day.

But he knew Fana wouldn't call. Fana's family must have 'Net phones, at least, but she never used one, just like she never used video feeds. She never talked about her home life either; her family *definitely* had something to do with the government. Dad refused to say anything about that visit seven years ago, except to grunt when Johnny mentioned it. For the first time in his life, Dad had managed to keep a secret.

Caitlin had been out of touch with Fana, her best friend? Johnny hoped Caitlin wasn't in trouble. He scrolled the rest of his ShoutOut posts to make sure a note from Caitlin hadn't been buried, too. Nothing. Damn. Johnny's heart pounded, flushing warm blood into his palms.

He recognized his symptoms: He was still stuck on Caitlin.

Caitlin had enrolled in Berkeley first, so he'd decided he would go there, too, breaking a three-generation chain of Wright men who attended Florida A&M. Johnny still hadn't heard the end of *that*. But he'd thought it would be worth it to be near Caitlin, finally.

It's just sex, Johnny. Caitlin had warned him right from the beginning. He had still been a virgin his freshman year, and she'd said she felt sorry for him living like a monk in Tallahassee. *Welcome to the world,* she'd said, straddling him for the first time, and he'd seen stars. He'd been ecstatic to explore the novelty of a girl's body and touch, but it hadn't just been that. He'd fallen for her, hard. Sweaty palms. Dancing heartbeat. Maybe it was because he'd struggled so hard with the conflict between what his church taught and what his body wanted: He hadn't realized it would be so hard to wait. But why *couldn't* he marry Caitlin one day? He'd stayed away from other girls just in case his devotion would matter to her.

But it hadn't. Maritza had mattered to Caitlin, and now Maritza was dead. A month ago, someone had kidnaped her from a South Beach clinic and killed her. Probably because of Glow.

Johnny shivered. He had never known anyone who'd died a violent death, and memories of Maritza gave him a chill. He had cried with Caitlin when she'd first called, hysterical, wailing her lover's name. He had been waiting to be of use to her since he was twelve. But now that terrible voice wormed into his head: *Hey, Wright, maybe now you'll have your chance.*

He could forget it. Caitlin would only be pissed when she heard about Ryan's visit. Johnny had said too much about Glow. He had said too much about her.

Johnny had always thought Caitlin was just paranoid. But what if he was wrong?

Omari was waiting for Johnny on the steps of his dormitory, leaning against his backpack in a sliver of shade. Cornrows wound around his glistening scalp in a succession of U's, the style worn by the rap-per Bizkitz. Students glanced curiously at Omari as they climbed the stairs, since he was barely five-foot-two and looked like he belonged on a playground instead of a college campus. No one would guess he was fifteen.

He was two hours early. And he was sweating.

"Hey, little dude, how long you been out in this sun?" Johnny said, trotting up to him. The sun had a clear sky in its favor, so it must have been eighty degrees.

"Thirty minutes. Maybe forty," Omari said. With a lanky arm, he grabbed the iron bannister to pull himself to his feet. Omari needed extra support, the way an old man might.

Johnny gave him a one-armed hug. "Why didn't you call me?"

Omari shrugged. "I didn't wanna' pull you out of class. Ain't nothin, man."

The first time Johnny took Omari to McDonald's on their assigned Saturday after he'd joined Big Brothers/Big Sisters in Oakland, Omari had kept his face mean. Making conversation had been like mining for diamonds. "So, want some ketchup?" *"I'm just doing this for my mama, so don't try to be my friend."* "So, how do you like school?" *"I'm just doing this for my mama, so don't try to be my friend."*

That was six months ago. Everything had changed when Omari had learned of their mutual interest.

As soon as Johnny had said he was premed, Omari bombarded him with smart questions: *"Hey, man, what do you think about gene therapy? And how come all this money gets spent on cystic fibrosis research, but way more people have sickle cell? What's up with THAT?"* Omari knew more about sickle-cell anemia than Johnny did. He had to.

"How'd you get here so early? You've got school, too," Johnny said.

Omari shrugged, dismissive. Omari was so bright that he was probably gifted, but his grades were awful. He missed too many classes with sick days, and he was allergic to homework. "When I'm sixteen, Mama say I can take the GED."

"You still have to learn how to study. To go to college, you have to know how to work."

Anger broiled Omari's face suddenly. "You think it ain't work gettin' my Uncle Lem to drive me twenty miles outta his way when he can't hardly pay for gas?" Omari said. "I didn't bring my ass here to get preached at. And what the hell makes you think I'm goin' to *college*?" He spat the last word.

That didn't sound like Omari at all. Omari wanted to be a doctor, and the only reason he visited the campus was to make his dream feel real. Had something happened at home? Omari's mother said there had been staff cuts at the hospital where she worked as a nurse. Even with health insurance, Omari's medical bills didn't leave room for surprises. If his mother was out of work, they wouldn't be able to afford the chronic transfusion therapy that was the only thing replacing Omari's sickled blood.

"You want to see the lab?" Johnny said. "We're early, but we can still probably—"

Omari shook his head. "Nah. Let's just sit and chill. Ain't your room right here?"

Johnny hesitated. A month ago, he had toured Omari through the campus, only stopping briefly at his own room. Zach's lifestyle was too wild, and Johnny didn't want to take the chance that Omari would go home and tell his mother he was being exposed to sex and drugs. Johnny wanted to make a difference in a kid's life, not end up on the nightly news.

"Bad idea, little dude," Johnny said.

Anger melted from Omari's face, and suddenly he looked like a child. "I gotta' lie down." He was wincing, shifting his weight.

"Pain?" Johnny said.

Omari bit his lip and nodded, but he avoided Johnny's eyes.

"Bad enough for a doctor?" Johnny said.

Omari shook his head. "Nah. All this walking, that's all. This school's like a damn city, man. I just wanna rest." Johnny could tell Omari was used to reassuring people, trying not to be a bother. His forehead was wrinkled with private agony.

"OK," Johnny said, patting his pocket for his key card. "But I'm calling your mom."

In the lobby, Omari headed for the stairs, but Johnny motioned him around the corner to the elevator. Johnny hadn't remembered the elevator the last time Omari had been here, and the kid had climbed two flights of stairs without a word. Had Omari been in pain then, too?

With Omari's gingerly steps, the walk to room 314 took a long time, but Johnny knew better than to offer him an arm to lean on. Omari was a proud kid. At his door, Johnny motioned for Omari to wait. "Sorry. I've got to check it out first."

"Like I ain't seen weed before," Omari muttered. "I can smell it out here."

"I have rules, Omari. Just hold on."

Johnny knocked and didn't hear anything, so he swiped his key card and opened the door just wide enough to stick his head through. The room was smoky. Shit. Two-fifteen in the afternoon, and Zach and his girl were still in bed. Classic *Boondocks* episodes played from Zach's computer screen on his desk, and Zach lay spread-eagled in his boxers. with his bong propped on his bare chest.

"Hide the bud and put on some clothes," Johnny told them quietly. "Omari's here."

Behind him in the hall, Omari sniggered.

"Sure, man," Zach said. He slipped the bong between his bed and nightstand, sweeping stray leaves into his drawer with his palm.

"I gotta' go anyway. Rehearsal," the woman said, climbing from beneath the sheet wearing only a T-shirt and white panties. Once she was dressed, she breezed past Johnny into the hall, stopping short to snake her finger across the top of Omari's head. She traced the patterns in his scalp. "Ooh. The work of an artist," she said. "Welcome to college, kid."

Omari didn't smile. His eyes were vacant.

"If it's hard for you to get around, there are ways to deal with that," Johnny said as they went into the room. Johnny stopped short of using the word *wheelchair*. He had yet to practice medicine, but he knew that was a word nobody wanted to hear. Especially a kid.

Sitting on Johnny's bed, Omari didn't answer. Zach slung a towel over his shoulder and excused himself to hit the shower; only then did Omari sink back, until he lay across Johnny's mattress, his feet still on the floor. He hadn't wanted a stranger to see how bad he felt.

Omari hissed. He had once told Johnny the pain was always

there; it just got worse sometimes. Sickle-cell anemia meant that Omari's red blood cells weren't shaped right. His blood cells caused his body problems everywhere they went. His own blood made his life hell.

"Your mom will just tell me to take you to your doctor," Johnny said, dialing his cell.

"Lemme talk to Mama. We got a system. No doctor unless it's eight. I'm only at a six."

"Six what?"

"How bad is the pain, between one and ten? It's a six." Omari sounded impatient.

"It looks like more than a six to me."

"Then I guess you don't know what pain looks like."

That probably was true enough, Johnny thought. Caitlin had said something like that once, during an argument. *You're a mama's boy who's never lived in the real world a day in your life,* she'd accused. After joining Big Brothers, Johnny thought he had seen enough reality to make up for it. He had asked to mentor a kid with health problems; he didn't want to turn into one of those robotronic doctors who forgot the whole point. Already Johnny realized he wanted to be a pediatrician. Omari was teaching him that.

Johnny listened to Omari's end of the conversation as his mother quizzed him on the telephone. He understood her worry: Omari was especially vulnerable because he'd been getting monthly blood transfusions for three years. Omari's body might be getting overloaded with iron, his mother had confided, so she was always on the lookout for signs of organ damage.

"It's my legs. I told you already, dag," Omari complained to his mother. He suddenly handed the phone back to Johnny without a good-bye.

"Mr. Wright?" his mother said when Johnny got on, with the brand of formality Johnny recognized from his grandmother in Macon. "Omari says it's his joints, but you sure it's not his chest? No trouble breathing?"

"No, ma'am, not that I can see." Omari's face was still twisted with pain, but his breathing looked steady. Omari was absently flicking at the edge of the Jimi Hendrix poster hanging above him on the wall, the one from the Berkeley show almost forty-five years ago.

"You call me right back if he does, hear? Omari says he's at a six, but he knows good and damn well that when he has chest pain, he goes to the hospital. Understand? If he has a clog in his lungs and doesn't get enough oxygen, then we're looking at hypoxia." She was rushed, speaking in a low tone so she wouldn't be overheard. But she wasn't panicked. The mother of a child who suffered from chronic pain didn't have room for panic in her daily life.

"Yes, ma'am."

"Make sure he gets liquids. Water or Gatorade. It'll thin his blood and help his joints feel better. I'll call Lemuel and see if he can't come by and pick him up early."

The woman was impressive. "Omari's lucky to have a nurse for a mom," Johnny said.

She breathed into the phone, and he couldn't tell if she was amused or annoyed. "Luck ain't got nothin' to do with it. My boy needed me, so I went to school. You take good care of Omari, Mr. Wright. God bless you."

"Yes, ma'am. God bless you, too."

When Johnny hit End to hang up his phone, Omari was still playing with the poster without looking toward him. Johnny pulled up his desk chair and sat beside the bed. Telltale moisture dampened the bridge of Omari's nose, and seeing his tears made Johnny's eyes smart. What if he wasn't helping this kid at all? What if he was only showing Omari his limitations?

"It's just a bad day," Johnny said. "You can come back."

Omari's chin trembled slightly before he caught it. "What for? Mama don't have college money. It all goes to food, gas and blood. And with me like this? Ain't no way."

"When we don't see a way, God finds the way," Johnny said. "It's up to us to bust our asses to get what we want, but God does the rest. He makes the way out of no way."

Johnny's grandmother in Macon might have quoted the Twenty-third Psalm: *The Lord is my shepherd; I shall not want. He maketh me to lie down in green pastures: he leadeth me beside the still waters. His*

Jaddah Jamilah, his grandmother who lived in Jordan, would echo the sentiment with her favorite Muslim prayer: *I know that Allah is able to do anything, and that Allah knows all. O Allah I seek refuge in You from the evil in myself and every creature that You have given power over us. Verily my Lord is on the straight path.*

"You should be a damn preacher, man," Omari said in a small voice. "For real."

"I just don't want to see you give up, Omari. I know you can do it. I *know* you can."

"How?" Omari's bitter tone was foreign. "You gonna' make a miracle happen?"

Suddenly, Johnny saw God's plan woven throughout his day: the visit from Ryan LaCroix. His thoughts of Caitlin. Now, Omari. God's message came to Johnny with such clarity that he marveled at people who insisted they couldn't see them.

Glow.

After she'd left Berkeley, when her paranoia had kicked into high gear, Caitlin had made Johnny swear never to mention Glow to her again. But if Ryan LaCroix was right—if Caitlin's Glow had cleaned out his blood—everything was different. Could he convince Caitlin to give him Glow one more time, even if it was dangerous? *"You gonna' make a miracle happen?"*

"Maybe," Johnny said. His heart and head thundered in unison. "Yeah. Maybe I can."

THREE

I've got Kush . . . White Light . . . Glow."

Caitlin O'Neal kept her voice low, as if she'd been talking to herself, as she haunted the storefront of Left Bank Books at Pike Place Market. Her cheeks stung from the cold wind spraying from Elliott Bay's waters just beyond the tourist shops. Her elfin body was nearly hidden beneath the drab green of her oversized militia coat from a thrift shop.

Someone was watching her.

He was sitting in the window of the coffee shop across the street, reading an e-book at a table. He was a black man with white hair and a matching beard, but he might be one of them. Wearing a disguise. Or he could be a cop, which was almost as bad. Almost.

Caitlin remembered a summer sleepover party, when she'd played one of the sequels to the ancient horror movie *Candyman* and all of her Long Island friends had jumped and screamed every time black skin had shown up on the screen. Pathetic. And now she was just as bad. Would she have even noticed the man in the coffee shop if he hadn't been black?

But Caitlin was almost sure she had seen him before. He looked like a man she'd noticed at the student union at Seattle U, where she'd ended up because she'd been low on cash. She could always find a student with a problem and a cash advance on Daddy's credit card. Last week she'd sold Glow to a law student who had just been diagnosed with Parkinsons. Only five hundred bucks, but his grateful eyes still put a smile on her face. She should have charged more. The money was already gone.

Caitlin prayed she wasn't being followed. She needed to get out of town.

"I've got Glow."

A flock of men in suits walked past her, fresh from a meeting. The last man turned around to glance at her over his shoulder. She kept her face blank, as always. Just in case. Nowadays, Glow was worse than moving bricks of cocaine. Vince and Lana were doing *fifteen years* in Georgia, and a nurse was up for a felony trial in Vegas. Vegas! It was an insult to be arrested in a city as corrupt as Vegas, and it was a bad time for a Glow bust anywhere.

"Got weed?" a scrawny teenager said hopefully, appearing from around the corner. She assessed him in a glance: Five-three. Awkward, furtive manner. A lightweight Insect skateboard under his arm. Not even fifteen. *Yeah, right.*

"Not for kids. Get ghost."

The boy gave her a sour, childish pout and moved on. The last thing she needed was a bust for supposedly trying to sell drugs to a minor. If he was old enough, he could get a prescription and go to a dispensary like everyone else.

Shit, shit, shit. It was late, and it was too dangerous to be seen in Seattle, especially since the Whitfields had moved to New York. After she interviewed Father Arturo, maybe he could loan her enough to take a bus. Or rent a car, if her dummy credit card still worked. She had six vials, and Laurel was waiting in Vancouver. Patients were dying.

Father Arturo Bragga had a personal recommendation from the Whitfields, which went a long way, and he had also passed his six-month assessment period and background screens. One last face-to-face with a conductor, then the five regional conductors would vote. The ones who weren't in jail, anyway. It would be great to have reliable Railroad in Seattle again.

Caitlin had volunteered for the trip north, mostly to stop thinking about Maritza. The Railroad brought out the sane part of her ever since Maritza was murdered. The words still didn't fit right in her head, so she must still be in denial. At least the rest of her head was still working.

Driving to Seattle had taken more than a week. Now that her

car's engine had finally died, she was stuck. Flying with Glow was out of the question, of course, and buses and trains were almost as bad. At least her problems kept her head busy.

Caitlin had only spoken to Father Arturo on the phone twice, never for more than two minutes. During her call from Portland yesterday, when she'd been hurting so much that she'd barely been able to pull a sentence together, Father Arturo had interrupted her with a long *"Shhhhhhh."*

"So often we blame God for the work of the Other," he said.

Damn right, Caitlin thought. Caitlin had seen Evil the night she'd identified Maritza's butchered body at the morgue. Someone had stabbed Maritza fifty times.

Caitlin retrieved her denim duffel bag from the shadows beside the storefront and hunched her shoulders into the wind on First Avenue. She walked fast, just in case the guy in the coffee shop really was a tail. She had to lose him.

Is this how it started with you, Mari? Did you see someone who didn't belong?

At Pioneer Square, the city reverted to red brick and cobblestones. Caitlin vanished into an alleyway near the warren of underground buildings that lingered from the city's nineteenth-century subterranean past. The alley was deserted, a tomb behind the plugged rush-hour streets. The few cars parked here looked abandoned. She circled three times, keeping an eye out for her tail, and she thought he was gone. She hoped he was.

Caitlin never showed up for a meeting anywhere she hadn't cased first, but this alley had looked safer three hours ago, in daylight. Caitlin stopped in front of the unpainted metal door at the end of the row of brick buildings. NEW DAYS, read small, faded letters stenciled on the door in white. She looked around once more to make sure she was alone. She heard the muffled sound of a baby crying from upstairs, behind one of the closed, cracked windowpanes.

One second. Two. Three.

She didn't see anyone, so she tested the doorknob. Locked. From her back pocket, Caitlin fished out the key Father Arturo had mailed her. She slipped it in.

Not much light inside, only a bare forty-watt bulb doing its best at the far end of the hall. The dimly lighted hallway was lined with cast-off furniture, mildewed boxes and dirty plastic crates piled with canned food and children's toys cast from their homes. The hallway smelled mildewed.

"Father Arturo?" she said, whispering into the quiet.

No answer.

Caitlin wished Father Arturo had been able to get away from his parish and meet her during daylight. With only twenty bucks left in her pocket, all she wanted was a greasy cheeseburger and a bed at the shelter. After all, wasn't she homeless, too? *You can't call it home if you're afraid to go back there.*

Caitlin couldn't wait to get the hell out of Seattle, so close to Fana. Should she go down to Berkeley and see her friends on her way to Arizona? Johnny was trying to call her, and he kept leaving text messages, but she wasn't sure it was safe to talk to him. *I need some candy,* he'd written, improvising a code for Glow, and she wanted to strangle him. Why had she ever shown him so much? Were her instincts failing her?

Too many mistakes, and mistakes had cost Maritza her life. Maritza hadn't died randomly—someone had been trying to get *her.* If Johnny didn't watch out, he might be a target too.

In the shelter's kitchen, Caitlin found open food containers and double sinks filled with dirty dishes. The large fridge was disappointingly empty, except for rows of soda cans. Caitlin grabbed a Coke and opened it, swallowing in hungry gulps.

Good. Sugar and caffeine. Next best thing to a meal.

When Caitlin closed the refrigerator, she nearly walked into the black man from the coffee shop. He appeared like a hallucination, not even a foot from her. For a moment, all she saw was his white beard, nearly close enough to touch her.

Caitlin's brain froze. Then she recognized the man, despite his phony beard and white hair. His hair wasn't white. Couldn't be. He was one of them. Caitlin considered pretending to be happy to see him, until his knife was at her throat.

He clamped a heavy palm across her lips. She felt her heart

pounding against the blade. "*Quiet,*" he hissed into her ear. "Hide in the pantry. Now."

"Oh, G-God," Caitlin stammered through his palm. "I'm sorry—"

"I said *quiet,* you fool." He shoved her toward the pantry, and she almost flew off her feet.

"It's not my dad's fault. He doesn't know what I'm doing," Caitlin said in a shaky whisper she didn't recognize. "P-please don't do anything to hi—"

He slapped her, hard. Caitlin felt her bladder loosen as a realization swamped her: *Maritza was killed with a knife.* Caitlin sagged, losing control of her muscles. She had never felt a sensation like it. Only the man's support kept her upright, and she should be running from him as fast as she could, even if he was her best friend's father.

"You're in danger," Dawit Wolde said. "Do as I've said, or I'll kill you myself."

The rules for a police bust were easy: *Don't resist. Call the lawyers. Say nothing.* But this was different. Caitlin didn't have rules for being discovered by Fana's father.

Caitlin dropped her soda can and ran, holding her burning cheek with both hands. She knocked over a metal mixing bowl, making an explosive clatter against linoleum. Caitlin vanished inside the pantry, slamming the door. *You have to hide the Glow.* Caitlin fumbled with the flaps of her knapsack and dug inside the bag for the can of hairspray with a false bottom she used to hide the vials. Her hands shook.

Father Arturo's voice came from the hall. "Caitlin?"

Caitlin saw Father Arturo in her imagination from his photograph: long-faced, about thirty, a Mediterranean man with a thick Florentine accent. Large, kind eyes. She had to warn Father Arturo, but her body wouldn't budge. Her mind was stuck on three words: *He killed her.*

Three heavy footsteps. Father Arturo must be in the kitchen. Bottles on the shelves rattled behind her as she hid her stash behind cans in the dark pantry. She heard a sudden sound, like a harsh breath. Then, silence. Caitlin's heart thrashed.

"Who sent you?" Dawit's voice said.

Caitlin tried to think of a lie.

But he wasn't talking to her. A sudden, agonized man's scream came, an Apocalypse on the other side of the door.

"Answer, and you'll see a doctor," Dawit said. "Who sent you?"

Was Father Arturo dead? Caitlin couldn't hear anything over the din of her heartbeat.

"*Per favore,*" Father Arturo said. "I d-don't know what you mean. We have n-no money . . . We're a shelter for homeless w-women and children . . ." Father Arturo was alive, but he was coughing. He might be talking through his own blood.

"*Basta!*" Dawit said. "Begin again. The truth, this time. *Ora.*"

"I'm a p-priest!" By now, Father Arturo could only wheeze.

"Why the gun?" Dawit said. "*Dimi.*"

"*Sicurezza. P-protezione,*" Father Arturo said, hardly a whisper. "We have r-robbers."

Caitlin heard another scream, but this time it was hers. She couldn't see beyond her tears, but she felt herself come flying out of the pantry. "*Stop! You're hurting him!*"

Everything was blurry at first, but as she blinked the scene came into focus: Father Arturo lay helpless on the floor, and Fana's father was kneeling on top of him with his knee pinned to Father Arturo's chest. The priest was already impaled with a knife beneath his ribs, pushed to the hilt. Blood dribbled from the priest's lips. He groaned, writhing.

Caitlin shoved Dawit with all her strength, but not hard enough to push him away so Father Arturo could breathe. "He's a *priest*. That's Father Arturo!"

Suddenly, Dawit's elbow snapped out at Caitlin, jabbing into her stomach with enough power to topple her to the floor and steal her breath. Caitlin blinked with tears of pain. Even with the room robbed of all its oxygen, Caitlin clawed toward Dawit again.

"He had a gun, Caitlin," Dawit said, pushing her away. Again, she fell back, this time hitting her head against the kitchen counter. The room swam in a way that made her realize she was stunned. But she pulled herself up again, scrabbling for the counter.

"Caitlin, you know th-this man?" Father Arturo gasped. Momentarily, his struggle ceased.

For a hysterical instant, it all seemed like one tragic misunderstanding. It must be. *Dawit Wolde, meet Father Arturo. Father Arturo, meet Dawit Wolde.*

But Caitlin O'Neal couldn't say a word.

Father Arturo tugged at Dawit's jacket pocket, and for the first time Caitlin saw the gun. Caitlin watched a horrifying maelstrom on Dawit Wolde's face. This man was not Fana's father. He was someone she didn't know.

"I'm a p-priest!" Father Arturo cried, his arm flailing toward the gun.

"A dead one," Dawit whispered.

Father Arturo's neck broke with a damp, muffled crack. Dawit was nearly panting, his face wet with perspiration as he held the dead man in a perverse embrace, his arm locked tight around Father Arturo's neck long after the priest's head dangled in his collar, silenced. Finally, Dawit pushed him away, as if the corpse disgusted him.

Caitlin watched the impossible scenario unfold, her thoughts banished. She felt warm urine dribbling into her shoes.

"I won't hurt you," Dawit told her, carefully sliding his knife into his pocket. He held up his bare palms to her. His voice was gentle. Caitlin was shocked at how much she needed to believe him. He said he wouldn't hurt her. He promised.

"Everything is fine, sweetheart," Dawit said. "It's fine."

Caitlin sobbed, giving him a baffled look. *Everything is FINE?*

Dawit Wolde covered his eyes with his hands and sighed a grieved sigh, his fingers trembling as much as hers. She might have felt sorry for him if she hadn't been so petrified.

He looked like a fallen angel wondering how he could ever confess his sins to God.

Four

Longview, Washington
Monday
12:35 p.m.

Fana, *stop!*"

The Blazer lurched to a halt with a shriek of brakes, jolting forward. Jessica Jacobs-Wolde braced herself with a palm against the glove compartment. A yellow school bus from Longview Public Schools drove past, hardly a foot from the Blazer's age-faded hood. Small palms and noses pressed against the bus windows to see the car that had nearly broadsided them. Some of the children were smiling, as if car crashes were only a spectacle on their GamePorts.

"Didn't you see the red light?" Jessica said. "Pay attention when you're driving."

Fana flung her head casually to sweep her dreadlocks away from her face, but Jessica noticed that her daughter's hands clung to the steering wheel so tightly that paths were drawn by her veins. Fana was terrified. "How am I supposed to see the light way over there?" she said.

Jessica took a quenching breath, the way she did when she began her morning prayers an hour each dawn. *Give me patience, Lord.*

There were parking spaces in front of the stately homes beyond the intersection, across the street from Lake Sacajawea Park's inviting rows of Douglas firs. A place to rest. "When the light changes, pull over and give me the keys," Jessica said. "You need a break."

"You mean *you* need a break."

"When the light changes, pull over, Fana."

Fana had been in a snappish mood all day, and it wasn't like her.

But first things first. First, you need to get those damn keys away from her. Jessica tried not to bring her thought's conclusion to consciousness, but it nudged free anyway: *. . . before she kills somebody.*

Fana gave her a look that could melt glass. Then she yanked the car's gear into park and pulled the keys out of the ignition. "You want the keys?" She flung her car door open and jumped out, slapping the keys onto the seat. "There. Now you know I won't kill anybody."

The stoplight on the pole turned green as Fana's car door slammed behind her.

"Fana, where—," Jessica began, right before the rear door opened and Fana climbed in back. At five-ten, Fana was nearly as tall as her father. Dawit had also bequeathed his red-brown complexion and exotic beauty, with only the bulb of Fana's nose to remind Jessica that this was her child, too. And Fana was definitely as moody as Dawit. No question about *that.*

Jessica sighed. Two cars were visible in the rearview mirror, waiting patiently. One was Melaku's familiar black Orbit, the driver idling at the requisite distance while he followed. Fana was never allowed out without at least one tail, and there were probably others nearby. Jessica had learned what it might feel like to be the president, flanked by Secret Service.

Jessica started the engine. "Tell me what's wrong with you today."

Silence. Fana's favorite retreat.

From the time she was three until she was nine, Fana hadn't spoken a single word aloud. Jessica had prayed her daughter's silence would be temporary, like Maya Angelou's in *I Know Why the Caged Bird Sings*—and luckily, Fana had snapped out of it at the dinner table one day, asking for mashed potatoes like it was no big deal.

That had been one victory, but there would be a long, hard war ahead.

"Sweetheart, when I was your age, I nearly drove Mom into a canal," Jessica said. "That's what happens when you're learning. Let's stop at The Brits and have lunch."

"I'm not hungry," Fana said. "Let's go back."

Jessica had not expected to hear the words *"Let's go back"* from a girl who complained incessantly that her world was too confined. They were only thirty-five minutes south of home, but it would have been smarter to put off this field trip after Dawit had gotten called away. And safer.

"Fana, you're supposed to talk to me when you're having a problem."

Stoic silence. Fana twirled the thin end of one of her ropy dreads around her index finger. Dawit was better with Fana when she was like this, with the endless patience he reserved for his children. If Jessica hadn't been so grateful for his mastery, she might have been jealous of their bond.

Jessica hoped Dawit would come home today. He'd promised during his too-brief call last night. Before he'd left, he'd been vague about where he was going, and last night he'd been more vague about where he had been. But Dawit didn't trust phones, even sat phones, so she would get more out of him later. Dawit had sworn to her years ago that there would never be another secret between them.

And there was something he didn't want to talk about. Like father, like daughter.

"Fana, if you tranced out while you were driving, just say so. Stop pretending with me."

In the rearview mirror, Fana blinked, looking downward. "I didn't trance out," Fana said quietly. "Everything got . . . blurry. Just for a second."

Jessica had never known Fana to have blurred vision. This was something new, another unforeseen problem. It was both a blessing and a never-ending trial that Fana was so different.

"When did the blurriness start? On the Interstate?"

"*No,* or I would have said something. I said it was for one second. At the light."

"Did you feel dizzy?"

"Should we call the pediatrician?" Fana said, her voice coarse with sarcasm.

In seventeen years, the only doctor Fana had seen was Jessica's sister, who had ushered her into the world. Fana would never need a doctor. Once, Jessica had believed that was enough for a lifetime's peace of mind. But she knew better now.

"I just want to know what's wrong, Fana. Let's see Teka when we get back."

"Let's not," Fana mumbled. She was tired of her teacher's intervention, and Jessica couldn't blame her. Teka's methods seemed too intrusive sometimes. Oftentimes.

"We'll have to tell your father. He should be home today."

Unless Jessica imagined it, Fana's face in the rearview mirror grew sullen. Usually, mentioning her father was the surest way to make Fana smile.

"Don't bother," Fana said softly. "I know what's wrong."

"What?"

"There are too many people here," Fana said, gazing through her window at passing cars full of strangers' faces. A sad defeat sat across her daughter's lips, and Jessica had never seen her daughter look defeated. "I need to go back home, Mom."

Fana said the word *home* as if it had been acid on her tongue.

Sometimes, it seemed to Fana that she knew every fir tree along the roadway.

She knew every shade of green, every pattern in the bark, each patch where the stands thickened or thinned. She had every highway sign memorized, knew every turnoff. The Five. Exit 60. The 505. She always knew exactly where they were, as if they hadn't been moving at all.

How did that song by Phoenix go? *My soul gets cold from standing still / If I can't test my wings I'll die. / Don't wanna die for a while. / I think I'll fly for a while.*

A prophetess with a piano. That song had been on Fana's mind all day, and she hummed the melody under her breath while she sat behind her mother and watched the same trees go by. She would be a shut-in if not for the I-5 corridor from Toledo down to Longview— or up to Seattle, when her parents were feeling adventurous. She would be an eccentric hiding in the woods, sheltered by the silence of the trees. Like the others.

I think I'll fly for a while.

Fana's sigh burned her throat. She would never fly like the girl in the song. She couldn't even drive a car. A school bus carrying forty children had blurred her eyesight and made her brain short out. She had only been away from home for two hours and twenty minutes, and she was so anxious to get back that her palms were sweating.

What had made her think she could go driving and have lunch in town like a normal person? Dad had taught her five languages, but *normal* wasn't in her vocabulary in any of them. The thought of her father made Fana's stomach cramp, and the song on her breath died.

Her father had been in her dream.

It was just a dream. Dreams don't always mean anything, she'd told herself when she'd realized that sweat had soaked through her pillow while she'd slept.

Her father stands in a large ornate room, all marble and glistening gold. A priest in white ceremonial regalia and a cardinal's cap kneels on the floor before him, grasping a golden chalice full of blood. Her father walks behind the priest in slow, measured steps. A girl who might be Caitlin stands watching in the darkened wings, her hands clasped before her face as if she is deep in prayer, but her eyes are wide and frightened.

"I'm a priest," the man in the white robe says.

"A dead one," her father says, and swiftly breaks his neck. The chalice's spilled blood soaks the corpse's white robe crimson . . .

This dream meant something. Fana had nightmares at least once a week—nightmares *worse* than most people's, she was sure—but this dream had felt more immediate. She had been a witness last night, not a dreamer.

Mom knew something, too, even without a dream or any gifts beyond intuition. Fana allowed a few of her mother's thoughts to slip past her protective veil, and Mom's anxieties pricked her like a swarm of tiny insects. Like bees.

MY FAULT WHAT CAN WE DO TO HELP HER

Feeling like an intruder, Fana shut Mom's thoughts away. It was harder work all the time, but Fana could ignore the noise in other people's heads. Usually. Besides, Mom didn't have answers, only questions. The answer, Fana knew, lay within the dream.

As fiercely as she fought against remembering most of her

dreams, Fana fought now to make sense of the latest vision thrust on her by her unconscious. She wished she knew how to order her dream the way Teka had tried to teach her, dissecting the symbols.

Her mind went back to the chalice. The blood.

That part was simple, suddenly. *Dad knows,* Fana thought, understanding.

"Oh, no," Fana said aloud. Her heart throbbed as her body went cold.

"What, honey?" Mom said.

Fana shook her head. Her abrupt insight had surprised her so much that she'd forgotten she was riding in a car with her mother. She tried to keep her panic from her face.

"I'm sure it's no secret to you," Mom said evenly, her brown eyes sad and steady in the rearview mirror, "but you're worrying me, Fana."

I'm worrying me, too. "Sorry. I'm just tired."

She should tell her. She had no choice. But Fana's lips stayed melded together. Slowly, she sank far back against her seat, wrapping herself in a tight embrace. Fana was slipping into a grimly familiar place now. She wanted to vanish. To trance out.

The green sign proclaiming Toledo appeared. Fana heard the placid clicking of the Blazer's blinker as Mom prepared to exit the Interstate and take her on the road home. Behind them, Melaku's car followed, as always.

"Mom . . . ," Fana began, ready to confess. But this time, her mother didn't hear her.

I was right. None of them will understand, but I was right.

Remembering her resolve calmed Fana's muscles, unwinding them. She had known this day would come. It was miraculous that they hadn't been caught before now. Three years was a long time. That was why Caitlin had been in the dream, she realized. Caitlin was in trouble!

But why a priest? What did that part mean?

More than ever, Fana felt like a prisoner as the Blazer jounced from the main road to the dirt path leading to the wooded colony that was the only home she could remember. There was a gate farther up the road, where the land's original owners had once welcomed visitors, but their destination veered east, two miles' drive on a narrow, barely navigable path that had once been a horse trail, through dense stands of old-growth forest that hid the colony from the world. Western red cedars. Cottonwoods. Douglas firs.

But there was more to this land than five hundred acres of freely growing nature. Webs of trip wires were invisible to the eye, but Fana knew every leaf, stump and mound of soil that hid them. The colony's security measures were meant to keep unwanted visitors out, but to Fana they had always seemed designed to pen her *in*. She had made a game of learning how to slip past the hidden traps unseen, the rare times she took pleasure in exploring her gifts.

Three years ago, she had made it all the way to the paved road leading to town without alerting anyone to her feat, her biggest triumph. To meet Caitlin there.

As the Blazer neared the clearing where the houses stood, Fana sensed the four men who lived among the trees, sentries as fleet as deer who had no thoughts other than protecting the colony of twenty-eight people. No thought except protecting *her*.

She was home.

Fana didn't recognize the silver hydro sedan parked ahead of them, probably a rental, but she knew her father had driven it. The car was empty, but its hood would be warm if she touched it. Dad had beaten them here by only a minute or two. Her muscles clenched tight again.

"I hope that's David . . . ," Jessica murmured. Her mother veered between calling her father *Dawit*, the name his Brothers used, and *David*, the name she had first known him by. Mom called him *David* most often when he was away, her name for his memory.

The path from the woods ended at the Square, which was really a hexagon and served as their tiny colony's nexus. The Square's centerpiece was a large fountain and its large twin marble lions, the maned male and his female mate, who seemed to stand guard while water arced from their open mouths, shooting skyward. The two streams of water crossed in the air like liquid swords. Her father had sculpted the lions—another talent he'd had no luck passing on to her. The exquisite black marble fountain was Fana's favorite part of her home.

Since it was one o'clock, the younger children were in school instead of playing in the Square, so all Fana heard as she climbed out of the car was the hairy woodpeckers fussing in the trees. Someone—not Gramma Bea—was cooking. She smelled stewing meat, a scent that always made Fana feel ill.

She felt sicker than usual today, but not because of the meat.

Not more than five acres separated any of the structures at the colony from any of the others. They all lived within shouting distance, as Gramma Bea liked to say. For safety.

Fana's house, which she shared with her parents and grandmother, was at the end of the cobblestone garden path. Her aunt Alex and uncle Lucas lived in the elegant wood-frame house closest to theirs, and the Duharts lived with their three children east, on the other side of the fountain. The remaining buildings were the meeting hall, the library, the schoolhouse, the lab, and—set back farther in the woods than the others—a long, dormitory-style Council Hall shared by eight men her father had known longer than any other men had lived. Those men preferred each other's fellowship best.

Fana could make out a huddle of people walking toward the Council Hall, almost out of sight behind the black walnut tree. She recognized her father's walk first, Teferi tall above them, and then wiry Teka. Fana saw pale skin, too: Caitlin was here, and her father.

Seeing Caitlin made Fana forget her own problems. No one was touching Caitlin, but she and her father moved reluctantly. Caitlin and her father had been *brought*.

"Dad is here. And Caitlin." Fana sprinted after them to confront her fate head-on.

"Caitlin?" she heard her mother say in delighted ignorance. "That's a nice surprise!"

When Teka turned because he sensed Fana's approach, the group's progress halted. They all stood still, watching Fana run toward them. Justin O'Neal, Caitlin's sandy-haired father, was dressed in a rumpled three-piece suit, his tie hanging unwound. His face was devoid of the smile he usually welcomed her with. There were no smiles from this group—especially from her father.

Dad's eyes slowed Fana's feet.

Caitlin broke into a run toward Fana that made Mr. O'Neal

stiffen. Fana saw her father rest his hand on Mr. O'Neal's shoulder, holding him in place.

Even before Caitlin was within ten yards, Fana felt her friend's frantic thoughts punching her: *OHMYGODOHMYGODOHMY-GOD* Caitlin's cheeks were bright red, and tears filled her eyes as she tripped, hugging Fana.

"Oh, God, Fana," Caitlin whispered. "They—"

"It's all right if they know," Fana said calmly, hugging her. "I'll say it was my idea."

"P-please don't let them hurt me and my dad. *Please.*"

Caitlin's memories charged into Fana's head. Suddenly, Fana saw an inversion of her dream: A man dressed in black held helpless, an arm wound tightly around his throat, then his neck cracked with a wrenching motion, like juicing an orange. The image replayed itself in a frenzy; it had been the only thing on Caitlin's mind for hours. Suddenly, Fana saw her father in Caitlin's memory, too—he stood behind the man wearing black, his arm wrapped around his neck. Dad's face was a mask of rage Fana had never seen.

Fana looked at her father, who stood watching her beside Caitlin's father on the path to the Council Hall. Her father's face churned with hurt. And anger. Maybe a trace of shame.

She had brought trouble to Caitlin. She had brought trouble to all of them.

Fana forced herself to reclaim the images from her dream, hoping to find solace there.

A priest in white ceremonial regalia and a cardinal's cap kneels on the floor before her father, grasping a golden chalice full of blood. Her father walks behind the priest.

"I'm a priest," the man in the white robe says.

"A dead one," her father says, and swiftly breaks his neck. The chalice's spilled blood soaks the corpse's white robe crimson.

The priest's bloody robe flutters, and he stirs.

The corpse isn't dead at all.

Five

A Camel wobbled between Caitlin's thin fingers as she sat on the bare bed with her legs hiked up like a child's, close to her body. Thanks to Gramps, Caitlin O'Neal had been chain-smoking since she was sixteen. He'd let her smoke her first cigarette when she was seven, the same year he'd died. Gramps had not been a nice man. If Caitlin had been able to go back in time, she would have kicked him in the balls. But the habit had outlived him, and the nicotine beat back the panic trying to fill her throat. *Calm down, Caitlin. There's a way out of this. There has to be.*

Where was her father? It had been an hour since Uncle Teferi had taken him away.

Uncle Teferi had called this narrow room the "guest quarters," but since there was no window and only two narrow twin beds, it was just a cell. She'd been afraid of being locked up since the night she'd first met Fana at the border of the woods, when Fana had given her a backpack hiding an ounce of her blood. But she hadn't expected to be locked up here, a place that had been a second home most of her life.

Casey had warned her. Even without really knowing, her twin had known about the Glow. *You're looking for a quick trip to jail, or worse,* Casey had said a month before Mari had died.

Caitlin's heart bucked when the door opened.

Fana slipped inside. As the door closed behind her, Caitlin saw the shadow of a man who must have been a guard. *Shit.* They weren't going to let her leave.

Caitlin choked, coughing. "Thank God it's you," she said. "Where's my dad? They—"

"He's fine, I swear. They're asking him questions."

Fana looked like she had been crying, too. Caitlin hadn't seen Fana in three years, since the night she'd gotten the blood, and Caitlin was surprised at how tall Fana was now. She didn't look like a kid anymore. Fana hugged Caitlin; and it felt good to be hugged. With Fana here and a nicotine bath, Caitlin felt safe for the first time since Seattle, like being in her mother's arms.

"I promise I'll get you out of here," Fana said. "Just tell me what happened."

"We're busted, that's what happened. I nearly got killed. But Dad doesn't have anything to do with it. He doesn't know anything."

"Tell me everything, Caitlin."

"Are you sure I should?"

"Of course." Fana looked hurt, but Fana was one of them. Caitlin couldn't forget that.

Right before Caitlin had gone to college, when Fana was fourteen, Fana had announced that Caitlin was her best friend—and she'd wanted to show her true self. As it had turned out, Fana's "true self" had included freaky mind-tricks. And the blood.

Fana had told her the truth about Dad's work: Caitlin's father was using his corporation as a front to help Fana's people distribute their blood in secrecy to heal sick people in parts of Africa and Asia. Caitlin had thought it was the most miraculous thing she'd ever heard. She used to.

Caitlin had tried to put the awful sound of Father Arturo's cracking neck out of her mind, but now she had to relive it as she spoke in a hush directly into Fana's ear. She'd be a fool not to think the room was bugged. "It's Sunday night, and I'm meeting with Father A. People I trust vouched for him, and he was about to pass his six-month screen. That night, I went to meet him at his shelter for battered women. After I got there, your father broke his neck. I *saw* him do it."

Fana's eyes swam, lost. "I don't understand. Why would Dad do that?"

Caitlin shrugged. "You tell me."

Fana looked away from her, as if she'd been slapped. Fana was a

Daddy's girl to the bone. Some subjects were best avoided between them—especially the bloody day in Florida when their families had met for the first time. That day, Gramps had died, and Fana's aunt and uncle had nearly died, too. Dad said that Dawit Wolde was the most frightening man he had ever met.

He killed her.

Maritza's face came to Caitlin's mind suddenly; a perfect oval, like a doll. The thought of Maritza brought the memory of her hair's smell; sweet milk and vanilla. Caitlin almost turned around to make sure Maritza wasn't sitting behind them on the bed.

Fana reached over to squeeze Caitlin's hand, and Caitlin held on tight.

Fana's face had been the first to appear on her mobile video phone the night Maritza's body had been found, not even ten minutes after Caitlin had gotten the news from the Miami Beach police. The memory of that night was still a cold blade in Caitlin's stomach. It was the only memory worse than seeing Father Arturo killed.

Caitlin wiped her eyes. "I think they killed Maritza, Fana. Your p-people."

"Why would they do that?"

Caitlin bit back her anger at Fana's naivete. "Because she was counseling AIDS patients, and . . ." Caitlin's voice broke off. She could not talk to Fana here. She couldn't tell Fana how Mari had cleaned out thirty men, women and children, setting them free of the system, unless Fana mined it from her head. "Maritza was a good person, Fana."

"I know she was."

Caitlin took a deep breath. "Your father—"

Fana cut her off. "Dad didn't kill Maritza. He wouldn't do that."

For all of her amazing gifts, Fana lived in a dreamworld, Caitlin thought. Just like Mari, who'd been laughing on the phone instead of using the right codes. Mari had never learned how to hide, to the point where patients had knocked on their apartment door late into the night.

"Do you really know he didn't?" Caitlin said. "Or do you just hope not?"

"Something like that would have . . . come through." Fana lowered her eyes. She always looked embarrassed when she talked about the way she had access to people's heads.

Could Fana hear what she was thinking now? *Your father is a fucking murderer. Wake the hell up, Fana, or he and those other freaks will kill my whole family.*

But Fana's face didn't change. Fana hadn't heard, or she was ignoring her.

"Are you sure you know your father?" Caitlin said.

"I'm . . . pretty sure."

So much for all-knowing. Caitlin shook her head, almost chuckling. "Don't be."

The weight across Fana's eyebrows made her look like she wasn't sure of her own name.

Stealing. That word made Justin O'Neal clear his throat and pour another glass of water from the crystal decanter with an unsteady hand. No matter how much he drank, he couldn't kill his thirst as he sat across the large oak table from his questioners. The large hall's cedar scent was as sharp as incense, burning his throat.

Yesterday, Justin had gone to his office at Clarion World Health overlooking the East River on Wall Street like it had been any other day. He'd been preparing for a lunch with the ambassador from Ghana when they'd come with the news about Caitlin. Just yesterday.

Today, he and his daughter might be about to die. Caitlin had told him she'd seen Dawit kill a man yesterday. A priest! How did he know that Caitlin was still alive now; that they hadn't killed Caitlin as soon as she was alone?

"I took five milliliters," Justin said, his voice shaky. "Half a vial."

"That was an intricate plan, Mr. O'Neal." The man's voice was almost congratulatory.

Two weeks ago, Justin had been in Ghana to inspect the two clinics in the Volta region, and he'd been pissed and scared: After he'd spent ten years helping them build their distribution network, these men still wouldn't let him keep a few drops of the blood for his family's safety. Their bigotry against anyone without the blood was infuriating. He wasn't asking to live forever—he just wanted an emergency supply. How could they expect him to help thousands of other patients and leave his own family vulnerable?

But Justin never would have taken the blood if he had known Caitlin was selling Glow.

Justin raised his eyes to face the five dark men dressed in matching white tunics who sat in judgment in the tomblike, unadorned Council Hall. Justin kept his eyes on the small-boned man who had recited his offenses, the one they called Teka. Teka's slight frame and immature face made him look like a boy, and his eyes were the only compassionate ones.

This was a trial, all right, but not by his peers. Could they even be called human?

Justin had been a defense lawyer before he'd gone corporate. He'd always been paid well for his ability to paint a bright picture, but he couldn't choose a strategy. How could he keep Caitlin out of trouble without getting himself killed?

Justin glanced at Dawit Wolde, and the immortal's eyes drove him away. He was wearing white hair and stage makeup, but Dawit's eyes hadn't changed.

"Remind me," Dawit said. "How much do we pay you a year?"

"Two million, sir."

"That's a lot of money, even for someone with your expensive tastes," Dawit said. "And how did we treat you when your wife had cancer?"

Justin's hands curled into fists as he remembered the scare with Holly four years earlier. Ovarian cancer. She'd been so far along that her young doctor had blanched when he'd probed Holly's insides with his hand. "You treated us well, sir. You saved her life."

"Did Teferi refuse you what she needed? Did any of us object?"

"No, sir. Teferi treated me like a son." Justin's voice broke. "Dawit, it was *half a vial*—"

Dawit rose to his feet. "Yes. Half a vial. After we warned you that we do not tolerate theft of our blood. After we explained that we take the matter very personally, and that you must petition for personal use. We said this rule was *cardinal*. And you agreed, did you not?"

"Yes, sir. I broke that rule."

Dawit gave him a bitter, steel smile. "In your father's footsteps," he said, glowering. "None of us need wonder why your daughter has so prodigiously taken up your family tradition. Caitlin far outshines you, I might add. Her offenses are far more impressive."

He and Caitlin were both dead if they would be judged by his father!

More than a decade ago, long before Justin had imagined himself in this place or known about these people, Dad had prodded him into an outlandish plan to try to find "magic blood" he'd believed to be a part of their family history. Justin had thought his father had lost his mind, but as it had turned out, he had not. His medical reports had proven it: Dad had found a miraculous cure.

But Dad had always been greedy. He'd bullied Justin into hiring mercenaries to track down a clinic in Botswana for sick children—which, unfortunately, had been run by Dawit's wife. The mercenaries had narrowly missed abducting Dawit's wife and child, but they'd found blood. A lot of it.

They had also captured a scientist and a physician, a woman. Tortured and nearly killed them. The woman had been Dawit's sister-in-law. During her rescue, Justin's father had been shot and killed before his eyes.

Of course, Dad had had it coming. Justin knew that. But some of the dead had been innocent, undeserving of the massacre. They had died because Justin had made a telephone call, doing his father's bidding. Justin was only alive to remember his shame because Teferi had pled with the other Africans to spare him after discovering that Justin was his direct descendant, two hundred years removed. And his position at his company, Clarion, had made him useful to them.

The choice is clear to us: Trust you or kill you, Teferi had said. *We choose trust.*

Now their trust was gone.

"Do what you want with me, but please don't touch my family," Justin heard himself say. "I'm begging you. Whatever Caitlin's told you, I talked her into it. She never wanted to have anything to do with the blood. I convinced her."

A burly African who hadn't spoken muttered something in a melodic language Justin didn't understand, and the others chuckled. The chuckles horrified Justin in a way Dawit's eyes had not. Was he only a plaything to these men?

"Justin." Teka spoke quietly. The small man's voice was fatherly, and Justin felt his fear melt away. Such a caring voice promised a reprieve. Teka went on: "In this Hall, among my Brothers, deception is your worst course. Each lie is known to us and serves as a deeper insult. Never lie to us again."

Justin gazed at the knowing eyes around the table and felt scalded by the truth of Teka's warning. These men not only had remarkable blood and lived for generations but they also knew when he was lying? Now he didn't have to wonder how they had found out about the stolen vial!

"Jesus help me," Justin whispered. His mind felt cast adrift. *Our Father who art in Heaven, hallowed be Thy name* . . . Justin couldn't remember what came next in the prayer. He hadn't been to a church in years.

"So, to clarify . . . ," Teka said. "You did not supply your daughter with diluted blood being sold outside of this colony. You did not know Caitlin was involved in the sale of this blood."

Justin could only shake his head. His tongue was a useless lump in his mouth.

"Show him the photograph," Teka said.

A color photo appeared on the table in front of him; Justin was so dazed that he didn't see who had given it to him. An autopsy photo. Justin saw a nude, dark-haired woman, visible to midchest, her mouth hanging open in a face streaked with blood. Her chest was a collection of dark bruises and punctures that looked like knife wounds. Too many to count. The poor woman looked like a speared fish, her wounds gaping and fresh.

Then Justin recognized her face.

His stomach flew into his mouth, and he vomited a stream of warm water to the floor. His shaking limbs nearly threw him from his chair. Justin tried to straighten again, but he couldn't move. His muscles were locked.

The girl in the photograph was Maritza, Caitlin's girlfriend. Maritza, who'd called him Papi and had promised him a grandchild one day. Caitlin hadn't even told him Maritza was dead until the memorial service had been over. Maritza had been a baby herself.

"Maritza Colón," Dawit said. "She was selling Glow on South Beach. She received blood from Caitlin. She's a very dead girl now, as you can see."

"Jesus God, please help us . . . ," Justin whispered, still bent over the floor. His tears spilled freely as the room spun above him and beneath him. *He killed Father Arturo right in front of me, Dad. He's a monster.* That was the first thing Caitlin had said when they'd had a minute alone, when his daughter had been desperate to prepare him for what he would face.

"We didn't kill Maritza, Mr. O'Neal." Teka's voice cut through the fog threatening to make him faint. Justin sat up slowly in his chair, wiping spittle from his lips. He wanted to believe Teka. He *did* believe, somehow. Justin's tears softened from grief to gratitude.

"But her death raises a question about you," Dawit said. He stood up, standing over Justin. "What would you do to save your daughter's life?"

"Anything."

"Anything?" Too gently, Dawit cupped Justin's chin in his hand. "Yes, you *would* do anything. That was the fate of beautiful, dead Maritza here. She betrayed her beloved to try to save her life, and now Caitlin is being hunted. If someone took Caitlin, how long would it take you to tell them everything you know about us? A day? An hour? Five minutes?"

Justin couldn't think, much less answer. Dawit's presence over him felt like a death sentence. Dawit was impossibly quick with a knife; Justin had seen that the day they'd met. The mercenary whom Dawit had killed hadn't even seen his knife coming.

"You've made your point, Dawit," Teka said.

Dawit took his seat after a last glare, and Justin exhaled with force.

"Kill me, then," Justin said. "But not my family. They don't know anything, except for Caitlin. You know I'm not lying. Fana told Caitlin, so let Caitlin live here with her. Let them all live here, or anywhere you say. Please." He had convinced Holly to move to Johannesburg to keep his family as far from the colony as possible. For their protection.

The room's silence was broken by a chuckle from one of the Africans, a harrowing sound. Justin's family meant nothing to them.

"Be silent, please," Dawit said. "Just go."

Go? Justin sat frozen, confused. *Will they let us go free?*

Dawit waved him away. "To your room, you fool."

"Go be with your daughter," Teka said gently.

Justin leaped to his feet, seeking balance on weak knees. He was surprised he wasn't given an escort, until he remembered that escape from this hall was probably impossible. Caitlin had told him that even the forest was booby-trapped.

Desperation gave Justin courage. As he passed Dawit, he leaned down for a private plea: "I'm begging you, one father to another. Caitlin wasn't in this alone—Fana *gave* her the blood. Don't destroy my family. Our children are friends. Don't do this to your daughter."

Dawit's dark eyes didn't soften. He gazed at Justin with an indifference that was worse than anger, as if Justin already didn't exist.

Six

Jessica found her sister sitting on a low stool beyond rows of storage supply cabinets, computers, blood screen racks and tubes lighted by bright fluorescent bulbs overhead. She was shoving papers, magazines and computer files into boxes so quickly that she looked like she was late for an appointment with a moving van.

Alex didn't look up when Jessica came in. In Alex's lab, the world disappeared. The lab was her shrine to medicine and music, plastered with crooked posters: Bob Marley. Phoenix. Los Van Van from Cuba. African salsa played from the CD player on the counter closest to her; Alex and their mother refused to give up CDs, just as they had clung to vinyl long ago. Alex's bad leg was splayed out to the side for comfort while she worked. Alex liked to pretend the leg didn't bother her, but Jessica knew it did. Her sister's limp grew worse with time.

A metal lockbox landed in Alex's plastic crate with a thump.

"I see you heard," Jessica said.

Alex jumped, startled. She gave Jessica a long gaze over her shoulder. "I've heard Caitlin crying. Saying your husband is going to kill her. Saying . . . he already killed someone."

"I don't have the facts yet." There was no point in answering to a rumor.

"Why are they being held here, Jess?"

"The Brothers consider that their right. The O'Neals haven't been hurt."

"Not yet. What's our position? Do we have one?"

Sometimes the balance between Jessica's family and the Life Brothers felt just right, miraculously so. Not this time. Their mission needed constant tending. *Was this how Esther felt in the Old Testament, married to the king?*

"Dawit and I will talk after dinner," Jessica said. "We'll resolve it. Caitlin can probably sleep at the house with Fana. That should help."

"We haven't used our guest room yet," Alex said wryly. "Her dad can sleep with us."

Considering that Justin O'Neal had once stood and watched while a mercenary had burned Alex's face and arms with cigarettes to try to force her to tell where the blood came from, Jessica was surprised Alex could even joke about it. But Alex wasn't joking; she was offering the man sanctuary. Age must have mellowed her. At fifty-three, Alex's lifelong Afro was mostly silver, with only a few stray strands of black.

"I'm not sure what we can do for him," Jessica said. "He stole from them, Alex. With Caitlin, they would see it as naivete. It's different with Justin."

"Naivete that's spreading all over the country. And Canada. Getting into the news." Alex sighed. She suddenly cupped her palm to her ear. "Do you hear that sound, Jess? That's the sound of the shit hitting the fan," Alex said. "They found a security breach with Justin, and then Caitlin's picked up with Glow in Seattle—two hours from here. This is the end of the mission. Me, I'm packing some research I'd rather keep closer to home. Not that it'll do any good, if someone wants to come take it."

"Nobody's taking anything from anybody," Jessica said. "I have the blood, too. And so does Fana. Not to mention your own *husband*, Alex. And Dawit could change yours any time. It's not just theirs anymore."

As usual Alex, as stubborn as their mother, didn't address the offer for the blood. At least Alex had finally started using herself as a test subject, injecting drops of blood even if she would not agree to Dawit's Life ceremony. So far, ironically, the blood had not helped heal Alex's leg.

"If we have to, Lucas and I can go out on our own," Alex said. "We'll find our own way to work with the blood. That's what we've always planned, one day. You have a bigger fish to fry, Jessica. Her name is Fana, and she's plenty pissed off."

Before Jessica could say anything, a voice surprised them from the rear doorway. "I knew I'd find you in here talking foolishness," their mother said.

Bea's cane *clack-clack*ed across the floor. Perspiration shone on her forehead.

"Mom, for God's sake . . . why did you walk all the way over here?" Jessica said.

It was a long walk from the Big House to the lab, over a knoll without a paved path, and Beatrice Jacobs Gaines had relied on a cane since breaking her hip on her back porch steps five years ago. A heart attack last year had sapped the last of her spryness, despite Alex's care. Bea had enough trouble navigating the kitchen nowadays, much less outdoors.

Her mother's deterioration pained Jessica. This frail old woman had once been the belle of Gadsden County, Florida, with knockout legs and a face Jessica only saw glimpses of beneath its canopy of wrinkles. Bea was eighty-four now, taking daily pills for everything from arthritis to high blood pressure, and she wouldn't accept a drop of her own daughter's blood.

Sometimes Jessica wondered if her mother had dementia, too. Couldn't she see she was dying, day by day? Why choose man-made medications above a gift from God?

"Alex, don't you even think about going off by yourself," Bea said.

Jessica shared a secret glance with her sister. They could not talk freely in front of Bea. She held onto everything tighter since Daddy Gaines died, especially her ideas.

"Nobody's going anywhere, Mom," Jessica said. "We're just talking."

But it was too late to cover for Alex. Their mother had heard enough.

Leaning hard on her cane, Bea walked six painstaking steps to Alex and stared her eldest daughter earnestly in the eye. "Baby, let them tend to their house. They tend to their house, we tend to ours. That's what keeps the peace. You're not going anywhere on your own, you and Lucas. You wouldn't last. That's crazy talk."

Alex's face itched for a rebuttal, but Jessica gave her sister a gentle, appeasing smile. *Leave it alone.* Any arguments sent Bea into a frenzy, and there was enough arguing ahead.

Jessica still had to talk to Fana, after all, even if she couldn't think of what to say. How could she condemn in her daughter what she would have done herself?

Fana was their colony's only common ground—the meeting place. Compromises would be brokered. Hard choices would be made. And with the battle ahead, Jessica couldn't spare any energy to referee between Alex and Bea. Not tonight.

Besides, she agreed with her mother this time: Their only safety was in numbers. That was the reason she had compromised so much already.

"Jessica?" Alex said to Jessica, ignoring Bea. Her eyes were solemn. "Look after Fana. She's mad her friend is locked up. That situation needs to change. Soon."

Jessica nodded. It was dangerous to upset Fana. They all knew that.

"Alexis Jacobs Shepard . . . ," Bea said, never one to allow a subject to be changed beneath her feet. "Don't you come to my dinner table spreading worry. I don't want you riling up that hothead redneck, Cal. Sometimes when people think the sky is falling, it's really only rain."

I hope so, Mom, Jessica thought, remembering the shame she had seen in Dawit's eyes. *But just ask Noah: Once the rain starts, sometimes it goes on for forty days and forty nights.*

"Simpering fool," Dawit Wolde muttered in Amharic, rubbing his temples. Justin O'Neal's rambling had given him a rare headache. "He should have died with his father."

His voice whispered against the walls of the Council Hall.

"Agreed," Melaku said. "You know where I stand."

"And me," Berhanu said. "I'd never have allowed him among us."

"Perhaps it was a mistake," Teka said, forever placating. "But mistakes can be rectified."

"Yes," Dawit said. "Preferably with the point of a dagger."

But Dawit did not enjoy killing, even if he wished he did. Caitlin O'Neal's frightened eyes still haunted him. And how could they blame Justin O'Neal for his mortal nature? Mortals would choose any course but death. He and his Brothers would have been no different, once.

Dawit longed for the time he'd lived by the Covenant he and his Brothers had once sworn their lives to: *No one must know. No one must join. We are the Last.*

He and his Brothers had changed too much, too fast.

After five hundred years in Lalibela, ensconced within a brotherhood of fifty-nine men, only a fraction of his Life Brothers had reassembled themselves on the shores of the New World. No maze of caverns protected them from the eyes of others, as it had in their sacred home. No underground fortress walls proclaimed their history in murals and secured their kind from the world of curious mortals above. Dear Khaldun was not here to swear fealty to, nor Khaldun's Covenant. All of it, gone. And what were they creating in its place?

Their tallest brother, Teferi, strode from the hallway into the meeting room, snuffing the last chuckles. "If this gathering represents hope for mankind's sick and unfortunate, then God help them all," Teferi said, taking a seat. "Justin is terrorized. And you reek of hypocrisy, Dawit. You should be ashamed for the way you've treated them both. As if you're not guilty of worse."

The colony had been created when Dawit had disobeyed Khaldun, refusing to leave his wife and first daughter behind two decades ago. He had done worse than share his Living Blood with Jessica—he had invoked the Ceremony to generate it in her veins, breaking their colony's Covenant with Khaldun. In doing so, he had created a child in Jessica's womb with gifts that went beyond his own. And he had fractured his Brotherhood in Lalibela, scattering them apart.

"The O'Neals are Teferi's descendants," Teka said. "Even Dawit would agree that one's children cannot always be controlled."

Teferi nodded. "It's not a decision for this table. I call for a colony-wide vote."

Berhanu shook his head. "Why should we vote? We are the majority."

"My vote certainly does not stand with yours, Berhanu," Teferi said.

And mine is uncertain, Dawit thought, although he tried to hold the thought close. Despite how he felt about Justin O'Neal, Jessica and Fana must share his decision. Hell was waiting for him across the path, at home.

Berhanu's jowls shook with anger. "I will *not* have our blood stolen. Never again. Why do we sit here awaiting disaster? Are we simply mad, or has it been too long since one of us was left in a cage to bleed for the pleasure of others?"

Dawit felt his heart surge in agreement. He and Berhanu had spoken many times about the blood mission's risks not only to them but to Fana, as well. Dawit never doubted Teka's wisdom, but he heeded Berhanu's, too. Berhanu was a warrior, and a battle was on the horizon. There were more signs all the time.

In the past six months, there had been four abductions; the first in Vancouver, British Columbia, another in Ann Arbor, one in San Francisco, and the last in Miami. The first victim, who had turned up dead two weeks after being reported missing by his mother, had been an insignificant drug dealer with no connections to anyone in Dawit's circle—hardly worth noticing. Dawit would not have noted his killing at all, except for the web that connected him to the rest.

A biology professor at the University of Michigan. An artist with a Haight-Ashbury studio. A social worker in South Beach. All of them abducted and then murdered. Each abduction higher in the chain, skillfully reaching closer to the supplies they risked their freedom for, to sell on the streets in the so-called Underground Railroad.

Somewhere, an enemy was too close for comfort. Much too close to home.

"Tell us what happened in Seattle, Dawit." Teka sounded uncommonly weary.

In silence, his brothers turned to him, waiting. *Now, it comes,* Dawit thought.

"Aloud, please. Your thoughts are disordered," Teferi said, crossing his arms. "A guilty conscience, I hope. Poor Caitlin tells a ghastly tale of a priest with a broken neck."

Dawit's headache amplified, ringing in his ears. With such sudden unison, his brothers' mental probes were uncomfortable. "I regret his death," Dawit said. "I bear the responsibility."

Dawit felt a soothing mental hum; his brothers understood. Sometimes innocents died.

"What went wrong?" Teka said.

"My mind art failed me."

Teka nodded. "That was my biggest fear when you left. The art is too new to you."

He might have succeeded if Teferi had been with him. Teferi was far more advanced, but the Brothers had decided that Teferi should be excluded from surveillance involving Caitlin. He was too attached to her, by blood.

ANOTHER TRAGIC BIT OF NONSENSE, Teferi's voice niggled in Dawit's head, purposely amplified for effect.

Dawit ignored Teferi and went on. "I knew someone was waiting for her . . ."

As soon as Dawit had stepped into the hallway of the shelter in Seattle, he had known that he and Caitlin O'Neal had not been alone. The sensation had been like slipping his head through an invisible film, a faint pulse between his ears. Someone had been hiding ahead of him, no farther than fifteen feet from where he'd stood. The stranger had a gun ready in his hand.

Dawit had known all of these things in the space of a single breath. The certainty had not been of his eyes, nor his ears, nor any sense he had relied upon until only a few short years ago. Dawit's perceptions had invaded the other man's, sluicing words and images that had nearly drowned his own thoughts. Myriad perceptions had made Dawit's heart race.

A nickel-plated revolver. A bloodied white robe. A syringe.

But something had gone wrong.

Dawit finished: "All I knew for certain was that he had a gun, and he waited for Caitlin. Nothing more. I should not have gone alone. I was vain."

If only he could have brought Teka! There was no one among them more masterful at thought translation, but Teka never ventured from the colony. His demanding meditation schedule alone made trips outside difficult. Teka had brought much-needed weaponry from Lalibela, but Dawit knew he would be reluctant to put the weapons to use.

"This priest had a gun?" Teka said. "I find that significant."

"This nation is armed. Their children shoot each other at their schools," Dawit said. "He said the gun was for protection. You would do well to model him."

Teka ignored the chide. "What other thoughts did you find?" Teka said. "Show me."

Dawit offered his memories to Teka, slipping into his teacher's familiar mental stream. He remembered himself in the shelter's kitchen, when his thoughts had been overrun by the injured priest's cascade of English and Italian words barely ordered enough to decipher. Only one word had leaped uncluttered into his consciousness: *Sangue*. Blood.

Then, images again: a crimson ribbon wound through a medallion imprinted with the unmistakable patterns of a cross and a crest he knew too well. The medallion had lain on a path within the smoking ruins of a village, evidence of killing. Burned huts. Charred remains.

"What startled me most was . . . the medallion of Sanctus Cruor," Dawit said. "I saw a vision of it, from a burned village I came across during the war."

The end of the nineteenth century had wearied Dawit to his soul, between being thrust into the American Civil War and then Ethiopia's war with the Italians on its heels. The nation of his birth had nearly been destroyed by a quest for their blood, even if the history books told another story. Sanctus Cruor had been a small sect, but its high-reaching influence had served as an enduring example of the danger to their kind if their blood was ever traced to them.

"Brothers . . . I believe I lost control," Dawit said. "I felt transported to another place. An earlier time. There is no excuse."

"When you delve in the memories of others, you are likely to unearth your own," Teka said, one of his most oft-repeated warnings. "Still, we must consider the possibility that the priest was involved in these killings. We'll begin with him."

"Father Arturo Bragga lies at the King County morgue, a martyr to our noble cause of healing the poor and infirm," Dawit said. He raised his drinking glass in a mimicry of mortals' customary dinner toast. "A true man of God should welcome such a selfless death. Shall we make a contribution to his church?" he asked, half in earnest, half in jest.

Teferi's face was so grim that his skin was ashen. "I see the killer in you is wide awake, Dawit."

Was Teferi, like Teka, another who hoped they could give away blood without taking blood in return? Teferi had fought by his side in Miami fourteen years ago, fending off a rich man's mercenaries. In the 1700s, Teferi's own son had slit Teferi's throat, as if he had been slaughtering livestock, draining his father's blood into a bucket for days.

"The killer in me is my most practical aspect," Dawit said as gently as he could.

It was the worst of timing.

Suddenly Fana stood in the room, watching Dawit. Her tear-streaked face glowed with hurt that looked too much like the pain he had offered his wife long ago. Dawit's stomach felt sheared.

The room hushed. Fana rarely entered.

Dawit's Brothers rose to their feet, their heads lowered in deference. Dawit rose as well, but not as an acolyte. Dawit had vowed never to make that mistake, no matter what the temptation. This was his *child*.

Dawit left his Brothers' table, reaching out to take his daughter's slender, delicate hand into his. In Amharic, Fana's self-chosen name meant *"light,"* and Dawit felt the light endowed by her touch. She drew away at first but relented when he clasped her hand again. She allowed him to escort her away from the table.

He had been mad to think he could kill the father of his daughter's friend. To kill either of the O'Neals would kill a piece of his child's heart. And what of his own?

"It's time for me to go home, Brothers," Dawit said. "To my family."

No one would have dared argue even if they objected.

Seven

Gramma Bea always said grace at the dinner table, her face knit in concentration while she shared her heart with her most trusted old friend: "Lord, you have brought us all through many storms, and we need Your hand to guide us through all future tempests too. We love you, Lord. We eat this food by your blessing and live with no other calling except to carry out service in Your holy name, and in the name of Your son, Jesus Christ. Bless the Blood, Lord. Amen."

"Amen," said ten people at the two tables shaped like an L in the dining hall, and silverware began its happy chorus. But Fana didn't have any appetite.

All these years, Fana had been afraid to be angry. *What a sweet child you are,* Gramma Bea always said. Quick to forgive. Last to judge. Now, Fana was the angriest she could remember, and the feeling surprised her. Anger didn't feel hot the way people said. Instead, it made her insides cold. Detached. That was why she wouldn't be able to eat a bite.

If not for Gramma Bea, Fana wouldn't have come to dinner. During the years Fana had been lost inside her head, Gramma Bea had always left an empty chair for her at the table, the way Jews leave an empty seat for Elijah the Prophet during the Passover seder. Gramma Bea had always known she would come to the table one day, and Fana had known she was waiting.

Fana deliberately looked away from her parents, who sat left of her. Mom and Dad would never discuss Caitlin in front of the others, and it would be too hypocritical to talk about anything else. It was an outrage that Caitlin had been held this long! If Fana didn't have so much respect for Teka, her teacher, she would have screamed obscenities at the Council.

Fana wanted to dive into her father's head and search for the truth about Maritza's death, but even now, that kind of invasion felt wrong. Besides, he was masking himself. Her father's thoughts were a silent wall beside her.

"There's no meat in the greens, Bee-Bee. Just pepper and peanut butter," Gramma Bea said, passing the steaming bowl. She never called her *Fana*, the name Fana had chosen when she was three. Fana had been named Beatrice after her grandmother, and Gramma Bea liked the sound of that just fine.

"Thanks." Fana's stomach growled, but she felt nauseated. She tried to smile for her grandmother, scooping herself two healthy spoonfuls she knew would sit on her plate. Then Fana's mind swam beneath the table's babble of voices and quiet thoughts.

Aunt Alex was joking about nearly getting thrown by a horse, but Caitlin was troubling her mind. Cal and Juanita Duhart, at the next table, were concentrating on making sure the twins ate, and they didn't know a thing about what was happening at the Council House.

There were a lot of things Uncle Lucas and the Duharts didn't know.

"Put that down *right now*," Juanita Duhart said, pointing her fork toward fourteen-year-old Hank, whose eyes were hidden behind his GamePort goggles. Hank was biracial; like Uncle Lucas and Jared, his skin had been buttermilk pale, but had turned golden brown over the summer. Hank made whistling sounds under his breath, battling whatever he was seeing in the game's three-dimensional fantasy world.

The Duharts lived on the grounds and ate with them, but they didn't have the Blood. Uncle Lucas was not from the original colony of immortals, but the Ceremony Dawit had performed had made him a part of the circle whether the elder Brothers liked it or not. Sort of.

But not the Duharts. Like Caitlin and Justin O'Neal, they weren't the same.

Caitlin had a nickname for mortals: *Shorties*. Short-timers.

Like Grandpa Gaines, any one of them could vanish while she slept.

Mom was just a faraway voice in her doorway, and Fana was so angry that she could barely listen, much less speak. Sometimes it was hard to sift her thoughts fast enough to get them out.

When she was thirteen and began complaining that other people's dreams kept her awake at night, Dad and Cal Duhart had taken down two walls and put up a new one to build her a wing to herself. The eight-hundred-square-foot space had a wall of windows, its own library, and a corner cordoned off by an Asian screen, where she sat on pillows and meditated, surrounded by potted pygmy date palms. The trees nearly reached the ceiling with their wide fronds, so they made her room look like an indoor jungle. The trees would be too tall to keep inside soon.

Fana's favorite historical icons gazed down from framed photographs: Gandhi, Mother Teresa, Harriet Tubman, Martin Luther King, Jr., Rosa Parks, Nelson Mandela, Eleanor Roosevelt and Ethiopia's Empress Taitu.

But Fana felt lost from her heroes' guidance tonight. Lost, period.

Her parents stood beside each other in the doorway, as if waiting for an invitation.

"You have to talk to us, Fana," her father said.

Caitlin said it would take just a word from her to solve this, and she was probably right. Fana didn't need to attend Council meetings to know she had a place at the head of their table. Maybe her word counted more than it should, but now she no longer felt crushed under the weight of the Brothers' awe.

"Let them go," Fana said. "I mean it. Right now."

But this wasn't the Council Hall.

"Watch your tone, Fana," Mom said. "Why were you giving Caitlin your blood?"

"You know why."

Mom had never been able to hoard her blood either. That was the life her parents had chosen for them once she'd begun sharing her blood. Flight, then hiding. *And death,* Fana thought. Death had followed her family since before she was born.

Jessica sighed, one hand planted on her hip in a pose that made her look like Gramma Bea. "Fana, we have a carefully crafted *network*—"

"Yes, and our treatment is only available in six countries, not including the one where we live," Fana said. "Six! I don't care about this country's drug laws—or the Brotherhood's. People get sick here, too. They should have the blood."

Mom only rested her hand against her cheek, sighing.

"You put her in danger, Fana," Dad said. "All of us are more vulnerable now."

Fana had heard enough. "I want Caitlin here. She's going to sleep in my room with me tonight. Tomorrow, you're going to let her and her father go."

She had never spoken to her parents this way, but when had they ever behaved so badly?

Her father was inside her room suddenly, looming above her. He had never looked so upset with her. "Because Caitlin was selling the blood you gave her, her friend was tortured day and night, stabbed fifty times by the sadists who kidnaped her. Was that a part of your plan?"

Her father's words hurt, but Fana was relieved. *At least he didn't do it himself.*

Fana gritted her teeth as tears glided down her face. "You think I don't know I had a role in the suffering of those people?" she said. "But at least I'm not like you, Dad. Unlike you, the killer in me is not my most practical aspect. *Your* words."

Knowing exactly which words to use was a devastating advantage. Fana's father was silenced, and her mother looked aghast.

"I'll have Caitlin brought to you," her father said. "But you will never again give away blood to be distributed outside of this colony. You'll promise me this, Fana."

"Or what? I'll be grounded?"

Jessica sighed. "Fana, please . . . haven't you learned anything from what I told you about Botswana? Our nurse died. Her brother died. All because we didn't take the right precautions. I know it feels like a sin to walk around with this blood—"

"*Yes,*" Fana said. "A sin. The worst kind."

"But we can't do this as individuals," Mom said. " We need structure. And protection."

Dad had moved to her window, staring out toward the Council House. "Fana, you'll get your friend killed. I can't say it any more plainly." It sounded like a vow.

"Oh, that's right," Fana said. "Sometimes people get killed. Don't they, Dad?"

He flinched. *Good,* Fana thought. He was afraid of what she might say. Inspired by his fear, Fana heard what he dreaded most escape through her lips. "Father Arturo didn't see you in the kitchen. You could have taken his gun away and left it at that, but you decided it was more prudent to butcher him to get him to talk."

Dad turned to look at her as if he didn't know her voice. The light had left his eyes.

Fana tried to stop herself midway through, but the words came anyway, shattering her rule: Never say things that hadn't been spoken aloud. Never use private memories as a weapon. "While he was bleeding to death, you kneeled with all your weight on his chest to cut off his breathing, in case that might make him talk faster. 'Dying men forget how to lie,' you told yourself. He begged for his life with tears in his eyes. He said, 'I'm a priest.' You said, 'A dead one.' And then you broke his neck. A very clean break. You're *very* good at killing. Does Mom know you killed her friend Peter without blinking your eyes?"

At first, when her parents' faces didn't change, Fana dared to hope that maybe the awful words had only been a loud, angry thought beneath the surface, not brought out into the room with them. Sometimes, she couldn't tell the difference.

But Mom's eyes pooled with tears. Dad opened his mouth but didn't speak. Mom lurched toward the door, as if she'd lost her balance. Dad tried to touch her, but she snatched her arm away. Mom was in the hall, then gone.

Now Fana remembered what she hated most: She hated knowing.

"S-sorry," she whispered. She wished she was still angry instead of only horrified at herself. "I didn't mean to say that."

What she had said was unforgivable, but what she had done was worse. People had died because of her. Caitlin had lost Maritza because of her.

Dad pinched his forehead, his face knotted. "I can explain."

"There's no need." Fana shook her head. "Really. I understand. You were afraid."

In the time before Mom knew the truth about Dad and his people, he had killed to protect the secret of his blood. One of the men he'd killed had been a newspaper reporter Mom had worked with, a man named Peter, Mom's mentor. He had done nothing wrong. Peter's death had sprung from an ugly web of coincidences and bad luck that had ended with his throat being cut.

Mom knew her friend had died in the front seat of his vintage Mustang, his throat slashed so wide open that his blood had coated the windshield red. Fana had seen the Mustang herself, because Peter's dying place crossed Mom's mind from time to time. Dad's, too.

Mom and Dad never talked about Peter. That was part of their uneasy truce.

But Mom hadn't known that the man who'd died yesterday had been a priest.

"I was going to talk to her later tonight, Fana," Dawit said. "I wish you hadn't said that, especially that way. But I wasn't going to keep it from her."

"I know, Dad."

He sighed, rubbing his forehead again. "I'm sorry I frightened Caitlin."

"I'm sorry I didn't tell you about the blood."

There. Almost all of this wretched episode felt better, except for that very last part. The last part didn't have an answer, unless she could make Mom forget what she'd heard. Mom told her she had done that once when she was three—simply made her forget the deepest heartaches of her life, for a minute or two anyway. She could probably do it again.

"Don't interfere, Fana," Dad said quietly. "It's my mess."

He had been inside her head, and so gently that she hadn't even noticed. Usually, she felt the air prickle when someone tried to probe her, and she could swat the sensation away. Fana wasn't used to masking herself in her parents' presence. The only place she didn't mask was at the Big House. At home. Now, she would have to be more careful.

Dad was better at mind arts than he believed he was. Maybe he had been right to kill the priest. Maybe that was what the dream had been trying to tell her.

"She's very upset, Dad."

"I know she is."

"This won't get better right away."

Dad gave a defeated smile. "No."

Fana wondered what it would be like to have a mate who loved her the way her dad loved her mother. How would she ever know?

She and Dad could be outcasts together. They deserved each other, her and her father.

"I love you, Dad."

Dawit's eyes were red. "I love you too, Fana. And you're not like me. Not in that way. You don't have to be afraid of that."

But that wasn't true.

She didn't remember the time, but she knew the stories.

Fana had killed almost as soon as she could walk.

Jessica knew she should be outside meditating. Finding her balance. Perspective.

Instead, her hands were shaking as she rearranged the items on her bedroom dresser. The cream-colored dresser with gold-paint trim had come from Bea's house, matching the canopied bed Jessica had had as a girl. The worn dresser merged her lives, old and new.

Before the Living Blood, and after.

Jessica needed to remember who she was. Sometimes she was in danger of forgetting.

She touched her fur hat from Botswana, a patchwork of textures and colors. The hat was precious to her because it was a gift from a child who had lived near her Botswana clinic and hadn't had much to give. Today, he was a physician to his people. The hat from Moses reminded Jessica of why she was here. And why she had the face and body of a twenty-seven-year-old woman when her birth certificate knew full well she had just turned forty-six.

Jessica held a child's toy, a Troll with wild purple hair her friend had given her years ago. *WRITE ON,* it said on its overstuffed belly. Sweet, thoughtful Peter.

Dawit had killed again. And, yes, Fana was right: He was good at it.

Peter Donavitch had been one of the most gentle and generous people she'd ever known, and he had accidentally planted himself in Dawit's path. *Painless,* Dawit had insisted. How could anyone who'd seen all that blood on the windshield believe there had been anything painless about Peter Donavitch's death?

Even after eighteen years of prayer and meditation, Jessica could not forgive Dawit for Peter's murder. But she'd done the best she could. She had learned to live with it, even if her throat sometimes felt bloated from all the poison she'd had to swallow. And maybe it was her fault, for not knowing the truth herself. For being so blind.

But now Dawit had killed a *priest?* Had it happened the way Fana had described?

A small, frail sob caught in Jessica's throat before she shoved it away. *No.* She had sworn years ago that she would never shed another tear over David Wolde. He was gone, a lie. She forgot that sometimes, since Dawit was so much like the man he had created to fool her into an ignorant marriage. But she could never forget. He was Dawit now.

"I miss you, David," she whispered.

"I'm here."

Jessica didn't turn. She felt her muscles and limbs slowly coating themselves with armor, like the passage in Ephesians. *"Put on the whole armour of God, that ye may be able to stand against the wiles of the devil . . . ,"* If Jessica closed her eyes, she could imagine being in their old bedroom in Miami, sharing a cramped space full of promise and normality. And in the room beside theirs, a lost daughter named Kira was five years old, sleeping peacefully in her bed. Awaiting her long, untroubled life.

Jessica could taste the sour poison in her mouth, threatening to spill.

"You're here to explain. Then explain." Jessica didn't recognize her own voice.

Dawit's silence told her what she already knew: There was no way to explain. And if he couldn't explain, there was nothing but air beneath her feet.

"There has to be a *why*," she said, turning around to look at him. Her husband's face usually had the power to wipe her mind clean, capturing all the beauty she had seen in him when she'd first met him in his classroom, dazzled by his knowledge of the world. But not this time. His white-haired disguise hid him from her.

Dawit was near tears. "I only wonder if you would understand. If even I do."

He crossed the room to their bed, sitting at the edge as if he were winded. Legs wide, he folded his hands between his knees, staring at the floor. "I saw a gun. I thought I was protecting Caitlin. Protecting all of us. I made a mistake."

"Like when you killed Peter."

Dawit sighed, lowering his voice until she could barely hear him. "Jess, you have to remember that time. Our family was in danger. My Brothers had threatened to kill everyone I loved. You saw how they tried to kill your sister."

Jessica hadn't mentioned Alex's name first for fear of what Dawit might confess. Alex had nearly died the instant Jessica had told her about her husband's blood, the first time she'd unknowingly waged Alex's life for the knowledge. It was pure fluke that Alex had survived an attacker's push from her apartment balcony with only a lifelong limp.

"What really happened with Alex that day?" Jessica said.

Dawit didn't answer, looking puzzled.

Damn him. He was going to make her say it. "Were you the one?"

Dawit rose to his feet. "God, no, Jess. I promise you. I knew nothing of Alex's attack."

"But it could have happened if she'd confronted you. As soon as I told her, she said we should beg you to heal people with your blood. What would you have done?"

"I don't know." He didn't even take time to think about it.

"You would have killed her if you'd thought you had to, Dawit. That's who you are."

"Jess, it's who I *was*. Please remember that time."

"*How the hell am I supposed to forget that time?*" Her rage, voice-less before, rang in the walls. It was as if she'd hated him all along, and only now was remembering how much, how deeply. His ritual had given her provisional immortality, but he had stolen her world in the process. She could forget that for years at a time, but tonight Jessica's memory was sharp.

Dawit kept his distance, waiting until the walls no longer rang. Then, his voice was all quiet rationality. "I thought he was a threat to me. I couldn't risk being discovered. I couldn't face the thought of leaving you and . . ."

Kira. He was still afraid to say their daughter's name.

A feeling as powerful as a bolt of lightning set down in the room, tethering them. Kira was in a place beyond blame. Dawit's hands might have killed her in his quest to give her immortality, but Jessica shared in his complicity. She had not protected Kira. She had not left Dawit when she'd learned the truth about who he was. And she had hesitated instead of finishing the Ceremony Dawit had started, choosing to send her child's soul Home rather than exiling her forever in the land of the living.

Despite the miracle in her own veins, Jessica never would have married Dawit if he had told her about his blood, his history, the danger, and his hidden Brotherhood of men who didn't die. If she had left him when he'd first told her, Kira would still have been alive—and Fana never would have been born: an impossible choice for her heart.

"*But Jesus said, suffer little children, and forbid them not, to come unto me: for such is the kingdom of heaven.*" Sometimes, knowing that Kira had made it to Heaven was Jessica's only joy. Would Kira have to represent them all there?

Both of them had killed Kira. Both of them would have to raise Fana. Somehow.

"Why didn't you tell me about the priest?" Jessica said.

"I was going to. When we were alone."

Jessica realized that she didn't want to be alone with Dawit tonight. Dawit might have heard the thought, but that was all right. The more he improved his mind arts, the less she would be able to hide from her own feelings, constantly twisted between then and now.

"Bring Caitlin to Fana," Jessica said. "She never should have been treated that way."

"I'll get her now. But the Brothers won't like it."

"Does that matter?"

Dawit almost smiled. For years, they had wondered what else might trigger a repeat of the awful events from Fana's early childhood, when she'd left a trail of corpses.

Jessica sighed. "We have to assume Fana knows everything about us."

Dawit nodded sadly. "Yes."

"Then I need to know, too. Who else, Dawit? How many others have you killed?"

Stark alarm swept across Dawit's face. He didn't answer. *Are there that many?*

"All of them," Jessica said. "I want to know."

Dawit's eyes implored her, as if she was torturing him. "Jess . . ."

"Do you even know, Dawit? Can you count them?"

Something foreign stole into Dawit's eyes. She suddenly saw the five-hundred-year-old man he was; unknowable. How could she ever have mistaken him for David? He was nothing like the college professor she had stood with at the makeshift altar in her mother's living room.

"Let me see . . . ," Dawit said, sarcasm lacing his voice. "When I was twelve, I hit a man with a stone so hard that the side of his head caved in. I did it to save my master's son, because I was a slave and a soldier from the time I was a boy. That's the one I remember best."

"How many?" she whispered. She felt like she was prying now, but she wanted to know.

Dawit's eyes brightened with an anger that hollowed his cheeks. "Then ask me as my *wife,* not my interrogator. I've fought in wars, Jessica. Shall I tell you about the pimply-faced boys I stabbed with my bayonet in Gettysburg? Or the Italians who murdered old men, women and children in search of my blood? Who blubbered for their mothers as their guts spilled out? How many did I kill? Not enough, by far."

For a moment, neither of them spoke. Her husband was shaking. But maybe she was, too. Jessica allowed herself a single tear.

"He was a priest, Dawit. Did you know that before you stabbed him?"

Dawit only blinked. The answer, clearly, was yes.

Jessica's mind expanded when she prayed each morning—she could feel herself stretching in all directions—but she still could not understand her husband. She wanted to love him the way she had when he'd only been David, but she had no idea where to start.

"Then *why*?" she said. Her voice trembled.

"He was a man with a gun. He was waiting for Caitlin. That was what was in my mind."

Jessica sifted her fingers through the wiry hairs of Dawit's phony beard. She looked away from his unknowable eyes. "Doesn't God mean anything to you?"

"There are many gods in this world, Jessica," Dawit said. "The greatest being I ever knew was a man named Khaldun, who gave me this blood. I have yet to choose my God."

"And the Blood?" she whispered. Khaldun had claimed the Blood came from Christ, but Jessica rarely spoke those words. All of them in the Big House believed it: Her mother. Alex. Cal and Nita Duhart. Maybe even Lucas, despite himself. What else could explain it?

"Khaldun told a story about the Blood, yes," Dawit said. "Khaldun told us many stories. In one story, he cast himself as Judas, the most misunderstood disciple. In another, the man you worship on the cross was another Life Brother, no different than any of us. Under other circumstances, the Gospels might have been written about Fana. Or me. Or you. Khaldun is a wondrous being, Jessica, but not all of his stories are true. Why shouldn't I assume the Blood was Khaldun's all along?"

"Then why are you here?"

Dawit blinked, and a sheet of tears fell across his eyes. "My Brothers believe another of Khaldun's stories . . . that our daughter is a deity," he said. "Whatever she is, like you, I want to nurture her heart.

I want her to feel zeal and drive and passion for this world. With my Brothers standing with us, the blood mission can be more than the naive fantasy of very young immortals who haven't lived long enough to know better. But I must confess: I prefer the peace of Lalibela. I'm here only for you, *mi vida*. I've always been here for you."

Standing so close to Dawit but still missing the man she had married, immersed in his unchanged scent, Jessica felt sadness with no end.

In her long silence, Dawit walked away from her to the foot of their bed and picked up the small black flight bag he still hadn't had time to unpack. He held it against his chest, waiting.

Jessica couldn't ask him to stay, even though her anger had been replaced by a hole.

"I don't know you, Dawit. Still."

"You can, Jess. You will," he said. "But please remember this: When I first found you giving your blood away, I warned you nothing but heartache was ahead. I told you there was a reason we had lived so long in secrecy and had shunned mortals so."

That was true. Jessica could never say he hadn't warned her.

"Your heart compels you to use the Blood to heal, and I fight for your wishes every day," he went on. "But let's not forget the truth of it, because you know all too well: The Blood heals, and it brings death. I learned this generations before you were born. If killing gives you pause, you need a new calling. I promise you, more will come."

He was the same rash man who had killed her friend when he hadn't had to.

"Then it's lucky that the killer in you is your most practical aspect, Dawit," Jessica said.

From Dawit's face, no weapon could have injured him more.

Eight

Her parents' argument was far from Fana's ears, beyond several closed doors and sturdy walls, but its spirit filled the entire house. Even with Caitlin sitting beside her on the bed with an avalanche of intrusive thoughts, Fana's mind was rooted to her parents.

No wonder she avoided anger. She was clumsy at it, even cruel.

Fana heard her father's sure footsteps in the hallway, then down the stairs. He was leaving the house. He usually tapped on her door to tell her good night at ten o'clock, but this time he avoided her room. Caitlin was afraid of him.

Dad would sleep in his Brothers' quarters tonight.

Except for Dad, only Teferi and Jima kept separate houses with mates and children; the rest lived in a communal state as they had in Lalibela, another habit that had been conditioned into them over centuries. But Dad had never slept outside of these walls when he'd been in town. What if she had shorn the fragile thread between her parents?

Caitlin nudged Fana's shoulder. "We have to get my father, then we all need to *get the hell out of here*. That means you, too. Your teacher wants you to meditate four hours a day? Come on! That's *bullshit*, Fana. I'd rather die when I'm sixty and be free instead of living forever cooped up in the woods."

"They can't stop me from giving you blood, Caitlin."

Caitlin's mouth fell open as she gaped, disbelieving. "God, I hope you're not that naive."

Fana sighed. The Life Brothers could make Caitlin vanish, and probably her entire network. That would happen unless Fana was willing to fight ugly—and she wasn't. She had fought ugly as a child, and she couldn't survive that again. She wouldn't even know how.

"We can't even make plans," Caitlin said. "You said your teacher can get in your head."

Fana and Teka never spoke aloud during their daily lessons anymore, one of the few times Fana practiced her mind arts consciously. "Not if I'm careful."

"What about me? They can force me to name everyone I know in the Railroad. They probably know everything already. And they won't let me go, Fana. My dad either." Caitlin's lips shook. "Do you know how *scared* Dad is right now? He's throwing up. And it's our fault."

The Underground Railroad. The North Star. Nicknames for the network of Glow distributors in the United States, Mexico and Canada. Fana's blood was the only source of Glow in North America. If Caitlin's supply was cut off, that might end the healing for a continent. Caitlin was as important in her world as Fana was in this one.

Fana knew there were other reasons the Life Brothers would never forge meaningful ties with the Underground Railroad. Fana sometimes heard the Brothers' comments, as she had tonight in the Council room, but their thoughts were worse: *Leave the monkeys to themselves,* Berhanu often thought. But Fana hated to admit her people's bigotries to Caitlin.

"It's the drug laws," Fana said instead, which was mostly true. "They have to work with cooperative governments. Places where they can cover their trail."

With enough secretiveness to hide the immortals' existence— but with the blessing of a handful of national health ministers—her parents' network practically had obliterated the raging AIDS problem in Botswana, South Africa, Ghana and Nigeria. Other nations would follow soon. The blood's effects were so powerful that a little went a long way.

But it was different in the United States. Glow had been classified as a Schedule II drug—the most dangerous—because of corporate meddling and fabricated reports of fatalities. There were even new rumors cropping up in the news that Glow was related to terrorism.

With so much controversy and mystery, Fana knew that Glow would never get past the FDA for legalization. For now, the prevailing theories were that Glow contained synthetic blood cells or nanotechnology, but it wouldn't take forever for outsiders to realize the truth.

Then catastrophic times would begin.

Every month, there were drills to make sure all of them could vanish in minutes, leaving their homes to retreat to the underground shelters. *The price of helping people,* Mom always said. The children had turned drills into games, racing each other.

"You need to see what's going on out there, Fana," Caitlin said. "Health care is shit, and it's getting worse. Insurance is a scam. The only reason there are laws against Glow is because the multinationals don't know how to profit from it. The health corps get richer while people are *dying*. Without us, the people are trapped in the system. We can set them free."

Fana had seen plenty on the internet about the health care crisis: hospitals dumping the indigent on the streets. Families losing their homes. Children and the elderly dying for lack of care. That was why she had decided to tell Caitlin about her blood three years ago: She couldn't sleep at night knowing she was only hiding in her room, doing nothing.

Fana's heartbeat quickened. "Even if we did make it out of here . . . where would we go? My mind shorts out when I'm around too many people. I've told you that."

"There's people in the Railroad who give shelter," Caitlin said. "Please, Fana? I think Dad and I might die if we don't go. Or worse."

"What would be worse?"

Caitlin blinked. "Failing. If we couldn't get Glow out in the world."

Fana stared at the photograph of Harriet Tubman that had been taken in the 1800s. Grim-faced Tubman was resolute in a formal dress, her head wrapped in a scarf, fighting her way into history. Tubman had run and led others to freedom. Sometimes running *was* the answer.

"We have to leave your father," Fana said.

Caitlin's face went flat, stunned. "No."

"We have to. He's under guard, and our chances are better alone."

Berhanu would not allow them to take Justin O'Neal from under his nose. Fana didn't even dare probe him from a distance. Berhanu's mind arts were nearly as strong as Teka's, and she would never dream of trying to pull that trick on her teacher. She wasn't ready, not by far.

Caitlin's head fell forward, as if the bones in her neck had collapsed. Fana took her friend's hand. Gramma Bea liked to say that touching her was like squeezing the sun, a burst of light. She hoped that was true for Caitlin, too.

"I promise you, they won't kill him. I *promise*," Fana said.

"Please, Fana. Please please please?" Caitlin whispered. "We have to go get him."

"Either we leave without him or we stay. There's no other choice. If you're right, staying here means your network could disappear. Look at me, Caitlin: During slavery in the American South, do you know why more slaves didn't run away?"

Caitlin's weary, frightened eyes alarmed Fana. She had never seen Caitlin so broken.

"They were . . . afraid of getting caught?" Caitlin said.

"No," Fana said. "They didn't want to leave their families. They were worried about what would happen to them. They didn't want to be alone. Neither do I. But I'll do it for you. For Glow. To heal. And you have to make the same sacrifice."

Caitlin's head hung again, and her shoulders shuddered with a stifled, keening sob. That was how Fana knew that she had made up her mind.

Fana jumped from the bed and found an empty Miami Dolphins duffel bag her cousin Jared had given her. He would tell her she should stay until she was older, but that was easy for him to say. He didn't have the Blood. And he was already gone, tasting the world outside.

The current of blood pounding through her veins made Fana dizzy. She was going to do it. After years of fantasies and wishes, she was going to leave.

"Come on, help me pack," Fana said. "If we're going, we have to go tonight."

Glow had transformed Caitlin into a revolutionary, Fana realized.

She heard her friend crying softly, but the sobs were only quiet, huffing exhalations as she trotted behind Fana, keeping perfect pace. Caitlin was focused on escape.

The darkened schoolhouse appeared in front of them at the edge of the eastern woods, the small brick building where Fana had studied before Teka had become her sole teacher. Fana had enjoyed many happy moments in this building, when she'd finally felt like she'd had a normal life like Caitlin and the kids outside.

The school building was her last piece of home before the woods.

Fana grabbed Caitlin's arm, ducking them around a corner where they would not be seen from houses, nor by the sentries who lay in the darkness ahead of them. Fana leaned against the wall, slowing her breathing, and Caitlin followed her lead. Fana had stuffed only a few clothes and snacks into her Miami Dolphins duffel bag, but it was heavier than she had expected.

Caitlin's fear and grief smelled bitter in her perspiration.

"He'll be fine," Fana said again. "They're not cruel."

Caitlin sniffed hard to clear her nose. "Right."

They couldn't worry about Caitlin's father now.

Before they left, Fana had drawn out a map for Caitlin in her bedroom, showing her the route she'd used to escape the colony three years ago. The firefence was sure to be different now—its patterns changed several times daily—but their general route would be the same, ending on a mile-and-a-half dirt road that would take them to Toledo. They would have to stay clear of the paths, even the horse trails, because they would be more easily spotted there.

"Remember . . . ," Fana whispered. "I run, I find cover, and crouch. It takes me time to sense what's around us, and I have to be still. If we get separated, go to the nearest cover and *don't move*. That's the most important thing. Just don't trip the firefence. I'll find you."

Caitlin nodded, wiping her nose with the sleeve of her Berkeley sweatshirt.

"What happens if I trip it?" Caitlin said.

"Best-case scenario, they know exactly where and *who* you are. Worst case . . . I don't know. There's a charge. It might just knock you out, or it might do worse."

Caitlin nodded, accepting. Her life was full of danger now. "What else?"

"It's a workout. Your legs will burn from crouching," Fana said. She had been shocked at how tough the exertion had been last time.

"'If you are tired, keep going. If you are hungry, keep going,'" Caitlin whispered.

Harriet Tubman's words, the conductor of the original Underground Railroad. Scholars said the words were a fiction created by one of Tubman's biographers, but Fana knew they captured Tubman's spirit. Fana clasped her friend's unsteady hand, finishing the quotation: "'If you want to taste freedom, keep going.' We'll be free, Caitlin. We'll free the world."

Her only answer was another quiet sob in the dark.

Fana was afraid, too. Sometimes dreams and premonitions guided her, but she didn't know what would happen to Caitlin's father. She didn't know what the Life Brothers would do once they realized she was gone. And now she would have to spend all of her days in hiding, always expecting to be found.

Fana felt Caitlin's resolve in their clasped hands, and she knew Caitlin could feel hers. Their belief in their mission burned through their skin, a fire to warm the lonely night.

"Let's move," Fana said.

As Fana launched herself from the wall to sprint toward the woods, she ran headfirst into someone walking around the corner. Her arms and legs tangled with another's, and she heard a woman gasp with surprise as they lost their balance and fell in a heap.

Fana knew her peppermint smell even before she sorted through her startled thoughts.

"Lord have *mercy* . . . ," Aunt Alex said. "Fana?"

"Oh, sh— Aunt Alex, I'm so sorry," Fana said. Her mouth moved on its own, because her mind had come to a standstill from seeing Aunt Alex in such an unexpected time and place.

"'Oh, shit' is right. What are you doing back here so late?"

A flashlight beam glared into Fana's eyes, and she shielded her face. How hadn't she noticed an approaching flashlight from around the corner? Why hadn't she sensed anything at all? "Caitlin? You're out here, too?" Aunt Alex said.

"Just taking a walk, thinking things through," Caitlin said. She shoved her hands in her pockets. Although Caitlin's face glistened with tears and mucous, she sounded amazingly nonchalant. Glow had turned her into an actress, too.

Fana recovered her mind and voice. "What are you doing up so late, Auntie?"

"I came back to grab my lesson plan before morning. The older kids are reading *Lord of the Flies,* if you must know, and I haven't studied it since high school. But you're not the one asking the questions. I hope you girls aren't trying to do something stupid."

Aunt Alex knows. Fana lost her voice again. Even without telepathy, her mother and aunt had such sharp maternal perceptions that Fana was still startled by it.

"We're just talking," Caitlin said in a young-girl voice. "We wanted some privacy."

Aunt Alex's voice softened as she stroked Caitlin's hair. "Honey, I know you're worried about your father. But like I told you before: And this, too, shall pass."

Fana's heart raced. A plan that had seemed within their grasp before now felt ridiculous. They'd already been caught, and they hadn't made it as far as the cedar fence! Teka was deluded to think she had any valuable powers. She had only been lucky to make it through the property's hundreds of acres the first time.

But Caitlin's desperate look said *DO something,* and Fana knew she had no choice.

Her heart still pumping hard, Fana suddenly leaned over to kiss her aunt's cheek. Aunt Alex looked pleased but wary. "Unh-hnhhh. What's that all about?"

"Thank you for caring, that's all," Fana said.

"Of course I care—"

"But we have to go now, Aunt Alex. I won't see you for a while, and I'll miss you."

Fana jabbed gently at her thoughts. Aunt Alex scowled at her, stepping back.

I HOPE I HEARD THIS GIRL WRONG

"You didn't hear me wrong. Good-bye." Fana held her aunt's cheeks between her palms.

Fana pried at the stream of Aunt Alex's thoughts again, easing herself into the flow of incoherence Teka called *noise*. The sound was at turns shrieks and babbles. Most people would never hear noise or know it existed. Even for people who studied a lifetime, the ability to see auras was the closest they would experience to visiting someone else's mind. Noise was well beyond the auras, and noise was only the beginning.

Aunt Alex stiffened, pulling away. Her eyebrows lowered in puzzlement, then alarm.

Damn. Maybe she'd pushed too hard, fighting to separate her aunt's thoughts from Caitlin's. Fana tried to nudge her consciousness into her aunt's, past the squall of sounds. The noise suddenly separated into streams that Teka had taught her could be comprehended with thought "languages," the mental creation of meaning from the sounds. Suddenly, her aunt's thoughts were a loud drumbeat: *WHATINTHEWORLDISGOINGON*

Navigating thought streams was painstaking and difficult even when Fana had time to concentrate. Now, she felt herself jabbing and tugging, fumbling past the sound to the endless banks of images flying in her aunt's conscious and unconscious minds. Some of the neural pathways were familiar and easy to wade through, but most were foreign.

Finally, the solid world vanished, and Fana was swallowed in the surge of her aunt's myriad memories. Pigtails in the mirror. A red Radio Flyer wagon. Her father's gap-toothed grin. Why did childhood memories always bubble so close to the surface, never gone?

Tonight, Fana thought, willing herself to discard what she didn't need.

She saw Chestnut, one of the horses, leaping over a fallen tree trunk. The dinner table. Aunt Alex at the Council Hall with her father, bringing Caitlin out of the holding room.

Now, Fana thought.

Suddenly, she saw through her aunt's eyes as she swung her flashlight, climbing down the back porch's steps. Fana sliced off the end of the stream, leaving only a white space. With more time, she might have constructed an alternate fantasy, but under the circumstances, this was the best she could do. Aunt Alex would remember climbing down the porch, and then . . . nothing.

But Aunt Alex will be fine. She's lost a minute's worth of memories, or two at most.

"Come on," Fana whispered, grabbing Caitlin's arm. "We have to go."

But Caitlin was staring, wide-eyed, as Aunt Alex stood frozen. Even in the dark, Aunt Alex's face showed the tendrils of alarm that had emerged when she'd felt Fana's intrusion in her head. She stood like a statue, hardly breathing. Caitlin waved her hand in front of her eyes.

Had Fana been too clumsy in her aunt's mind?

"Is she okay?" Caitlin whispered.

I'm so sorry, Aunt Alex. I hope you can hear me. I'm sorry.

Fana yanked Caitlin's arm harder. At the periphery of her awareness, she realized that her mental scent had caught Berhanu's attention as far as the Council House. If she stayed any longer, he might see through the decoy marker she had left in her room.

"Let's *go,*" she said over the new lump in her throat. Aunt Alex's vacant face made her stomach knot, but there wasn't time to mend the damage now. She would be fine. If Caitlin had to leave her father behind, Fana could leave her aunt. Mom would take care of Aunt Alex. Teka would take care of her.

This time, the sob Fana heard was her own. "Come on, Caitlin. Hurry."

The woods waited.

The cedar fence that circled the colony's buildings kept the horses from getting loose, and its quaintness gave the appearance of a gentle commune in the woods, bothering no one and not expecting to be bothered. Fana often let herself forget that she lived in an outdoor fortress.

The firefence was the colony's true defense system.

Fana had first seen the firefence long before she'd been old enough to understand what it was; she'd been lost in her head, spending hours staring out her window. When it had been dark, she'd noticed a faint orange glow in the woods, so fragile she'd had to stare hard to know if it had been real. When she'd been older— after her mind set her free to roam in the physical world like other children—she'd studied the woods and the light while she'd leaned across the colony gate.

The closer she got to the woods, the more crisp the light became, as fine as countless orange-gold laser beams. She had always been able to see the firefence. She'd confided this to Teka once, and he'd been incredulous until she'd gone outside with him after dark and pointed out its patterns one by one with the tip of her sneaker. Teka had been excited, claiming that her ability to see its rays had been further proof of her gifts. *And it is fortuitous for us, dear Fana, that the firefence is not intended to keep you in—only to keep others out.*

The Life Brothers had brought the technology for the firefence from the Ethiopian colony's House of Science, in addition to weapons that were hidden from the eyes of the others. Fana had often wondered whether Aunt Alex and Gramma Bea would sleep better at night, or perhaps not at all, if they knew the true power of the arsenal in their midst. Her father said the security measures were to protect everyone, but Fana knew they were to protect her.

She was the reason most of the Life Brothers had come, and she was leaving them.

But it was long past time for all of them to release their illusions about who or what she was. She wasn't worthy of worship. She might not even be worthy of forgiveness.

Fana felt renewed sadness as she squatted behind the swathing, feathery fronds of the bracken ferns with Caitlin panting beside her. They had already been running for an hour, and Fana could still see a faint glow from the Duharts' backyard solar light, as if they hadn't made any progress. Fana's upper thighs throbbed with pain.

And the farther they got from her house, the worse she felt about Aunt Alex. What would her mother think? And Gramma Bea? And Teka? What if she had harmed her aunt far worse than she knew, like so many people she had harmed when she was too young to remember?

She should turn back. With each passing minute, Fana was more sure of it.

But she couldn't.

Fana wiped tears and perspiration from her eyes so she could see. For an instant, the woods was all darkness. Even with a full moon that evaded the thick treetops above them, it was hard for Fana to separate one tree from another, and the firefence was nowhere in sight. *Patience,* she told herself when she felt panic rising. Her mother's mantra. So far, she was almost sure they had been undetected. That was something, at least. There was still a chance.

"How can you see a damn thing out here?" Caitlin said.

"Just can." Fana peered hard into the blackness, waiting.

"What about the flashlight?" Caitlin had liberated Aunt Alex of her flashlight so deftly that Fana hadn't noticed until Caitlin had confessed later. So much for Caitlin's concern about her aunt.

"You might as well send up a flare. *Shhh.* Ouch—"

Fana lost her balance in her crouch, and when she flung her palm back to catch herself, a jagged exposed root sliced into her skin with her pitching weight. She snatched her hand away and struggled not to yell out, but it was the worst pain of her life.

"You okay?" Caitlin whispered.

Fana breathed deeply, pulling her hand close to examine it: A pencil-thin root fragment had pierced her like a knife, missing her tendons but slicing a hole clean through the web beside her thumb. Runny blood seeped on her palm. Fana's eyes flooded with tears.

"Holy mother of shit," Caitlin said. She could see the blood even in the dark.

Gritting her teeth, Fana yanked out the wood sliver and tossed it to her feet. Another searing flash of pain. *One . . . two . . . three . . . four . . . five . . . six . . .*

Gone.

"Let me look at that," Caitlin said, grabbing her wrist. The flashlight flared in Fana's face.

"No light," Fana hissed, turning it off. "What's wrong with you?"

"You really hurt yourself," Caitlin said.

"I did, but now I'm fine. It's done."

Tingling overtook Fana's hand, and her fingers trembled. Instead of pain, Fana felt a cold-hot immersion, as if her hand had been beneath water with a shifting temperature. Her cells were knitting back together. Fana shoved her arm beneath her sweatshirt to wipe the blood away. She didn't want Caitlin to see the way her skin squirmed when it healed.

"Done?" Caitlin said. "You mean? . . ."

The blood wiped clean, Fana raised her hand to Caitlin's face, wiggling her fingers. The hole the wood had made was gone. Her palm was slightly numb, but that would pass within ten or fifteen minutes. It always did.

Caitlin grabbed Fana's wrist with both hands, staring. Fuck-eyed, as Caitlin would say.

"I told you I heal fast," Fana said. "Magic show's over. Let's get out of here."

While Caitlin muttered "*Holy shit*" in repetition, Fana stared into the dark for the firefence.

The moon grew brighter, and trees and brush leaped into focus. Fana could suddenly see every tiny pinnae on the fronds of the ferns in front of them. She also saw the delicate slivers of light that pierced the air in countless patterns. The woods was a light show of hexagons, polygons, triangles and Xs, with precious few untouched spaces between them for shelter. The lights stretched as high and far as she could see.

It was an effective system. The firefence was invisible even to infrared detectors, but no one was invisible to the firefence except the sentries. If one of the beams sensed her or Caitlin, the sentries instantly would know exactly where they were, how many of them there were, their size, how fast their hearts were beating, and a slew of other data. The firefence could also deliver a jolt of energy to knock them unconscious, or worse.

Fana didn't want to touch the firefence.

She breathed slowly, concentrating on the dark havens between the lines, looking for the biggest gaps, the ones closest to cover, the ones they could pass through. There weren't many. The best cover, a large juniper she could smell ahead of them, was twelve yards through a gauntlet of stabbing lights. But as Fana focused, she saw a winding polyline emerge, a path to the tree's base. *Very* narrow, but possible.

"This one's tough," Fana warned.

"Shit, what else is new?"

"Follow the leader," Fana said as she slipped from their cover.

Fana's first steps took her knees within four inches of the firefence, so she moved more slowly, encouraging Caitlin to mimic her creeping slide. So far, Caitlin had been keeping her shoulders low and angling her tiny body with enough precision that she avoided even what she couldn't see. Thank goodness Caitlin was five-two and small-boned. Mr. O'Neal never would have gotten through. They had been right to leave him.

"Watch your head," Fana whispered, eyeing a twig of light two inches above her.

Fana crept on, stooping. She jumped when her duffel bag hit her hip and swung toward the firefence's glow to the right of her. She clamped her arm down hard against the bag, whispering a curse. She should have left the bag, too.

At last, they reached the juniper tree. This time, they sat as they hid behind the trunk, resting. But they wouldn't be able to sit long. It was already 1 a.m. The property was five hundred acres, more than three-quarters of a square mile. Luckily, they didn't have to travel from end to end—just to the northwest corner—but their pace was too slow. At this rate, they wouldn't get to the road until afternoon. Fana wiped away the perspiration bathing her face and peered around the trunk to scout again, the routine she would repeat countless times tonight.

And she heard a man's clipped voice. Fana pulled back, and she felt Caitlin stiffen beside her. Fana raised a finger to her lips. *Shhhhh.*

It might be too late already. The sentries were bound to have refined mind arts, and the voice was no more than fifteen yards from them. Someone at a high level could perceive thoughts from farther than that. Teka and Berhanu could, and undoubtedly others.

Fana visualized a blanket falling over her, the way she masked her thoughts, and she spread her blanket over Caitlin, too. She might be terrible at rearranging memories, but she was expert at masking. Even Teka could not penetrate her thoughts if she didn't want him to, nor could he even realize that she was hiding from him. That was how she kept her secrets.

The voice spoke again, in Amharic. "*Esua konjo nech.*" She is beautiful.

He was speaking into a transmitter, Fana realized, communicating with another sentry. Was he talking about her?

Cautiously, Fana probed at him. His thought stream was only the smallest trickle, with very little noise. He was on duty, so he was masking too, Fana realized. She could not learn his name without a more assertive probe, and that would be dangerous. But small details emerged: Fana didn't sense any emotions or images to betray that he knew of their escape—a relief. He was alone. And he was groggy from sleep, or he would have noticed her approach.

He was at a campsite. A few more steps, and they would have stumbled right into it.

Suddenly, Fana wanted to *see* him. She had spotted sentries from a distance a half dozen times before, but she'd never been permitted to study the men whose vow to protect her drove them to a monk-like existence in the woods. They had once protected Khaldun and done his bidding as his Searchers; but now, Teka said, they had at last found what they'd been searching for.

Fana poked her head around the juniper's trunk, concealing as much of her face as possible. Caitlin tugged at her arm, confused, but Fana waved her hand at her. *Be still.*

Fana felt her pupils dilate, allowing in more light, and the forest came alive. She saw the firefence rays, pillars of Douglas firs, the craggy branches of big-leaf maple and western hemlock trees, and a riot of leaves beneath the pale moon.

The moon found him for her.

He was standing in a spotlight exactly fifteen yards from her. The man was slender but muscled, more than six feet tall, standing with one arm supported against what looked like a tree trunk. He wore dark, tight-fitting clothes that reminded her of what a diver might wear; clothes meant to make him invisible in the night. He was not looking toward her, but she could clearly see his silhouette, even at this distance; a long forehead, a well-etched onyx jaw. He looked like he was only twenty or twenty-one, Caitlin's age.

He was living art. All of him was breathtaking.

Because she had to know his name, her probe intensified until she fished it out: *Fasilidas*. The long-dead Ethiopian king, now reborn with this man's face.

Despite the perspiration that swamped her clothes and her racing heart, Fana felt a deep, sudden ache that had nothing to do with worries and guilt about Aunt Alex, the death of a priest she had never met, or her decision to leave home. The feeling was both new and old to her, but the sting had never pierced through every part of her at once.

The pain in her hand had ended before it had begun, but this pain never died, and never would.

This man loved her so much that he had moved to a strange land to undertake the never-ending task of preserving the colony's safety. Even if he had not been an immortal, he gladly would die for her. He was a true supplicant.

But Fasilidas could never be hers. No one could.

She could never love anyone who worshiped her. She might never be safe to give her heart and bed to anyone, even among the tiny, selective race of immortals. How could she know the difference between genuine feelings and those she might accidentally seed herself? Whose mind could be strong enough for her? Whose heart?

The man moved suddenly, straightening. "On my way now," he said, in Amharic.

Who was he talking to? Fana had forgotten to concentrate enough to learn what the other sentries' positions might be.

The sentry swept his arm down, and the tree beside him was

gone. Blinking, Fana realized he had never been standing beside a tree at all; it was a tangle of shrubbery growing atop a man-made entryway standing vertically. He had let it fall soundlessly against the forest floor, vanishing. Like their Brothers in the Lalibela Colony in Ethiopia, the sentries lived underground.

"Yes," the sentry said to his invisible Brother. "For the love of Fana."

For the love of Fana. He said it as if it was his customary good-bye.

Fana was so amazed by the sound of her name from his mouth that she nearly forgot her mask. Her surprise forced her to retreat from the sentry's mind faster than she would have liked, or her precious blanket might fail. Fana ducked behind the juniper, her eyes full from the sight of him. Did she dare probe him again? Would she ever see him again?

Not tonight, certainly. Tonight, she and Caitlin must sit and wait until her beautiful guardian was far from them. Then, they would continue their frog-hopping escape until dawn. As beautiful as he was, Fasilidas was an enemy tonight.

At some point later, Fana knew, the Brothers would piece together how she had circumvented the firefence. Teka had more than enough clues to determine their path. Soon, it would be known that they had passed under this poor man's nose.

Silently, Fana whispered apologies to her sentry, which he would hear only later, while he slept:

Do not feel shame, fine guardian. You performed your duties well. You could not have turned me back.

It was my time to go.

Nine

Seattle

No matter how many clothes he wore, Stefan could not get warm. His feet were numb, especially his toes. Were toes the last to come to life?

The security employee's oversized pants and shirt had warmed his limbs enough to stop his violent trembling, and he had found his way to the door of the freezing prison where he had awakened. He had also found a white doctor's coat and Mariners baseball cap before he hurried outside into the night. Undetected, by sweet blessing. In his weakened state, Stefan lacked the thought for evasion. His walk was barely more than a stagger on two dead feet.

Stefan searched up and down the street for a place to disappear from sight.

Bright signs behind him identified the King County Medical Examiner's Office and Harborview Medical Center, a sprawling campus. A screaming ambulance raced toward the emergency room, lighting Stefan's coat in red as he hugged himself in the night chill.

Suddenly, Stefan knew exactly where he was from the domed brick towers of St. James Cathedral five or six blocks north. He mourned that there would be no sanctuary for him inside that church, even if he had once been welcome with warm smiles and instant fraternity. How he would miss those magnificent organs! All of his years of work were lost now. Father Arturo Bragga was dead at last. His body was drenched in the odor of formaldehyde to prove it. He had been so close! The girl had come to him willingly. How had that black man surprised him? How had he been discovered?

The ancient text's warnings were valid; if he had ever doubted, he now had further proof. The Blood's enemies were powerful beyond imagining. He must talk to Michel right away.

Stefan lurched toward the row of businesses across the street, seeking rest. And sustenance. Without food, he would faint. It was a wonder he was on his feet. The sandwich shop would have to do. Nothing else was open.

The restaurant was empty, and the college-age girl behind the counter looked happy for company. "Hard night, Doc?" she said, grinning. "Welcome to Subway. How can I—"

Stefan waved his hand, silencing her. "Make me three sandwiches. No, four," he said. "Mostly meat. Bring them to me in your rear storeroom. Otherwise, I'm not to be disturbed."

The girl nodded eagerly and grabbed a loaf of bread in each hand from the oven without hesitation. Her grin never left her, and Stefan was relieved. If he'd been too weary to control her, he would have had to kill her, the way he'd killed the security guard. His son was impatient with Stefan's erratic telepathic skills, but he was glad to spare this girl.

Killing the young was hardest. She could wait until The Cleansing.

The Miami girl had been different. They'd had to make an example of her.

Stefan grabbed an armful of milk cartons from the refrigerated case and stumbled past the counter into the restaurant's storeroom. He drained the first carton so greedily that much of the milk splashed across his chin and clothes. Opening a second carton, Stefan found a small desk in the cramped room's rear and collapsed into the chair. The telephone beckoned him. Another blessing! He had taken the dead security guard's cell phone, but it was better not to use it.

He tore open a bag of potato chips from the crate beside him and began dialing. The plaintive violin in Pachelbel's Canon in D filled Stefan with hope. Michel's ringer.

"*Pronto?*" Michel said, anxious.

Stefan was so relieved that he wept. "It's me," he said, finding his voice. "I'm well."

Michel let out a river of exclamations. "I've been so worried,

Papa!" he said. "I know you asked me to stay away, but I felt your spirit when you died. And I saw you on the news! I'm on my way to you now. Those fools Romero and Bocelli were detained in New York. Expired passports! I've been petrified you would end up in an incinerator, or buried somewhere."

"No, don't come here," Stefan said, tasting the salt of his tears. He wiped his eyes. "It isn't safe for us. We are exposed."

Stefan was shocked to hear the sound of his son's raucous, child-ish laughter. "Then you don't know!" Michel said, and laughed again.

"Speak your thoughts. I'm not like you, to hear them from so far."

Michel lowered his voice to a whisper. "It is *we* who have found *her*."

The counter girl arrived with the first of Stefan's sandwiches, and none too soon. Stefan felt himself slipping from his chair. He gnawed off a bite of bread and meat, trying to hurry sustenance to his healing-ravaged body. A large chunk of beef nearly caught in his throat before he forced it down through sheer force of will. Had he dreamed his son's words?

"Again," Stefan said. "I don't understand."

"The man you met was her *father*, Papa. Do you see? He touched your mind. He touches hers. She touches his."

"You mean? . . ."

"He has brought us together! *You* have, Papa. You did not suffer in vain. I can see her now. Not only in dreams, like before, but I can see her in waking hours. She's mine. If you don't need me, I'll help sort out Romero and Bocelli. We'll go to her now. She has left her home. There will be none to challenge us."

Stefan's confused heart thundered with renewed life. All of these years since the Chosen girl's birth, Michel's abilities had been inad-equate to find her. Had their exile in the wilderness of ignorance finally ended? The receiver nearly slipped from his palm. Stefan dropped his food and fell to his knees on the hard floor, crossing himself.

"Thank you for blessing Your poor, tired servants so . . . ," he whispered.

"With some credit to me, I hope," Michel said.

Stefan had battled his son's arrogance for fifty years, since before the boy could speak aloud. All glory was due to the Witness. Stefan could never forget that, or he was lost.

"They butchered you, Papa," Michel said, his voice sober. He had been so preoccupied that he had overlooked Stefan's memories, until now.

"Autopsies are a daily hazard," Stefan said. "I destroyed my samples, but I'm so tired, I can barely walk. The attack was a torture. Not since the war . . ." Stefan didn't go on. He was not proud of the war; the memory of his deeds felt more heinous in light of their failure. He prayed for the souls he had killed, hoping to bring them peace, but he had nothing to show them for their sacrifice.

And then the suffering! First a spear, and then his harrowing recovery from fire.

"What was his name, Michel?" Stefan said. "The one who stabbed me?"

"Dawit." Michel didn't hesitate. Truly, he had learned what had been unknown to them.

Stefan cringed, remembering the knife's torment. "Ethiopian. I met him once, I think."

"If you did, he didn't remember you. He believes he killed you in error. How lovely when irony plays a hand," Michel said. "So much more is known to me now, Papa. Even the couriers! All of them. It will be nothing to do away with them, and quickly. We will not fail this time. I promise you, we shall have what is ours to safeguard. And Fana is *beautiful*."

"There is no beauty in the work remaining for us, Michel," Stefan said. "I pray you understand this. Sometimes Father God demands sacrifices upon His altar, as Abraham offered Isaac. There is no gentler way to uphold our sacred duty."

"I've had no illusions, Papa," Michel said. "What choice was I given? My sensibilities are not as delicate as you like to pretend."

It was a jubilant day, but Stefan felt sadness, too. Each day, he thought of Michel's mother, Teru, and how she had begged him not to take away their extraordinary child. She sat imprisoned even now, kept comfortable in the castle in Tuscany, lost in the gentle dreams Michel wove for her from a distance. Even with all the death behind

Stefan in the name of Sanctus Cruor—and the death yet to come—
Teru had been Stefan's greatest sacrifice.

But Michel would know love even if he could not. Michel would
have the mate the ancient text had preordained for him. His only
equal. His divine match.

"Travel safely," Stefan said. "Your destiny is soon fulfilled, my
good son."

"And I am ready for whatever Destiny may ask of me."

"*Ciao*, Michel. *Benedetto sia il Sangue.*"

"*Benedetto sia il Sangue,* Papa."

Bless the Blood.

Ten

The sun outside was awake to light a bad day. Teka stood posed in front of the stone fireplace in the living room of the Big House, smiling as if he could blunt his report with a pleasant face. Lucas Shepard had never believed the tiny man's expressions looked quite right, as if they'd been chosen at random. Bea was absent, upstairs at Alex's bedside.

His wife had been catatonic all morning. Now maybe Lucas would learn why.

"Fana has run away with Caitlin," Teka told the group of five. "Alexis encountered Fana and Caitlin as the girls were on their way to the woods. I imagine Fana only wanted to quiet her long enough to pass safely."

"Quiet her?" Nita Duhart said. Fear thinned her voice. "What does that mean?"

Lucas stared at Jessica and Dawit, who sat on the love seat directly across from him, but they avoided his eyes. Jessica looked as shell-shocked as Lucas felt, holding her husband's hand. Jessica and Dawit were strangely silent; they knew more than they had let on. Cal and Juanita stood behind the sofa above Lucas, each resting a hand on one of his shoulders.

"There is an injury to Alexis's memory centers," Teka said, exactly the way he had explained it to Lucas earlier, which had hardly been an explanation at all. "It is akin to . . . a stroke, I suppose. A mental paralysis. I will work with her to restore what I can . . . but I believe Fana herself is the one who can bring Alexis back as she was."

Teka raised his eyebrows, as if to say *Will that be all?* Lucas's limbs tensed with anger, but he was sadder than he was mad. He felt spent.

"*Bullshit,*" Cal said to Teka. "Tell us what the hell you did with Alex and Fana."

Lucas noted the flicker of annoyance across Dawit's face, and something else in his brother-in-law's eyes he didn't like. But Teka's polite smile remained. "Fana is very special," Teka said, surveying their group. "What she has marred she can also repair, with time. I know this to be true. But I'm prepared to say no more. My apologies for your confusion. I dare not proceed without my Brothers' agreement."

"What's he talking about?" Nita said to Jessica. A plea.

For the first time, Jessica spoke. "I've told you Fana has gifts."

Beside her, Dawit sighed, as if she had already said too much. How dare they conceal information that the rest of them had a right to know!

"*Gifts?*" Lucas said, rising halfway from his seat. "Yeah, you said she had gifts. You never said she was going to fry my wife's goddamn brain." Dawit's face got tight, and Jessica blinked fast.

"Lashing out at us helps no one," Dawit said. "We're concerned, too. Fana's our child."

Lucas sighed, rubbing his face. "I get that, Dawit. And Alex is my wife."

"And my sister," Jessica said.

Teka raised both hands to his chest level, palms out, as if in surrender. He gave a low, courtly bow; his forehead almost touched his knees as his spine folded. "I've said what I can. I think the concerns of this household are best discussed privately among its members. If no one objects, I must return to the Council House."

"Yeah, you do that," Cal said sarcastically. "Thanks for clearing this up."

Cal's taunt had no visible impact on Teka, whose smile never faltered.

Silence hovered in the room while Teka made his way to the front double doors. Lucas heard Hank and the twins whooping in the dining hall. They sounded like they were chasing each other around the room instead of eating their breakfast as they'd been told, but neither Cal nor Nita moved to quiet their children. No one spoke a word until they heard the front door open, then close. And then they waited nearly twenty seconds after that.

Cal went to the foyer to peek out of the door's lace-covered window. "He's gone," he said. "Now maybe someone can tell us what the hell is really going on here."

Dawit stood up to block Cal's return path. "Cal, don't ever let my Brothers hear you address Teka with such disrespect. I give that advice in the strongest possible terms."

Cal's face turned bright red. His hair had gone white, but he was still full-faced and thickly built, and suddenly his chest was thrust out like a bar brawler's. His eyes flared. "Or what?" he said, pouring on his thick Georgia twang.

"Cal . . . ," Lucas warned. He met Cal's eyes to telegraph a message: *Careful.*

Jessica reached up to gently pull back on Dawit's arm, and he took his seat again, eyes on Cal. The sadness and shock on Jessica's face turned to alarm.

Something had happened here overnight. Despite all of their differences with the Life Brothers, yesterday this had been a single colony with a unified mission. Today, Lucas felt like a stranger. An outsider. And Alex had known much more than she had told him, even after all they had endured together. Lucas felt pissed off and betrayed, which only sharpened his grief.

"This is a hard day, and we're all emotional," Jessica said. "But we've been family for a long time, so let's not turn on each other. Ask me your questions, and I'll answer them."

"Shouldn't Sharmila and Abena be here too?" Nita said. Two of their colony's other women were married to Teferi, and they lived in separate houses on the western side of the colony, ensconced in their own lives. Their three children attended school with Hank and the twins, but the women rarely socialized. Lucas knew there would be no privacy if they were here.

"Let's keep this to just us, for now," Lucas said.

"If it's privacy you want, I'll join Teka," Dawit said, meeting

Lucas's eyes so squarely that it was as if the man had heard his thoughts. "Will you be all right here, Jess?"

Jessica nodded, resigned. Dawit leaned close to Jessica's ear, but they could hear him. "Alex will be herself again. I won't rest until Fana is home. Please don't complicate matters."

Jessica closed her eyes as Dawit left the room. Her face was at war.

"They're thick as thieves," Cal muttered, watching the front door close behind Dawit.

Nita sat down beside Jessica, taking Dawit's place. She clasped her friend's hand. "Honey, I'm sorry . . . ," Nita said. "I know you're hurting and Fana is your little girl, but you need to talk to us. We're all very nervous right now."

"Scared to death is more like it, Jess," Lucas said.

"And when did Justin and Caitlin get here?" Cal said. "That's news to me."

"First things first," Lucas said. "Tell us about Fana, Jess. Please. Everything."

"Everything is a long story," Jessica said.

"We quit our day jobs a long time ago, sugar," Nita said. "We've got nothing but time."

Staring at the braided rug four feet ahead of her, Jessica didn't look like she was ready to talk yet. Nita got up and went to the kitchen, angling her wide hips through the French doors; she'd gained forty pounds in ten years, blaming Bea's cooking. Lucas sighed and glanced at Cal, who gazed back with lips pursed hard.

The French door flew open, and Nita came back with a tray of slightly burned biscuits and coffee, remnants of the breakfast Bea had been starting before her daughter had been carried to her doorstep. A lump in his throat, Lucas reached for a cold biscuit and buttered it. Cal and Nita followed his example. The biscuit was a rock in Lucas's mouth, but at least the coffee was warm.

Once, Lucas had been naive enough to think that he had lived to see almost everything: raised in Georgia at the end of segregation, an MD degree from Meharry, an adventure in the Peace Corps, and a Lasker Prize for his smallpox research. He'd gone through hell when his first wife had died, but Cal and Nita had helped him through it.

He and the Duharts had lived across the street from each other on a shaded Tallahassee road.

Then Jared had been diagnosed with leukemia. Lucas had gone to Botswana to chase down a rumor about a clinic with blood that could heal anything. Everyone, including Cal and Nita, had thought he'd been acting out of desperation. For a while, he'd been afraid they were right.

But he'd found Alex, and the blood. Or, rather, Alex and the blood had found him. Chaos had come crashing into his life on the heels of his discovery, and the trauma of that time had torn a hole in his memory. But Alex remembered. Sometimes, Alex woke up trembling and sweating with memories of torture. She was afraid it might happen again.

Lucas had died, after all.

Lucas hadn't been surprised that awful day when he'd felt a gun's nozzle against the back of his head. He'd heard a bullet cycle into a chamber before the explosion behind his ears. As an end to one's life, Lucas's had been extraordinary: Mercenaries. A hurricane. And miraculous blood.

Lucas remembered the eerie few seconds of consciousness after he *knew* he would die. He'd felt his thoughts go white and his body sink into stony paralysis. A euphoria had swallowed him, much more intense than the mental rush from a shaman's *ayahuasca* he'd once sampled in Peru. Jessica, Bea and Alex would say he'd felt the first welcoming winds of Heaven. But it had been DMT, of course. Dimethyltryptamine. Humans experience the release of DMT twice in their lives—at birth and at death. Nature's way of easing the transitions.

Lucas didn't remember the rest. Dawit had brought him back with his blood, as he had once brought back Jessica. The cost had been high, but the blood's rewards, it seemed, were boundless. The blood had overtaken Lucas's system, rewiring his cells so that they forgot how to age. And the healing! When Lucas was cut or bruised, he healed in eight to ten hours *without a trace of injury*.

And the blood could help others. Trace amounts were slowly reaching select rural portions of the world, controlled and contained. In their lab, Lucas and Alex kept a computer model of the raging impact of AIDS, whole nations and regions painted in bright red, and they watched the statistics fading before their eyes.

Fewer orphans. Fewer young people cut down. More industry. Botswana had rebounded so quickly, no longer saddled with its health crises, that it was second only to South Africa in its regional influence, creating one of the best universities on the continent. It only made sense: When your people are sick, what else matters?

Lucas had more influence on world health than he had ever believed possible. But five years ago, the Brothers had banned Lucas from visiting clinics and officials in Ghana and China because he'd become too easy to recognize. That damned Lasker Prize and his renown when he'd worked for the National Institutes of Health had stripped him of the anonymity he needed. Too many people recognized him as Dr. Lucas Shepard.

Dr. Voodoo, he'd been called. His fame had outlived its usefulness.

Long ago, Lucas had torpedoed his career because people had thought he'd believed in magic, and now he couldn't say *Told you so.* Lucas had made his peace with that. Hell, he'd planned to retire in his sixties anyway, and he'd just turned sixty-nine. He wished he'd gotten the blood when he was thirty, but freezing time at fifty-five wasn't shabby. And he had a gorgeous lab to study his blood.

Lucas had joked, cajoled and begged Alex: *You've earned the right to this blood. Tell Jessica and Dawit to give you the Ceremony so you'll be like us, too. Put my worries to rest.* But, like her mother, Alex had refused. Would Alex ever have the chance now, or had he just lost another wife? Lucas didn't want to live a single day without Alexis, much less hundreds of years.

"Jess?" Lucas gently prodded his sister-in-law, who was still staring at the floor. "Please."

Jessica looked up and nodded, sighing.

"Fana isn't the only one who can reach people with her mind," she said, pausing between sentences. "The Brothers are telepaths. The Blood seems to open up a new mental receptivity, depending on how much it's nurtured. Some, like Fana, have a more natural talent than others. That means, among other things, that they know what other people are thinking. I don't know yet if I can learn it—or you, Lucas. It takes years, Teka says."

Lucas's mind went blank, just like the day he'd felt the life leaving his body. The room was so silent that it was as if no one had heard.

"You mean like aliens?" a voice said. Hank was leaning into the entryway, eavesdropping. At fourteen, Cal's son was stocky, just like him. "Vampires?"

"Where's your brother and sister?" Cal snapped.

Hank ignored the question. "Look, I know something happened to Aunt Alex. I have a right to hear, too." He reminded Lucas of Jared as a young boy, when illness had made him old for his years. Cal, Nita and Jessica shook their heads in unison.

"Go mind Maya and Martin. Pronto," Cal said.

"Look, I'm not a little kid," Hank said. "I just want—"

Nita shot to her feet. "So help me, if you don't get moving right now, I will break off a switch and wear your behind out. I don't care how old you are," she said. "*Go,* Hank. And don't come back in here." She sounded like Alex, except for the terror hidden in her voice.

Jessica mustered a smile as placid as Teka's for the boy. "Alex will be fine. Really," she told Hank. "Do what your mom says, hon. This is a meeting for the grown-ups."

Hank gave them a nasty look, but he retreated. Cal nudged Hank along, then watched his son walk to the playroom on the other side of the house. Lucas heard the door slam. Hank was getting close to the age when he would want to decide more things for himself.

"He still doesn't know where the blood comes from," Nita said softly. "Not really."

"Keep it that way," Jessica said. "Ignorance is his protection."

"Not in my experience," Lucas said. "Go on. You say they're tele-paths . . ."

Jessica spoke rapidly, still in a hush. "They can hear what you're thinking, if they want to. They can send thoughts into your head, especially the stronger ones, like Teka."

Lucas remembered the eerie sensation of hearing Teka's voice in his sleep when he'd woken up that morning. His skin suddenly felt frigid, as thin as paper. Teka had roused him from sleep without making a sound!

"Dawit too? He can read your mind?" Nita said, taking her seat beside Jessica. When Jessica sighed and nodded, Nita gave her a sympathetic, disbelieving look.

"What are Fana's capabilities?" Lucas said.

Jessica didn't blink. "Teka says she's the strongest of them, in that way. But Fana's never done anything like what happened last night. Not since . . ." She stopped talking, as if she'd forgotten what she wanted to say.

Lucas's heart bounded. "Since when?"

"Since she was three. She hurt people." When Jessica gazed at Lucas, her arms fell flat at her sides, as if she were awaiting judgment. "People died, Lucas."

The entire morning had felt like a dream, but now he was getting lost inside it.

Jessica gulped at her coffee, as if for strength. "When she was three, unexplained things started happening. We lived in Botswana then, and a neighbor boy had an argument with Fana. That boy fell into a state very similar to Alex's now. Alex told me she thought Fana had something to do with it, and she was right. Fana admitted she'd put the boy to sleep. When we confronted her, Fana woke him up. That was how it started."

Fana woke him up.

Lucas's brain struggled to keep pace with Jessica's story. Could blood create an actual link to the nervous systems of others, or was it a conduit for some other unknown human functions? He had always assumed that telepathic claims were bullshit.

"Dawit and I weren't together during that time . . ." Jessica's voice became more strained. "I didn't know what to do with Fana, so I took her to the original colony to find Dawit. I can't say where it is, but the visit was a mistake for Fana. Going there scared her, and we weren't welcome. They resented Dawit for changing my blood and for creating a child they considered a mutation. But we learned more about the immortals. There are fifty-eight of them left. Only a few of them came here, following Fana. I was warned that Fana is powerful."

"Warned by whom?" Lucas said.

"The leader of that colony. You haven't met him. He gave all of them the blood. That's all I can say about him. I'm sorry."

Khaldun was his name, meaning "eternal" in Arabic. Alex had mentioned that much, at least. Khaldun claimed to be two thousand years old, according to Alex. But apparently Jessica had decided to keep that part of the story to herself; that was the way of life here. Lucas knew better than to say some things to Cal or Nita, but he hadn't realized how ignorant he was too.

Jessica went on. "Our only allies there were a small number of Life Brothers who were most loyal to their leader. Teka was one of them. He's been a friend for a long time, and I believe he cares for us. I don't think we have any reason to be afraid of him."

"Duly noted," Cal said, impatient. "Go on."

"Most of the others only ignored us, but a few were hostile. One of them attacked me. I was hurt, and it was a horrible thing for Fana to see. I lost my left hand."

"Lord have mercy . . . ," Nita whispered, rubbing Jessica's knee. She stared at Jessica's hand, now restored and folded with her other hand across her knees.

"Fana saw the attack, and she was hysterical. I really don't believe she ever had conscious control, but . . . she killed the man who attacked me, without touching him. He bled to death."

Lucas's mouth went dry. "Fana killed who? An immortal?"

"They're not immortals. We're not. It's possible to die, it's just much harder. Fana drained the blood from the body of the man who attacked us. She wasn't even in the room with him, but I believe to my soul that she did it. The colony's leader said she had killed others, too. I don't have evidence to support it . . . but I believe him."

"Why the hell would you believe that about your own kid?" Cal said.

Jessica rubbed her cheeks with her palms, then went on. "Hear me out, Cal. This was when Fana's catatonia began setting in—the way she was when you first met her, Lucas."

Lucas nodded. In the beginning, he had thought Fana was autistic, since she'd been withdrawn almost beyond reach. He and Alex had tried every therapy technique they'd been able to research, but she'd rarely responded. Only Teka had made headway with her, and now Lucas knew why: *Teka could communicate with her using his mind!*

"Dawit and I realized we had to leave the colony for Fana's protection. After we got back to the clinic in Botswana, we found it in shambles. Alex was gone, and there was blood everywhere. I thought Alex was dead . . . and Fana probably knew everything in my mind. She began having episodes . . . like epilepsy. She made objects move from across the room."

Jessica sighed. "The bed jumped. The television screen blew out. Violent things happened when she was scared or mad." Jessica swallowed hard, flicking away a tear. Lucas felt the nagging sense, again, that Jessica had left out part of the story.

After a pause, Jessica went on. "Fana doesn't remember any of it, and we kept quiet for her sake. It would have influenced Fana's feelings and beliefs about herself if the people closest to her were afraid of her. It *does*." Jessica lowered her eyes, almost wincing. Then Jessica looked up and smiled. Her smile looked sincere but misplaced, like Teka's. "But whatever happened behind the school, I know Fana didn't mean to hurt Alex. It was an accident. And if Teka says Fana can heal her, she can. I've seen what Fana can do."

Spoken like a true convert, Lucas thought. Other than that, he didn't know what to think.

"What's Teka teaching Fana, Jess?" Lucas said. "I've never understood that."

"I don't know all of it, I admit," Jessica said. "Teka gives me generalities: Focus. Thought literacy. Stillness. Fana has trouble expressing her lessons in words. She's helped me with my meditation—when we meditate together, she guides me. She tries to show me some things, but . . . mostly she's too far beyond me. Her mind is different. Except for the telepathy, Fana says she doesn't have any power. But I know that's not true, and so does Teka. She's just buried her access to it. Teka says she has to learn conscious control or she might hurt someone."

Amen, brother, Lucas thought. He took a deep breath, and his lungs cinched. Mist cleared from his mind, a realization. "Whatever happened with Caitlin must have been pretty drastic," Lucas said. "Otherwise, why would Fana run? She had to be desperate, to hurt Alex that way."

Jessica looked at him with sad, grateful eyes. "Yes, Lucas. She had to be."

"What scared them off?" Cal said.

Jessica looked at the floor again and told them the story Alex had told Lucas last night; Caitlin O'Neal's Glow and Justin's theft in Ghana. Suddenly the whole tragedy made sense: Fana had run away because the O'Neals were in jeopardy, maybe the whole family. Cal cast a long glance Lucas's way, as if to say *Are you hearing this?*

"Was Caitlin right to fear for her life?" Nita said.

Jessica paused so long that Lucas's heartbeat sped. Her silence sounded like a *yes*.

"Lord have mercy," Nita said.

"I know they wouldn't have killed Caitlin," Jessica said. "She's Fana's friend. But . . . they might have been planning to take other action against the O'Neals. Dawit says there was evidence that Caitlin was being followed, that someone looking for the blood got too close to her. She's considered a danger now. She *is* a danger now. To all of us."

"What does . . . '*take other action*' mean?" Cal said in a long drawl.

"What will they do when they catch her?" Nita said.

"And her father?" Lucas said. Justin O'Neal's future suddenly seemed highly pertinent.

"I don't know," Jessica said. "I'm trying to see to it that we'll all have a say in that."

If we don't have a say, Justin O'Neal is the least of our problems, Lucas thought.

Nita wrapped her arms around herself suddenly, gazing at her husband, and Lucas knew what she was thinking: Nita was content at the colony because she was writing successful mystery novels under a pseudonym, but Cal was restless. He'd amused himself with his building projects, especially the plank-by-plank re-creation of Lucas's old Frank Lloyd Wright house in Tallahassee, but he complained he felt useless at the colony.

Jessica had lobbied the Brothers to allow Cal and Nita to build a house in Antigua, and every winter their family spent eight weeks there. But for Cal, that wasn't enough. Hank either. Hank was older than the other children, except for Fana, and he wanted more friends. Jared had made the same complaint before he'd gone to Oxford, moving as far as he could from the woods where he had been raised.

"What if me and Nita want to take the kids and leave for good?" Cal said. "What then?"

Jessica sagged where she sat. The question wearied her. "Cal . . . we've talked about this . . . "

"That's right, Jess, we've talked about it," Cal said. "And every time we do, you talk me out of it. But what if we made up our minds to pack up and go? What would they do?"

"You agreed to stay," Jessica said. "It was the primary condition when you—"

Cal gritted his teeth. "Let's make believe we changed our goddamned minds."

"You're part of our mission," Jessica said. "You're helping to change the world."

"Cut the company line horseshit, Jess," Cal said. "Just tell us straight."

In the long silence, they heard muffled arguing from the playroom. Maya let out a shriek.

"They would never risk letting you go with what you know," Jessica said. "They can send someone with you to Antigua once a year, or shadow Jared in England, but they can't spare lifelong minders for you."

"And who the hell wants a minder?" Cal said. "What are you saying, Jess?"

"They would expect guarantees," Jessica said delicately.

"Meaning what?" Nita said, although Lucas thought the meaning was plain.

"A case of amnesia," Lucas said. "Don't you get it? They'd make us forget, folks."

Cal's face went ashen, and Nita jumped as if he'd fired a gun in the room.

Jessica nodded. "Yes, Lucas. I think they would."

Jessica watched from behind the fountain as Dawit and Teferi emerged from the Council House carrying small black leather suitcases. They didn't see her, walking instead toward the parked Orbit at the end of the driveway. They wore bland jeans and T-shirts, the clothes of the outside world. Dawit was still hidden behind his white beard.

Jessica wished Dawit didn't have to go.

Four of the Brothers had left when Lucas had brought Alex to the Big House, as soon as Jessica had knocked on her daughter's door and realized Fana was gone. Jessica had recognized Alex's stare—the same stare she had seen from Fana's friend in Botswana after she put him to sleep.

They had to find her. Soon. But finding Fana wouldn't be easy.

Teka said Fana had left behind a false marker so he wouldn't know she was gone. The impression was like a mental scent, Teka explained. To him, Fana's presence still filled her bedroom, calm and sleeping, even when his eyes said differently. Jessica didn't understand, but she wondered if it was anything like the way she had stuffed pillows under her covers as a young girl, when she hadn't wanted her mother to know she'd been out of bed.

Jessica's worry about Fana had boiled over to the point of numbness. What if something went badly wrong? With Fana, badly wrong might mean very, very bad. Jessica was so worried about Fana that she hardly had room in her heart to fret over Alex.

Alex wasn't gone. Jessica didn't believe it, not after everything she had seen.

But Bea was in bad shape, and she needed someone to look her in the eye and tell her everything was all right. Otherwise, this day might kill her. After Daddy Gaines had died in the ditch, with all the second-guessing about how the blood might have saved him, her mother had made Jessica swear on her King James Bible that she would not give Bea any blood, no matter what.

Lord, please give us all the strength to make it through this day.

Jessica watched from behind the fountain as Dawit and Teferi loaded their bags into the trunk of the car. Clothes, surveillance equipment and weapons, no doubt. They never traveled without weapons. Maybe they were Soldiers of the Cross after all, or striving to be.

Dawit looked around suddenly, spotting her. Had he heard her thinking about him?

Dawit slammed the trunk shut, said something into Teka's ear, and walked toward her.

Jessica couldn't catch hold of last night's rage and hurt. In the late-morning light, she saw Dawit Wolde as the only person in the world who shared her heart. There was no accusation in his eyes. No fear. No mistrust. Only worry for the child who would bond them for eternity.

Dawit clasped her hands while water spewed from the marble lions' mouths and roiled in their ears. There was no time to say everything that could be said, so she settled for the necessities.

"We owed them the truth about Fana. Some of it, anyway," Jessica said, answering the question in Dawit's eyes. She hadn't told them about the hurricane, and so much more. Cal would have been much more upset if he had known the most personal secret she kept from him: Teka had erased Cal's memory of the Brother's telepathic gifts long ago. The Brothers had insisted.

And when Khaldun had spoken of Fana in Lalibela nearly fifteen years ago, his language had terrified Jessica: *Fana is both salvation and destruction. She will be either our most awaited friend or our most fearsome enemy. . . . A child born with the power to stand between mortal and immortal, the two races of man.* Should she have told the others that part, too? Would anyone have believed her?

"I had to say something," Jessica went on. "They're my friends, Dawit. Our friends."

Dawit spoke gently, without reprimand. "Adversity has no friends. It was a mistake."

"They're scared."

"More scared now than before, I'm sure," Dawit said, and he might have been right. Nita had barely made eye contact after the talk in the living room, and Cal was probably off somewhere cursing a blue streak. "My Brothers are anxious, too. I wish we had peace today."

"Then I guess you need to bring Fana back," she said, squeezing his warm palms.

Dawit brightened, nodding. He thrived when he had a plan, no matter how dire the situation. He was the most efficient person she knew. Too efficient, sometimes.

"We'll bring her back," Dawit said. "Berhanu's already picked up a trail. The girls stole a car from a parking lot in Toledo early this morning."

Jessica's heart leaped, flushing her with relief. "Let's hope Caitlin was driving," she said, and even managed to smile. But Jessica didn't smile long.

Had they forced Fana to run away by thrusting too much weight on her? Had she understood better than they did how much her presence made a difference? *Come back to us, sweetheart. Forgive us our rashness. I know you didn't mean to hurt Alex. Do you think you could ever do anything I wouldn't forgive?*

Dawit sat on the smooth edge of the fountain, patting the space beside him. More bad news, Jessica realized. After she sat, Dawit leaned close and slipped his arm around her shoulder. Last night, she never would have believed that Dawit's touch would comfort her again.

"The Brothers have decided what to do about Justin O'Neal," Dawit said quietly.

All relief vanished. "No vote?"

"A vote would only serve appearances. We are the majority, Jess." More and more often, when Dawit used the word "*we*" he was referring to his Life Brothers, not his family.

Jessica gazed at meticulous rows of cedar planks on the Council House walls, just visible through the trees that separated them. "Appearances matter, Dawit," she said. "They can't just kill O'Neal, not for theft. There has to be due process. An open trial. Testimony and evidence."

"They're not going to kill him," Dawit said. "It's a memory wash. Twenty years."

Jessica closed her eyes. Thank God for that, at least. She remembered how it had felt when Fana had tricked her memory when she was only three: Jessica had felt like herself in every way, except that she had forgotten Kira, her first child. For a minute, maybe two, Jessica had stared at Kira's photograph and not recognized her own little girl. She had forgotten the agony of rocking her dead child in her arms.

Losing the memory hadn't been the hard part; the hard part had been having it back.

But Justin O'Neal's daughters were barely past twenty. With that much memory loss, he wouldn't know them anymore. And O'Neal was a better man now than he'd been twenty years ago. Jessica hadn't known him then, but she was sure of that.

"Teka agreed to this?" Jessica said.

"Yes, as a compromise. He'll do it himself. He has a gentle hand, more practiced than Fana's. O'Neal will fare better than Alex."

Jessica's throat flared with pain, but not long. No time. "What about Caitlin?"

"Caitlin would have to agree to stay with us. Away from her family. The Brothers won't allow another family of mortals here."

"Of course she can stay with us."

Dawit squeezed her hand. "Then that's decided. I'll take it to Teka."

Alex joked that Jessica and Dawit should be called *Your Highness,* since they thought they were king and queen of the colony. Together, they had created a nearly impossible union of peoples. But Fana and Caitlin would have their own ideas, if Fana was even willing to come back. "What if you don't find her?" Jessica said, the thought she had tried to silence all day.

Dawit kissed her forehead. "We will. Probably today. Maybe tomorrow."

"But what if you don't?"

Dawit sighed, nodding. The Searchers would have found anyone else already. Fana wouldn't be easy to find if she could misdirect them with mental scents. There were probably a thousand ways she could elude them.

"Then she's a woman, Jess," Dawit said, shrugging. "Her life begins."

Was it really that simple? Maybe it was. All parents faced the day when their children wanted to leave, and most parents thought their children weren't ready. But all parents didn't have killers hunting their child's blood. All parents hadn't looked into their child's eye in the midst of a hurricane and seen something staring back that hadn't been the slightest bit human.

Please, Lord, don't let her hurt anyone else.

"What about Alex?" Jessica said, her throat tight. Would she be forced to forever remember that she could have heeded the warnings but hadn't—just like with Kira?

"Teka will work with Alex if Fana doesn't come back," Dawit said. "But we'll find her. If you have any worries while I'm gone, talk to Teka."

Without Teka here, Jessica knew she would be as nervous as Cal, Nita and Lucas. An hour ago, when Jessica had asked Teka if there was anything he could do for her mother's nerves, the man had stood outside of Alex's room, where Bea was sitting vigil, and made Bea stop trembling. Jessica had watched it happen. She had *seen* the fear lift from her mother's face, with Teka's single thought. If Teka wasn't a true friend, so be it. He was close enough.

"I'll find her," Dawit said and lightly kissed her lips.

Jessica stayed at the fountain, watching as Dawit walked back to the car, where Teferi was waiting. She waved as the car pulled around the driveway. Both men waved back, although neither smiled. Dust followed them on the unpaved path into the woods.

Was Fana powerful enough to hear her now? Jessica knew she had squandered her opportunity to talk to Fana last night, when it had mattered, but she had been talking to her daughter in her head all day, like she had when Fana was three. The night of the storm.

Come home right away, Fana. We need you here.

Remember Teka's lessons, Fana. Remember mine.

Respect your gifts.

Never lose control.

UNDERGROUND

On such a day

who would dare think of dying?

So much Freedom means

that we'll postpone

   dying

until the morning after.

—Kofi Awoonor, *Until the Morning After: Collected Poems 1963–1965* (Ghana)

Eleven

Vancouver, Washington

The first miracle had been making it to the road while it had still been dark, out of sight of two pickups that had ambled past them on their way to Interstate 5.

Exhausted but infused with new energy, Fana and Caitlin walked half a mile to the Minit Mart in Toledo, where Caitlin hoped they could find a car. The choices were stealing a car or hitchhiking, and neither of them liked the idea of climbing into a car driven by a stranger. Fana didn't want to steal, but what else could they do?

"It's not for us—it's for Glow," Caitlin reminded her, Caitlin's rationalization of choice. Too many rationalizations were dangerous, but a few were indispensable.

The store lights were already on, although it wasn't quite dawn and the sign in the window said Closed. Even if the store had been open, they had agreed not to go inside. Too close to home. Fana had never shopped at that store a day in her life, and today wasn't the day to start. She was masking her presence as well as she knew how, but the Minit Mart would be the first place her parents, and the Searchers, would look for her.

Caitlin spotted a brand-new red Orbit parked against the brick side wall of the parking lot. Better yet, it was unlocked. Caitlin got in, and the car started right away. No more crouching and running or hiding from cars driving by. They drove off without a soul seeing them.

With a car and a seasoned driver at her behest, Fana was free for the first time.

On Interstate 5, the clear, open space hit them like a shock wave, and they laughed together as if they were drunk. Above them, the dawn finally broke free of the night, casting a sheen of pink, orange and gold across the lush green forest on each side of the road. When had her head ever felt so quiet outside the colony?

It was the best sunrise Fana had ever seen. Freedom was a powerful intoxicant. For a short while, she forgot everything. The world was fresh and lovely.

The problems started when they approached the state line into Oregon, closer to Portland.

Fana could feel the approach of the city almost as soon as they drove beyond Longview; it was a tremendous vibration in her head. Cacophonous voices overpowered the threads her mind had carried from home: Whispers from Aunt Alex. Mom. Dad. Gramma Bea. Teka. She hadn't noticed how close their minds were to hers until the new voices began drowning them out. Fana hoped they could drive past Portland quickly.

But Caitlin wanted to stop at McDonald's.

"I can't believe you've never tasted a biscuit from Mickey D's," Caitlin said, pulling off the interstate when she saw the restaurant's arched logo in yellow. Then Caitlin rattled off her disclaimer about how she hated the way megacorps were poisoning the world with empty calories and saturated fat. Fana barely heard her as she struggled to find Aunt Alex's sleeping hum in her head.

But Fana was so glad to hear Caitlin sound lighthearted that she didn't object. Besides, she was hungry. She hadn't eaten since dinner, except for a few handfuls of almonds. Caitlin ordered a plain biscuit and a carton of milk for Fana, and two biscuits for herself.

One bite almost made Fana throw up. It wasn't the *taste*, since her tongue had celebrated the salty flavor at first. But the scent of the frying meat charging through the drive-thru window overpowered her taste buds.

The euphoria faded, replaced by a shocking realization. Home was gone. Familiarity, gone. Then Fana heard Caitlin's panicked thought: *SHIT THERE'S PROBABLY A CAMERA HERE DUMB-ASS.* And she was right: There was a camera at the drive-thru window, aimed right into their car. It was a barely noticeable black minicam planted on the side of the cash register like an oversized bug with one unblinking glass eye beneath a pinprick of red light.

Caitlin was still waiting at the window for her sole credit card—their financial lifeline—but Fana saw Caitlin's hand grasp the gearshift suddenly, as if she was about to run. Caitlin's face was slack and bloodless. Scared. Between the unpleasant taste in her mouth, the growing hive-like hum from the large city looming just south and Caitlin's fearful face, Fana's mind knotted.

Pop. The minicam's red light went off, and a single crack shattered the camera's eye in half. Fana blinked, shocked. During her sessions with Teka, she had stirred enough mental energy to make paper flutter, or blow a ball of dust. But nothing like that!

Fana didn't have time to celebrate. Her headache started then. A bad one.

WHATINTHEWORLDISGOINGON

Fana's head squalled with Aunt Alex's voice, a loop from behind the schoolhouse. Aunt Alex's thoughts were still frozen in confusion and terror. Fana had done that to her, and Fana was helpless to soothe her. She could have helped Aunt Alex if she had stayed at home, but she had chosen selfishness. Childish impulse.

She tried to say *I need to go home,* but her words were trapped in the echo chamber of her mind. *I'm sorry, Aunt Alex. I'm sorry.*

A series of sharp images stole Fana's thoughts, appearing like a 3-D movie—*indistinct, bloody writing on a wall. Spots of blood on clothes. Dark skin spurting blood from a wound.*

Suddenly, Fana saw a face: Johnny Wright. He looked so close to her that she gasped.

"You OK, Fana?" Caitlin said, grabbing her arm.

Suddenly, Fana realized she no longer knew.

Berkeley

6 p.m.

When his arm vibrated, Johnny glanced at his phone's screen, where the letters shone in royal blue:

Get outside. Don't b tailed.

Johnny's heart jumped. There was no name signed, but the curt message could only be from Caitlin. Finally! But how did she know where he was?

Johnny imagined he could see Caitlin far across the cafeteria at the soda machine; there was a girl with Caitlin's face under jet-black hair that looked more chopped than cut. But after a stream of students walked in front of him, the girl was gone.

Johnny shoved the books from his Death, Dying & Medicine class into his bookbag, slung the bag over his shoulder, and melted into the pack of undergrads walking outside, matching their pace until he peeled off past the crowded bicycle rack to round the corner toward King Union. Papier-mâché figures of President Goodard and Vice President Salazar bobbed above a crowd that was just dispersing from a protest, the lingerers stubbornly shouting, *"No more war! No more war!"* like generations of yearning hearts before them.

Johnny used to go to the protests, but he'd learned last year that the protests didn't do any good. The war wasn't going to stop; it was more ancient than most people wanted to admit. He could kiss his financial aid good-bye as soon as the Selective Service office figured out he'd checked the box marked *No Thanks,* but Johnny could live with that. He just couldn't live with being sent to some desert to shoot another kid with a gun, busting his soul wide open for life.

Fuck that. If Uncle Sam didn't like it, he'd move to Toronto.

Johnny trotted behind two tittering girls wearing red wristbands from the protest, fashionably dressed in low-slung jeans that formed a tantalizing V right below their tailbones. *Crack pants,* people called them, since only skinny girls without asses could get away with it.

Johnny checked his pager again. No new message. Damn.

He typed fast, his elbow bent so he could reach the keyboard as he passed the protesters:

WHERE R U? CALL ME.

Johnny jogged toward Bancroft. Four blocks west, a BART train could speed him anywhere Caitlin wanted to go. He wasn't going to take any chances of leading someone to her.

Johnny's arm vibrated again, and this time it was the telephone.

"Where are you?" Caitlin said on the speaker, her version of a greeting.

"Shattuck. On my way to the train."

"Perfect," she said. She sounded pleased with him for once. "Stand at the southeast corner of Shattuck and Bancroft. Don't be tailed. And never put me on speaker again."

"You're here?" he said, elated. His voice sounded whiny at the end, like a child's.

Luckily, Caitlin had already hung up.

After ten minutes on the corner scouting every face, cyclist and passing car, Johnny wondered if he had failed Caitlin's test. The temperature was dropping rapidly as the afternoon sun fell, and Johnny wished he had his jacket. His textbooks and ultra-thin Blade notebook computer seemed heavier now than they had when he'd left King Union.

Johnny looked at his watch. Four. Shit. He was late for Death & Dying.

Suddenly, Caitlin's voice was behind him. "Don't turn around. Let's walk. Fast." She was pressed against his back. She had been running. He smelled her sweat and skin, and he felt a surprising surge of desire. But he walked.

Johnny dared a glance, and there was jet-black hair beside him.

"I saw you at the union," he said.

"Did anyone else?" Caitlin sounded scared shitless. Maritza's death had wrecked her.

"I doubt it."

"Don't talk. Just keep walking."

Johnny didn't ask where they were going. He didn't ask any of his fifty questions, because he was trying to decide what to do about Caitlin's nervous breakdown. If he said the wrong thing, she might go ghost on him. It was better to ride out Caitlin's storm.

"Your hair's different," he said.

"Please don't talk." Caitlin's voice softened, a plea instead of an order. "Not yet."

In front of Starbucks, Caitlin tugged on Johnny's sleeve. "Here," she said.

Great! Caitlin wasn't usually the Starbucks type, but Johnny hoped a cup of Ethiopian coffee would give him the chance to talk her down from whatever emotional ledge she was teetering from. But Caitlin walked past the barista without a glance. Toward the back door.

Cars crammed the alley. A row of hybrids claimed the reserved spaces, while the gassers were squeezed at the end. Caitlin kept walking. She headed toward a battered, older-model PT Cruiser parked against a wall. The car's grill and front bumper were splattered with mud.

"I thought you hated gassers," Johnny said.

"Get in. Hurry." The door's locks clicked upward as they approached, even though Caitlin wasn't holding a key. By now, she was running toward the driver's door.

Inside, Johnny saw a tangle of wires beneath the steering wheel. Had someone broken into her car? Caitlin hunched over, playing with the wires. Johnny had already closed his door before he realized she was hot-wiring the car. Impossibly fast, the engine roared. Caitlin shifted into reverse. Her foot jammed on the accelerator, and the car leaped backward.

"Caitlin, what the hell?" Johnny said. "This car is *stolen*?"

"Just look in the backseat," Caitlin said.

Bracing himself with the handrail while the car beeped chides for not wearing his seat belt, Johnny glanced at the tarp covering the backseat. There was something underneath, bulky enough to be a human being.

"What's going on, Caitlin?" Johnny said, genuinely afraid to look.

Caitlin didn't answer, her eyes intent on the road as she roared out of the alley, racing a bus. "She can't be around too many people. It's hurting her head. She's gotten worse."

Psychotic episode. Johnny had studied it all in psych last year. The first chance he got, he was going to sneak a call to Caitlin's mother.

"You can't call anyone, Johnny," a tiny voice whispered from the backseat. The tarp shifted, rising. Johnny stared as the tarp fell, and he saw long dreadlocks underneath, twice as full as his. A brown face and unblemished skin. He knew her voice from her email messages, of course, even if he couldn't quite believe she was here.

Fana?

"Everything you think you know is a lie," Caitlin said. The tires squealed as she turned toward the 510. She was heading out of town.

"What?" Johnny said.

Between Caitlin's dizzying driving and Fana huddled in the backseat, he felt fuck-eyed. Had Caitlin kidnaped Fana? Was he going to have to fight for the wheel?

Caitlin turned to look over her shoulder, staring back at Fana. "What's he doing now?"

While her eyes were off the road, Caitlin was bearing down too fast on a minivan. Johnny saw every smear of grime on the rear window ahead. "Watch it!" he said, yanking on his seat belt.

Caitlin braked, and Fana was jolted forward. She must have been wearing her seat belt beneath the tarp, or she would have been flung into the front seat. Fana closed her eyes, her face wrenched, as if she were in great pain. Concerned, Johnny reached back to touch her wrist, and he was so jarred he almost pulled away. Fana's skin felt electric; warm static shock. Fana gritted her teeth, eyes still closed.

"There's a GPS," Fana said, her voice weak. "On the phone. He's . . . checking."

"*Shit.*" Caitlin looked at Johnny wildly. "Throw your phone out of the window. Now."

"Wh-what?" Johnny said.

His phone was still on his arm, and Caitlin snatched it. Her window was down in a zip, and she tossed the phone onto the freeway. Johnny looked back in time to see a silver wink before his phone was crushed beneath the tires of the semi truck behind them.

That snapped Johnny from his stupor. "What the *hell*? That phone cost—"

"They're tracking you," Caitlin said. "*Wake up,* Johnny, or get the fuck out of this car."

Traffic had stalled, so Caitlin held his eyes this time. He wasn't used to seeing her without her layers of black mascara; she looked younger and more fragile, only scared instead of judgmental. *Who IS she?*

"There are people looking for us who will kill us if they catch us," Caitlin said.

As much as Caitlin sounded like she was having a psychotic breakdown, Johnny felt a rising terror that maybe she wasn't. But he was more worried about Fana, for now.

Fana didn't look good. Her face was shining with perspiration. Her eyes were closed, her cheeks and brow wrinkled, almost converging. She was hurting. Johnny pressed his palm to Fana's forehead, and the strange static sensation jittered across his skin again. Her skin might be a little warm. Maybe. He was glad she didn't have a raging fever.

"What's going on, Lil' Cuz?" he said gently. "Are you OK?"

"Too much noise," Fana said, her voice far away.

"Stay focused, girl," Caitlin said. "What's up with Berhanu?"

"I don't know . . . ," Fana said. "He's gone. Maybe he's too far now."

"We've only gone ten yards," Caitlin said.

Fana just shook her head. "Maybe he's masking. He's gone. There's too much noise."

"Who's Ber . . . hah . . . noo?" Johnny said, buried under yet another layer of confusion.

"A Searcher," Caitlin said. "They knew we might come to you. You're a friend of Fana's. They've probably been reading her Shout-Out posts."

Each sentence Caitlin spoke was more bizarre than the last. He couldn't talk to her.

"What are you doing here, Lil' Cuz?" Johnny said, matching Fana's kitten-soft voice. He stroked the top of her head, running his hand down her soft ropes of hair.

Fana opened her eyes then, as if she'd just realized he was there. She smiled at him, and her dimples were unchanged from the day he'd met her when she was ten. If not for the sweat and the fact that she was outside the state of Washington for the first time since he'd known her, Fana looked like everything was fine.

"We were worried about you," Fana said. Her eyes were dewy.

"Why? What's going on?"

"She's liberated, that's what," Caitlin said. "The revolution has begun."

Fana clasped Johnny's hand. He didn't feel the static this time, but her skin glowed inside of his. Hadn't he felt some kind of glow the first time he'd touched her, too? She looked like a fragile little angel. He wanted to protect her in a way he had never wanted to protect anyone.

"I ran away," Fana said.

Johnny sighed. "Look, I know you're bored at home, but—"

Fana's eyes silenced him, burning with a flurry of emotions. Something terrible had happened. "You're not safe because of me."

"What are you talking about?" The car was moving, but Johnny's world fell still.

Fana blinked. She spoke again, louder than before, but this time her lips didn't move. His rational mind fought his eyes as he stared for six seconds, and the illusion didn't go away: Fana's mouth was still, but her voice filled up his head, louder than any of his own thoughts:

PLEASE TELL CAITLIN TO DRIVE FASTER SO THE NOISE WILL STOP.

Twelve

Tallahassee, Florida
8:37 p.m.

When his phone rang, Garrick Wright was waiting.

His wife always made it a point to be home when Johnny called, but tonight a cracked crown had sent Tahira to her dentist. She had left Garrick instructions to remind Johnny to explain his missing Selective Service card at the financial aid office. Garrick hoped the government fuss wouldn't ruin their trip to Jordan to see Johnny's grandmother this summer.

Garrick had already finished half the conversation with Johnny in his head before he picked up the phone and heard Lucas Shepard's voice instead.

"Garrick?"

Five years ago, Lucas had said he would call him next week, and this was his first call since then. Garrick sat at the edge of his back-yard cedar picnic table, swatting a fly from the bridge of his nose. He saw swarms of insects in the light from his solar lamp, which silhouetted his yard's live oaks, strung with tendrils of moss. Garrick hoped Lucas's call had nothing to do with the newspaper and video files he kept on the laptop locked in a safe under his bed. Lucas Shepard wouldn't call about something trivial.

Garrick tried to think of the worst-case scenario but couldn't. "What happened?"

"It's Johnny," Lucas said. "He vanished from the Berkeley campus late this afternoon."

Garrick felt rocked by a series of unfamiliar emotions that made it hard to catch his breath. The strongest was anger, in the end. "Why haven't I heard about it?"

"His roommate doesn't know yet. We only know Johnny vanished because . . . he was being watched. My people found his cell phone on the 510." Lucas didn't sound like a friend anymore, talking with such detached efficiency about a telephone Johnny had loved.

When Lucas hadn't called him back and the number had gone out of service, Garrick had guessed that the government had taken over Lucas's work. He shouldn't have been surprised that his son was under surveillance, yet he was. Shocked, even. But shock gave way to a creeping sickness. He couldn't think of where his questions should begin.

Lucas went on, more gently. "I'm sorry, Garrick. We have a security problem, and Johnny's disappearance might be related to that. He was being tailed as a precaution. Someone might be tracking us. I'll tell you what I know . . ."

For the first time, he sounded like Lucas again.

"Please." The wind chimes Tahira's mother had sent them from her village near the Dead Sea hung outside the window, robbed of music without a breeze. Trip approval from the State Department had just arrived that morning. Johnny didn't even know yet.

"Fana and Caitlin have run away," Lucas said. "The girls were selling Glow."

Of course. Garrick had suspected that Glow had something to do with Lucas's work. Once he waded past the anti-Glow propaganda exaggerating its dangers, the effects of Glow sounded too similar to claims sending bloggers into a frenzy in Ghana and China. And Nigeria.

"The Underground Railroad," Garrick said.

"Yes. I'm not accusing Johnny of selling, but—"

"He might have been if Caitlin was." Garrick hoped his honesty would be contagious.

Garrick and Tahira had talked about Caitlin many nights the first year they'd eaten alone at the dinner table after Johnny had gone to Berkeley. Johnny would have followed her anywhere.

"Caitlin's roommate was abducted and murdered last month," Lucas said.

Like Garrick used to tell his journalism students, Lucas had buried the lead.

Garrick stood up and began pacing, and the weathered patio floorboards creaked under his weight. He couldn't sit still with that information in his heart, not when Johnny's voice wasn't on the phone. His heart stalled, so his mind took over. "I've been following it as best I can," Garrick said. "I read about a girl in Miami. Colón. That one? And a guy in Michigan—a UM professor? I figured it might come together, since Glow was involved. Who's doing the killing?"

"We don't know." A pause, then Lucas added, "We think Johnny is with Caitlin and Fana. They left within twenty-four hours of each other. But we really don't know where he is. That's the truth. I'll call you the minute I hear anything, good or bad. I promise you, Garrick."

Did Lucas think he was just going to hang up the phone? Garrick's heart thrashed. He didn't have to look at his caller ID to know that Lucas was calling from somewhere he couldn't reach. "I'm flying out to Berkeley," Garrick said.

Lucas sighed. "I'd advise against it."

"I have to call the police, Lucas."

"They won't want that yet."

"*They*" were the scientists, the Africans. The masters of Lucas's new world.

Lucas was telling him to sit and do nothing. To trust in the people who did not trust him.

"I'm having trouble with this, Doc," Garrick said.

"Me too." Lucas's voice cracked. His day wasn't going much better, from the sound of it.

Garrick couldn't imagine living the way Lucas had chosen, no matter what the cause. There were times over the years Garrick had wished that he'd accepted Lucas's offer to live at the colony, where he might have chronicled it all from inside, capturing history fresh. Now he was sorry he had ever laid eyes on that compound in the woods.

"I'm thinking back a few years, Doc . . . ," Garrick said. "I remember when your son was sick and you thought you had to go to Botswana to get a cure. A miracle drug. You did what you thought you needed to do, and nobody could tell you otherwise. Remember that?"

Before Lucas had left Tallahassee, he'd come to Garrick's house for a few beers and told stories about his son's recovery. Said he'd seen spontaneous remission on a steady basis. Said he believed it was possible to eradicate AIDS within a decade. Hinted that the bigger truth was impossible to believe, that he was living proof of a medical miracle.

Finally, he'd invited Garrick to a meeting. Garrick and Lucy Keating and Three Ravens Perez and the South African nurse Shandi Shabalala had traveled to the Pacific Northwest to hear about a new blood-based drug. The Living Blood, the woman Jessica had called it. But that had been the last meeting, the last he'd heard about blood. No explanation of its origins.

Garrick wasn't a doctor, but he wasn't a fool, so he could guess at what he didn't know. Either the blood was manufactured or it was organic, or some combination of both, but blood was at the heart of the health movements overseas. And now Glow was out there, too. For all the precautions the scientists at the colony had taken, their genie was out of the bottle.

The silent phone line left Garrick's history with Lucas Shepard unspoken, and Garrick realized Lucas couldn't talk. Garrick wondered if his family's phone had been bugged all this time. Garrick felt a physical tremor, the ground sinking beneath him.

"I'm asking you to trust me," Lucas said finally. "Stay under the radar. At least wait until somebody else reports him missing."

"That might not be until tomorrow."

"Might not. But I'm asking as your friend, Garrick. I know how hard this is."

Lucas Shepard hadn't been his friend for a long time, but Garrick didn't dwell on that. Lucas was busy changing the world, one way or another. For better or worse.

"I have to tell Tahira," Garrick said. "How am I supposed to meet her eyes?"

"Give me twenty-four hours to get you some news. One hour at a time, Garrick."

"*Shit.*" Garrick's hand shook, and the telephone receiver was unsteady. He was terrified Lucas would hang up, that he would never know what happened to Johnny. "How's Jared?"

"Good." Lucas's voice loosened. "We're bringing him home from Oxford."

Oxford. Not bad. Garrick tried to say *Keep him safe,* but his words caught in his throat.

"My wife's on her way back," Garrick said.

"Please don't say anything to her, Garrick. It isn't safe." Lucas was begging. "If Johnny is with Fana and Caitlin, he's fine. They have safe houses, like the original Underground Railroad. My people will find them before anyone else does. My people are good. They're fast."

"Is that what's best for him?" Garrick said. He had to ask. The answer depended on who Lucas worked for, and how "his people" felt about Glow dealers. Garrick had read about prison sentences that would destroy his son's life before it began if the feds were involved.

"Tell me if you hear from Johnny," Lucas said. "That's what's best for him. We need to find them before the bad guys do."

"You're asking a lot for what you're giving," Garrick said.

"I know, but . . . I only called to tell you about Johnny. We need to get those kids home." Lucas sighed again, and Garrick wished they were sitting on the back porch together instead of thousands of miles apart, in every way. "This is my fault, Garrick."

"I won't argue."

"I'm so sorry. Give Tahira a hug. Just don't say it's from me."

Then Lucas hung up, gone as suddenly as he'd reappeared.

Another dramatic exit with no forwarding number. A kick in the stomach.

Bring Johnny out with you, Lucas had told Garrick five years ago, before that last phone call Garrick had finally stopped waiting for. Lucas had thought he could convince Garrick to move out to the colony once he showed off the new houses, the lab, and the children lined up at school. The colony had been doing wonders for Lucas: He'd looked like he hadn't aged a day in ten years.

Lucas had strolled those peaceful wooded grounds as if God had whispered The Answer To Everything in his ear. Garrick had never seen a man look so contented. He had thought he would have had to cross to his Father's Kingdom to see the joy he'd seen right there on Lucas's face. Garrick had been tempted to join Lucas and build a house just like Cal Duhart and his family, with a creek out back.

Was it science? Was it a religion? The journalist in Garrick Wright had needed to know. Something in his *soul* had needed to know.

But Tahira would never have agreed to leave Tallahassee. And no matter how many children lived there, Garrick hadn't been able to imagine raising Johnny out in the woods. It hadn't seemed like a well-rounded life, with all the secrecy. For his family's sake, he had chosen caution.

Johnny had only visited once, for two days, but it had been long enough. Long enough to meet Caitlin O'Neal. Long enough to meet Fana.

What is It? Where does It come from?

Garrick might have sacrificed his only child and never know why.

Bea had stopped shaking, but she looked far from all right.

Jessica gazed sadly at her mother, who sat in the armchair near the window in Alex's room with her eyes closed, her chin bobbing slightly as she fought off sleep. Her lips were pinched shut, the only sign that she was awake. Bea looked like a woman sitting in a burning room, her face full of focused pain. This was the half-waking state Bea had been sinking into more and more often in the past few years, as if the effort of consciousness wearied her. Today precious hours of Bea's life had been stolen from her early. Jessica could see it in her face.

Alex lay in the Victorian-era maple bed, her head resting on two pillows, as if she were sleeping. Lucas had dressed Alex in a pink gown Jessica knew her sister would hate—silk with lace fringes, no less. *Wake up, hon, and tell your husband to go bring you a decent T-shirt.* But at least Lucas had tried to dress Alex like a queen.

Jessica only remembered that Lucas was still in the room when she heard him sigh behind her. He was sitting in a wooden chair near the closet. He slipped the black satellite phone into his jacket pocket, stood up, and carried his chair to Alex's bedside. Lucas shouldn't be calling anyone, but she understood. He had to talk to his friend, considering the news that had just come.

"How'd it go?" Jessica said.

"Awful," he said. "He was a friend, I couldn't tell him everything he deserved to know, and I think I just lied to him. I don't know if I should bring Jared back here, much less Garrick's kid. But he said he'll wait to call the police. Until he hears more from me."

Thank goodness. Maybe there was still time to fix it before it became worse. Before outsiders got involved. *Damn, damn, damn.* This was their worst day in a long time.

Fana and Caitlin were gone, and now Garrick Wright's son was, too. Garrick was a good man, but the Brothers had refused to allow further contact with him and the others. The Lalibela Council had threatened to shut them down by force if they brought in more out-siders, and Dawit had made concessions to avoid conflict. She hadn't minded the extra precaution; she'd known the price of carelessness. But as much as they had all tried to shield their children, clearly the younger generation had been touched by the mission, knowing what had rarely been spoken. Radicalized by it, maybe. *And a little child shall lead them.* Jessica wished she felt proud instead of scared.

Alex had tried to warn her. Jessica clasped Alex's hand, feeling her sister's warm skin, the calluses in her palms. *I miss you, Alex. I need every counselor today, and you're my best.*

Jessica gazed at Lucas, who shared the one bond with her that even Alex did not. Lucas was as tall as Teferi, almost six-foot-six. Lucas was the big brother Jessica had always wished for, and he had arrived just in time.

"It's happening tonight," Jessica told Lucas. "Justin will lose twenty years of memories."

Lucas shook his head with a forced chuckle. "Then we better hope Alex doesn't wake up, or she'll beat us both senseless."

Jessica wished she could laugh too, but she was closer to crying. She hadn't cried since waking to realize that her sister was in a kind of coma and her volatile little girl was gone.

"Can we try to appeal it?" Lucas said. "Would Dawit support us?"

"Do we really want to try, Lucas?" she said quietly.

Jessica had never been able to like Justin O'Neal, and she had been trying a long time. He had a weak character, a dishonest nature. *And the Old Testament says Moses was a murderer before he found God—so what's your point?*

Lucas rested his head on his wife's gently breathing chest. His eyes shimmered. "Listen, Jess, that man and his father held me and this lady at gunpoint. He didn't do jack shit while a man burned Alex's face with cigarettes. Almost got me killed. Hell, no, I don't like him. So would I lose any sleep if they make him forget his own name? Probably not."

"But . . . ," Jessica said. She knew there was more.

Lucas glanced at Bea, who was so still that she might have fallen asleep at last. He lowered his voice. "Telepathy? Thought manipulation? They can do things to us we can't do to them, and they've kept it from us. You hid it, too. And Alex. I know you told your sister."

Lucas's voice was raw with hurt, and Jessica understood more than she wanted to admit. They needed the Brothers' support for the mission, but it came with a price.

"I've never liked all of their demands, Lucas," she said. "Alex hated keeping secrets from you."

Lucas sighed, impatient with her coddling. "So they can jump in and out of our heads at will? A polygraph that never quits, is that it?"

"They wanted open access to the minds of any of us working with them. Especially people who don't have the blood. . . ." Jessica couldn't use the word *mortals,* the shorthand Dawit and his Brothers used freely. That word sounded too much like a wall between her and the people she cared about. "They promised not to abuse it."

Lucas smiled wryly. "Ten to one they're just pissed off Justin out-smarted them."

"They're pissed off because Justin lied, abused his position and stole their blood. That vial he stole was intended for thousands of patients, and now it's lost to them." Jessica felt her temper surge. "Alex was right last night: The mission might be in jeopardy because of Justin and Caitlin. Everything. I think we should demonstrate to the Brothers that we're willing to allow them to protect them-selves—really, to protect all of us who have this blood."

Some days, Jessica didn't believe the words she heard from her own mouth. *If Alex hears this, she's going to sit up and slap me.* Was she offering Justin O'Neal as a sacrifice?

"First it's Justin, next it's Cal. Or Garrick's son, Johnny. Or any of us. You know that."

Jessica couldn't pretend that most of the Life Brothers felt any warmth for them. It was as if empathy had somehow gotten switched off after hundreds of years. Or were they just too different? "Potentially. Yes."

"I don't trust them, Jess."

"Teka promised me that Justin will still remember most of his life," she said. "Maybe it's a just sentence. And if it is, we look petty for putting up a fuss."

"If we don't, we look weak."

"We are weak, Lucas. As long as Fana is gone. Is this the time to provoke them?"

Bea's voice spoke up suddenly: "Let them tend to their house," she said. Her mother wasn't sleeping after all, although her eyes were still closed. She looked like she was squinting into the light from the window. "I feel badly for the man, I do. But you reap what you sow. He knew there were rules. We forgave what he did before, and maybe we shouldn't have. You two leave it be." Her voice was tired and sad.

Her mother must have overheard many conversations when they'd thought she hadn't been paying attention. But then again, her mother's insight had been surprising Jessica all her life. Bea's body was fading, but not her mind.

Was acquiescence really the answer? If so, why did it feel so much like cowardice?

Jessica thought she saw Alex's mouth twitch. Maybe, knowing Alex's mind, she'd only imagined it. Alex wouldn't tolerate the Life Brothers' decision, whether or not it was Justin O'Neal. The cost for protection was too high, Alex said. She must be screaming inside.

"There's another way," Jessica said as the answer came to her.

Dinner was delicious, the kinds of foods Justin O'Neal never saw on the menus of the five-star international hotels where he spent too many of his nights on the road. Roast chicken cooked with a Cajun spice rub. Mashed potatoes. Homemade biscuits. Turnip greens flavored with peanut butter. Jessica and Nita had explained that the food was only leftovers, but after two nights in a cell, the dining room at the Big House was paradise.

Justin hadn't expected to have an appetite, but he piled up a second plate in the room's stony silence. Even with Teka sitting across the table, the food hadn't lost its flavor.

The others were eating, too, although without his enthusiasm. Lucas Shepard hadn't eaten a bite, and Jessica, Cal and Nita weren't doing much better. None of them looked like they wanted to be here, not even Teka. It was hard to catch anyone's eyes.

Is this my last meal? If so, Justin couldn't complain. If that was peach pie he smelled baking, that would make up for a multitude of sins.

"There's cobbler in the oven," Nita said. "Peach. Want some ice cream on that?"

"Yes, ma'am," Justin said. "You just read my mind."

Lucas and Jessica gave each other a look, mournful and significant. Whatever was about to happen here, Justin hoped it would wait until after dessert.

Justin got his wish. The cobbler *was* the best he had ever tasted. Hands down.

"You have a decision to make, Justin," Jessica finally said while Nita poured coffee.

Suddenly, all eyes were on him, and Justin suddenly noticed the ticking of an old-fashioned clock from the living room.

"I didn't think this was for the pleasure of my company," Justin said, smiling to put Jessica at ease. She might be the only reason he had lived this long.

Jessica nodded, returning his smile, but sadly. "The Life Brothers have passed a sentence on you, but the rest of us might choose to oppose it. If we oppose them, win or lose, tempers will flare. The outcome for you and your family might be worse than the original sentence."

Do you want door number one or door number two?

"So I need to decide if it's better to take the sentence," Justin said.

"Yes."

"If I do . . . is the safety of my family guaranteed? Even Caitlin?"

"If you agree to the sentence? Yes," Jessica said, not hesitating. As she spoke, she stared toward Teka, as if for confirmation. "We wouldn't harm Caitlin. We would protect her."

Teka assured both of them with a slow, sober nod.

Finally. His reckoning. Either he was about to die, or he would disappear from the world in a prison cell somewhere. No price was too high for a guarantee that Holly, Casey and Caitlin would be all right, but how could he take their word?

"What's the sentence?" he said.

"You would forget you know us," Teka said. "You would forget everything that has happened to you for the past eighteen years. Perhaps twenty."

They'll fire me and let me go? Justin's armpits prickled with disbelief. Jubilation.

"Of course," Justin said, tears stinging his eyes. "I would never say a word."

Jessica leaned forward, shaking her head. "No. You won't *remember*."

Six faces stared at him with dead certainty, waiting for him to see the point.

"Some kind of . . . brain surgery?" Justin said. His stomach ached suddenly, pulled too taut.

"Tell me what you just ate," Teka said.

Justin stared at the small man, dumbstruck. Was this a joke? Were they playing with him? He could still taste his food in his mouth. He'd had . . .

Justin's mind was a blank sheet.

He stared down at his plate. Chicken bones. A pastry for dessert? Was that melted ice cream? He couldn't remember, although he remembered enjoying the meal.

"I . . . don't . . ."

Lucas stood up, as if he were a defense attorney at a trial. "That's enough."

"What's the point of playing with him?" Nita said.

Justin was suddenly on his feet, too, his eyes locked with Teka's. He took a step backward, stumbling into a chair. Teka's eyes weren't normal. Those eyes were *alive,* and Justin couldn't look away from him. His heart hammered against his ribs. *What the FUCK?*

"You've been asked to give up eighteen years of memory," Teka said. "I want you to understand what you're being asked. I can do what I have claimed. You will forget."

Justin wished he hadn't eaten so much of whatever he'd had, because he felt sick to his stomach. Was this a dream?

"I wouldn't do it," Nita said. Her voice quavered.

He heard the others' angry voices, but they blended in his mind as one. They were trading mundane legal points the way he would at a jury trial. Not a dream. Not a fantasy. *Real.* This was their inner world! Justin's heart raced.

Eighteen years. What would he lose in eighteen years? He would remember the twins' birth, but little else of them beyond that. He would have to get to know his daughters again. He would have to get to know himself again.

"You'll remember all of your childhood," Teka said.

Justin almost laughed, a glimmer of sanity. "That's the part I can do without."

The others chuckled uneasily, but their eyes weren't laughing.

"How did you do that?" Justin asked Teka. "Scramble my head?"

Teka shrugged. "It's a skill I've refined over time."

"Tell me who you are."

"If I tell you more, your sentence is decided."

Justin forced himself to stop and think. He couldn't be mesmerized by this man's dancing eyes and the knowledge brimming there. "What would happen to Holly and my girls?"

"Holly and Casey will live undisturbed. Caitlin must give up her memories, or live here."

"You mean like . . . reading and writing? Language? She would lose it all?"

"No. Most of her cognitive learning would be intact, with some gaps. The memories most affected will be experiences. Nothing conscious will connect her to this colony or its people. She'll remember nowhere she has lived during that time. She will remember no one she has met since she was six or seven, yet she will remember how to compute an algebraic equation she learned as an older girl. In your case, you would remember yourself as a younger man. Your job. Your home. Baby daughters. The contrast will confuse you at first, but you will adjust with time. If we're satisfied that your wife and daughter pose us no threat—"

"They don't know anything about the blood. I mean that."

"We know," Teka said, with a smile so certain that it chilled Justin.

But of course Teka knew. Teferi had always known everything in his mind, too. Justin had always sensed that, and he'd even joked to Holly about it. But that wasn't why he had never betrayed this colony's secrets to Holly and the girls: To explain the blood, he would have had to explain all of it, starting with the people who'd died. Holly thought the colony was a health-conscious family retreat, and he was happy to keep it that way. Caitlin must have found out about the blood from Fana, because he never would have told her.

"Let me at least wait until Caitlin is back. To say good-bye. To see her safe."

The others' eyes went to Jessica. Gently, she shook her head. "I'm sorry."

Jessica and the rest must have argued for leniency, he realized. He owed them his life, and they didn't have room for negotiation.

"Promise me she won't be hurt," Justin said to the mother of Caitlin's closest friend.

"Never. Not by us," Jessica said. She reached across the table and clung to his hand. It was the nicest gesture she had ever made toward him, genuinely warm. As if they had been friends all this time and he hadn't known it.

Oh, God. He was thinking about it. He had made up his mind. Justin's heart drilled him; even the idea made him dizzy. Justin sat down again, and the room stopped rocking.

"Are you all right?" Nita said. A glass of ice water appeared in front of him. She raised the glass and helped him drink it.

Justin stared again at the faces around the room. Could he really forget them?

Justin had seen his father shoot Dr. Lucas Shepard in the head point-blank. Had seen Shepard's brain tissue spray on the wall. Yet here the man was, sitting at the table with a coffee mug in his hand as his advocate, if not a friend.

Jessica Wolde had something like love in her eyes, even though her face usually cracked any time she tried to smile at him. He had led violent people to her family once. He was responsible for her nurse's death, and nearly her sister's.

Cal and Nita Duhart had never liked him much either, but at least Cal had invited him squirrel hunting once. Cal couldn't look him in the eye now. The old woman and her daughter Alex weren't here, maybe because he'd nearly led Alex to her death.

All he had to do was forget?

"I've never felt square with you," Justin told Lucas and Jessica.

Jessica smiled at him, and her face didn't crack this time. "You've made up for it, Justin. Your work has shown us who you really are."

"The past is done." Lucas extended his hand. "You've worked hard."

"Thank you." Justin shook the scientist's hand, surprised to be overcome with gratified tears. Without him, it might have taken the immortals decades to accomplish what had taken Clarion only a few years. *He* had helped them do that. If they hadn't been so cautious, they could have reached half a billion people by now instead of only thousands.

But maybe they'd been right to be cautious. Maybe he was proof of why.

"Where do you come from?" Justin asked Teka. "What makes your blood this way?"

"Tell me your decision," Teka said.

"I agree to the sentence," Justin said. His tongue felt too big for his mouth, but he got the words out. "I'll lose the years. I knew the risks. I can't say I don't deserve it."

Nita Duhart sighed, shaking her head as if he had just agreed to an execution. Without a word, she left for the kitchen, with the French doors swinging angrily behind her. Still, Justin sensed relief in the glance between Lucas and Jessica. They were glad to avoid a fight.

"Are there others like you?" Justin asked Teka. He was just trying to buy extra time in his own head, the way Caitlin and Casey had tried to stall him at bedtime when they were young. Another glass of water. Another toy in their cribs.

Teka's voice sounded closer; his singsong speech was lulling him somehow.

No. Not speech. Teka's lips weren't moving. He was talking to Justin with his eyes.

THERE WERE FIFTY-NINE OF US TO START, AND THEN CAME JESSICA AND LUCAS. AND FANA. OUR FAMILY GROWS. WE LIVED TOGETHER FIVE HUNDRED YEARS, AND I WOULD LIKE TO THINK WE SHALL LIVE TOGETHER AGAIN. OUR BROTHERS DO NOT SUPPORT OUR BLOOD MISSION. THEY ADVOCATE SEPARATION.

"Could it be your own people after Caitlin? The murders . . ." Justin's voice fell to a whisper to match the gentle voice in his head.

For the first time, emotion gave way on Teka's face. Sadness. *WE PRAY NOT.*

"Don't give up the mission," Justin told him.

Teka smiled, noncommittal. *ALL THINGS END.*

"Where's Teferi?" Justin said, wishing he had said good-bye to his oldest living forebear.

This time, Jessica broke in, her voice snapping the eerie link he had felt with the man across the table: "He's out looking for Caitlin. They think she was in Berkeley today. A boy named Johnny Wright may have left with her. Caitlin is with friends. Teferi will find them."

Thank God. He could trust Teferi to keep her safe. Caitlin was Teferi's blood.

Justin had never felt so much peace. Was Teka helping him with that, too?

Justin drained his water glass. Cold and crisp. Perfect.

"What happens now?" Justin said. Was he only imagining the shimmer in Teka's eyes?

YOU GIVE ME YOUR BLESSING. MEMORIES ARE EX-TRACTED BEST WHEN THEY ARE OFFERED RATHER THAN STOLEN. THE MORE FREELY YOU RELEASE THEM, THE MORE GENTLE I CAN BE.

The anxious fear Justin had felt in his cell came back, and his body went rigid. How could he make himself hand over the past eighteen years? He would need to be drunk for that. Justin's hands were shaking, so he flattened his palms against the tabletop. He couldn't meet Teka's eyes again. He was afraid of Teka's eyes now.

They were immortals. Telepaths. A race of them! If Greek mythology was any lesson, mortals and gods had never lived well together. Justin hoped he would still remember Atlas and Prometheus when he was cast from this Garden, even if he forgot Dawit, Teferi and Teka.

"Will it hurt?" Justin said. He felt only Teka's presence. Needed to hear Teka's voice.

YOU WON'T FEEL ANYTHING, SO LONG AS YOUR MIND IS CALM.

"What should I think about?" Justin said.

THE DAY YOUR TWINS WERE BORN, Teka said. A whisper across his heart.

Justin saw the same golden late-afternoon light he'd seen in a shaft across his wall when he'd opened his eyes after he'd heard Holly call him. He'd been lying facedown on the bed in his suit, so tired he hadn't taken off his coat and hat even though he'd been sweating. Chicago winter.

"I can remember that," Justin said to someone, or maybe he only thought he did.

He's too tired to move, but he's sure he hears Holly calling him from downstairs, excited and a little scared. He gathers his strength and pulls himself to his feet. Holly needs him. She grins, gritting her teeth through her pain, when she sees him on the top landing. The light catches her face from the second-floor window, that perfect golden glare, and he knows this is the most important day of their lives.

"I want painkillers," Holly says. "Lots of them."

Anything you say, Holly. Anything for the twins. Anything for Caitlin. Anything so you won't get hurt, sweetheart.

Thirteen

Casa Grande, Arizona
Wednesday
6:25 a.m.

When the PT Cruiser finally reached the beige bungalow at the end of a cul-de-sac, Caitlin steered left of the driveway's rows of narrow cactus to stop under twin green acacia trees. Fana had told her not to underestimate the Searchers, so Caitlin wasn't taking any chances. She didn't want anyone to be able to track their car from the air.

Mitchell and Sheila Rolfson had moved to Casa Grande, halfway between Phoenix and Tucson, last year, saying they wanted to live in a smaller city; thirty thousand instead of more than five times that. The new house wasn't as big as their last, which used to have enough beds for a dozen travelers at a time, but Caitlin could already see why it was a good place to hide. The suburban street was cookie-cutter and could be anywhere, except for the paved lawns to compensate for a lack of rainfall. And the Sonoran desert's purple morning light.

Fana needed the quiet.

Thank bejeezus Mitch and Sheila moved out of Tempe. Caitlin wished she could have stopped at the safe house in Vegas instead—it was three hours closer than Casa Grande—but if Fana hadn't been able to handle Portland and Berkeley, Vegas might have made her head explode.

Most of the houses on the street were dark, with cars safely parked at home for the night. The street was sleeping. *Oh, God. We made it.* The promise of rest made Caitlin's hands shake.

Caitlin dialed Mitchell's number from memory, using the cell phone she'd bought from a street vendor in Berkeley. The phone rang twice.

"Come on in," Mitchell said before she could speak, and the white aluminum garage door rolled open with a subdued whir, revealing a neat garage with plenty of space. The only thing parked inside was a black Kawasaki painted white in desert dust. Caitlin sighed. Mitchell should have listened for her voice and run it through his analyzer before he opened his door.

But that was Mitchell. He hadn't changed in six years.

As soon as the door was clear, Caitlin sped inside the garage. The sudden motion woke Johnny, who had finally fallen asleep after a sleepless night. He looked around, shielding his eyes against the garage's bright fluorescent glare. Behind them, the door was already on its way down again. They were hidden from sight.

For the first time in two days, Caitlin's muscles unclenched. *Safe. We're safe.*

"Where are we?" Johnny said.

Caitlin glanced back at Fana. Good. She was sleeping.

"Where we're supposed to be. Stay in the car with Fana. I'll be right back."

Johnny suddenly grabbed her arm, yanking her back toward him. His eyes were bleary but angry. "Hell, no, Caitlin. You're not leaving me here until I know where we are."

They shouldn't have gone to Berkeley. They never should have brought Johnny. Caitlin hoped Berhanu hadn't picked up Fana's mental scent in Berkeley, when he had been so close. What if Fana's masking hadn't worked? Fana had been so overcome that she might have lost her concentration. She could be leading the Searchers right to the Rolfsons.

"It's a safe house, like I told you," Caitlin said. "We can rest and plan our next move."

"*What* next move?" Johnny said. "Look, maybe you treat your Glow people like shit, but I'm not just anybody else." His eyes softened from anger to a deeply grooved hurt.

"I *will* tell you," Caitlin said, for what she was sure was the hundredth time. She was so tired that she wanted to cry. "We just have to make sure we're OK first. Trust me, that's the most important thing right now."

Johnny looked sulky, arms crossed as he stared away from her, but at least he was quiet. Caitlin wanted to talk to him like a friend, but she only had the strength to open her car door. After twelve straight hours of driving with only one bathroom break, Caitlin's knees were shaking. Crumbs from the vanilla wafers she'd been quieting her stomach with fell from her lap when she stood. She wished she had a stun gun, at least. She felt naked.

But thank God it was Mitchell and Sheila. She had known them since she was fifteen.

There was a doorbell beside the door inside the garage, glowing in inviting white, but the door swung open before Caitlin could raise her finger. She was washed in the overwhelming scent of frying bacon. And pancakes. Caitlin's stomach flipped, and saliva flooded her mouth. She was so hungry that she felt sick to her stomach.

Mitchell's beard was trimmed low, and his curly brown hair grew to his shoulders like his hero, rocker Jimmy Page; he hadn't changed much from when she'd been in high school and he'd been Mr. Rolfson, her philosophy teacher in the gifted program. He was lanky, with a spray of pale freckles across his nose. It still amazed Caitlin that her former teacher had decided to change his life, uprooting his entire family, because of her.

"That was fast," Mitchell said. He gave her a tight hug and kissed the top of her head. The gesture made Caitlin miss her father so much that her throat clenched. "You made it, Cat."

"There's two more in the car. My friend isn't feeling well."

Mitchell glanced eagerly toward the car. "Justin?" he said, relieved.

Caitlin just shook her head. She had told him that she and her father were in trouble, but she couldn't talk about it now, and not just for the sake of secrecy. Squeezing her elbow, Mitchell didn't press. "Sheila's got breakfast on for anyone who's interested, and beds ready for those who would rather sleep. Another traveler beat you here, and we just got the table set."

"There's a traveler? From where?"

"Canada. Vancouver."

Laurel Reid in Vancouver was one of the best conductors in the Railroad, single-handedly responsible for the Glow that crossed north. After all Laurel had been through, she would never send anyone to the Rolfsons without a thorough screen. But procedure was procedure.

"Before we come in, I want to see the traveler's file. Name?"

"Charlie Dominguez." Mitchell's head listed to the side as he shrugged impatiently. His tone said *Oh, come on.* "He's Laurel's. I just talked to her ten minutes ago."

Caitlin loved Mitchell, but he had the same tendency to skate over details he'd had as her teacher, when she'd thought it was cool that he didn't sweat anyone about missing class. In the Railroad, everyone had been conscientious in the beginning, but most people had loosened up. Life under high alert was joyless, and most people didn't have the stomach for it. Maritza hadn't.

"Why's Dominguez here?" Caitlin asked.

"Pinching. First Phoenix, then Vegas. Laurel's been dry for three months."

When Glow supplies were low, couriers were sent to "pinch" Glow residue from conductors around the country—everything from old vials to IV bags to hypodermic needles—hoping to salvage trace product. Most pinched Glow was too weak to cure a cold sore, diluted to nothing. But Caitlin knew why Laurel was dry in Vancouver: Laurel's godson, Ethan, had been abducted and murdered, just like Maritza. Half of Laurel's supply had disappeared with him, never recovered. This had been a hellish year for the Underground Railroad, but Laurel hadn't quit, and neither had any of the other conductors. Even with four people in jail, no one had talked. Caitlin felt herself trembling again; part nerves, part fevered jubilation.

You can't stop us, you bastards. There are too many of us. And now we have Fana.

"Send his file to my phone. My friend doesn't go near anyone I don't know," she said. "And you have to get rid of the bacon. My friend is sensitive to the smell."

"You call the shots, *mi capitan*. We only cooked it for you."

Caitlin would check Dominguez out herself before they set foot in the house, accessing the encrypted database a sympathetic MIT professor had set up for the Railroad. Names. Faces. Histories. A legit courier would be registered, and Caitlin didn't trust anyone's eyes but her own.

But if Charlie Dominguez was who he claimed to be, today was Canada's lucky day.

Johnny glared when Caitlin came back to his window. She answered by staring away from him, the closest she ever came to apologizing. She was typing into her phone, barely looking at him. "That was Mitch. His wife's name is Sheila. She's a Unitarian minister, one of the coolest people on the planet, and he was my teacher in high school. I trust them with my life, and they cooked pancakes."

"That's all I'm talking about, just some respect," Johnny mumbled. "Shit."

"Excuse me for my lack of bedside manner, but my father might be dead right now."

"He's not dead," Fana said from the backseat. She raised the tarp above her eyes to cut the light. She still looked sleepy, but she didn't seem to be in pain anymore.

Caitlin finally stopped the manic scrolling on her phone, giving Fana a sharp, skeptical glance. "You look better. Be right back," Caitlin said and vanished inside the house.

"Is she always like this?" Johnny asked Fana.

Fana rubbed her face, trying to wake up. "Way worse since Maritza."

"Who killed Maritza?"

"We're not sure."

"But you think the same people could be after us?"

"We have to assume they are."

"But why?"

Fana gave him a heartbroken smile. "Glow. When it's real, it works. It's valuable."

Johnny remembered his brush with violence from Ryan LaCroix.

He touched Fana's forehead again, gauging her temperature. Fana's skin was unlike any he had ever felt—warm, but not just that. Her skin seemed to vibrate beneath his fingertips.

"Well, Doc?" Fana said playfully.

"You'll live," Johnny said, trying to smile. "What's going on with Caitlin's dad?"

Johnny couldn't mistake the shadow across Fana's face. "Let's get settled first," she said.

In other words, you ain't gonna' tell me shit, Johnny thought.

"Trust us," Fana said, grasping his hand with such sudden urgency. "We have to tell you enough so you can protect yourself. Anything else would be irresponsible."

Finally, Fana seemed to be talking sense. "Deal, Lil' Sis," he said, and squeezed her fingers. Maybe he was only imagining it, but he felt better every time he touched Fana. Less pissed. Less scared. Less convinced that he had just been kidnapped. *But what about that weird feeling? What about when you thought you could hear her voice talking in your head?* Johnny wanted to ask Fana about it, but the question felt ridiculous in a hundred ways.

The door to the house opened suddenly, and Caitlin waved them inside.

"All clear!" she called out. "Sorry for the smell, Fana."

Johnny hadn't realized how hungry he was until he climbed out of the car and the scent of breakfast made his knees go weak. Bacon! What the hell was Caitlin apologizing for?

A middle-aged man and woman were waiting on the other side of the door, in their kitchen. They were a grinning welcome party, still dressed in robes and slippers. The bearded man's long hair made him look like an escapee from the 1973 cast of *Jesus Christ, Superstar,* and his much shorter wife had a round, ruddy face that was the Webster's dictionary portrait of *perky.* She looked like a farmer's wife, a bit chubby with blond hair in a bowl cut. Johnny liked her cheerful, active eyes. They each held a bundle of clothes wrapped in plastic.

"Road kit," the woman said, offering her bundle to Johnny. "Sweatpants. Arizona State Sun Devils T-shirt. Undies. Toothbrush. Welcome to Casa Rolfson."

"She's Mitch. I'm Sheila," the man said, then he winked at them. "Or something like that. We've been up since four-thirty. Who's hungry?"

So, *this* was the Underground Railroad, Johnny realized as he introduced himself and shook his hosts' hands. Like abolitionists fighting slavery in their own quiet way in the 1800s, Caitlin's network took in fleeing strangers. Johnny couldn't imagine what it had felt like to be a runaway slave who'd found food and shelter after a long, harrowing journey, but he was plenty grateful now. Even the cool air in the house was a welcome change; Caitlin had left the AC off in the car to save gas. At six bucks a gallon, she'd said they couldn't afford to waste a drop.

"I'm Beatrice, but my friends call me Bea-Bea," Fana said quietly. She looked sick again; her hand was pressed to her stomach. "Is there anywhere I can just? . . ."

Johnny moved toward her, feeling an instinct to scoop her up and carry her into the house. Caitlin beat him, hugging Fana with one arm and guiding her out of his reach.

"Sorry," Caitlin said. "She gets carsick."

"Poor baby," Sheila Rolfson said, about to whirl away. "Nate, too. I've got Dramamine."

"No need. Sleep will do it," Caitlin said. "Mitch, can you take us down to the beds? I'll come right back. Why don't you guys go to the table? Don't wait for me."

When Johnny started to protest, Caitlin gestured that he should go with the Rolfsons. Caitlin followed Mitchell, leading Fana across the kitchen and around the corner, out of Johnny's view.

Alone in a stranger's kitchen, Johnny felt self-conscious and nervous. He noticed a pea-green phone mounted on the kitchen wall. Three or four days might go by before his roommate missed him, but his parents had expected him to call yesterday. They must be worried even if Zach wasn't.

"Can I use your phone?" Johnny said. "I have a calling card."

Sheila Rolfson's expression soured. Her bright eyes held his. "We're not big fans of phones here, hon," she said with an iron smile. "Let's grab a bite while it's hot."

Sheila gently took his arm like a nun with a wayward student and led him out of the kitchen, toward a hallway. Johnny was startled, then angry. What kind of hospitality was this? But he didn't pull away. It was her house, after all, so he'd have to abide by her rules. After breakfast, he'd find a phone somewhere else. *God, I miss my cell.*

"Whoa—about time!" a teenager's voice said as they reached the family room.

It was a sunken room, one steep step down to pile carpeting and dark wood-paneled walls. Antique lanterns and typewriters were set on shelves beside the CD player, game consoles and recorders. There was a large flat-screen TV mounted on the wall, playing morning network news at a low volume; a weather map. Above the TV hung a painting of religious symbols—a cross, a Star of David and a Buddhist yin-yang symbol, side by side. The rest of the room was lined with books, with one wall dedicated to DVD cases with their covers displayed: *Pulp Fiction. The Seven Samurai. The Exorcist.* Johnny and his dad could spend days in this room.

Two teenage boys sat at the scarred, round wooden table big enough for six behind the sofa. The lanky, older boy, about Johnny's age, was studying a faded road map. He had deeply tanned skin and curly jet-black hair cropped short in back, a military-style contrast to his leather biker jacket. The younger boy was about fourteen, but it was hard to see his face past his GamePort goggles. All of Johnny's cousins were GamePorters, too, engaged in wireless medieval quests and deep space battles with other addicts around the globe.

The older boy shifted position, leaning on one elbow to get a better look at the map. "I'm Charlie," he said, a grunt. He only glanced up toward Johnny.

"Nate," the younger boy said, not lifting his goggles to show his eyes. "Let's eat."

"Excuse Nate's bad table manners," Sheila said, embarrassed.

"I'm in a tournament," the boy said. "Me and two Maori guys. It's dinnertime in New Zealand, but the sore losers won't pause the game. I'm finally beating Tama."

"And *such* a good excuse it is," his mother said, rolling her eyes. Then she smiled at Johnny, probably trying to make up for practically yanking him away from her phone.

Johnny gave her a thin smile as he took his seat. Sheila Rolfson bit her bottom lip as she leaned over to offer Johnny a bottle of syrup, and he realized they were all scared. Charlie's laserlike eyes were fixed on his maps. Nate's leg bounced beneath the table nervously, making the milk in their glasses quiver. *Maybe I should be scared, too.*

Johnny remembered the kitchen phone again. But he was hungry, so he reached for the stack of pancakes. He smelled bacon, but there was none in sight. Too bad. Johnny's mother was Muslim and didn't serve pork, but he'd discovered bacon in college and liked it.

"Did you hear about this? It's awful," Sheila said suddenly. She snatched up the television's remote on the table. "Someone stole that poor man's body."

"Stole a body?" Johnny said, confused. "From where?"

"From a morgue," Charlie mumbled, dismissive. Like it was obvious.

The TV screen showed a Catholic mass at a large church. The pews were full. The television's volume was suddenly loud with a crisp female announcer's voice: ". . . still no clues or explanations in the theft of a priest's corpse from the King County Medical Examiner's Office on Tuesday night, leaving parishioners reeling. Father Arturo Bragga—"

"Jesus," Caitlin's voice said suddenly.

Johnny hadn't seen Caitlin and Mitchell come back to the family room. Caitlin walked until she stood two feet in front of the TV screen, blocking it.

The announcer's voice went on: "The first shock came Monday night, when parishioners at Saint Mary Magdalene Parish learned that a beloved assistant pastor had been murdered at their church-run shelter for battered women." The screen showed a photograph of a grinning dark-haired priest in his collar; about thirty, with a long face.

"Twenty-four hours later, a cruel twist: An intruder killed a King Medical Examiner's Office security guard, Heath Crowley, in the cooler where Father Bragga's body was stored, then removed the priest's body. Now investigators are wrestling with a question even more puzzling than the murder of a priest: Why did a killer steal a priest's body from the morgue?"

"Oh, God," Caitlin said. Her hands trembled at her sides.

"Cat?" Mitch said.

"*Shhhhhh*," Caitlin said. The room hushed. Even the tinny sounds of battle from Nate's headset were gone. Nate slowly lifted his goggles to stare at the television set.

An older, white-haired priest appeared on-camera, barely composed as he read from a statement with unsteady hands. "To endure one senseless crime and then another even harder to understand . . . is a great deal to bear," he said, blinking fast. "But we rejoice that our friend's soul is safe. He is not lost. He is found."

"Amen," Sheila Rolfson said.

Caitlin didn't move even after the story was over and a cereal commercial came on.

Sheila zapped off the television. Her skin had gone gray. "Cat?"

Caitlin turned around, her face red and tear-streaked. "F-Father Arturo," she said, swatting tears from her cheeks. "I w-was . . .." Caitlin didn't finish, sobbing.

Mitchell and Sheila encircled Caitlin while Johnny stood. Charlie and Nate both came to their feet. Nate's goggles lay on the table, forgotten.

"Was that guy one of ours?" Charlie said.

Mitchell held up his hand, a gentle gesture for quiet. Mitchell and Sheila led Caitlin to the sofa, sitting on either side of her. Sheila hushed her, stroking Caitlin's hair while she sobbed on her shoulder. Mitchell patted her knee. They could have been her parents.

The sight of Caitlin melting like a rag doll scared the shit out of Johnny. He'd ignored all of the other reasons to be worried as long as Caitlin had seemed so sure of herself. He had trusted her all the way to Arizona. *Now* what? He didn't want to be even slightly involved in whatever Caitlin O'Neal had dragged him into, Glow or not.

Caitlin shrieked, a sound of inconsolable sorrow that made Johnny's toes go rigid.

"That's right, let go of it . . . ," Sheila said, rocking with Caitlin. "It's all right, Cat. You're here. You're with friends now."

Johnny knelt on the carpeted floor at Cat's feet, afraid to hear more.

"I'll get water," Nate said, sprinting toward the kitchen. His voice had aged a decade. Johnny wished he had thought of it first. His brain was only working at a crawl.

After two minutes, Caitlin's crying calmed. She accepted the water from Nate and nearly emptied the glass. Then she bowed and shook her head. "I was there," she said. "Father Arturo was supposed to meet me, but someone else was waiting. I saw him get killed. It was because of Glow. I th-think the same people killed Maritza."

Johnny was surprised he was the first one to speak. "Did you go to the police?"

"He's right, Caitlin," Mitchell Rolfson said. He flipped his hair out of his face, tying it into a ponytail so he could meet Caitlin's eyes. "You have to say what you know. How else will the killings be stopped?"

"Who is it?" Sheila said. "Who's doing this?"

Caitlin shook her head. "I can't tell you."

"Why not?" Sheila asked, looking shocked. And hurt.

"They have Dad. He's a prisoner. Fana helped me get away, but . . ." This time, Caitlin stuffed a sob back into her throat.

Sheila Rolfson shot to her feet. Her hand rested on her throat, her eyes horrified. "Cat, where's Justin? We have to help him. Whatever it takes, that's what we'll have to do."

Caitlin shook her head. "I don't even know if we can help ourselves," she whispered.

Johnny was sure he had heard wrong, because Caitlin O'Neal would never say that.

"That's bullshit," Charlie said, and Johnny noticed his Hispanic accent. "They tore out my friend Ethan's guts like a pig, and he was only sixteen! If you know where they are, let's take out the fuckers and get Glow back on the streets. We can do it ourselves."

Johnny felt a dreamy sensation, like eavesdropping on someone else's life. How could he be standing anywhere near this conversation?

"The Railroad is a nonviolent organization," Mitchell said.

"Yeah, and see what it's getting us?" Charlie said. "They're picking us off!"

"Charlie?" Sheila said. "Keep your composure, kid. Theatrics won't help right now."

Charlie paced beside Johnny, his face angry. His biker jacket reeked of cigarettes.

"I don't understand why I'm here," Johnny said. "I never met that guy. I don't know anything about any murders. I just want to call my parents and tell them I'm OK."

He sounded like a pussy, but so be it. The situation had felt wrong from the first time Caitlin had appeared in Berkeley in a stolen car.

"Grow up, man," Charlie muttered behind him.

"I'm sorry your friend died," Johnny said, "but mind your fucking business."

"Boys . . . ," Sheila warned, "we're a family when we're under this roof."

Caitlin reached out for Johnny's hand, and he took it. She squeezed his fingers. "I'm sorry, Johnny. You'll implicate your parents if you call them," she said. "Like I did my father."

"Why did you bring me here?" Johnny said. He hated how close to tears he sounded.

Caitlin leaned closer to Johnny. Her lips grazed his earlobe as she finally told him the truth: "That guy Ryan you told me about last year? The football player? Fana knew his name, Johnny. She *sees* things sometimes. She has premonitions."

Johnny shook his head to clear his hearing. Her words were a jumble. "What?"

Caitlin's grip tightened. "Fana said Ryan was going to get drunk and try to make you tell where you got the Glow. That's why we had to get you. We only wanted to help you. The others would have come after you next, and they're worse than Ryan. I've seen what they do."

Caitlin's eyes were strangely emptied, like Dad said his uncle Reggie's had been after he'd come back from Vietnam. All Johnny could think about were those first confusing words Caitlin had spoken to him after he'd climbed into the PT Cruiser in Berkeley on the road to Arizona.

Maybe Caitlin had been right.

Maybe everything he thought he knew was a lie.

Fourteen

The Underground Railroad would have fresh blood for the first time in three years.

Fana and Caitlin found their retreat from the others in the tiny basement bathroom. Fana sat on the toilet, seat down, while Caitlin stood over her beside the plastic shower stall with the half-filled bag of blood cupped in her palms. A tube hung between them, flushed crimson. Fana's mother had told her that she and Aunt Alex used to hide away from everyone when it was time to refresh their blood supply in their little clinics in South Africa and Botswana.

That tradition would be preserved.

The hidden basement wasn't pretty, or even finished: The ceiling was low, with unpainted concrete block walls and bare floors. But it was sanctuary. The basement was large, almost a thousand square feet, and the Rolfsons had built a concrete wall to separate the genders, for added privacy. A door at the top of the stairs was hidden behind a bookcase in the house. The bookshelf was crammed with books, mostly paperbacks, which made the door hard to open; but if the police ever raided the Rolfsons, no cursory search would detect the door.

Fana felt almost like herself for the first time since leaving home, thanks to two hours' sleep and a fat soy butter sandwich on homemade multigrain bread. For now, she was no longer reeling from the maelstrom in her head. But a sick, doomed feeling followed her. She hoped it was only the shock of being away from home, but she was afraid it was something bigger than her silly adventures. Something to do with the priest.

Fana heard the boys' muffled voices from their bunk area outside of the bathroom door. Johnny and the other boy, Dominguez, had been talking about nothing except the priest since breakfast. Fana had heard their chatter during her nap, at the fringes of consciousness.

Fana just wished she felt safe here. She didn't. Dad, Mom and Teka had told her not to tell anyone—not *anyone*—what flowed in her veins. Trusting Caitlin didn't make Fana feel any less vulnerable. What if someone was spying on them? She didn't sense any cameras in the bathroom, but she was learning the hard way that her perceptions were unreliable. She hadn't sensed Aunt Alex only a few feet from her two nights ago.

Take it an hour at a time, Fana reminded herself. Teka had warned her that immersion in the outer world would take practice, and her flight with Caitlin was a crash course. She had to be patient, like Mom was always saying.

Caitlin needed to learn patience too. Since the newscast, Caitlin hadn't given Fana a direct glance. Fana wished Caitlin would learn the difference between truth and appearances.

"If you're thinking my father took that priest's body, you're wrong," Fana said quietly. When Caitlin gave Fana an icy look, Fana realized she sounded like she was snooping. "That's just a guess," Fana said. "I don't always know your thoughts, unless I try."

"I don't want to talk about it," Caitlin said, eyes on her task. "Tell me about Dominguez. Can you read him?"

"It's harder to read someone who isn't right in front of me."

"That isn't what I asked." Caitlin's tone was snappish, but Fana forgave her. Caitlin reserved her greatest reproofs for herself, constantly calling herself names and chastising herself. How could she be more kind to others?

Fana imagined herself walking through the bathroom's closed door, around the corner and to the side of the room where Dominguez and Johnny were talking. Their voices became amplified, bypassing her ears.

"*Fifteen hours straight.*" Johnny.

"*That's nothing. Try three days on a bike. Oh yeah, and one whole night in freezing fucking rain.*" Dominguez.

Boys were always in competition, Fana thought. Her probe grazed Johnny, and she saw a mossy tree above a cedar deck. His backyard? Faces appeared, eyes wide and worried: an olive-skinned woman with long, dark hair and a black man with a gray moustache.

GOTTACALLGOTTACALLGOTTACALLGOTTACALL

As usual, Johnny was thinking about his parents. His desperation made Fana feel misplaced, too. Did either of them belong here?

Quickly, Fana withdrew and redirected her probe at Dominguez. Usually probing caused a prick, but her mind slipped into his like a knife through soft butter. Easy. Warm.

Fana saw Charlie astride his motorcycle, speeding through a rainstorm. Worn, brown leather biker boots. A silver cross on a chain hanging beneath his shirt, across a nearly hairless chest. The image shifted: She saw his face distorted by tears as he hugged a rail-thin white woman whose mouth hung open in agonized shock. They were both mourning a teenage boy lying on the ground, covered to his shoulders by a sheet soaked with blood. Dead.

She smelled Charlie then: sweet perspiration. Tobacco-scented breath. Earthy clothes.

"He's brave," Fana said. "Committed. More scared than he wants to show anyone."

"Join the club," Caitlin muttered. "Anything else?"

Fana shook her head. There was plenty more, but nothing Fana felt it was her right to learn. Charlie's raging heart moved her, and she wanted to squeeze his hand. Or press herself against him in a hug? Fana smiled. Her sudden longing to hug Charlie surprised her. She was glad to have something to think about besides Aunt Alex, her parents and Caitlin.

Charlie's mind was fascinating. Soothing. She didn't want to leave. But she had to.

"Are we giving him blood?" Fana said.

"As much as you can spare. Can you do another pint now?"

Fana felt dizzy, but she knew it didn't have anything to do with her blood. Sometimes withdrawing a probe too quickly jarred her. "I'm fine."

"Good. Mitch has just enough saline to get us by. Charlie'll have to carry about thirty bags of Glow, but he looks like he's up for it."

"Oh, he is," Fana said, and Caitlin gave her a puzzled look. Had she said it too eagerly?

Caitlin shook her head. "You're so seventeen."

"Too bad you never gave yourself that luxury."

Caitlin smirked. "Hey, I had my fun in college. For a while. But in my life, being childish gets you killed. Forget Dominguez, Fana. He'll be gone by morning. We'll be gone soon after."

Caitlin had slept with Johnny a few times at Berkeley. Fana had sensed their past intimacy from Johnny almost the instant he'd gotten in the car, a vibration beneath and above everything else. Johnny believed he loved Caitlin, and Fana felt sorry for him. As Gramma Bea would say, Johnny was barking up the wrong tree. Caitlin was convincing herself she would never love anyone the way she had loved Maritza.

"Where are we going next?" Fana said.

"Mexico. There's a tunnel in Nogales. We'll leave tomorrow."

Caitlin's clipped, businesslike tone pained Fana. Tentatively, Fana let her thoughts reach toward Caitlin for what Teka called a "massage," a subtle mood adjustment. She imagined herself fanning away thick clouds of smoke from Caitlin's face until she could see a smile through the haze. Just a small one. It was a personal violation, but sometimes emotions were a barrier to the things that needed to be said.

Fana noticed her friend's shoulders slump. Unlocking.

That's it, Fana thought. *Just relax. You're my best friend, Caitlin. Don't wall me away.*

"We have to talk about the priest, Caitlin."

Blue eyes fixed on her, unblinking. Stubborn. "Yeah. I guess we do."

"I know what you believe, and I understand why. You saw my father do something terrible, and I know he's done awful things before. But why would he take the body?"

"To destroy evidence. Why else?"

"Be objective. Aren't there other explanations?"

"Like what?" Caitlin said. "Father Arturo got up and walked away?"

Fana felt gooseflesh across her arms. "Yes," she said.

Caitlin's jaw flexed. She didn't want to listen, but she would. "Go on."

"The night before Father Arturo died, I had a dream. I saw you in my dream, and a priest I didn't recognize at the time. In my dream, you were watching while my father broke the priest's neck." Amazement clouded Caitlin's mind. Fana massaged Caitlin's thoughts again so Caitlin would hear the rest of her story above her inner chorus of *OHMYFUCKINGLORD*. The memory of the damage to Aunt Alex haunted Fana; this time, Fana's touch was as soft as a kitten's fur.

The cacophony in Caitlin's mind quieted.

"But that wasn't all," Fana went on. "At the end of my dream . . . the priest woke."

"What does that mean?"

"I wasn't sure before, but now I think he may be like the Life Brothers. An immortal."

"Then why wouldn't your father know him? You said they're all from the same place."

"Maybe there are others."

There are others. How hadn't she realized it before? She must have given too much credence to her father's stories about Khaldun, the underground colony in Lalibela and the original fifty-nine Life Brothers. Others had never occurred to her. Dad would have mentioned the other immortals if he had known about them. So would Teka.

I have to warn them, she thought. But she didn't dare say it aloud.

Caitlin shook her head. "I think you're reaching. It's denial, Fana."

"Caitlin, my father thought he had to kill Father Arturo to protect you. He sensed danger from him. And maybe there was more he *didn't* see. Maybe the Railroad was infiltrated by other immortals who disapprove of Glow even more than my parents do." Her voice was hushed.

A sudden knock on the bathroom door made them both jump. Caitlin nearly dropped the bag she was holding. Three droplets of blood spilled to the bathroom's unfinished concrete floor.

"*Fuck,*" Caitlin said.

"Hello?" Charlie's voice said. He turned the knob, found it

locked. "Hey, I know girls like to go to the bathroom together, but this is *loca*. Can I get a turn? I'll pay five bucks."

Caitlin didn't answer. She dropped to her knees, directly above the spilled blood, as if it needed protection from the bathroom's flickering fluorescent light.

"Please use a bathroom upstairs," Fana said. "We're busy."

Even through a closed door, Fana visualized Charlie's flirtatious grin. "It's none of my business, but I think this other dude is jealous."

Fana heard Johnny clearly from across the room: "Man, why are you trying to start shit?"

"'Cause you make it so easy, that's why," Charlie said. "I'm just playin', *hombre*."

Fana heard herself giggle. Even with the gravity of her conversation with Caitlin, she wanted a release, no matter how small. Dad had once been as silly as Charlie around Mom. She had seen glimpses of it in his memories, and sometimes even in her mother's.

Caitlin shook her head slowly, still gazing at the blood on the floor. *I'VE DIED AND GONE TO HELL,* Caitlin thought with so much force that Fana couldn't help overhearing. *I'M SURROUNDED BY INFANTS.*

Stifling her giggles, Fana put her hand on Caitlin's shoulder and squeezed. Caitlin needed her touch. "Go away, Charlie," Fana said to the door. "Please?"

Charlie grumbled to himself in Spanish about flighty women, half joking. And left.

Caitlin still held the bag of blood, her eyes darting around the cramped bathroom. "I need something to pick it up. To salvage it. Hold this."

Caitlin thrust the bag into Fana's hands, careful not to interrupt the flow from the tube. She grabbed an empty plastic bag from the sink and knelt down, dabbing the blood. Her nose nearly touched the floor.

"Caitlin, we have a whole bag. And lots more where that came from, remember?"

Caitlin looked up at her, eyes disbelieving. "Do you have any idea how many people this could help?"

"But it's dirty. It's on the floor."

Caitlin blinked, and tears came. She looked down again, working carefully. "You don't get it, Fana," Caitlin said, voice unsteady. "You completely take it for granted."

"Why do you think I'm here? I left my whole family. You think I don't want to help people?" Fana was angry. If Caitlin didn't believe in her, Fana never should have left the colony. Aunt Alex had been hurt for nothing.

"That's not what I mean," Caitlin said softly. "To you, it's a few drops of blood. To us, this dirty blood is somebody's life."

Fana was tired of Caitlin's Us and Them mentality. Tired of being treated like a child. Caitlin shoved everyone into categories; that was why it was so easy for Caitlin to believe the worst about Dad and the Life Brothers. Mortal. Immortal. Good. Bad. Nothing in between. The more Fana thought about it, the more annoyed she felt. She was tempted to revisit Caitlin's mind and try to loosen up a few of those rigid places. But she wouldn't, of course. It was wrong to mess with people's heads. *Not like that stopped you a minute ago.*

Fana closed her eyes. Like Mom would say, she should try walking a mile in someone else's shoes. Didn't Caitlin have every right to be upset? Wasn't her father a captive?

Fana tried to make herself float the way she vaguely remembered from when she was very young. She could almost remember touching a cloud with her mind, coaxing rain. And if she could touch a cloud, how much farther could she travel? Teka had told her that Khaldun could send his thoughts across miles and see events across the ocean. Even the future! Teka thought she had that power, too. Only with stillness, he said, would she find it again.

Had she found it when she'd broken the camera at McDonald's?

Fana didn't think so. She'd only had a fearful impulse, just like when she was three, and what good was a gift she couldn't control?

As Fana felt her warm blood emptying into the bag in her palm, she tried to be still. To see Aunt Alex. Caitlin's father. Or Teka! Was Teka meditating now? Could they reach each other in the place where dreams meet?

YOUR GIFTS IN THEMSELVES ARE NOTHING TO FEAR.

Teka's voice came alive. Was he talking to her now, or was it only a memory?

ONLY IN STILLNESS CAN YOU BE CERTAIN THAT THE POWER YOU WIELD IS YOURS AND YOUR CREATOR'S ALONE. ONLY IN STILLNESS WILL YOUR PUREST GIFTS MANIFEST.

When Fana imagined the woods, the colony, she thought she felt Aunt Alex's sleeping mind, waiting to be released from its last moment of surprise and fear. And Justin O'Neal . . . changed somehow. But alive. The impressions were so faint that they might exist only in her imagination. Teka said she could regain her childhood gifts and more, but even now, when she needed her gifts the most, they were hidden from her. Fana breathed slowly, searching for stillness within the house's havoc and her own doubts.

Can you hear me, Teka? There are others like us, and they mean us harm. Warn your Brothers to protect the colony. Warn my mother and father.

Silence taunted Fana. A white shroud of nothingness.

Then a thought crashed into Fana with such power that her breath caught, trapped in her throat. Her eyes flew open from a ringing inside her ears that was so loud she expected Caitlin to look at her as if she'd heard it, too. But Caitlin was still kneeling, scouring the floor for blood.

The thought was like none Fana could remember, yet it felt like a current carrying her somewhere she had been once, long ago. It filled Fana with a terror she had no name for.

Four words, unmistakable, in an unhuman voice she did not know.

AND BLOOD TOUCHETH BLOOD.

"So, wait . . . ," Charlie said, exhaling sweetly scented clove cigarette smoke from the corner of his mouth. He lowered his chin and gazed at Fana with unblinking dark eyes, hugging a pool cue to his chest as he leaned against the patio wall. "Explain to me how someone survives seventeen years of life without ever playing pool."

"Where I live, it's quiet," Fana said. "No pool table."

"And where's that?"

An innocent question, but one Fana could never answer. Not for

anyone. Even someone with fascinating, tight locks of raven hair spilling across his brow, resting above two lush eyebrows and lashes almost
too long for a boy. Not even someone whose skin was dark bronze, or
who was wearing tattered jeans revealing a patch of his thigh, tight
enough to beg her eyes to examine the stitching more closely.

"A quiet place," Fana said with a coy smile. "There are a lot of
things I've never done." Her daring shocked her. Pleased her. She
had never witnessed this side of herself. Charlie brought out aspects
of her she could hardly believe.

Only two hours ago, she'd been in bed again, where she'd been
nearly all day trying to fight off the unsettled, claustrophobic feeling
that had haunted her in the bathroom. She'd talked herself out of
bed because she didn't want Charlie to think she was an invalid. If he
was really leaving in the morning, why waste the few hours they had
left? Already, it was almost dinnertime. The scent of Sheila Rolfson's
vegetarian gumbo on the stove seeped onto the patio through the
family room's open glass sliding door.

Across the patio, Johnny cleared his throat. He pretended to
be ignoring them, studying the plants, but his attention rarely left
them. Johnny was like her cousin Jared and Fasilidas in the woods.
A guardian. "Where she lives is quiet, all right," Johnny said with
exaggerated familiarity, striding toward them. "Beautiful, too, right,
Bea-Bea? Her parents are awesome."

Charlie smirked. "If it's so awesome, what's she doing here?"

Fana felt her face flush. A lifetime of being ignored by the opposite sex, and now she had two boys hovering over her! Three, if she
counted the shy approaches of Nate, who had never been more than
a few yards from her since she'd come upstairs from the basement.

Balls clicked on the pool table. Nate was bent over, already posed
for his next shot, one eye closed, the other staring down the brown
ball teetering at the edge of the corner pocket. Nate was a fast and sure
player. When he gave Fana a quick glance over his shoulder to make
sure she was watching, Fana realized he was showing off for her.

Nate and Charlie were both good players, so they each had long
turns. Charlie took advantage of his lulls to sidle beside Fana. Every
time Charlie came within a couple feet, as he was now, Fana felt the

strangest gentle burning sensation across whichever arm was closest to him. At first, she'd mistaken the feeling for another ailment after her sudden trip. But the condition only got worse each time he came near. And it wasn't unpleasant. Not at all.

So this is what it feels like when your skin wants to touch someone else's, she thought.

Charlie squashed out the last of his cigarette in the ashtray he'd made from a soda can. "Maybe I should ask the lady herself," Charlie said, his eyes back on Fana's. He shifted position suddenly, a hair closer, and her arm sizzled again. His faint accent was heavenly. "What would make you leave a quiet, beautiful place to live like this?"

"I believe in Glow," Fana said. "I believe in what it can do for humankind."

"And you're not afraid?"

"Of course I am," she said. "We all are—even you. But like you, I won't give in to fear."

Johnny was not only saddled with fear but he also felt deep shame because of it. Aunt Alex had been Fana's first mistake, and maybe Johnny had been her second. He would have gotten hurt at Berkeley—Fana had no doubt—but she wished they had thought of another way to help him. Johnny felt the most alone of any of them, without any tribe.

Nate took his shot, and the white ball went wild, jumping to the floor. He turned to walk up to her so fast that Fana wondered if he had missed the shot on purpose.

"I've got a story," Nate said. It was the first sentence he'd spoken to her all day. Nate waited for Charlie to leave her side, then he leaned against the wall in Charlie's place before going on. The sizzling feeling died.

Nate went on. "When we lived in New York, there was this kid at my dad's school whose car crashed. The valedictorian, right? He'd been in a bunch of my dad's classes, really smart. It was this huge tragedy, because he was in a coma and wouldn't wake up. My dad was really down about it. So one day he talks to Caitlin . . ."

Nate suddenly had Johnny's attention, too. Nate only had to utter Caitlin's name.

"Caitlin went to the hospital with my dad to see this kid. They waited until they were alone, and"—he mimicked the motion of pressing the plunger of a hypodermic needle—"bam. He's awake. Now that kid's at West Point. That's my Glow story."

"I have a story just like that," Fana said quietly, smiling at him. "My cousin."

Jared had been in a coma when Mom had gone to him in Florida and brought him blood. Fana could almost remember talking to Jared even before she'd met him, in his sleep. They had been destined to become family; they had known each other before they'd met.

Like her and Charlie, maybe.

"AIDS is the big one for me," Charlie said, studying the landscape of the pool table. He settled on the green ball Nate hadn't sunk, readying his cue. He turned the cue over in his hands, fondling it like a friend. Fana noticed how wide his palms were, how long and slender his fingers. "It blasts the shit out of AIDS. That's why we call it Blast, and that's why the government wants to ban it. So we'll stay sick. So we'll stay poor while the rich party on."

Charlie didn't say it, but Fana suddenly realized that Chalie had been diagnosed with HIV when he was fourteen. He had tried shooting heroin only once and had been infected by a friend's needle, contracting the resistant strain pills didn't help. Last year, he'd met Ethan at his high school, and Ethan had told him about Glow. Ethan had saved his life, and now Ethan was dead, murdered.

Fana knew without trying; the story was practically on Charlie's lips.

"What about sickle-cell?" Johnny said.

Fana nodded. "Thousands of people have been cured of sickle-cell in Africa. AIDS, too. It works best on blood diseases." She almost blurted out *Because it's blood,* but she stopped in time.

"I have a friend with sickle-cell," Johnny said. "I want to get him Glow."

Fana smiled. "He'll have it. We just need a little time, Johnny. I promise."

No need to touch Johnny, or give his mind a massage; her words alone made his face lose a layer of anxiety, replaced by something like rapture. He believed her. *Omari.* That was his friend's name. Just like that, Johnny found his peace. To him, whatever he was going through was worth it if he could help Omari.

"Yeah, Glow's worth fighting for," Charlie said. He took his shot, and the green ball dropped as smoothly as if he'd blown it in with his breath. "But there's still The Big Question . . ."

"What's The Big Question?" Johnny said.

Charlie turned to scowl at him. "What do you think?"

"Where does it come from?" Johnny guessed.

"*Exactamente,*" Charlie said. "I have a theory. Ready to hear it?"

Fana nearly squirmed. Her ears burned, and not in the pleasant way.

"Scientist revolutionaries," Charlie said. "They probably work for the U.S. government, which had the cures all along. So now these guys are giving it away to the masses. As my man Che Guevara would say, *Viva la revolución.*"

He sounded like Caitlin, except that Caitlin knew the truth.

"Yeah, that's what my dad would say," Nate said. "But check it: What if it's like a care package from an alien civilization? They're sharing their advancements with us, but they don't want us to know they're here."

"Why not?" Charlie said, giving Fana a private glance. Humoring Nate.

"Simple," Nate said. "If we knew, we'd destroy them."

"But you said they're helping us," Charlie said.

"Haven't you ever seen any sci fi movies?" Nate said. "*The Day the Earth Stood Still*? Come on. Welcome to Earth—POW. The aliens always bite it, whether they're helping us or not."

Fana felt herself trying to sink into the patio's tiled floor. She was desperate to change the subject but didn't dare. Her voice might give away how close to home their musings had drifted.

Charlie laughed. "I've seen some movies where the aliens did all right," he said. With hardly a thought, he sank a red ball with an elegant shot. He nodded toward Johnny. "How 'bout you, college boy? Where does Glow come from?"

Johnny was controlling his nerves by tying and retying his sneaker, one foot propped on a patio chair. "There's a long answer and a short answer," he said. "The long answer explains the how.

Who's making it? When did it start? What are its components? We'll find out one day, but no one knows yet. Not for sure. But I know the short answer."

"What's the short answer?" Nate said.

"Simple," John said and glanced skyward. "From God."

Fana's arms quivered again, but in a different way entirely. No one argued or joked. Even Charlie reached over to pound Johnny's fist, making Johnny grin for the first time all day.

By the time Caitlin came and told them dinner was ready, something had changed. The worries in the house had gone nearly silent. Charlie and Johnny rushed toward the dinner table, talking like old friends as Charlie explained how powerful Johnny would feel the first time he realized he had cured his friend's disease.

Nate lingered last, beside Fana. He gently took her arm. When she looked at him, his eyes widened slightly. Nate seemed to have forgotten what he was going to say.

"I . . . like your dreads." His words were nearly garbled beneath heavy breaths.

Fana smiled. "Thanks. I've had dreadlocks almost my whole life."

"Sorry if this is bad to ask, but . . . can I touch one?"

"Sure," Fana said, not hesitating. When she was growing up in Botswana, she remembered being baffled by the sight of a white boy with freckles at an airport. Maybe Nate had never known anyone with dreadlocks.

With care, Nate rubbed the end of one of Fana's dreadlocks between his fingertips, gently tracing the patterns woven in her hair. With his pug nose and clear braces, Nate reminded her of the curious child she had been.

"Thanks for putting up with that," Nate said, resting Fana's hair across her shoulder with both hands, as if it were a sleeping snake. "My mom said I might offend you if I asked."

"A lot of people would be offended, maybe. But it takes more than that to offend me."

Nate's ears blushed red. "You're pretty, Bea-Bea," he said, his eyes darting away. Before Fana was sure she had heard him right, Nate Rolfson slipped into the house.

Inside, the others were taking their places at the table with a hum of familial chatter that made Fana think of home. Her eyes stung as she looked for her seat at a new table. Fana didn't have to wonder where to sit: The empty chair between Charlie and Caitlin beckoned.

Charlie leaned over to whisper in her ear. "Can I touch your hair too, *negra*?"

Her parents had taught Fana enough regional Spanish to know that *negra* was a term of affection in the Caribbean that had nothing to do with skin color. But Charlie's tone seemed to give it a layered meaning, embracing all of her in a single word.

Fana's fledgling tears vanished. She usually couldn't stand the smell of cigarettes, but Charlie's breath perfumed the cloves. Pursing her lips to keep from smiling, Fana gave Charlie a scolding pat on the knee.

Quick as lightning, Charlie's palm trapped hers and held it there. Was his skin electrified? Fana felt lava flowing from his large palm. Moisture drenched her hand. As her heart inflated with warm air, Fana did not pull away. She gazed at their hands; her darker one, and the subtle contrast of bronzed skin and fine dark hairs atop hers. A man's hand.

Maybe Charlie would kiss her tonight. Her first kiss! Would he have the chance?

Sheila Rolfson beamed at everyone at the table. "Well," their hostess said, sounding breathless. She met Fana's eyes, knowing. "Can we all hold hands?"

Charlie locked the web of his fingers against Fana's, more electricity. Fana glanced toward Caitlin on the other side of her and squeezed her hand with meaning: *Your father is fine.*

Caitlin nodded, knowing Fana's message even if she couldn't hear it. Caitlin laid her head on Fana's shoulder; part resting place, part apology. Then Caitlin reached for Johnny's hand on her other side and gave his wrist a tiny kiss. Johnny looked taken aback. Then he smiled, too.

Was the good feeling Charlie had given Fana contagious?

"I'll try not to be long-winded, but I'm a minister," Sheila Rolfson said, and everyone laughed. "This is a special night. I think we can all feel it."

Everyone at the table nodded, agreeing.

Sheila went on. "There's a lot of bad stuff going on in the world right now—some of it not so far away—so I'm just glad my family is safe. And we've made new friends in a time of pain. Dr. King said, 'I believe that unarmed truth and unconditional love will have the final word in reality. That is why right, temporarily defeated, is stronger than evil triumphant.' With that, I'm done. You want a sermon, come to First Unitarian at eleven on Sunday."

Nate pretended to choke. "Oh my God. Less than a minute. A record, Mom!"

Mitchell Rolfson nodded, ignoring Nate. "Ditto what she said. I've known Cat forever, but we just met Charlie, Johnny and Bea-Bea. You kids . . ." He stopped suddenly, and a tear slipped from one eye. He rubbed it away with a brush of his shoulder. "I taught high school for fifteen years. You remind me of the kids in Birmingham. And Soweto. And last year in Beijing. History wouldn't be the same without you. It's a privilege to know you all."

"Even me?" Nate said.

"You most of all, kid," Mitchell said and leaned over to kiss the top of his son's head. "Although I didn't recognize you without your GamePort. Your turn."

Nate grinned. "Well, first of all, I'm thankful I'm holding my dad's hand right now, so I won't get in trouble for giving him the finger." Laughter. "And I'm glad my parents give a damn about the rest of the world and not just themselves like my friends' yuppie loser parents."

Sheila and Mitchell Rolfson shared a painful glance. Fana suddenly knew what they had been discussing with Caitlin in the kitchen: They were closing their doors to the Underground Railroad. Between Maritza's death and Justin O'Neal's capture, they thought it was too dangerous for Nate. They hadn't told Nate yet, and they weren't looking forward to it. Fana cast her eyes down at the table, embarrassed to have learned so much about people she hardly knew. She would have to learn how to filter better!

Charlie lifted his wine glass skyward. "*Muchas gracias, Dios, por el Glow,*" he said quietly. "Thank you for helping me make sure Ethan

didn't die in vain. Thank you for returning what was stolen from us."
Charlie's easy eloquence brought a tear to Fana's eye.

The rest took their turns: Johnny was thankful he would be able
to help his Little Brother get rid of his pain. Caitlin was thankful
because she believed her father was all right. "Don't ask me how I
know," Caitlin said, gazing at Fana. "Just faith, I guess."

"What about you, Bea-Bea?" Sheila Rolfson said. "What are you
thankful for?"

"For meals prepared with love and a place to sleep," Fana said.
"You've given us the world in one day and a night, and I'll never
forget you."

Mitchell and Sheila Rolfson nodded. Their decision to quit had
been hard.

"Damn right," Charlie said, clinging to Fana more tightly. "Let's eat."

The homemade French bread was so soft that it nearly fell apart
in Fana's hands. The gumbo teemed with okra, bell peppers and
mushrooms, and no one complained about the missing meat. Sheila
Rolfson served white wine with the meal; even Nate was allowed
to have a few sips. While they ate, Mitchell Rolfson showed off his
sound system with old-school music that veered between Aero-
smith, Led Zeppelin, Prince and Funkadelic.

After dinner, Charlie tugged on Fana's hand and invited her to
dance on the family room floor, as if he knew how much she loved
"1999." Grudgingly, Caitlin allowed Johnny to pull her out of her
seat for a dance, too. When Mitchell and Sheila Rolfson joined them,
they forced Nate to get up with them so he wouldn't be left alone at
the table. Prince's irresistible beat called to Fana, shutting off her
mind while she watched Charlie. He was a fluid, practiced dancer,
hips, waist and shoulders all alive at once. Fana could have watched
him dance all night.

The Temptations' "Just My Imagination" came on, a slow song,
and Caitlin peeled away from Johnny as fast as she could, making
up an excuse.

Charlie tried to hold Fana's hands and bring her closer, but she
pulled away, too. Fana could feel Nate's eyes on the back of her neck,
and she couldn't torment him by slow-dancing with Charlie before

his eyes, no matter how much she wanted to. Even if this was their one and only chance before Charlie was gone.

Instead, she let Charlie carve her a piece of pound cake, and they watched Mitchell and Sheila sway to the ballad, both of them mouthing the lyrics as Sheila gazed up high into her husband's eyes. Fana had never seen her parents dance that way. Not once.

"Sorry you have to witness this," Nate said. "They get ridiculous sometimes."

"It's not ridiculous," Fana said. "It's beautiful."

Since the next day promised to be trying, the evening lingered; no one was ready to end a pleasant night. But Fana couldn't forget her worries about Aunt Alex or the missing priest.

She noticed Nate's GamePort goggles on the coffee table. Fana knew more about GamePorts than she wanted to. All players had user names, and they could communicate with any other players in the GamePort network to invite each other into games. Hank Duhart had a GamePort back at home, so Fana could ask Nate to send a message to HANKTHEKING. If Hank was playing—and Hank was *always* playing—he would see it right away. She wanted to do it so badly that she nearly reached for the goggles half a dozen times.

But she didn't. It might bring trouble to Nate. It might bring trouble to the colony. She didn't know who was monitoring the networks. She couldn't take the chance.

"*Pssssst,*" a husky voice said.

Charlie was beckoning from just beyond the open patio door.

Fana glanced around the room: No one was looking her way. Fana slipped outside, and Charlie silently rolled the glass door closed behind her. Outside, she heard only crickets and lizards' throaty mating songs, with no light other than the full moon. At last, stillness.

Charlie sat down beyond the far end of the pool table, and Fana sat beside him. Close. The patio's tiles were still warm from the sun, although the sky was dark.

Even if someone glanced outside, they would have had to open the door to see them. Charlie gently slipped his palm into hers, playing with her fingers one by one. Her fingers seemed to expand beneath his touch, her nerves thrilling.

"I understand," he said.

"What?"

"Why you didn't want to dance close to me. Because of Johnny?"

Fana shook her head, smiling. "No. Nate, actually."

Charlie chuckled, leaning his head back against the table. She watched his Adams' apple dance in his throat. "That's *so* sweet."

"Don't make fun of me."

"No, really. That's what I like about you. Never a bad word about anybody. Eyes always watching to see how people are feeling. Like . . . a hall monitor at school."

Playfully, Fana tried to pull her hand away. "It would have made him feel bad."

That was when it happened: Charlie's lips were on hers, impossibly soft flesh barely touching her mouth. His sweet breath washed through her. He sank against her with moisture and resolve, and Fana's mouth responded as if she had been craving him for years, yielding wide. The tip of his tongue darted against hers, and Fana felt something pop open at the pit of her stomach, flooding her abdomen until it shook. His tongue tasted a bit like tobacco, but mostly like juice from raw sugar cane. She saw cane fields and modest cement block homes with windows open wide to let out the music, and lush, gorgeous countryside. *Boricua.*

His kiss showed her his home.

Both of them forgot to breathe, absorbed in kissing. Charlie's hand rested across her ribs, a few conspicuous inches beneath her left breast. He did not move to touch her further, and Fana wasn't sure what she would do if he did. Her heart churned with possibilities that had never occurred to her before tonight. But she was glad he didn't pressure her.

Charlie pulled away, studying her face in the moonlight. He captured one of her dreadlocks and wound it slowly around two fingers, until his wrist lay against the side of her face.

How could she feel so sad saying good-bye to someone she had just met?

"Come to Vancouver sometime," Charlie said. "Caitlin knows how to find me."

Fana nodded. *Hell, yes,* she would go to Canada. Maybe tomorrow, if he asked her to.

"There's bad things happening," Charlie said. "You stay safe, Bea-Bea."

"You too," she said. "Motorcycles are dangerous."

Charlie smiled, and his teeth looked brilliant in the night. "If I crash, I'll have Glow. Nothing can hurt me." And he kissed her again.

To Fana, his kiss never ended.

That night, as she lay on a thin mattress beside Caitlin's cot in the basement and tried to sleep, Fana used her gifts to replay her kisses with Charlie in her imagination. Felt his lips on hers. Tasted the ridges of his sweet tongue. The knowledge that Charlie was just on the other side of the wall made it impossible to close her eyes. Was he thinking about her, too? She wanted to visit his mind, but she wouldn't allow herself to.

When the tingling between her thighs became unbearable, Fana rested her fingers atop the warmth there with just enough pressure to quiet the clamor. A gentle pulsing answered her.

Then Fana gave herself over to sleep.

The smile on her lips wilted, until she was grimacing instead. She twitched in her sleep. Howling, churning winds clogged her ears.

That night, Fana dreamed of a hurricane.

Fifteen

What's a . . . patty melt?" Teferi said, staring at his menu.

Dawit sighed. He would starve waiting for Teferi to choose a meal! Teferi had insisted on stopping when he'd seen the diner on the 60. *Hunger impedes my abilities, Dawit.* At every turn, a new excuse: Hunger. Ill temper. The time of day.

They must have lost the girls' trail by now, if indeed Teferi had ever found it. Teferi was slow to admit failure, but he would have no choice by morning. They should have followed Berhanu to Los Angeles. The theory that Teferi's tracking might be improved because of his blood ties to Caitlin seemed preposterous now. Those genetic ties went back more than two hundred years, altered many times over. Berhanu was much more likely to find the girls.

And Berhanu would never stop his search for a leisurely meal at a diner. The diner was boxy, like a train car, the walls crammed with bric-a-brac that looked like trash.

"There's hardly a hair's difference between these dishes," Dawit said. "Meat. Bread. Cheese. Grease. Close your eyes and point."

"You make poor company, I hope you've been told." Teferi closed his menu. "A patty melt it is, then. Your thought projection is improving, so our time together may not be as wasted as you fear."

Dawit sipped from his glass of nearly melted ice cubes and water that tasted like silt. "After we eat, we turn back," he said.

"No." Teferi's face tightened. "Not yet. I had them before. But they may be asleep."

"Why should that matter?"

"I don't know, but perhaps it does." *FANA MAY BE MASKING THEM IN SLEEP. TEKA SAID IT MAY COME NATURALLY TO HER.* Teferi explained the rest in silence.

Another of Teferi's excuses; each was more novel than the last. Dawit raised his hand to get the attention of the female server behind the counter, the evening's sole employee except for the man tending the grill. The woman wore a ponytail too young for her sun-beaten face, her hair swinging from side to side as she pivoted between passing notes to the cook and ringing up the cash register. She tried to keep pace with the steady flow of customers jangling through the cheerful glass door despite the late hour.

What would he give for his daughter to walk through the door next?

"And if you're wrong," Dawit said, "someone else might find them first."

"You might imagine, then, that finding them is more important to me," Teferi said.

OUR BROTHERS WOULD NEVER HARM FANA. BUT CAITLIN?

Teferi's projection was clear and elegant. Dawit could not yet lapse in and out of thought language without great effort, so he only lowered his voice. "I'm sorry I treated Caitlin as I did," he sighed. "There is no plan to harm her. How often must I say it?"

"Ah, yes," Teferi said. "And plans never veer astray."

A voice spoke from above their table: "One has veered astray this very moment."

Arabic. A voice Dawit knew like his own.

Dawit's finger tightened around the trigger of the weapon hidden in his lap, and he instinctively curled his wrist beneath the table, aiming at groin's height left of him. Teferi made a similar motion, his eyes iron. They snapped to look at the man standing over them.

Dawit saw the bump of a nozzle beneath Mahmoud's white sheepskin and denim jacket, It was aimed at his head. Their Brother wore a beard and a white skullcap, like home.

"Yes," Mahmoud said softly. "All three Brothers have weapons, it seems."

How could Mahmoud have surprised them without Teferi feeling his presence? Had Mahmoud learned to mask himself too?

Dawit had left Mahmoud in Lalibela fourteen years ago, when Mahmoud had tried to bar his family's escape from the Ethiopian colony after Khaldun had disappeared into his meditations. When Khaldun had relinquished control of the Brotherhood, Dawit had been left to fend for himself. The entire Brotherhood had been enraged at Dawit for breaking their Covenant and siring a child Mahmoud called a mutant: born with the Living Blood. Fana had driven Mahmoud away with the miraculous mind arts she'd had as a child, besetting him with a swarm of bees. Fana had been better able to defend herself then. Now she was more a child, virtually helpless.

"Where is she?" Dawit said, rage shaking his jaw. He returned Mahmoud's Arabic, since their conversation was unfit for the ears of strangers. Mahmoud had cost him one daughter, in Miami. "If you have touched—"

"I will kill you in pieces and see you buried forever," Teferi finished, also in Arabic.

"*Salam*, Teferi," Mahmoud said, not hiding his amusement. Peace. "You've grown brittle since last I saw you. Be careful you don't shoot yourself in the balls, Brother."

"There's only one pair of balls in his sights . . . *Brother*," Dawit said. "Where are they?"

"How crass you've become here," Mahmoud said. "No invitation to join you?"

Suddenly, the long-absent waitress swooped to their table, stabbing Mahmoud with an openly wary look. She held her Bic pen toward him the way she might a weapon. "Excuse me, gentlemen," she said to Dawit. "Is this man bothering you?"

Her lips curled over the words "*this man*." Between Mahmoud's olive skin, dark beard and white skullcap, he must have looked like a Wanted poster in her terrorist-addled eyes. The woman's western twang reminded Dawit of different times. This nation's fear of the Arab had replaced fear of American blacks indeed.

Dawit grinned at her. "This man is my best and oldest friend." He wished it had been a lie.

The waitress didn't seem comforted, but she was happy to let it rest, her duty done. "Y'all ready to order?"

"One patty melt, one grilled cheese," Dawit said quickly. "And . . . American apple pie for my dear friend here. Not too hot. I'd hate to see him get hurt."

Mahmoud's eyes churned. He might kill the woman for her impudence, or to spite Dawit. Not to mention at least fifteen other diners. Dawit could not sanction endangering so many.

"Please," Dawit said to Mahmoud with a dolphin's friendly smile. "Sit with us."

YOU ARE MAD! Teferi said, squirming.

Dawit softly nudged Teferi under the table. *Be still,* he tried to say.

Mahmoud glared down at Teferi, waiting for him to make room in the narrow booth across from Dawit. Teferi finally slid aside, lips pursed, sitting far against the diner wall, where rows of absurd, elaborately carved cuckoo clocks hung above his head.

Mahmoud had been Dawit's brother long before they had imagined a future spanning centuries. Dawit had known Mahmoud before he'd met Khaldun, when they'd been traders between Abyssinia and India. Dawit had married Mahmoud's sister, Rana, only to watch both his new wife and his first son die during the rigors of childbirth. When he and Mahmoud had met in the 1500s, a man had lived a long life if he'd survived to thirty-five. For a soldier, life was often snuffed out by eighteen. At thirty, he and Mahmoud had been old men when they'd accepted the Living Blood.

"I feel unwelcome still," Mahmoud told Dawit. "Tell Teferi to drop his gun to the floor."

"You'll not take mine," Dawit vowed.

"I didn't ask for yours," Mahmoud said. "But Teferi might maim me with a sneeze."

Teferi didn't move.

Drop your gun, Teferi, Dawit strained to tell him. *Don't make him wait.*

Teferi made a soft growling noise at the base of his throat. Then his gun fell to the floor with a *ping* against the iron table leg. His breathing sped out of frustration and anger.

CAITLIN IS SURELY DEAD. AND WHAT OF FANA? came Teferi's anguished thought.

Be calm, Dawit answered. *I know Mahmoud's ways. I will finish this.*

Mahmoud leaned forward until his face was only inches from Dawit's. He smelled of home, too; incense of myrrh, frankincense and a blend of other oils from the Lalibela Colony. "I'm lazy in my mind arts, Dawit, but I'm not deaf," Mahmoud said. "I've been practicing, too. If you know me, you know not to antagonize me."

Dawit did not know Mahmoud. His very presence meant Dawit had misjudged him. After the negotiations with the Lalibela Council, Dawit had thought he and his Brothers had reached an accord. He and Mahmoud were not friends, certainly. No more. But not this.

There would be bloodshed, Dawit realized. There was no avoiding it.

But he must try. "She's the kindest child you will ever meet, Mahmoud," Dawit said.

"She did not seem so kind to Kaleb as he died in a pool of his own blood."

Such amnesia! Dawit might have laughed, except that laughing would inflame Mahmoud. "Kaleb burned me alive and tried to kill Fana and her mother," he said. "Would you have her sacrifice herself on Kaleb's wishes?"

"Nor, I imagine, did she seem kind to six hundred souls in the Caribbean on the night of a certain storm," Mahmoud said. "Did you think Khaldun said nothing of it?"

Dawit had never understood how Teka could believe that Fana had somehow been responsible for Hurricane Beatrice, the deadly storm that had killed so many in the West Indies. How could a *child* summon a hurricane? But if Khaldun himself had said so, he had to reconsider. Jessica had always insisted that Fana had made it rain a week before the hurricane, in the midst of Botswana's dry season. Perhaps nothing to do with Fana was impossible, and everyone knew it except him.

To him, Fana was still the girl who had sat on his knee for hours at a time, smiling at him.

Angry talk about Fana had subsided in Lalibela, according to Kelile, who had moved to the Washington colony within the past year. Kelile reported that there had been long debates about Fana in the chaos after Khaldun's departure, but most of the Life Brothers were scattering and mating with mortals themselves. As if waking from a long nap.

But Mahmoud had tried to kill Fana twice before—once when she'd still been in Jessica's womb, and once when she was three. If Mahmoud had been as zealous this time as he had been the last time Dawit had seen him, God only knew what horrors might have befallen Fana.

"What have you done to her, Mahmoud?" Dawit whispered.

"You think too highly of me, Dawit," Mahmoud said. "I've abandoned most of my principles, and the rest are a nuisance. I would prefer to be attending my own affairs rather than counseling a Brother who has grown bafflingly incapable of protecting his own. What happened to the practical friend I knew?"

"He has a gun trained to your belly," Dawit said. "Where is Fana? I won't ask again."

"Ask Sanctus Cruor," Mahmoud said.

Teferi's breath caught—a gasp—or Dawit would have thought he'd heard Mahmoud wrong.

"We killed them in Adwa," Dawit said. "And in Rome. To their last man."

Mahmoud raised an eyebrow. "Did we?"

The waitress returned. A plate of apple pie landed before Mahmoud. None of them moved as she delivered their food. No one answered when she asked if she could get them anything else. All Dawit could manage was a small shake of his head. He had never expected to hear the words *Sanctus Cruor* bound to Fana's name.

But in Seattle, he had seen the raised image on the medallion! A cross with a large teardrop of blood at its center. He *had* seen it in the priest's mind, not just in his own memories.

During his last call home, Teka and Jessica had told him about the vanished corpse in Seattle. If Mahmoud was telling the truth, Fana was in greater peril than he had known. And with so many

Brothers away searching for Fana, the colony was exposed. Jessica and the others needed to move to the shelters or leave the colony altogether. Not tomorrow. Tonight.

AND I MOCKED YOU, Teferi's thought came, sorrowful.

"Apparently, they have found the Blood they seek," Mahmoud said. "Some of them wake as we do. Look at that priest! We do not know how they obtained Blood and learned the Ceremony, and we do not know how many of their sect remain. Are they a few, or are they an army? Do they still hold sway with the Vatican? We are, you see, quite ignorant, or have been made to be. But Sanctus Cruor still lives. It never died."

The priests who had created Sanctus Cruor believed themselves to be the only true guardians of Christ's blood, and no act was too heinous in their mission to collect what remained of their Savior on Earth. They burned villages alive in search of immortals who might wake, to have the Blood. Their influence among Vatican officials had steered Italy toward war with Ethiopia, their search carried out in the guise of conquest.

The decisive victory in Adwa and the expulsion of the Italians had been the first time an African nation had repelled a European army, a feat unto itself. But that had not been the end.

After the war had been won on Ethiopian soil, Dawit, Mahmoud and Berhanu had traveled abroad: Istanbul. Gdansk. And Rome, of course. Dawit had been assigned to slay a Vatican official the Searchers had identified as a Sanctus Cruor collaborator hoping for power and immortality. Two others had died in Rome that day, at Mahmoud's hand.

Sanctus Cruor was supposed to have been finished. *To a man,* Khaldun had said when he'd finally emerged from his meditations two years later.

Now Dawit understood the torture. The murders. It was Sanctus Cruor's way.

"How did you learn this?" Dawit said.

"A Brother sent them to you, Dawit," Mahmoud said. "He never agreed with the Lalibela Council's vote to allow you to distribute the Blood. The priest who died in Seattle is surely Sanctus Cruor. I wager your little colony is not far from where he was found."

"Who would betray his own?" Dawit said. "Who would be coward enough to sell us to our enemy rather than take us himself?"

Mahmoud hesitated, his face pained. He was silent.

Dawit's throat locked. Jessica already believed Mahmoud was a monster because of the horrors he had committed against their children and her sister, but those actions had been in service to the Covenant, not out of malice or cruelty. Dawit would not know what to think if Mahmoud had sent Sanctus Cruor to him.

Dawit's hand holding his gun went rigid. "If it is you, Brother, our talking ends now."

Mahmoud shook his head. "*Salam*, Dawit. Not me. Negash."

Grief overwhelmed anger, but it was tinged with relief. Dawit believed Mahmoud; he thought he could feel the truth of his words in the gentle murmuring of his thoughts, not unsettled with lies. Negash! He had been one of Khaldun's most diligent pupils in meditation. What had Sanctus Curor offered Negash?

"Did you think there would be no consequences, Dawit?" Mahmoud said, almost gently.

"Of course I knew," Dawit said. He stared at his plate of cooling food.

"Then you shouldn't look so surprised, Brother. And I come bearing congratulations: According to Negash, your daughter is to be married."

Dawit's heart froze. "What do you mean?"

"Don't toy with him about Fana," Teferi said. "Have decency, Mahmoud."

Mahmoud shrugged, discovering the dessert before him. He plunged his finger into the heart of the pie and tasted. "Scalding," he said. "And you gave specific instructions."

Dawit jabbed Mahmoud with his foot. "Tell me about Fana."

Even if Mahmoud had come as a counselor, a kick was a taunt to him. "Tread gently, Dawit," Mahmoud said.

Dawit didn't blink. "My patience has been epic. I must be kindred to Christ after all."

If they must shed each other's blood tonight, so be it.

AND WHO ELSE IN THIS PLACE WILL SUFFER FOR YOUR

MUTUAL VANITY? Teferi's voice said. *I PREFER NOT TO SPEND THE NIGHT IN JAIL OR A MORGUE. IF MAHMOUD COMES AS A FRIEND, GIVE HIM A BERTH TO PROVE HIS FRIENDSHIP.*

Mahmoud half-smiled. "I was too slow to catch some of that, Teferi, but the gist tells me you're a wiser man than when I knew you."

"We have all changed," Teferi said. "New times compelled it."

Dawit softened his voice. "Tell me about Fana, Mahmoud."

"Sanctus Cruor is on a holy mission to find her," Mahmoud said, avoiding his eyes. "Teka and the Brothers who followed you here aren't the only ones who consider the girl divine. But Khaldun misled us."

"Misled us how?" Dawit said.

"Fana was not the only one born with the Blood," Mahmoud said. "There is another."

"How?" Teferi said, sagging in the booth. His face was mystified. Crestfallen.

"Sanctus Cruor," Mahmoud said. "They manipulated their Blood in ways Khaldun would not have sanctioned. A child was created—the child of a woman they passed the Blood to while pregnant. She gave birth to a boy who came into the world much as your child did."

Dawit never would have passed Jessica his blood if he had known she was pregnant, for fear of the Ceremony's unknown effects on a fetus. Fetuses did not share blood with their mothers, so when Jessica's heart had stopped during the Ceremony, a fetus might simply have died in the womb even after he'd injected Jessica with blood. Instead, Fana's tiny unborn body had been rejuvenated as a part of her mother, her dead limbs brought back to life before she was born.

Mahmoud went on. "Sanctus Cruor considers Fana to be his rightful mate, according to writings they adhere to, something about 'mates immortal born.' It has the ring of Greek myth: Hera and Zeus, or the Yorubas' Obatala and Odudua. I'm no student of Christianity, but their text is some sort of Apocrypha. It is not from any of the eighty-one books in the Ethiopian Orthodox canon, and it certainly was never approved at Nicea. I have never seen it, but Negash believes the Sanctus Cruor document. Negash sends his apologies for any pain he has brought to you. He is a true believer, I think."

An apology did nothing for Dawit now, but he was glad his Brother retained that much honor, at least. "We were all true believers once," Dawit said. "We believed in Khaldun."

"Yes, some of us more than others," Mahmoud said. He pushed the apple pie away from him, toward Dawit. "You see what came of that."

No one must know. No one must join. No women in the colony. No race of immortals to multiply ungoverned, ruling over mankind. Khaldun's wisdom was clearer each day.

"When was the other child supposedly born?" Teferi said.

"Fifty years ago," Mahmoud said. "In Italy. Perhaps Khaldun knew, perhaps he did not. In any case, your idolization of Fana would seem misplaced, Teferi. The boy came first."

"Born into monstrosity," Teferi scoffed.

Mahmoud glanced at Dawit over his paper napkin. "And what does that make Fana?"

Dawit blinked. "My child. My only one."

Teferi's thoughts crashed through Dawit: *POLICE ARE COMING. THREE.*

Teferi's eyes motioned left, and Dawit turned around to gaze through the picture window. He saw a parking lot lighted only by the diner windows. Two sheriff's cruisers had pulled up in the darkness. A trucker spoke to three deputies animatedly, gesturing inside. The deputies wore cowboy hats, a scene out of a movie western.

Almost simultaneously, the trucker and three police officers met Dawit's eyes through the glass. The deputies were young, no doubt overzealous and easily frightened. The worst luck.

Mahmoud followed Dawit's eyes. "A nest of pests," he muttered.

Dawit slid his gun back inside his jeans. "We must leave."

TOO LATE, Teferi said. *LET ME WORK ON THEM, I BEG YOU.*

The door jangled, and the three deputies were inside in a carefully spaced procession, only yards from the table. Trying to flee would be futile. Two of them, the ones hanging back a few steps, already had their hands floating comfortably close to their weapons, holsters unlatched. Dawit kept his hand on the butt of his gun. If they couldn't flee, he should draw. Mahmoud would follow his lead, and their problem would be solved.

"Work on them how?" Dawit asked Teferi aloud, in Arabic. "To influence them?"

Teferi nodded, looking uncertain, and Dawit's spirits fell. Was faith in Teferi their only hope of avoiding arrest, or worse?

EASE YOUR FACE. SMILE. I'LL WORK ON THEM. KEEP MAHMOUD CALM. Teferi's smile was congenial, but not enough to compensate for Mahmoud's hostile scowl.

With his best grin, Dawit released his gun. He slowly moved both of his hands to the tabletop and folded them in a docile pose.

Mahmoud's eyes mooned as if he thought Dawit mad. Then, slowly, Mahmoud's hand retreated from his pocket and drummed on the tabletop. Mahmoud smirked.

"Help you, Officers?" Dawit said in his easygoing American accent, second nature by now.

EASY WORK

Mahmoud's projection was clumsy and full of noise, but Dawit heard his meaning.

We will try another way, Dawit tried to tell him with his eyes.

Dawit held his smile steady for the deputy standing over their table, whose tag identified him as Sgt. Hayes. His face was Nordic and square-jawed. He was only about twenty-six, but he was the eldest of the three and carried himself with confidence and experience. This one had seen combat, Dawit realized. A military reservist. He wore a wedding ring.

It would be a shame if he died over nothing.

"Everything all right at this table?" Sgt. Hayes said. He scanned each of their eyes, but his gaze fell on Mahmoud. To Sgt. Hayes, Mahmoud looked like a bad memory from Baghdad.

Mahmoud returned his gaze, not blinking.

"Can I see your identification?" Sgt. Hayes said. He spoke to Mahmoud and no one else.

Dawit's heart caught. If Mahmoud reached into his jacket, he would bring out his gun.

"I don't understand," Dawit said, his tone steady. "We're just sitting here talking, Officer. Is this some kind of profiling?" The word made Sgt. Hayes's lips twitch.

Sgt. Hayes and Mahmoud grappled with their eyes. Sgt. Hayes's fingers fanned out across his hip, looking for his holster. Was Teferi's mental work entirely useless?

Remembering his white-haired disguise, Dawit engaged the deputy as an elder. "Son, excuse my friend," Dawit went on, his tone almost jovial. "You think he's looking at you in a disrespectful way, and I understand that. He has an attitude. He's a first-class asshole, in fact. He was my student at Yale, and he was an asshole then, too."

The deputy didn't smile. But he also didn't interrupt.

Dawit went on: "He just flew in from LaGuardia today, and he said airport security's gotten so bad that he got scanned three times, pulled out of line twice. He's exhausted and he's hungry, and he feels discriminated against every day. So when you officers come in here like this and head straight for this table, it makes him very upset."

Dawit didn't expect his babbling to turn the deputies away, but at least he might gain enough time for Teferi's mental manipulations to find some footing.

Sgt. Hayes looked at Mahmoud, considering him. "Yale, huh?"

"A long time ago," Mahmoud said, his face softening into a smile that was hardly better than his scowl. "All of my professors were exemplary, except one. That one was a fool."

"May I reach for my wallet?" Dawit asked Sgt. Hayes, hands held up in clear sight.

Slowly, Sgt. Hayes nodded. The deputy's reflexes seemed to have slowed, unless it was Dawit's wishful thinking. Was the deputy allowing himself to be led?

Dawit leaned forward, exaggerating his motion as he reached into his back pocket for a leather wallet. His collection of phony identification was elaborate, down to staged photos with his "grandchildren." Credit cards colored in gold and platinum bespoke money. No one wants to incite anyone with money, and Reginald Hutchins had money.

"As you see, I'm Reggie Hutchins," Dawit said. "I'm a deacon at my church, I'm on the faculty at Yale, and I write books. I was practicing my Arabic with my former student. My friend Cedric and I here have been studying Arabic for years. We always thought it might come in handy one day if we could understand people who don't know we're listening. Amen?"

Sgt. Hayes didn't move. Dawit was almost certain Teferi must be working on him, softening his impulses. The other two deputies shifted nervously, waiting for Sgt. Hayes's lead.

The diner's other patrons watched in uneasy silence. Since he had an audience, Dawit raised his voice to be heard: "Now, these fine folks sitting around us, I'm willing to bet there isn't an Arabic speaker among them. So when they heard the language, it came as a shock. Most of us only hear it on the news, spoken by people who are our enemies. I know what that's like. I'm not ashamed to say I don't much care to hear people speaking Spanish around me. No offense to anyone here. But it just always seems like they're talking about *you*."

Laughter from the patrons, none of whom, apparently, were fond of Spanish. Shared bigotries create fast friends. The laughter quelled the itching in the younger deputies' eyes.

"Sir," Sgt. Hayes said to Mahmoud, "are you an American citizen?"

"I sure am," Mahmoud said. His accent sounded Kansas-bred.

Sgt. Hayes almost winced. "I'm sorry you had a rough time at the airport, but I need to see your ID. Please. I apologize for the inconvenience, and I won't take up too much of your time." He glanced at Teferi, an afterthought. "You too, sir. Sorry."

Teferi smiled and nodded. "Of course."

Dawit's eyes pleaded with Mahmoud. "He asked with great respect. I'm sure that if you show this man your identification, he'll be reasonable and go on his way. Don't be so sensitive, my young friend."

Mahmoud's lips curled downward as he slowly reached for his back pocket. Dawit prayed no gun would emerge. Instead, Mahmoud brought out a driver's license, dangling it for Sgt. Hayes to see. "I live in California," Mahmoud said. "San Francisco."

Sgt. Hayes studied the license, then Mahmoud's face. Then the license again. "And you are . . . Mr. Habib? Frank Habib?"

"If that's what it says."

Dawit nearly groaned. Teferi's eyes closed; his effort was too great to conceal.

Sgt. Hayes flipped to Dawit's license next. Then, Teferi's. Dawit knew that he and Teferi had impeccable identification, but he had no idea if Mahmoud's alias was registered in the five-year-old national database. The national ID scanner all police officers wore hung from the deputy's belt, but Sgt. Hayes didn't reach for it. Instead, he handed the licenses back to them, one by one.

"I am truly sorry, gentlemen," he said. "Very sorry. In fact . . ." Sgt. Hayes slipped his hand into his own back pocket for his wallet. He pulled out a twenty-dollar bill and laid it on the table. "That's all I've got on me. It may not cover the whole meal, but I hope this helps take the bad taste out of the interruption. Enjoy your stay in Buckeye." And he raised his hat.

His eyes still closed, Teferi smiled.

The younger deputies flocked to Sgt. Hayes with questions, but he shrugged them off. The deputies went outside and consulted while Dawit watched them through the window. After a lively discussion, both police cars drove off.

Once the cars were safely gone, Teferi breathed. He leaned down to retrieve his gun.

Mahmoud laughed. "Money from his pocket?" he said, tucking the bill into his own wallet. He slipped a cigarette between his lips. "Teferi, I'm shocked by your sudden usefulness."

Dawit patted Teferi's shoulder. "You must teach me that."

"You can only teach yourself," Teferi said. "All I did was whisper in his ear. He thought the voice he heard was his own."

"You are skilled enough to find Fana," Dawit said. "I will not doubt you again."

The waitress was back, her lips wrenched tight. "Sir, there's no smoking in here," she said as she dropped the bill in front of Mahmoud. She whirled away, not waiting for his response.

Mahmoud glared after her with a flick of his match. "How have you avoided prison, Dawit? I could not live here, bossed about by chattering monkeys."

"Life presents its challenges daily," Dawit said.

LET US GO, BEFORE THE POLICE RETURN, Teferi insisted. THEY WON'T IGNORE THEIR BETTER JUDGMENT TWICE.

Dawit stood. "Come, Mahmoud. You must share what you've learned with Teka."

Mahmoud sighed. "Only if your esteemed prophet can refrain from his proselytizing."

Teferi drove Mahmoud's car behind them while Mahmoud sat in the passenger seat of Dawit's Orbit and repeated his story to Teka on the satellite phone. Dawit was careful to make sure his headlights were on, driving the exact speed limit although his mind and heart raced.

How could he tell Jessica something so awful when she was already reeling?

"I'm sorry, Jessica," Dawit whispered, navigating the dark road. With more than a century between him and his last meeting with the fanatical sect, he'd never imagined he would have to explain Sanctus Cruor and the heritage of her new Blood.

Sixteen

Clouds of angry, well-fed smoke fanned across the rocky mountainside, and Dawit knew what they would find at the village.

In the lead, Dawit rode at a gallop on his black mare, while Mahmoud and Berhanu thundered closely behind. The sturdy-legged horses kicked up dust on the path already worn in the soil by the caravan of warriors, priests and servants making the unprecedented journey toward Adwa to stand with the emperor and empress against the Italian forces. War was upon them, and war meant that warriors were called from every corner. Emperor Menelik and his commanding Rases had marshaled troops from across the nation. For some, the pilgrimage had taken nearly half a year over difficult terrain. Yet they'd come.

If Ethiopia was victorious, it would be the greatest victory in Africa since the time of Hannibal, an example to the world. But if Emperor Menelik was as low on provisions as the reports claimed, even a fevered nationalism unlike anything Dawit had ever witnessed might not be enough to stave off the Italian forces.

Signs of camps lined the path: fire pits, dung piles left by donkeys and mules, broken walking sticks, and the dried bones of slaughtered livestock. Dawit could make out a line of about fifty stragglers about five kilometers distant, marching east toward Adwa while he and his Brothers rode west, toward the smoke.

Dawit and his Brothers would follow the warriors soon. Even

the reclusive Life Brothers, who worshiped no mortal's flag, were Ethiopians today. Man and horse alike were dressed for battle; Dawit wore a nobleman's robes and a crown of ostrich feathers, and his bridled horse wore colorful adornments across her mane. Dawit's sword, spear and guns were ready.

But first, they must heed Khaldun's vision.

The smell of charred flesh told Dawit that they were close. At least two dozen had died in the village they'd just passed, with no one left to tell the tale. War had reached these remote villagers already. Most of the dead had been slashed to pieces.

THERE. Berhanu's voice charged into Dawit's head, as fluid as his own thoughts. *NESTLED BETWEEN THE HILLS. NOT A HUNDRED METERS.*

Craggy rocks reached toward the sky like grasping fingers on the path. Smoke plumed behind tall, umbrella-shaped acacia trees. The trees were nearly hidden in the foggy smoke, but as his horse galloped closer, Dawit saw a human form hanging from the farthermost tree. Upside down. It was a boy, not yet a man. Perhaps twelve years.

The boy's feet were lashed with ropes to the tree, his arms bound behind him. He was naked, his throat slit from end to end, his face a mask of dried blood and flies. The dry earth had greedily swallowed his blood, with only a large brown-black stain beneath him. Enshrouded by fog, the boy looked like a wretched memory from Louisiana fifty years ago: Dawit had watched, helpless, as his dear Adele had been hung from a tree. Her death had impelled Dawit to Gettysburg.

Dawit raised his hand, and Berhanu and Mahmoud slowed behind him. Berhanu's horse whinnied, as impatient as his master.

"Rome's cowards slay children, too?" Mahmoud said.

"Italy's army isn't this far inland," Dawit said. "These are from Khaldun's vision."

I HEAR SURVIVORS. WE WILL LEARN WHERE THEIR ATTACKERS WENT, Berhanu said, and yanked his horse's bridle to take the lead on the smoky path to the village of the dead.

The pathway was littered with corpses. Ash floated everywhere, and at least twenty dead lay in the ash, some of them burned beyond gender recognition. Dawit steered his horse around the body of a girl whose belly protruded with an unborn child, now dead like its wide-eyed mother. A bundle of sticks she had been carrying lay crushed and scattered around her. Next lay a white-haired old woman, wrapped in a fetal position in a puddle of blood. The village's huts were scorched. The cylindrical stone shells still stood, blackened, but the thatch roof-tops had all burned away. Belongings inside the huts still smoldered.

Something ominous on the path made Dawit dismount so he could look more closely. From a distance, it might have been a bloated snake.

But no. When he kneeled, he saw that it was a severed arm. A child's. Charred.

Beside the limb lay a golden medallion with a crimson ribbon. Dawit picked up the medallion—a European-styled cross with a garnet in the center. The inscribed words were in Latin: *Ordo Sanctus Cruor.* Order of the Holy Blood.

Just as Khaldun had prophesied! Khaldun's visage had appeared to Dawit, floating above Dawit's bed, and now Khaldun's warning filled Dawit's ears anew: *They know that men walk with the Living Blood. They believe themselves to be holy, but their hearts lust only for the power of our Blood. They would destroy a nation, or a world, to hoard it.*

With the power of Italy's forces behind them, this Order could march straight into the heart of the nation, to Lalibela. Already, only two hundred and fifty kilometers separated them.

Dawit heard children's screams.

Berhanu, still on horseback, uncovered a nest of survivors hidden in the brush beside their burned-out homes. A dozen young children fled, the older children pulling the younger away from the giant of a man on horseback. Mahmoud's lighter skin terrified them more.

Dawit lay down his sword and raised his hands as the flock of children trembled, trapped between the three of them on the path. "*Selam, selam,*" Dawit greeted the children, wishing them peace. "We will not harm you. We are here to help. Do not fear us."

To prove his intentions, Dawit reached into his saddlebag and found the provisions he had brought for his journey. Dried beef called *kuwanta.* Dried *injera* chips. Spicy brown *chiko.*

The younger children still wailed, but the eldest, a tall boy who might be ten, snatched the food from Dawit's hands and passed it to the younger ones. Dawit gave the boy a skein of water, and he took only a sip before offering the skein to the younger children, who quarreled over it.

"What is your name?" Dawit asked the boy.

Warily the boy eyed Dawit, and then Mahmoud, before he answered. "I am Amare."

"Where are the others in your village?"

Amare's haunted eyes searched the ruins. "My grandfather . . . is dead. My grandmother. My cousin. All dead." Tears watered his face.

Dawit saw two or three mature women among the dead, but most were very young or very old. Dawit knelt to talk to the boy at eye level. "Where is your father, Amare?" he said.

Berhanu's thoughts blared: *ARE YOU THIS YOUNG MONKEY'S BIOGRAPHER?*

"My father has gone to fight," Amare said. "All of our fathers have gone. Our mothers too. The elders were left here with us."

"Your *mothers*?" Mahmoud said, skeptical. "Gone to war?"

Amare glared at him, offended. "We have brave mothers! They are like Empress Taitu. If they do not fight, they will cook and nurse the fallen with herbs. Was your mother so brave?"

Dawit smiled. Amare was brave, too, to stand up to Mahmoud. Dawit wondered what it would be like to raise a strong son, to teach a child what he knew instead of leaving him for his mother to care for alone. If he and Adele had raised a child, would he have been as worthy as Amare?

Such pointless thoughts! Khaldun would never permit it, and Adele was long dead. It was the worst folly to love mortals, only to watch them die.

Dawit held Amare's hand. "Tell me . . . who has done this to you?"

The children answered in a cacophony, but Amare's voice was loudest. "They came like you, on horses! They were ghost-men. Their skin was white like the clouds. They shouted at us, saying to tell them about the magic blood."

"What magic blood?" Berhanu said.

Amare shook his head. "They asked us about men who could not be killed, like the stories my grandfather tells the little ones. Everyone came from great distances to hear my grandfather's stories of flying lions and men who live a thousand years with magic blood, who cannot die by spear nor sword. They were only stories, but these ghost-men thought they were true. They hung my cousin from a tree to make my grandfather tell. They cut off Hakim's arm with a sword to try to make us say where the magic blood was. But how could we? It was a story!" For the first time, Amare sobbed. "Now where are my grandfather's stories?"

Dawit sighed. An old storyteller's fertile imagination had brought a plague to his village. If the villagers of Lalibela were subjected to the same tortures, they might speculate about the priests among them who never seemed to age. Some of his Brothers' faces were known.

"How many of these ghost-men came?" Dawit said.

"They were like a swarm of bees," the boy said. "Too many to count."

I SEE HIS MEMORIES, Berhanu said. *I COUNT THEM AT FIFTY.*

Fifty was a formidable number against three, even with advanced weapons. More of his Brothers should have been dispatched, Dawit realized. They had misjudged the threat.

Amare suddenly squeezed Dawit's hand tightly. "Come help me," the boy said. "I need to cut down my grandfather. And my cousin. The ghost-men left them and said they would return to see if the dead would wake. But priests say the dead must be laid to rest."

FORGO THESE SENTIMENTALITIES, Berhanu complained. *I SEE IN HIS MEMORIES THAT THE ATTACKERS TRAVELED EAST. THEY ARE WEARING WHITE.*

"And we will follow them . . . soon," Dawit said to Berhanu aloud. Then he turned back to Amare's waiting eyes. "Hurry, boy. Take us to your grandfather."

The old man was strung to a rock face outside the village. He hung upside down several meters above the ground, his legs splayed open, each ankle tied to the trunk of a sapling. Like the boy on the acacia tree, his throat had been cut, and his blood painted the rock's surface in a drying stream to the soil. Someone had used the dead man's blood to write a crudely drawn message on the rock, in Italian: *AND BLOOD TOUCHETH BLOOD.*

Old Testament scripture, King James's Book of Hosea. Khaldun's vision was true!

Dawit had witnessed horrors as a boy, and he grieved for these children. No violation could match being stripped of one's childhood by violence. Amare had lost more than his family.

Dawit picked up a crying girl who looked like she was about three. He passed her up to Mahmoud on his saddle. Mahmoud took the child, holding her tiny waist in his outstretched arms like a sack of teff.

"Let the young ones feed sugar to your horse," Dawit told him. "Keep them back while we cut this old man down. Their eyes have seen too much already."

Mahmoud and Berhanu looked at him grimly but nodded.

TEN MINUTES, Berhanu said. *NOT A MINUTE MORE, OR WE RIDE WITHOUT YOU.* Amare waited below while Dawit and Berhanu climbed the rocks to cut his grandfather's broken body down. He remained at Dawit's side to receive the corpse while Berhanu held the ropes to lower the old man to the ground. Amare also helped them at the acacia tree, when it was time to cut down the hanging boy. Tears streamed down Amare's face, but he never sobbed. Dawit glanced skyward, then at his pocket watch. It was 6 p.m. They must go, or the sect would target another helpless village. Dawit collected enough provisions from his Brothers to last the children a week. A nearby stream was almost dry, but it was enough for them to drink. There was no time to help these children bury their dead.

AT LAST! Berhanu's voice boomed in his head. *NO MORE DELAYS.*

Dawit took one last look at the severed arm on the path to the village. He would carry the memory of the butchered child to their attackers' trail, and then on to Adwa.

The younger children wailed when they realized Dawit was mounting his horse to leave. "No!" they cried. "Stay with us! The ghost-men will come back!"

Dawit met young Amare's eyes and handed the boy his sword. The weapon was almost too big for Amare's hand, but he clutched it like a seasoned warrior. The blade was one of Dawit's favorites, forged in Spain, but the gratitude in Amare's eyes dulled the sting of the loss.

"Your grandfather told the truth," Dawit told Amare. "There *is* magic in this world—in that very sword. As long as you keep it, no more harm shall come to you. We will ride after the ghost-men who came to your village, and they shall answer for what they have done. We will send word of what has happened here, and your mothers and fathers will return to you."

Amare shook his head. His pain-reddened eyes didn't blink. "*No*," he said. "Tell our parents to stay and fight. Tell them they must not return until Ethiopia is free."

His arm trembling with weight he could barely lift, Amare raised Dawit's sword above his head. Miraculously, the children began to sing, their voices thinned by tears: "*Send the invaders away! / The flying lion will rise up and lead us to victory! / Our warriors are too mighty to die!*"

The stories Amare's grandfather had told still lived in song.

As the crying children sang behind them, chasing their speed-ing horses, Dawit knew the future even without Khaldun's gifts of prophecy: Ethiopia's battles ahead were already won.

The trail of hoofprints was easy to follow through a narrow ridge hidden in the hills.

Dawit kept his eyes trained for scouts; the viewers from the House of Science gave him enough vision in near-darkness to see a flea on a man's neck from two hundred meters. Sure enough, he saw two scouts mounted on the hilltop above them, up ahead. They, too, looked like fresh-faced boys—one African, one European, both wearing golden Sanctus Cruor medallions pinned to their white shirts.

Killers rarely looked as despicable as their deeds.

"I'll take them," Mahmoud said and galloped on a separate trail toward the lookouts.

USE YOUR TRANSMITTERS, Berhanu reminded Dawit, mildly mocking. Berhanu often complained that too few other Brothers could trade thoughts with him during battles. But Berhanu was a rarity, to have mastered arts in both the mind and body. Most Brothers had the patience for only one path or the other. There was no advancement in mind arts without meditation, and prolonged meditation bored Dawit to tears.

Dawit clicked on his transmitter so Mahmoud would hear the gentle beep in his ear.

"Wait for our word to advance," Dawit told Mahmoud. "We don't know their number."

"*Almighty Berhanu can't pluck such simple knowledge out of the air?*" Mahmoud said sarcastically in Dawit's earpiece, taking advantage of his distance from Berhanu. Their more advanced Brother could hear thoughts from thirty meters, but not beyond.

Dawit and Berhanu slowed their horses, riding close to the ridge wall to be out of the lookouts' sight until Mahmoud could dispatch them. This time, the thin smoke floating toward them in the wind was from campfires, accompanied by the smell of coffee and cooking food.

There was no clear view of the camp; there were too many twists in the scrubby trail.

I WILL TRY TO FIND THEIR LEADERS, Berhanu said. *WE MUST DISCOVER THEIR NUMBER, AND HOW THEY LEARNED OF THE BLOOD.*

"Then they will taste the suffering they brought to that village," Dawit said, his palm tightening around the base of his spear.

WE FIGHT FOR OUR OWN PRESERVATION, DAWIT. FORGET YOUR ANGER.

Dawit gazed through his viewers again. The two lookouts posted high on the hill had not moved. Both wore Remingtons. Dawit motioned for Berhanu to rein his horse. If they advanced farther, they might come into sight.

"*They're within my range,*" Mahmoud's voice said in the earpiece.

As always, Mahmoud was fleet. But as long seconds passed, the men's position did not change. Dawit saw them talking, sharing coffee.

"Are you waiting for dessert, Brother?" Dawit said, half to himself.

Suddenly, one after the other, the men fell forward. Neither had time to raise a shout. The air pistols from the House of Science had a more limited range than conventional rifles for a lethal blast, but they were devastating in their silence.

Dawit saw Mahmoud's head emerge where the lookouts had stood.

"*They are arrogant enough to camp behind enemy lines,*" Mahmoud reported. "*They're supping around their fires. Some may be in tents, but Berhanu was right to guess fifty. Heavily armed with Remingtons and pistols. They are out of my range from here. We should wait until dark and attack from—*"

Dawit never heard the rest of Mahmoud's plan.

Berhanu gave a start a moment before his hurried thought came: *BEHIND US!*

Gunfire cracked, echoing in the ridge, and a rifle round chipped the rocky wall two meters beside Dawit's head. The attackers were on foot—three men running toward them at full speed, rifles firing. The shots would draw the others!

Dawit let his spear fly. Two of the men crumpled from Berhanu's pistol fire, and the third watched, frozen, as Dawit's spear flew into his chest, staggering him backward before he fell.

"*Their full forces are at a charge,*" Mahmoud's voice said. "*I'll move quickly to aid you.*"

"Quickly is not fast enough, Brother," Dawit said, spurring his horse toward the fallen men to retrieve his spear.

In such a narrow ridge, there were few places to run. A cluster of rocks ten meters behind the fallen men would serve as their cover. They would not retreat: They would stand and fight.

The man Dawit had speared lay prostrate, grasping wildly at the wood to try to free it from his chest. When Dawit yanked the spear free, the man screamed. He was more mature than the scouts, about thirty, with a long, deeply lined face. Instead of a medallion, he wore a large Sanctus Cruor emblem on a white coat. An officer.

"*P-per favore . . . ,*" the man wheezed, begging.

Dawit spat at his face. "What mercy did you show those grandmothers and children?"

WAIT—

Dawit fired his pistol with his free hand, stopping the fallen man's heart. Berhanu would berate him, but no matter: The man's injury was so severe that he would have been dead within seconds. There would have been no time to question him, nor to study his memories. They would be lucky to save themselves today.

Galloping hooves raced toward them, shaking the earth.

THE ROCKS, Berhanu said as Dawit dismounted. Dawit slapped his horse's flank to send her away from the approaching soldiers. Dawit did not want to lose her to gunfire. He would wake again, but his loyal horse would not.

"They are upon you!" Mahmoud reported breathlessly. "Fire on my word!"

The rocks were fortuitous cover, high enough to hide them, yet porous enough to fire through. As always before a battle, Dawit's heart shook his ribs and stanched his breath. Any sleep, however temporary, might bring the day when he would be buried alive, unable to free himself, doomed to wake and suffocate for all of time.

Dawit's fingers itched on his trigger as soon as the first horses raced into sight, carrying their pale-skinned riders.

"Fire!" Mahmoud said.

Air pellets sprayed the army, flinging riders from their horses. The soldiers were confounded by the silence. Bullets without sound? A few seconds' confusion cost two dozen men their lives. The rest were thwarted by the whinnying horses, who ran in confusion as their riders fell. Some of the quick-thinking soldiers took refuge behind fallen horses to aim their rifles, but they did not know where to fire. There were no muzzle flashes to betray Dawit and Berhanu. There was only death, in pitiless silence.

As a diversion, Mahmoud fired his rifle from the top of the ridge.

A symphony of rifle fire answered Mahmoud.

By the time the survivors realized the direction of the lethal air pellets, it was too late for them to save themselves. The rest of the killing was one by one; the dying boys screamed for their mothers. By the end, forty were dead. Thirteen still lived, if barely.

Berhanu walked up and down the row of wounded, probing their minds. The soldiers were not all Italian, as Dawit had believed. Some had features ranging from Asian to Eastern European, with a few Ethiopians scattered among them. All wore identical white shirts and golden medallions. Most were very young, made younger by their sobbing.

Dawit would not look at their faces long.

THEY KNOW VERY LITTLE, Berhanu said. THE ONE WHO MIGHT HAVE HELPED US, NAMED STEFAN, WAS AMONG THE FIRST TO DIE.

Dawit felt the weight of his responsibility. Had he killed too hastily?

"Are there others?" Mahmoud said.

Berhanu nodded. "I have learned a few names. Vatican officials. Merchants. We will have to take this fight far from home."

"Khaldun will give us guidance," Mahmoud said. "We will find the others."

"We can get nothing else from these?" Dawit said, frustrated. He would be ashamed to report to Khaldun that their mission had failed. "What is this sect? What is their goal?"

THESE WERE ONLY SOLDIERS, Berhanu said. THEY CRAVED THE BLOOD, BUT THEY HAVE NEVER SEEN IT. THEY DIED ON FAITH ALONE.

Dawit gazed at the collection of fallen young soldiers. If these men had died on faith alone, they were not the first. But their ignorance was maddening.

Soon, their flesh would feed a pyre to light the night, as if they had never existed. Whatever else would be written about Ethiopia's war with Italy, this battle in the hills would never be known. They could not leave survivors.

"It was the one I felled with my spear," Dawit said. "He would have told us more."

"We cannot change the past, Brother," Mahmoud said. "Only the future."

Still, Dawit's heart was heavy with dread. His Brotherhood might be known by outsiders with enough power to bring them harm.

Mistakes in the past eliminated one future and created another.

Somewhere, their new future had already begun.

Seventeen

As soon as Dawit appeared in her sat phone's viewer, Jessica's heart quailed. Bad news was written in Dawit's joyless face.

"What happened?" she said.

As Dawit told her Mahmoud's story, Jessica's eyes fought tears.

She saw a shadow move beside Dawit, and she realized Mahmoud was in the car with him. Mahmoud had maimed Alex, tossing her from her apartment balcony. He was responsible for Kira's death. He had tried to kill Fana and had helped ignite that terrible rage—that faceless being—that had controlled her baby girl. Jessica would never forget the shock and terror she'd felt when Mahmoud had held her and poor Kira at gunpoint, when her world had first collapsed. And then four years later, Mahmoud had pointed another gun toward Fana, in a twisted *déjà vu*.

Would she ever escape Mahmoud, or his memory?

"He's there right now?" Jessica said. She could only whisper.

"He's not the point, Jess," Dawit said. "Right now, it's his story that matters."

Jessica blinked and forced her tears at bay. "How can you trust him?"

"Teka has talked to him, and he is intrigued. We're trying to learn more, but that will take a day or two. A brother will fly out in person. Our Lalibela Brothers are difficult to reach."

Jessica saw the tiny orange glow of what she guessed was the tip of Mahmoud's cigarette, hardly two inches from Dawit's chin. In Miami, she had always wondered why there had been cigarette butts strewn around her backyard. She never could have guessed that an assassin like Mahmoud had been spying on her family.

"I won't talk like this," she said. "Not in front of him." Why did she even have to say it?

Mahmoud muttered impatiently in Arabic. The cigarette's glow vanished, and his car door slammed. How dare he complain! The loathing she felt reeled in her stomach. Was Dawit's friendship with Mahmoud so strong that even Kira's death couldn't sever it?

"I'm sorry, Jess," Dawit said. "I wasn't thinking. I had to warn you right away. You'll follow emergency procedures tonight. All of you. Tomorrow, you'll set out for the airport. Jima and Teka will fly you out on our plane."

"Fly us where?" Jessica said.

"It's best not to say."

Jessica hoped Dawit was exercising the same commonsense precautions with Mahmoud.

"I don't think Mom is strong enough to travel now," Jessica said. "And Alex—"

"You'll have all the assistance you need, Jess. But please do this, and make sure the others comply. Sanctus Cruor is all we've feared and more."

Jessica tried to catch her thoughts. "This other child . . . ," she began. As horrible as Dawit's story had been, nothing had made a bigger impression than the story of a child who had been born like Fana, immortal from the womb. "He wants Fana as his . . . mate?"

"That much is hearsay," Dawit said. "But it's possible that Sanctus Cruor is hunting us and may be close to you. The precautions may not be enough."

"How is that possible?" Jessica said. Fana had eluded the firefences, but Jessica doubted anyone else could. The underground shelters were intricately protected, both in their design and an invisible canopy that protected their property even from the noses of dogs.

"There are always unknown vulnerabilities, Jess."

The strobelike flickering from the alarm light above Jessica's door intensified, lighting her room with intervals of brightness. She shielded her eyes.

"Keep looking for Fana," she told Dawit.

Now it was his turn to whisper. "Yes. I know," Dawit said. His eyes glimmered.

"And don't trust him, Dawit. No matter what."

Dawit nodded. "Don't worry, *mi vida*. I have not forgotten."

Dawit raised his fingers to the phone's camera, a larger-than-life blur across the five-inch screen. Instinctively, Jessica raised her hand, too; her fingers brushed the brown image. All she felt was cool glass, but it was the next best thing to his touch.

"Go to the closet," Dawit said. "Get the case."

Dawit kept a spare gun in the closet—a weapon from Lalibela modeled to look like a standard .45 pistol but comprising a technology that did not exist outside of the Life Brothers. The gun was easy to aim, since it could sense human heartbeats even through walls. Instead of bullets, it fired bursts of compressed air. Silent and deadly. Dawit had taken Jessica shooting in the woods and in outbuildings many times. Jessica was good with Dawit's gun.

But that had been target practice. This was different.

"I'll get it," Jessica said.

"Don't hesitate to fire, Jess. They commit atrocities. If you must shoot, remember that anyone you think is dead might wake."

Like the priest. The memory of her last, horrible argument with Dawit stabbed Jessica. "Dawit . . . I'm sorry—"

The signal faded, and the viewer went dark.

Her heart pounding, Jessica waited ninety seconds for Dawit to call back. Had he hung up so abruptly? Had something happened to him? If there was a problem with the satellite, which happened occasionally, reception might not be restored for an hour or more.

Jessica pulled a stool into her master bedroom closet and climbed up to reach the highest shelf, pushing aside the dusty boxes of Monopoly, Scrabble and chess that had been left by the previous owners. A frigid breeze from her cracked window tickled her body with a wave of goose bumps, creeping beneath the knee-length South Beach nightshirt she slept in. The cold spurred Jessica's thundering heart. *Are we really being hunted by other immortals?*

Bea had been so weak today that Jessica hated to rustle her mother from bed and take her to the cramped quarters underground. And what about Cal and Nita? Were they gathering their kids to go to the shelters, or stubbornly locking themselves in their house? The latter, she guessed.

The loud knock on her door almost made Jessica lose her balance.

"Who's there?" she called. Her voice told her how scared she was.

"It's just me, Jess." Lucas.

"And me, Auntie." Her nephew Jared's deep voice came next.

Jessica hid the lightweight case under the pillow on her bed; she didn't want to open the door with a gun in her hands. Jared had only arrived back home right before dinner, and his life was in enough turmoil his first night back.

"What the hell's going on?" Lucas said, once she opened her door.

Both father and son wore sweatpants and heavy jackets. Lucas was only a couple of inches taller than Jared, who had towered over Jessica since he was thirteen. Jared had a well-trimmed moustache, and he had grown so pale in England that she had barely recognized him when he'd first arrived. Jared's brow was furrowed with annoyance, rare for him.

"Dawit got some intelligence," she said. "We have to go to the shelters."

"What kind of intelligence?" Lucas said.

Jessica glanced at Jared before answering. She knew Lucas talked to Jared, but she wasn't used to sharing privileged information with her nephew. "Another Life Brother warned them that an enemy may be close. I'll tell you more when we're settled. There's no time now."

Lucas peeked into the hallway, then closed the bedroom door behind them. "This has a damn funny smell to it, so soon after O'Neal."

"I know, and I can't help that," Jessica said. "But Dawit wouldn't lie to me."

"Auntie, Dad told me all about what happened with Justin O'Neal," Jared said. He sounded exactly like his father, except for the high-bred English lilt that had crept into his speech at Oxford. "You've both disappointed me. It was wrong."

Jared's pronouncement hurt. Jessica had given Jared drops of her blood and saved his life fourteen years ago, when he was ten. Jared had grown into one of the young men she most admired; bright, hardworking and good-hearted. She wished she had time to defend her position.

"I need to know what I'm dragging my son into," Lucas said.

"We've drilled dozens of times," Jessica said.

"So why does it feel like we're being taken into custody?" Lucas said.

"You're not." She took his hand and squeezed it between her palms. "There may be . . . another sect of immortals. They're violent and fanatical, and they're looking for anyone else with our blood. Dawit and Teka think we need to go to the shelters tonight, just in case."

Another knock, and the door eased open before Jessica could say anything.

A young, dark-skinned black man as tall as Jared stood in her doorway, dressed in a black wet suit. A stranger! *Sanctus Cruor?* Jessica gasped, turning to reach for her gun case. She was dismayed to realize that she was a full six strides from where she'd hidden it.

Teka peeked from behind the stranger in the hall.

"It's all right," Teka said quietly. "This man is with me."

"Forgive my intrusion," the stranger said and bowed deeply. "*Aznallō*. My most sincere apologies. My name is Fasilidas. I am guardian to Fana, She Who Is Most Holy. Now I will be guardian to her Blessed Mother. I beg you to move with haste. We must go to the shelters."

The man remained bowed low, both hands behind his back. Was he one of the men who lived in the woods? He must be. There were four of them, and tonight Jessica was glad of it.

"Rise, Fasilidas," Jessica said. By the immortals' custom, he would not rise until invited.

Jessica's nephew looked at her as if she had become a stranger before his eyes.

The house had no elevator, so the two immortals helped Lucas carry Alex down the winding staircase, heavy feet thumping and squeaking on aged floorboards.

The Life Brothers rarely mingled, but Lucas recognized the huskier man as Jima. The other was Yonas, Jared's minder from England. The house was mostly dark, except for dim alarm lights with eerie synchronization, like flashbulbs. With his flashlight, Jared led them down the stairs. Every time the hall lighted from the alarm, Lucas saw the panic on his son's face.

He had been a fool to bring Jared home.

Bea and Jessica were beside the door in the foyer. Jessica bent over her mother, speaking softly as she secured a heavy blanket over her. Bea sat in the wheelchair she had used after she'd broken her hip; the man who had called himself Fasilidas was pushing her. He was a shadow, appearing from thin air. Were there more Brothers here than he knew?

When they opened the door, Teka was waiting outside.

"We must go to Cal's, Lucas," Teka said. "There is trouble, perhaps."

Teka was the king of understatement, so that might mean anything. "As in?"

"Cal is packing his vehicle. He has vowed to leave with his family."

"Please go talk to him, Lucas," Jessica said. "I would, but I don't think it would help. It's too dangerous to send them out. They might be captured."

Jared exhaled sharply. "What?"

Jessica sounded more like Dawit every day, Lucas thought. "We're talking about Cal and Nita and their kids," he said. "Let's just let them drive straight up the 10 into Canada, all ties cut off. What are the odds that—"

"I don't know the odds, Lucas," Jessica said. "What were the odds of you finding my clinic in Botswana? What were the odds that my nurse would get murdered by an army of mercenaries? We should go down to wait out the night. I agree with Dawit."

That was when Lucas first noticed it: Aside from Teka, the other immortals were armed. Jima and Yonas had weapons beneath their tunics; he could see the impressions of the holsters under the fabric. Fasilidas had an ominous black baton strapped to his outer thigh. Even Jessica was carrying what looked like a gun case under her arm. These four men in this foyer were not his friends. If Cal and Nita wanted to leave, it was a damn fine idea.

"Being a prisoner won't sit well with Cal," Lucas said.

Jima said something impatient to Teka in Amharic.

"Prisoner is an unkind term," Teka told Lucas.

"My father raised me to call things the way I see them," Lucas said. "So if you expect me to go talk my best friend out of doing something I'm pretty damn sure I should be doing myself, don't expect me to coat it in bullshit."

Fasilidas and Jima shifted, startled. Fasilidas's eyes studied Lucas more carefully. The immortals didn't like anyone mouthing off at Teka, but too bad.

Teka's face fluttered, torn. "We cannot permit Cal to leave," he said. "Nor you, nor your son. If you must call it imprisonment, the facts render my arguments moot. I am sorry."

Lucas turned to Jessica, who looked more torn than Teka. "Was this supposed to be a part of the mission, Jess? What would Alex say about this?"

The last question was a low blow. Both of them had trouble keeping their eyes dry.

"They agreed to stay here," Jessica said, blinking. "All of us did."

"How can you make an agreement with people who don't tell you the truth?" Lucas said. "Cal had no idea who these people are."

"Don't you blame Jessica," Bea said suddenly, her head rising from its slumped position. "You knew this was a sacred commitment. Remember your Scripture from Joshua, Lucas. The Lord said, 'Be strong and of good courage; be not afraid, neither be thou dismayed: for the Lord thy God is with thee wherever thou goest.'" By the end, she was nearly breathless. Bea was in pulmonary distress. Lucas could hear it.

"It's all right, Mom," Jessica said, resting her hand on her mother's shoulder. "He has a right to his feelings. I concealed information."

"She needs oxygen," Lucas told Jessica.

"My breathing is fine," Bea snapped. Her voice was nearly a rasp.

Lucas held Jessica's eyes. "There are O2 tanks in my quarters. Alex and I stockpiled medical supplies. You take care of Bea." Lucas sighed. "I'll have a look at her. First, I have to see if I can keep Cal from getting his brain fried. Or worse."

A man who was like a brother to him might die tonight. That was plain.

"I'm going with you, Dad," Jared said.

"No, you're not," Lucas said. "Go down and see after your grand-mother."

In the flash of light, Jared's face was stone. "You heard me. I'm going."

Lucas had forgotten that Jared was a grown-ass man now, twenty-four. Adults had to be negotiated with. "Jared, your Gramma Bea needs you. Please. I'll be fine."

"Come on with us, baby," Bea's voice said softly. Only then did Jared's lips curl, relenting. The look he gave Lucas scorched him.

But that was all right. Jared didn't understand, not yet. Jared hadn't been sitting at the dinner table when Justin O'Neal had casually been stripped of the most meaningful years of his life.

Jared didn't have the foggiest idea what it was like to watch memories die.

Headlights shone from a distance as Lucas and Teka waded through ferns, taking a shortcut from the Big House to Cal's land five acres away, on the northeast side. Lucas stumbled on a stone in the dark-ness, twinging his ankle, but he didn't slow.

"Don't screw with his head, you hear?" Lucas said. "I mean it, Teka."

"Is it not dangerous—and cruel—to leave his fears unabated?" Teka sounded like a zookeeper debating whether or not to shoot an animal with a trank gun.

"Leave him his damn dignity."

"I will use all possible restraint. But dignity is the least of what's imperiled tonight."

The Blazer's rumbling engine was the only sound in the night. By the time Lucas reached Cal's ranch-style cedar house, Nita and the kids were already in the car.

Cal stood with one foot on the running board of the Blazer's open driver's door, a shotgun over his shoulder. Two immortals dressed in white looked ghostly just beyond the headlights' beam, blocking Cal's path fifteen yards down. The trees were too dense to allow Cal to drive around the men, and it was too dark for Cal to go out of his way to find another pathway. Lucas couldn't see if the other immortals were armed, but he'd better assume they were.

"Shit," Lucas muttered.

Cal waved toward Lucas. "Good!" he called. "Get in here, Lucas. We got plenty of room. Where's Jared?"

A thought froze Lucas in place: *What if Teka's controlling me like a puppet on a string?* For two heartbeats, he couldn't speak. If he couldn't trust that he was himself, who was he?

"Jared's in the shelter, Cal," Lucas said.

"Then you're out of your goddamned mind," Cal said.

Nita's window came down. She was in the backseat. In the dim light inside the car, Lucas saw the twins' round faces beside her, strapped into car seats. Hank was in the passenger seat up front, and Lucas realized Hank probably had a gun, too.

"Lucas?" Nita's voice was both gentle and stern. "Get in. We'll stop for Jared and Alex."

"I'm only here to ask you to stay," Lucas said. "Just tonight. There's a crisis. Please."

Cal stepped down from the running board, cracking a thick twig beneath his boot. He jacked a cartridge into his shotgun's chamber, a sound that echoed in the treetops. "Did they get to you too, Lucas? Got you rewired to do what they say?"

I hope to hell not. "No," Lucas said. "Cal, please put down the gun."

Cal took a step toward them, eyeing Teka. "That your new massa, Doc?"

"Cal, I understand why you want to do this, but they're not gonna' let you jump in your rig and go. Our situation needs fixing, but this isn't the way. Weren't you there with Justin?"

"More reason to get the hell out!"

"You planning to run those two men down?" Lucas said.

"That's their choice," Cal said. "I expect they'll be all right, by and by."

Lucas swallowed hard. He took two strides until he stood squarely in the beam of Cal's headlights. "I'm not worried about them. But you and Nita? Those kids? I'm worried plenty."

"I fucked up, Doc," Cal said. His voice was coarse, near tears. "I believed in something so much, I let myself go to sleep. But now I'm wide fucking awake. So I tell you what: I'm gonna' leave tread marks over any dumbass who isn't smart enough to get out of my way, present company included. Then I'm gonna' take my family somewhere far from here. End of story."

Lucas clasped his hands together, linking unsteady fingers. He had known Cal Duhart a long time, and Cal might run right over him.

"Cal, they won't let you go. I wish to God it weren't that way, but it is."

Teka spoke up. "These measures are only temporary. I assure you, Mr. Duhart, your concerns will be—"

Cal cut off Teka. "Doc, tell your new massa I'm full up on horseshit."

For the first time, one of the immortals farther down the path spoke up loudly enough to hear. "Be advised, monkey, to always address Teka with the honor he deserves." His basso voice filled the woods with thunder. Lucas's skin went cold. He had suspected that some of the immortals weren't fond of the rest of them, but the word "monkey" added a whole new level of clarity.

Cal pursed his lips, aiming his shotgun at the voice. The muzzle was rock steady. "Say one more word, you smug, superior sonofabitch."

Lucas's heart shook. "Cal . . ."

Inside the car, Nita sounded like she was praying.

"Last chance, Lucas," Cal said. "Do the smart thing, or God help you."

"My wife and son are here. My work is here." Those words felt weak, but the only other words he could think of were *Please don't force their hand,* and he knew those were pointless.

"Then excuse us monkeys, Doc. You better move."

Cal climbed into the Blazer, slamming his door. When the brights flicked on, flooding Lucas's eyes, he took a step back. His heart hammered at his throat.

"Move your ass, Lucas!" Cal shouted.

The Blazer lunged forward with a squeal, grinding and spitting stones. Lucas shielded his face, locking every muscle in place. *He won't hit me.* Light burned through his eyelids, and he felt heat baking from the car's monstrous grill. The engine was a roar.

The Blazer swerved just as instinct made Lucas leap. His leap came too late, and directly into Cal's path. Lucas flew.

Pulverizing waves of pain; first his left side when the Blazer clipped him, and then his right after he flew forever and landed against a tree. He heard himself say *"Oooomph"* as ribs collapsed, all air exiled. His head snapped back, more dizzying pain. Lucas was amazed, and dismayed, to still be conscious. He lay crumpled at the foot of the tree. He was in the worst pain of his life. He couldn't move, not even to moan.

Red taillights. The Blazer righted itself and sped away from him, toward freedom. *GO, Cal,* Lucas thought, fevered. *You can make it!*

But Cal didn't make it, of course. One last roar of the engine, and suddenly the Blazer slowed. Then stopped, rocking.

The last thing Lucas heard was Nita Duhart screaming her husband's name.

"So . . . how does it work?" Jared said, voice unsteady. Jessica's nephew's face was ashen.

Lucas lay stripped to his boxers on one of the three twin beds in the small, wood-paneled room in the shelter. He was unconscious, and his chest and pelvis were bloodied and battered, splotched purple and black. Lucas looked like he needed to be in an emergency room, not in a shelter fifteen feet under the ground.

Jessica looked at her watch. It was two-thirty in the morning.

"He may not be completely healed by dawn," she said. "But soon after. He'll be hungry, so I'll bring food for him. The food helped me when I lost my hand."

Jared shook his head. "I can't believe Uncle Cal would do this."

"Only because he knew Lucas would be all right."

Jared's jaw shook. "But he *didn't* know. Dad cut his arm with a razor to show me, but this is different. Uncle Cal might have killed him."

Jessica shook her head, sighing. "He chose his children first, Jared. Most people would."

"So I'm supposed to forgive him, too. Like I'm supposed to forgive Fana." He whispered Fana's name. When Lucas first told Jared that Fana was responsible for Alex's condition, Jared had cried for the first time since his arrival.

When Jessica stepped closer, Jared inched away. "I'm sorry for this, hon. All of it."

Jared ignored her apology. "I have a girlfriend, Issa. We were both going to apply for biology posts at the University of Dar es Salaam next fall. But I can forget about Oxford, and I'll have to give up Issa along with everything else. I never had a life of my own, did I?"

"That's not true, Jared. Like Alex would say, this will pass."

"I saw that look in Dad's eyes, Auntie. His best friend just rammed the piss out of him trying to get out, and you have no idea what's wrong with Alex. What if she doesn't recover?"

"She will, Jared. Fana—"

"Fana was *responsible*," he said, cutting Jessica off. "That doesn't mean she can fix it."

Jessica had never heard so much anger in Jared's voice; his adoration for her had turned inside out.

"I believe she can," Jessica said quietly. "With all my heart. It was an accident, Jared."

Jared sighed. "When Dad offered me the blood Ceremony, I told him I would think about it after my doctorate. Well, I don't want it."

Jared sounded like Alex now. When Jessica opened her mouth, he motioned her to be silent. "I'll help it reach the places it hasn't," Jared said. "I'll work in the clinics. If I have to, I'll give my life for it. I probably already have, Auntie. But I won't accept the double standard. I won't turn myself into something I don't want to be."

"Sweetheart, you'll always choose who you are, no matter what," Jessica said. "Blood doesn't change that. And if you need to reach your girlfriend . . ."

Jared shook his head. "I won't bring her into this," he said. "I'll stay here with Dad. Call me if there's a change in Mom or Gramma Bea, Auntie."

Her invitation to leave, Jessica realized.

Outside of Jared's door, the Life Brothers were waiting. Fasilidas and Yonas were talking quietly, but they snapped to alertness and bowed when she appeared. The Life Brothers' customs had embarrassed her once. Had the Blood changed her, as Jared feared?

"Make sure Jared has anything he needs," Jessica told Yonas.

"Of course, Blessed Mother," Yonas said. He might have been fifty when he'd undertaken the Ceremony, of older appearance than the rest. "It is my honor to serve the family of Fana."

It looked like midday instead of the middle of the night. The cement-fortified passageways had naturalistic lighting from bright lamps on sconces, and the hall flurried with activity. Six Life Brothers huddled in conference a dozen yards from her. The white-clad Brothers acknowledged her with inclined heads but did not speak. None smiled.

Teferi's wife Abena excused herself past Jessica, groggily shooing through a noisy flock of chickens as she led her children toward their quarters. Abena's three boys dutifully held neatly folded blankets up to their chins, each looking sleepier than the last. The boys all had Teferi's long, lanky legs. Jessica rested her hand on the head of Teferi's youngest, Miruts.

"You'll be in bed soon," Jessica told him and kissed his precious face. He playfully brushed the kiss away, and Jessica smiled. *They're safe,* she thought. *Tonight, anyway.*

Abena cast wary eyes back at Jessica but forced herself to smile. "Teferi says wives should trust their husbands, but why is there a drill at this hour?" Teferi's senior wife, an Indian woman named Sharmila, was bolder and often spoke for both of them.

"Teferi and Dawit are worried that an old enemy may be close. They're very protective."

Abena sucked her teeth. "Too much, I think." And she moved the boys along.

Jessica gazed across the hall at the Duharts' closed door. She could hear Maya and Martin crying inside their family's quarters. She wanted to go in and comfort the children, who were like a niece and nephews, but Nita didn't want to see her. Jessica hoped she would think of the right thing to say to the Duharts by morning.

"The Duharts' door stays unlocked," Jessica told Yonas, to be sure.

"Yes, Blessed Mother. As you have asked."

Fasilidas sprang behind Jessica like a cat when she walked toward her quarters. When she stopped abruptly, he nearly ran into her.

"I am s-so sorry, Blessed Mother," he said. Mortification shadowed his angelic onyx face. She felt a maternal instinct toward him, until she remembered his true age.

"My name is Jessica, Fasilidas," she said.

Fasilidas grinned. His teeth were large, scrubbed to shining. "As I know well, Blessed Mother. Jessica, daughter to Beatrice and Raymond. Stepdaughter to Randall. Granddaughter to Charlotte and John, and Lucille and Marion. Wife to Dawit. Jessica, a name from the tongue of the ancient Hebrews, meaning one who has wealth." His recitation was breathless.

She could forget about the call-me-Jessica routine, she realized.

"Wake me if Jared or the Duharts ask for me, no matter what the time," she said.

Another bow. "My honor, Blessed Mother."

Jessica's room was equipped with beds, a bathroom, and a corner kitchenette. The units all looked like modest hotel rooms, except for the fine woodwork. Cal had helped the Brothers fell the Douglas firs and maple trees for the lacquered walls.

Inside Jessica's room, Alex and Bea lay in the beds meant for her and Dawit. Teka still sat where she had left him, his eyes closed in the recliner beside her table.

Jessica stood over Bea's bed to watch her mother's sheets rise and fall with her breathing. Despite Bea's complaints, her nostrils had been fitted with oxygen tubes, as Lucas had advised. Jessica was glad her mother was sleeping. *Hurry and wake up, Lucas, in case she needs a doctor.*

"She is weak, Jessica," Teka said before she could ask. His eyes were open. "As Lucas feared."

Jessica's heart trembled. "How weak?"

"The excitement has had a toll. Her heart struggles. Her medications are useful, for now, but the heart is an unpredictable muscle in one so aged. It has already served her past its time. The Blood is her surest remedy."

Teka had all but said what Jessica had known for six months: Bea was dying. Now Bea would have no choice but to accept an injection of blood, once she understood her condition. Jessica expected the weight of Teka's words to fall on her, but she felt numb. Was Teka easing her emotional burden for her with his mind? Maybe she needed him to, just for tonight.

Teka smiled at her. "Your strength, Jessica, is not my doing," he said. His smile faded. "But I should have soothed Cal. I promised Lucas I would not interfere too soon—instead, I waited too long. Their suffering was so easily avoided." He clucked, shrugging.

"It's not your fault," Jessica said. "It's mine."

She should have encouraged Alex and Lucas to go as soon as the O'Neals had gotten in trouble. The Duharts would have happily left, and with Fana here, who would have stood in their way? And she never should have disclosed so much to Cal, Nita and Lucas, just as she should have found a way to delay Justin O'Neal's sentencing. Would she ever grow wise, or would the years pass her unmarked in every way?

"What about Cal?" Jessica said.

"I only made him sleep at the steering wheel before he could do more harm. He is awake again. But his mood—"

"Leave him alone, Teka. Lucas was right. He'll survive his mood."

Teka shrugged. "But will the rest of us?"

Jessica felt hot irritation. "God gave us free will, Teka. It offends us to our souls when it's taken from us."

"As it should, Jessica," Teka said, and he smiled. But Jessica knew what he left unsaid: Dawit had confessed that Khaldun had exerted a form of mind control over his colony for centuries. Khaldun had been the Life Brothers' example of leadership, and old habits were hard to break.

"I have had a message from Fana," Teka said.

"When?"

Teka's smile widened. "During my meditations earlier tonight, I sensed a presence close to me. I wasn't certain at the time, but now I believe it was Fana. Mahmoud's warning held great resonance because he confirmed what my unconscious had already learned from Fana's visit. She warned me of danger from others with the Blood."

"Then she knows?" Jessica said, elated. If Fana knew, she could protect herself!

"What else she knows, I cannot say. But this is very much to the good, Jessica. Fana is exploring her gifts. She will need them. We all may."

Jessica sat on the floor at Teka's knees, the student's position Fana often assumed, like the Japanese sitting style in yoga. Legs folded beneath her, she cupped her kneecaps with her palms. Jessica understood why Fana and the Life Brothers trusted and respected Teka so much; a foot in front of him, she could feel the incandescence of what might be his aura. She had felt nothing like it since her audience with Khaldun in Lalibela.

"Teka, tell me about the other child," Jessica said. "Dawit doesn't believe in him."

"He doesn't want to," Teka corrected her. "But he believes in the possibility, certainly."

"Did Khaldun know?"

"I would not presume to say what Khaldun did or did not know. He never said so."

"Would this other child . . . have Fana's gifts?"

Jessica saw something she didn't recognize play across Teka's lips. Was it fear?

"If he exists . . . he may. Yes."

"Would he be as powerful?" She almost said *dangerous,* the truer word.

"If he has had fifty years, as Mahmoud claims, he knows himself in ways Fana cannot. Especially if he has had a good teacher. But even without a teacher . . . " Teka closed his eyes. "Fana may not have the capacity to match him. Not yet. Her best hope is to elude him."

Jessica's knees shuddered against the floor. A being *more* powerful than Fana?

"What will happen to her?"

Teka's eyes opened. "I do not share Khaldun's gift for future sight, Jessica. But I will go to my quarters and sit in stillness. Perhaps she will find me again."

"What can I do for her?" Jessica had felt useless since the day Fana had disappeared into trance, where only Teka could truly reach her—and Khaldun, when he chose. But Fana said she had not sensed Khaldun in many years. Khaldun had left the Lalibela Colony after more than five hundred years, believing that Fana's birth had set him free. How could Khaldun remain so remote, when he considered Fana so vital? How could Khaldun abandon his legacy?

"Protect her home," Teka answered her. "Protect the ones she loves."

Jessica thought of Bea, fighting to breathe. Alex, piteously silenced. Lucas, bruised and broken. Jared's anger and disappointment. The horrible, unintended betrayal of the Duharts.

Yes, she wanted to protect the people Fana loved.

But protect them from whom?

Eighteen

Casa Grande
5:07 a.m.

Johnny hadn't slept all night. He heard Charlie's soft snoring beside him, and the mingled heavy breathing from Fana and Caitlin beyond the wall. How could *anyone* sleep?

He had to get out of here. Johnny had made his decision right after midnight, and he should have been up long before now.

His plan was simple: disarm the alarm, sneak out of the house, find a phone, call his parents. To make sure the call couldn't be traced to the Rolfsons, he would take a bus to another city, which would take most of the day. He'd find a wireless kiosk with 'net phones. He had one of his dad's credit cards, so the call wouldn't be traced to his name.

It wasn't a perfect plan, but it was the only one he had. Now he needed the nerve.

Johnny was good at creeping around his roommate, so he dressed without a sound. In his wallet, he found a business card he'd taken from someone offering him a summer job at Tallahassee Memorial. He sacrificed the hookup to write Caitlin a note:

5:10 a.m.—C, I DISARMED THE ALARM. MUST BE RESET.
WENT TO FIND A PHONE TO SAY I'M OK. SORRY.

Johnny was glad he wouldn't be here when Caitlin woke up and saw his note.

He crept to the other side of the room and recognized Caitlin's breathing from the bed closest to him. Caitlin's covers were pulled to her chin, bunched up as if to protect her. When she'd spent the night in his bed at Berkeley, she'd stolen all of the covers and wrapped herself around the wad like a fetus. A blanket hound. He could have learned to live with it, though.

Johnny stared at Caitlin's sleeping face until he could see her lips, loose and pink.

I might as well kiss her good-bye, he thought. Caitlin would never speak to him again.

But if he had to lose Caitlin's friendship to jump out of this insanity, fine with him. He wanted Glow for Omari, but he wasn't going to follow Caitlin to Mexico.

"Sorry, Caitlin," Johnny whispered. "This is too much drama."

If he got arrested for anything to do with Glow, no med school in the country would consider his application. Wouldn't he do the world more good by getting his M.D. degree?

Johnny slipped the business card as close to Caitlin's face as he dared, at the edge of her mattress. On the way to the stairs, Johnny walked softly past Fana's bed.

Fana slept flat on her back, her arms planted at her sides as if she had forced herself to sleep by pure will. Fana was in a deep sleep, but her face looked so troubled that Johnny wanted to shake her and take her with him. But fanaticism burned in Fana's eyes when she talked about Glow, like she thought she was Sojourner Truth or Harriet Tubman. Fana wouldn't turn back.

Johnny gazed at the bulb of her nose, the dip between her chin and lips, her high-hewn Ethiopian cheekbones and striking eyelashes. Fana wasn't little anymore, but she wasn't as adult as she thought she was. He'd ask Dad to call Fana's parents too, if he knew how.

A few strategic bumps with his shoulder, and the door opened with a quiet *swish* against the tiled floor upstairs. He was glad he was skinny and could slip through a narrow opening. No one in the hallway. No one in the darkened kitchen. Silence in the house except the humming fridge.

Johnny closed the hidden door and bookshelf quietly behind him. A dislodged hardcover bounced on his head, but he caught it before it hit the floor, his heart racing.

Johnny let himself breathe. So far, so good.

The alarm panel was near the kitchen entry. Johnny pushed Disarm, and a friendly green light came on. Now all he had to do was open the front door and disappear.

But he didn't. Johnny's nose caught an undercurrent he thought was from the kitchen, maybe from a meat package left on the counter overnight. But suddenly he realized the smell wasn't coming from the kitchen at all: It was from *left* of him. The hallway.

Johnny smelled blood. A lot of it. He'd never worked in an emergency room, cleaned up a car accident or stepped on a mine, but he knew the smell by instinct. Wet, rusting copper.

Johnny's peripheral vision sharpened, and he wondered how he hadn't noticed giant letters scrawled on the hallway wall behind him. There was just enough light thrown against the wall from the kitchen window for Johnny to see what was written:

AND BLOOD
TOUCHETH BLOOD

The two-foot-high letters took up much of the wall, two words stacked upon two in a script that would have been perfect except that it was runny at the loops and edges. The words had been written with great care. With effort and time.

In blood.

Johnny gagged. He pinched his larynx to stop its flailing. His fingers and neck pulsed with a manic call and response. *Where did that come from?*

The bloody writing on the wall was sharp under his nose, but it wasn't enough to fill up the hallway. Johnny was sure there was more blood close by. His heart whipped his rib cage, urging him to run, but his legs were locked, knees unsteady.

A doorway was open six paces ahead of him, on the left. Nate's room. Nate had invited him into his room yesterday to show him his collection of Zonehead graphic novels, Japanese manga. The deepest dread of Johnny's life burrowed into his stomach in the hall.

Just leave NOW. Johnny was shocked at how certain his inner voice sounded, without any worries for the welfare of others; a clean line of thinking.

"Nate?" Johnny called anyway. His voice was thin and wavering.

Johnny walked past the bloody message to Nate's waiting room, half-hidden in darkness.

Nate was lying on the floor, facedown in plush carpet. He was wearing brightly colored pajamas, Mutant Men. He lay not two steps from his doorway. Nate's bare heels were so pale that they seemed to glow in the dark. Nate wasn't moving.

Please let this be a joke, Johnny thought.

"Stop playing around," Johnny said. He nudged Nate's shoulder with his toe, and his shoe sank into moisture. He stepped away, leaving a dark footprint on the hall's white tile just outside of Nate's door. But Johnny saw a large purple ring in the blue carpet around Nate's head. The smell gave it away: The carpet was soggy with blood. A stain was creeping onto the hall tile beyond the room, like spilled paint.

"N-Nate?" Johnny said. His heart pummeled him. "You OK?"

Johnny knelt beside Nate and immediately felt blood seep through the denim at his knees. The blood was cold. Nate was definitely not OK.

But Johnny felt for a pulse anyway. His fingers slipped across Nate's slick neck. Nate's skin was slightly warm, but Johnny couldn't feel any sign that his heart was beating.

Johnny grasped Nate by his shoulders and rolled him over to start CPR.

Nate's face was painted red with blood. His eyes and mouth were wide open, all dribbling blood. His nostrils were caked with blood, runny. Bloody teeth grinned at Johnny. Nate's face looked waxen, cheeks hollowed, skin ghostly pale. Nate was dead. Nate hardly looked human.

For the first time in his life, Johnny screamed.

The next thing he exactly remembered was Caitlin crying. And arguing between Caitlin and Charlie. But that must have come later.

At some point he had opened every door in the house until he found the Rolfsons' master bedroom, which smelled of blood, too.

The husband and wife lay at arm's length from each other, both lying on their backs, bloody eyes staring, sightless, at their bedroom's wood-beam cathedral ceiling and a skylight above them; an uncaring eye of morning light. Mitchell Rolfson's hair and beard were so damp with blood that they were matted to his skin. Their pillows were crimson.

Behind him, Caitlin was crying. "Fuckfuckfuckfuckfuckfuck*fuck*."

When Caitlin wasn't crying, she was swearing. Pacing. Grabbing handfuls of her hair.

"Who did this?" Caitlin said. "Who could d-do this?"

Charlie was running around the room like a bandit, stuffing clothes into duffel bags, his hands in gardening gloves. "*Chica,* I don't know shit," Charlie said, "but we need to get ghost."

Caitlin suddenly looked at Charlie as if she had never seen him before. Wild-eyed. "Where were you last night?"

"Oh, sure, I came up for a drink of water and then I killed everybody," Charlie spat, red-faced. "What the fuck are you talking about? Ask this guy where *he* was."

Johnny had a headache, and the arguing was unbearable. His knees felt weighted with fifty-pound sandbags, as if he'd been bedridden. He walked to the Rolfsons' oak sleigh bed and turned on the nightstand lamp so he could see better.

Johnny tried not to notice the wedding photo on the night stand, smiling faces on a Hawaiian mountainside. He tried to forget that Sheila Rolfson was a minister, and that her congregation was expecting to see her on Sunday morning. And that their son was lying dead down the hall. Remembering those things only made him tired.

Johnny tipped the lampshade for an unflinching beam on Mitchell's face. This man had the same ghostly pallor as Nate. As if every drop of blood in his body was gone.

"There are no injuries," Johnny said quietly. "Just blood."

Caitlin and Charlie gaped at him. Caitlin had grabbed the sleeve of Mitchell Rolfson's sweatshirt when she'd first gotten to the room, but she hadn't come within five yards of the bed once she'd realized how much blood there was.

"Don't touch him," Caitlin said.

"Hey, man, don't leave fingerprints!" Charlie said. "Let the cops do that."

Five years ago, when Johnny had been a high school freshman, he and his classmates had lined up in the auditorium to file past a table where bored government clerks had taken their fingerprints. When he'd applied for a driver's license, he'd had to submit to fingerprints again. Dad had told him there had been a time when only criminals and government employees had had their fingerprints on file, but now everyone did. His fingerprints were all over the house. Charlie had been trying to clean their fingerprints away, but he would miss plenty. Johnny couldn't change that now.

"I'm just saying," Johnny said. He lifted up Mitchell's sweatshirt and found loose skin with no visible injuries; just the same pallor, glowing through uneven tufts of dark hair. "They bled out from their faces. Mouth, nose, eyes. None of us did this, unless it was poison. But I don't know a poison that makes people's eyes bleed. There's viruses, like Ebola. . . ."

He was babbling. Ebola was confined to faraway jungles, and no one in the family had looked sick yesterday. The Rolfsons had not died of Ebola.

"What are you, a damn doctor?" Charlie said.

Johnny shook his head. He didn't have time to tell Charlie that he'd been a science geek all his life. *I have to know. Maybe I can handle waking up to a house full of dead people if I can understand.* But he didn't understand. Something unnatural had happened to these people. Johnny remembered the eerie writing on the wall outside, and his hands shook.

Charlie walked behind Johnny and put his hand on his shoulder. "Hey, man," Charlie said. "I get it. You should have seen what they did to Ethan. They left him in the road like a dog. It's fucked up, but we're all in serious shit if we don't haul ass out of here. One, whoever did this may not be gone. Two, the cops will nail us for this. Think about it: Glow dealers murdered? With Ethan, they made it out like a turf war. We need to get out of here."

"Oh, God," Caitlin said, a deeper realization. A wail. Her eyes cleared, and she looked around the room, frantic. "Where's Fana?"

"Who?" Charlie said.

"Bea-Bea," Caitlin said. She rushed to the Rolfsons' bathroom to look for Fana.

But Fana wasn't in the bathroom. Johnny remembered clearly now, because he always noticed Fana: She had come stumbling out of the basement to see why he'd been yelling, and she's stopped short when she'd seen the writing on the wall. She'd stared and stared.

Then had been seen her slip into Nate's room and close his door, mumbling to herself.

Fana had been zoning, but he couldn't judge her. He was zoning, too.

"She's with Nate," Johnny said. "She said she would try to bring him back."

The bloody rooms were no worse than last night's dreams of wind, rain and death, if only this was a dream too. But the waking sunlight told Fana the truth.

No dream. She was awake.

And blood toucheth blood.

Fana sat on Nate's bed, her hands on her knees as she stared down at his body on the floor. The bed still smelled like freshly bathed skin, scented sweetly like a boy. His toys were everywhere: Action figures, games, comic books, trophies, a GamePort like Hank's at the foot of his bed. Gum wrappers on his nightstand, another pile on the floor. A pair of spotless white Nikes on a shelf beside his closet, treasured. The weight of his unfinished life.

And blood toucheth blood.

Fana felt herself turning to ash, flying away.

Trance. Trance out. Quiet.

"Nate," Fana said aloud, so she would not forget why she was here. Her eyes snapped open, full of the room's horror. Her call became more urgent. "Nate?"

FANA?

She heard Nate, faint but distinct. Somewhere else.

Nate was confused. Confusion was inevitable, at first.

When Grandpa Gaines had been killed in the ditch, Fana had

realized she could hear the dead. She had been in meditation, and his startled confusion had washed over her with a long gasp that had not originated from her own lungs. Through her, Grandpa Gaines had sucked at the air until she'd thought her chest would burst, filled taut with his last taste of the world.

And then he'd let her go. Let the air go. Let the world go. *Good-bye, Fana,* he'd said. She had heard his giddy glee, as if he'd been riding his favorite horse, Moonshine, at a gallop. He still visited her dreams, and sometimes he brought others with him, those he insisted she must meet properly: Randall. Lucille. Patricia. Charlotte, who answered to Lottie. John.

Nate had not found his place yet, nor his people. Nate's freedom confused him.

Nate was much farther from her than Grandpa Gaines had been when he'd died. Far, but not too far to hear. Unbound. Untethered. Leaving had taken him by surprise in the night, and her voice bewildered him more. She was a remnant, a memory of longing. Nate wanted to come to her because he knew nothing else yet.

WHERE ARE YOU? Nate said. A childlike whine.

She might have brought him back if she had come in time. Maybe she would have chased after his spirit if his heart hadn't already cooled in his chest, or if his mother had been wailing at the memory of him sucking at her breast. Fana might have convinced him it wasn't time yet, coaxing him back to the world of skin and sensation, away from the music and lights.

But it was too late. He was following the sound of his parents' laughter on the flight his grandparents had blazed for them. What right did she have to try to stuff him into a cold corpse, even if she could? For whose sake would she bring him? Her own?

Fana shivered. Her desire to bring him back despite everything scared her.

Too late. Her throat and face burned. She had forgotten how painful grieving was, the lesson she'd first learned at three, too late for a baby's oblivion, but too soon for her heart.

Good-bye, Nate. Travel well.

GOODBYE FANA

He was gone. All he'd needed was assurance. For an instant, Fana thought she smiled.

Then came the withering doubt and fear, unceasing. The barrage of questions.

Did I do this?

Was it me?

For the first time since she was three, Fana remembered how a man had died when her mother had taken her to the colony in Ethiopia. He had been a big man, and he'd frightened her. He had tried to hurt her, which had filled her with rage, and blood had seeped from his face and pores. Had she dreamed her rage? Had it come to life while she'd slept, rampaging above her, mindless?

Am I this awful?

Fana suddenly felt that the others were in the room with her. She didn't know how long they had been talking, or what they had said to her.

Hands clasping hers, indistinguishable. Colliding voices, murmuring.

Trance. Trance out. The questions hurt too much.

"Fana?"

A living voice brought her back. Eyes the color of Grandpa Gaines's saddle, and lashes like black down. His scent cradled her, fresh spring soap. His hands warm in hers.

"You're safe, *negra,*" Charlie said. "You're safe with us. We have to go now."

Fana rose.

Caitlin's chest jabbed her when she saw the hidden cabinet in the garage open, the broken lock on the floor. The lock had been pried off. *Shit.* She kneeled in front of the cabinet, and two barren shelves stared back.

All twenty-five bags of Glow were gone. The Glow had such a high potency that the mixture had been dark pink instead of clear. Those twenty-five bags could have been diluted to hundreds more. Thousands, handled properly. All of it, gone.

But that figured, Caitlin thought. The immortals always took back their blood.

Caitlin's nose and cheeks were raw from tears. It almost seemed funny now: On a morning like this, she had expected to find the Glow?

She still had Fana. There would be more Glow.

"You missed us, you assholes," Caitlin whispered. "We were right underneath you, and you missed us."

Despite the smudges of blood beneath Caitlin's fingernails, the dead bodies inside the house didn't feel real yet. Caitlin had washed her hands for ten minutes, but she hadn't been able to get all of the blood out, just like the scene from *Macbeth* she had first read in Mitch's tenth-grade class: "*Will all great Neptune's ocean wash this blood / Clean from my hands?*"

When a cigarette appeared in front of her, Caitlin snatched it without looking up and clamped it into her mouth. Charlie's lighter was there a heartbeat later.

Caitlin coughed, surprised by the taste.

"Clove," he said.

Caitlin took a deep drag. She didn't like clove cigarettes, but nicotine was nicotine. She felt guilty that she could salvage any pleasure on a morning as horrible as this, but feeling better was almost like feeling good, for a quick sip of time.

"Protocol says we split up," Caitlin said.

"I wish," he said quietly. "But Fana's zoning bad. She's pretty fragile for the Raiload, isn't she? And young. Whose idea was it to let a kid run away from home?"

Caitlin's face vibrated, as if she'd been slapped. Her eyes ached, but no tears came. She suddenly saw Mitchell grading papers at his desk a week after Lawrence Flanagan had been hit by that old man who'd run a red light, when his parents had been about to take him off life support. *I'm going to tell you something, Mr. Rolfson, but you have to promise you'll never tell anyone.*

Caitlin's stomach felt like it was bleeding. "Please don't fuck with me right now."

"Never mind," Charlie said, looking toward the Cruiser. Fana was sitting in the backseat with Johnny, her head on his shoulder. "I like her. I'm worried about her."

"Let me worry about her."

"We'll go together," Charlie said. "That's what Fana wants. All of us."

"And if we get caught together?"

Caitlin hadn't known Charlie long, but this morning had taught her that he was invaluable to Laurel's operation in Canada. She was embarrassed about the way she had gone off on him in the bedroom, accusing him of the killings. When she had whispered in Fana's ear to ask her if Charlie had done it, Fana had shaken her head. Fana would know.

"I don't get caught," Charlie said. "I'm ghost at the first sign of trouble."

Caitlin studied him to see if there was any irony in his eyes; there wasn't. Good for him. The Railroad needed survivors now.

"Ride your bike," she said.

"Right behind you."

Behind her. Why was he trusting her to lead?

"I like your idea about Mexico," he said.

"We're being followed. They knew where to look."

"They didn't know enough," he said.

"They might be waiting for us."

Charlie reached around to the back of his waistband, his hand returning with a nickel-plated .38. "I'll be waiting too," he said. "This was in Mitch's closet."

Caitlin remembered Sheila as a staunch gun control advocate, so she was surprised there was a gun in the Rolfsons' house. She was grateful, but sad. She wished she could go to the police and confess. She hadn't killed the Rolfsons, but she was responsible. If not for Fana, Caitlin would have gone to jail gladly.

"You're right," Caitlin whispered. "I shouldn't have brought Fana."

"Screw that," Charlie said. "Can't change it now. We've just gotta' make sure nothing happens to her. It's up to you and me."

"Johnny was going to sneak out right before he found the bodies," Caitlin blurted. It was a relief to have backup. She'd been on her own too long. "I found a note he wrote me."

Charlie's eyes widened. He glanced toward the car, where Johnny was sitting in the backseat beside Fana, waiting. "You think? . . ."

"I know there's no way Johnny killed those people," Caitlin said.

"Then how did the killers get past the alarm?"

"I don't know. Someone with skills could rig an override. I know Johnny, and killing isn't in him. But he did shut off the alarm this morning. Even if they were already dead, he would have left us exposed. He's definitely zoning too. So like you said, it's up to us."

Caitlin couldn't be mad at Johnny. Fresh tears burned her cheeks. She had hurt everyone she cared about. Caitlin wanted to tell Charlie everything, suddenly. About her father. About Fana and the immortals. About the blood. Caitlin's hands shook violently as she was overcome by the loneliness of the secret. She remembered her cigarette and took another drag. She should never have told Charlie Fana's name, she reminded herself. She was falling apart.

"I'll be fine once we're on the road," she said, trying to convince herself.

"Take a minute," Charlie said. "They were your friends."

Firmly, Caitlin shook her head. "We don't have a minute. No more mistakes."

"No such thing, *chica*," Charlie said. "There's always one more."

Always one more, Caitlin thought, newly terrorized as she realized what a holocaust her life had become. *Until the last one.*

Nineteen

Fana's eyes were dry from not blinking, but blinking was dangerous. Fana needed her eyes to stay open and take in the light. The
light kept her from drifting. She catalogued everything she saw as
the miles flew past her window: Eight Burger Kings. Five gas sta-
tions. Six Taco Bells. Ten Subways. Anything to occupy her eyes.

She looked for Charlie again, but he was nowhere in sight in the
heavy flow of midmorning traffic. Motor homes, eighteen-wheelers
and panel trucks blocked her view beyond a few yards in any direction. Fana's heart sped. Had he peeled off at the last exit?

If he had, he might be safer. Why had she asked him to come
with her?

They'll end up like Aunt Alex. Or Nate Rolfson.

Fana didn't want to stay awake to remember her carnage at the
Rolfsons' house. She was her friends' worst nightmare, in plain sight.
Worse than a nightmare.

She had to go home. To see Teka. Her parents.

But Caitlin would never agree to drive her home without inva-
sive mental prodding, and Fana couldn't drive herself. Johnny would
leave with her in a heartbeat, but how could she be sure she wouldn't
lead him to more trouble? And she didn't dare take a bus or a train
alone, where she might accidentally kill someone with a thought if
she slept.

Trance. Trance out.

A motorcycle's engine revved beside her, waking Fana's mind. It was Charlie, riding alongside the car. He ducked down, smiling at her: *You all right?*

Fana's insides warmed. She sat a bit straighter, not the hunched ball her body kept twisting into. Seeing Charlie helped her breathe.

Fana smiled back at him even though she didn't mean to; if she could stop smiling at him, he might go away. After a wave, Charlie fell away from them, drifting to the outer lane. He had been floating beside them since they'd left Casa Grande, in and out of traffic.

"'And blood toucheth blood,'" Fana said.

Caitlin glanced back at her, startled. "What?"

Fana's heart pounded. She hadn't meant to speak aloud. "That message on the wall, 'And blood toucheth blood.' I was thinking those words yesterday. I heard them, in my mind."

Caitlin's attention went back to the road. "Like your dream about the priest?"

"Except . . . much stronger. It made me feel sick. I had to lie down. I th-think . . ."

Could she make herself say the words?

"A premonition," Johnny said. His voice was weary to the bone as he stared out of his window. "My grandmother has those. Dreams that come true . . ." He looked like he wanted to go on, but he only sighed. Thoughts of his grandmother in Georgia were torture to him; he was afraid of shaming his family.

"I . . . killed them," Fana blurted.

Johnny's head bobbed with surprise. He peered at her with slitted eyes.

Caitlin's eyes locked with hers in the rearview mirror. "What?"

Fana's jaw shook. "I killed them," she said. "All of them."

Johnny shook his head. "Maybe it feels that way—"

"Don't say that, Fana," Caitlin said. "That's not true. They knew there were risks. Having a premonition doesn't mean you made it happen. And it doesn't mean you could have stopped it," Caitlin said. "But the next time you get that feeling, we definitely need to know. As *soon* as it happens, Fana. Understand?"

Fana had spoken the words she had been most afraid to utter, and neither of them had heard. Would they be more willing to believe if she told them about the man she exsanguinated in Lalibela? Or another she'd killed at the airport in Rome? *Da Vinci airport. A sick man staring at a little girl the wrong way. Staring at me.*

The past didn't seem so distant and hazy anymore. At the airport, Fana had stopped the beating of a man's heart simply by thinking the words *Bye Bye*. No wonder she'd made herself forget. Had it been that easy to her then? Could it still be that easy now?

Fana trembled. Her bones were trying to fly away from her, too.

"Hey, Fana . . . it's gonna' be OK," Johnny said. He was petrified, but his desire to comfort her made him sound so certain that she believed him. "I promise."

And blood toucheth blood. Fana was angry at herself for not telling Caitlin about the eerie words in her head, but what could Caitlin have done? Fana realized she had heard that gravelly voice before, when she was young. That voice had encouraged her to hurt people.

Fana wanted to stay far from that voice, but she had to find the source of it! Could the voice tell her more about the immortals who were stalking them? Fana's heart pounded. She probed as far as she could in any direction.

Her mind nearly buckled. She felt blind.

"They're close to us," Fana said. "One of them is masking. I feel it."

Fana gazed behind her, looking for Charlie. She could no longer see him clearly; he had fallen back several car lengths. There! He was coasting at a steady speed behind a Hummer, with the faded kneecap of his jeans occasionally drifting into sight. Even a nudge from a car could send him crashing to his death. She wished he'd been riding in the car with them. It would have been safer.

Fana remembered Charlie's last smile outside her window so clearly that she could see his face reflected back at her in the glass. The memory of last night's kiss plowed its way past the morning's horror and filled her stomach with a gentle glow. Her first kiss.

Fana tried to imagine a blanket over their car, and one stretching as far back as Charlie. Could she mask him? She hoped so, but she wasn't sure. He felt far away from her now.

"We have to hide," Fana said. "Somewhere secluded."

"You're damn right we do," Caitlin said. "First stop, Mexico. Then . . .

who knows? After I turn around some Glow, we can go wherever we want. *Anywhere*, Fana." Caitlin glanced back at Fana in the rearview mirror, bravely smiling while her eyes looked for police cars.

"Police aren't our problem," Fana said. "We have a tail. He's watching us."

The person chasing them was a man. Suddenly Fana was sure of it. She tried to refine the mental impression, but it only vanished. Gone. Fana scanned the faces in the cars behind them: Mothers. Businesspeople. College students. She knew them in passing: Running late. Lost a job. Pregnant. Dying.

As the collection of lives roared to life, Fana felt police nearby, too. The officers' thoughts were a clear drumbeat: *White PT Cruiser.*

"The police know what our car looks like," Fana said.

Johnny stared out the window. "I don't see any police," he said. "How do you know?"

"I told you," Fana said. "I know things."

"Can you do anything about it?" Caitlin said.

"I'll try." Fana closed her eyes.

Fana visualized her parents' Orbit, a deep, dark black. She imagined the Washington State tag instead of the California license tag on the PT Cruiser, and a random jumble of numbers and letters. A heartbeat later, she felt the police car pass them.

Fana opened her eyes in time to see an Arizona highway patrol car speed ahead in the lane to the left. Fana was relieved, but she didn't allow herself to be distracted from her larger task. The police were not nearly as dangerous as an unknown entity.

"Shit," Caitlin whispered. "First chance we get, I'm dumping this car."

"That's where you can drop me off," Johnny said. "I'm ghost."

"We're staying together," Caitlin said.

"Nobody's keeping me anywhere I don't want to be," he said. "Believe it."

Fana sighed and stared out her window again, searching the faces. The bickering between Caitlin and Johnny and the combined mental noise on the highway threatened to swallow Fana, but her mind ducked beneath the noise and kept probing.

Like Teka always said, noise couldn't hurt her.

I'm going to find you, Fana thought, projecting into the haze. *You can't hide from me.*

Michel slipped on his earpiece.

Telephones were a nuisance, but his father couldn't be reached any other way. Papa's telepathic skills were so rudimentary that he might as well have had none, and his two attendants were worse. Only his mate would be able to meet him across the miles for easy conversation.

Michel could barely hear his father's connection over the wind as he raced after the white car ferrying his precious cargo. The vehicle was out of his sight, but Fana's vibration was strong. This close to her, sometimes Michel forgot to breathe. He felt her clumsy probes skitter across his consciousness, repelled so gently that she could not feel him. Her probes were delightful.

She fit him. The only one. Their minds would touch over hundreds of miles.

"Where in the world are you, Michel?" his father's voice said on the flimsy earpiece. "Romero and Bocelli said the family was dead when they got there. And you evaded them."

"I changed the plan," Michel said. "Too many would have died. It would have brought her too much pain."

"Where in the world are you?"

"On my way."

The car was close. Michel heard the angry thoughts of Fana's two friends as they argued, misguided but faithful. Michel hoped he would not be cruel to them. Fana swept the road with another probe, and Michel's toes shivered.

"Fana is brilliant, Papa. I am fully concealed, yet she has taught herself to sense my presence. She cannot find me, and yet she knows I am here. She makes me work like no one else. The things she will learn!"

"Where is she?" his father said.

Michel could see her again. Fana was staring out the window.

Still looking for him.

"I am gazing at her lovely profile right now."

"Be careful, Michel. Wait until you reach us before any games begin."

Did all parents treat their offspring like perpetual children?

"Of course, Papa. You've said nothing about my triumph!"

Michel had killed the family without entering their rooms, wielding only his thoughts, as precise as lasers. All three had died at the same instant, pleasantly dreaming an identical dream about their last night together. No person could match such a feat except Fana herself.

Stefan sighed. "The bloody writing . . . was unnecessary."

It was exactly like Papa to ignore so much success and seek out a fault! Bocelli and Romero had recovered twenty-five bags of diluted Blood at the house. Blood stolen two thousand years ago was being recovered one drop at a time. Had there ever been a more effective servant of the Blood than he?

"If our time has come, why should we hide?" Michel spoke as Most High, not as a son.

"Those are the old ways," Stefan said, his voice placating. "So much spectacle is distasteful. It's best not to alienate our friends."

"They did not suffer, but their example had to be striking. They were thieves. 'By stealing . . . they break out . . . And blood toucheth blood,'" Michel said, reciting from Hosea. Next, he recited the Letter of the Witness: "'Let he who stands over the Blood . . .'"

"I'm familiar with the passages," his father said. "Since you're quoting the Letter, remember Chapter 4, verse 2: 'Any hand that toucheth the Blood with impure heart. . . .'"

. . . *will be damned to walk forever accursed.* Michel had memorized every page as a boy. What child would not delight in learning that a two-thousand-year-old Gospel had already been written about him? That burden made his father's rebuke sting all the more.

"So . . . I am impure?"

"Of course not, Michel. But do not reveal yourself yet. Your ways are foreign, and you'll raise questions. Romero and Bocelli should have done the killing. Conventionally."

Michel's father's voice was chopped by the wind, nearly inaudible.

"What kind of ruler, Papa, expects others to stain themselves with blood on his behalf?"

"Most I have known!" Stefan said, and laughed. But why shouldn't he be laughing? Untold numbers of men over time had awaited the New Days, only to be disappointed. God's glory would unfold through Michel at last. And Fana.

"Give me your location," Stefan said. "I'll send Romero and Bocelli."

"No," Michel said. "If I cannot bring her alone, I do not deserve her."

"Don't count on hiding from her," Stefan said. "Find a way to harness her, Michel."

What else could he expect his father to say? "I have no need to sully her will," Michel said. "Her every thought is naked to me."

Soon, the rest of her. Michel knew he could have had her last night if he had persisted, and their union would have been complete. Fana's body was at its ripest, a newly formed woman. Waiting was excruciating. But soon enough.

"When will I see you?" Stefan said.

"By sunset."

"I am eager beyond words to meet her. *Benedetto sia il Sangue.*"

"Papa! I've almost forgotten the most exciting news . . ."

But his father was gone. Michel almost activated Voice Redial, but he decided to wait. He would save the best news for his return.

Michel's mother refused to look upon Stefan or speak to him unless she was mentally compelled, which caused his father daily regret. But Michel would not be doomed to relive his father's tragic entanglement. Fana would stay with him willingly. Forever.

Michel sped up, racing in the narrow space between two vehicles. He was so close to Fana that he could hear her heartbeat. Michel revved his engine.

Fana looked around, surprised. Michel grinned at her.

Fana smiled back at him, the very face of Paradise. She lifted her lithe fingers in a small, tentative wave. *Hi, Charlie,* she mouthed, and her caring eyes brightened every part of him. *Be careful,* she said, tapping gently on the glass.

Would Papa ever believe it?

His dear Fana loved him already.

SANCTUS CRUOR

And let he who stands over the Blood

Take every worldly Measure

To wrest this Blood from the hands of the wicked . . .
—Letter of the Witness
Chapter 1, verse 5

Twenty

When the knocker sounded against the double doors, Stefan watched from the balcony as the two doorkeepers scattered to greet the visitors. The bright uniforms of red and white were the only visual sign of the future splendor of Sanctus Cruor's first church in North America. The regal coats looked out of place among the debris and tarp that lay in place of pews, but soon this church would gleam with gold, a beacon to visitors worldwide.

When the double doors opened, bright midmorning light unveiled sheets of dust motes floating in the vast space like blizzard snows.

Bishop Ian Paddock was pink-faced, winded from the steep walk outside. Cardinal Amadi Owodunni followed him, his crimson cardinal's robe aflame on black skin. Paddock lifted his crimson robe at the collar to invite in a breeze but Owodunni was from Nigeria and thus more accustomed to the sun. When the two visitors paused at the bowl to cross themselves, Paddock applied the holy water as if to relieve the heat.

He should take better care of his delicate mortal heart, Stefan thought.

Guided by the doorkeepers, Paddock and Owodunni carefully walked around a pile of lumber left behind by the work crew. The pews would be built of rare, expensive Amboyna burl imported from Southeast Asia. The floors, polished Italian marble.

Paddock and Owodunni were prime Sanctus Cruor followers—

one with the media's ear, the other sitting on the edge of St. Peter's chair. Owodunni enjoyed worldwide popularity, and Paddock was both a friend of the pope's secretary and well-liked by a wide array of conclave voters.

If these servants proved wise and true, mortal concerns would trouble them no more.

The doorkeepers drew pearl-handled handguns from the white leather shoulder holsters they wore above their robes, a ceremony that was as practical as it was theatrical. The guns startled Paddock and Owodunni. They did not yet understand.

If Stefan had known that Michel was bringing the girl today, he never would have scheduled a meeting with Paddock and Owodunni. But despite Fana's importance, this meeting could not wait. The New Days could not wait.

Michel would be ready to lead when the girl walked beside him. The Letter had prophesied it. Soon, miracles would be broadcast for the world over to see, and there would be only one church. After that day, all weapons could be laid to rest. All the world would bow in obedience and give thanks, at last, to its proper Master.

Until then, there was much business to attend to.

Stefan waved to his guests from above. "Do not judge us by our disarray," he called in English, their common language. "There is much left to do here. Please follow my good men to our temporary rectory."

The rectory was more finished, with gleaming African mahogany walls that still smelled of the wood's motherland. Scrolls of lambskin parchment lined the walls, written in Ge'ez. The sole painting was a ten-foot rendering of the golden Sanctus Cruor cross with a fist-sized ruby at its heart, representing the Blood. The painting stilled Stefan's heart with its beauty.

The men's eyes were hungry as they studied the rectory from his doorway.

"Do come in," Stefan said.

Owodunni sank to both knees, presenting himself in the manner reserved for the pope. Paddock followed the African's bow. "Most Excellent," they said, heads lowered.

Stefan knew enough about both men to have them

excommunicated—even arrested, in Paddock's case. Paddock had curbed his taste for rough carnal games with prostitutes only recently, after being named bishop. Owodunni was a corrupt thief, and he defied doctrine by working secretly with African leaders to distribute condoms throughout the continent; Stefan couldn't guess which actions his church would frown on more. Both men were flawed in their church's eyes, but they were believers in the Blood. Both had tasted the Blood's healing.

"Please rise, my friends," Stefan said, lifting his arms to fan out the sleeves of his crimson robe. Stefan sat in the leather chair beside his library table and crossed his legs. "For the moment, let us forget ceremony. I'm sorry your trip was such a hardship."

Both men protested that their travels had been no trouble, although Stefan knew they had spent hours stranded at the airport in Mexico City, and the mountain road to the church from Nogales was dusty and bumpy, still unpaved. Both of them were lying and didn't realize it. Casual sin was so easy, even to the vigilant.

"The conference went well?" Stefan said. The International Health Alliance meeting in Mexico City had been attended by religious leaders from throughout the world, the occasion that had brought the two men to Stefan's doorstep.

Owodunni grinned. "Praise God, there is finally cooperation from the United States."

"My calls are returned immediately, Most Excellent," Paddock said. "Extraordinary."

Stefan's friends at the CDC had helped mend relations between the U.S. and the clergy-led health alliance—for a price. Stefan and the CDC had history: The same friends had helped manufacture the U.S. government's case against Glow, fanning talk of bioterrorism. Stefan had learned the art of recruiting mortal allies a hundred years ago. The United States government and Sanctus Cruor had widely separate agendas, but it was always useful to have friends.

Paddock and Owodunni were two of his favorites.

"I owed you thanks for my last visit with His Honor," Stefan said. "Lolek was so ill. If not for your assistance . . ." He gestured delicately that it would have been too late.

Paddock's jowl trembled. "I am only grateful to have been of service. God rest his soul."

Lolek's death still grieved Stefan. The pointlessness of it all! If Lolek had embraced the Blood when he'd met him in Poland, Sanctus Cruor would have had the papacy years ago. But Lolek had been stubborn from the start, with no stomach for talk of Cleansing.

Stefan opened the crystal decanter on the library table beside him. He poured three shots of tequila, a drink he far preferred to wine. Stefan flung back his glass and basked in his throat's stinging. His visitors drained their glasses too, although their faces told Stefan that they loathed the taste. They were natural followers.

"Our departed friend was misguided," Stefan said. "Lolek misunderstood God's will. But times will soon be different, and God's will won't be mistaken. One day, the pope will never die."

"By the Lord's grace," Paddock said. His eyes were afire.

"What a blessing," Owodunni whispered.

Stefan poured a second round. "Our sitting pope is a ship's captain with neither map nor compass. He revels in his ignorance of the Witness."

Owodunni shook his head. "Such a sad dilemma."

Paddock sighed, exasperated. "His rigidity is notorious, Most Excellent."

"So when he, too, passes away from us . . ." Stefan said, ". . . the New Days will begin."

The construction workers pounded below, and Michel and his bride were on their way to lead the future church. The moment was a marvel, as much as the day the Letter of the Witness had first come to his hands. His acquisition had been as unlikely as the farmer's unearthing of the Coptic Gospels in Nag Hammadi, Egypt, or the goat herders' discovery of the Dead Sea Scrolls in the West Bank. Those frivolous texts were dwarfed by the prize Stefan had found in Ethiopia.

Stefan had spent hundreds of hours in prayer to ask God why *he* had been chosen. When he'd found the Letter, he had not attended church since he was a boy, having run away to fish the Red Sea when he was fourteen. A series of ventures had taken him from France to

Yemen and, finally, to Ethiopia, where he had made a living in the coffee trade in Harer.

But guns had sold better than coffee. It had been 1894, and war had been on the horizon. Italy had been encroaching upon Ethiopian soil, and Stefan had sold guns to all customers with currency or barter.

One day, Stefan and an Englishman who'd smuggled Remingtons with him had been ambushed by bandits. The mortally wounded Brit had begged Stefan to take him by horseback to a shaded area near Harer's wall, where he'd said he had buried a chest. The man had never given his name, only repeating that he'd wanted to retrieve something his father had given him. His father, he'd said, had been a soldier and a man of God, at odds with his conscience after the Battle of Maqdar in 1868.

Return what you find to its people, he'd said. And then he'd drawn his last breath.

Stefan had dug to retrieve a chest from the earth, hoping for treasure. Instead, he'd found a document so old that its parchment had felt like dust to his fingers. The pages had been written in Ge'ez. Stefan had realized that it must have been one of the sacred texts taken by English troops during the battle twenty-six years earlier. Hidden somehow.

Stefan had planned to take the document to London to have its value assessed, but one night his houseboy had seen him studying the parchment, and he'd offered to translate the ancient, holy script. For four hours, by lamplight, Stefan had first heard the Letter of the Witness.

And his life had been forever changed.

I am only a storyteller, not worthy of worship, the document had begun.

I was trading in the Jewish city of Jerusalem in the days before Passover with my stores of wine, grapes, figs and sheaves. I bought an ass to ride to Alexandria, but the beast was ill. I was arguing with the farmer when there came a commotion. There are many executions during Passover, to bring fear to the people. That day, the Romans executed two thieves and a rabbi. I was sorry for their agony, and I wished I could set their feet down on the earth to relieve their suffering. But what could one man do?

I slept against a wall because I had no lodging. A Roman soldier came to me in the night, running and short of breath. I expected him to berate me, but he treated me as a brother, showing me a goatskin skein full of blood. When I held out my finger, he poured a drop of blood to my fingertip that was as cold as rainwater. "Is this blood from a man or a beast?" I asked the man in great wonderment, very much afraid that the blood he carried would soon be mine.

The man said to me, "I woke from sleep with a message from God: The crucified Jew named Jesus will walk again. His Blood must be preserved."

The soldier said he knew not what the vision meant, but he had felt a great Spirit pushing him to the place where the rabbi still hung in the dark. His arms were no longer his own. His legs were not his own legs. He climbed on stones to be near the corpse, which did not move or make a sound. He punctured the rabbi's thigh and drained Blood into his pouch. All the while, he said he trembled like a dried leaf in the wind. And there his story ended.

"The Blood will live again," he said to me in his fever. "And let he who stands over the Blood take every worldly Measure to wrest this Blood from the hands of the wicked." I asked him the meaning of his words, but the soldier was so distraught that he wept on my shoulder. Then he went on his way, and I looked on him no more for three days.

On the third day, he came back to my sleeping place. He carried the same skein, but his face was as gray as a storm-cloud. He stammered his words like one afflicted by demons. He told me to feel the skein, and the goatskin was as warm as a human hand. He said he had slept on the skein as his pillow, and he woke because he felt a living thing against his ear. The skein was warm. He held the skein in his hands to see if it would cool, but its warmth lived.

The Blood lived.

The story had been mesmerizing even to an unbeliever, but Stefan still had not comprehended God's bigger plan until he'd reached the document's last page: There, a smear of blood, still slightly moist to the touch, had made the pages stick. Words proclaimed a Ceremony to give eternal life.

And God had brought the Blood to Stefan alone!

If only Stefan could have spared the houseboy's life that night. If only the excited youth would not surely have screamed the Letter's secret to anyone who would listen.

"The Most High speaks well of you both," Stefan said to Paddock and Owodunni. "He will want to discuss the future of the new church with his best servants. You, like Saint Peter, will be its architects."

The men only nodded, awestruck. These two men were not yet at the highest level of Sanctus Cruor, when the Blood would be revealed to them, but they had been brought closer to the Truth than any others of weak blood. If they proved effective, they might be the first new initiates in fifty years. Since Teru.

Stefan opened the library table's cabinet and pulled out his small ceremonial dagger of gold. The precious ore glowed on the eager men's faces in flickering shards of light.

Stefan pricked his index finger and squeezed a fat bead of blood to his fingertip. He pressed his bloodied finger against Paddock's forehead. Next, Owodunni's.

The men's eyes closed when he touched them, as if they could feel the heat from their Savior's body. Stefan felt Owodunni shudder beneath his touch.

"You are Sanctus Cruor," Stefan said. "Caretakers of the Blood."

Together, the two men recited the scripture he had asked them to memorize from the Letter of the Witness: "'And let he who stands over the Blood take every worldly measure to wrest this Blood from the hands of the wicked.' Bless the Blood."

"*Benedetto sia il Sangue*," Stefan said, and they repeated the Italian blessing.

Stefan raised his bleeding finger, and both men kissed it as if his Blood had been no more than a stale wafer or a sip of cheap wine.

They dreamed of the day when the Most High, the caretaker chosen by God, might allow them to glimpse the Blood with their own eyes. They imagined that Christ's blood was preserved on an aged shred of fabric salvaged from the hill in Calvary.

Their ignorance almost made Stefan smile. Their lips had already touched the Savior's promised immortality, and they still did not understand.

"Strong men are needed to lead the new church," Stefan said. "Men who are not afraid."

"Not afraid of what, Most Excellent?" Owodunni said, sounding nervous. The cardinal leaned forward to hear the words his heart had hidden from him.

Stefan slid his index finger into his mouth to taste the last of the Blood. He gave each man a fresh white handkerchief and watched as they wiped their foreheads dry. After the soiled handkerchiefs were laid in his waiting palm, Stefan's fingers closed tightly to clutch his Blood.

"Cleansing," Stefan said.

Twenty-one

Dawit slowed his car as he approached Floral Street. The police channels had been quiet all night, until 9:30 that morning. Since then, the chatter from Floral Street had been nonstop.

Day had dawned on the quiet street like a declaration of war.

The little beige house at the end of the cul-de-sac was surrounded by investigative vehicles, with cars squeezed on both curbs halfway down the block. A Pinal County sheriff's office van parked in the driveway was marked BIOHAZARD. Two ambulances were parked in front of the house, its attendants squiring three empty gurneys. Neighbors stood watching from the safety of their yards, holding dogs on leashes and their children by the hand.

An officer in the street in front of the house motioned Dawit on: *Nothing to see. Turn around.* Dawit complied, driving slowly, nodding at the officer from the anonymity of his beard.

"They were here," Teferi said, once they rounded the corner, out of sight. "I feel it."

"And now?" Dawit said.

Teferi shook his head, distressed. "I don't know."

Dawit made a U-turn and parked at the corner of Floral. He peered back down the street with his micro-binoculars, built within the lenses of simple reading glasses. The large white van parked in the house's driveway had a white plate with blue numerals. United States government. "An FBI mobile lab," Dawit said.

After the Lakeview Mall bombing in Salt Lake City, mobile

labs had begun turning up at FBI offices around the country—fingerprints, DNA, chemical and computer analyses on wheels. Cases that had taken days or months to process were now being analyzed on the spot by the boxy Mobile Comprehensive Analysis Vehicles, usually reserved for suspected terrorist attacks. They were still primitive, but a vast improvement over recent years. And cause for worry.

"Glow has captured high-level attention," Teferi said, anxious.

Mahmoud chuckled from where he lay reclined across the backseat, smoking. "Did you think that men were no longer afraid to die?"

"We had thousands of miles, and several continents, to enshroud us," Dawit said.

Mahmoud sat up. "You were fools," he said. "Anything of value is stolen eventually."

Dawit sighed. "We looked in the wrong places for the breach. Ghana. China. We never suspected the children."

"Ah, well," Mahmoud said. "As the Americans say, your chickens are home to roost."

Teferi pulled out his computer, the size and width of a paperback novel. "We'll use their lab to our advantage. I'll learn what they learn."

"Why haven't you sent in a Spider?" Mahmoud said.

Dawit bristled at the scolding. "I'm sending it now."

Spiders were a surveillance cameras created by the House of Science in Lalibela, once used by Searchers to locate Brothers who left the Colony to explore the world outside. Only half an inch long, nearly invisible to the naked eye, the black Spiders moved on thread-thin legs with the capacity to leap to designated locations with a highly sensitive camera. Mahmoud had no doubt used Spiders when he'd tracked Dawit down in Miami.

Dawit opened his leather pouch, pulled out two of the Spiders he had brought, and tossed them out of his car window. The first Spider hopped into the grass beside the curb, on its way to the house. The second only sat where it landed, atop a crumpled bag of potato chips.

Mahmoud gazed down at the device. "No one maintains them?"

"Teka does," Dawit said. "When he's not in meditation."

Mahmoud exhaled, impatient, but kept his criticisms silent.

With a gleam, the second Spider hopped behind the first. Gone.

"*. . . three bodies. One male, Caucasian, age 41. One female, Caucasian, age 37. And one boy, Caucasian, age 14 . . .*" A man's voice transmitted from Teferi's computer. Teferi had accessed FBI internal communications.

Teferi's face tightened. "Three dead?" he whispered.

"At least Caitlin is not among them," Dawit said. *And we won't have to rescue Fana from a morgue,* he thought. Although he might soon wish he could.

"You should eliminate that mortal girl," Mahmoud said. "She is your undoing."

Dawit avoided Teferi's eyes. He agreed with Mahmoud, but Dawit hoped that Mahmoud would respect Teferi's grief for his descendant. They needed Teferi's wits intact.

"*. . . more latents coming your way, MCAV,*" Teferi's transmission went on. Fingerprints.

Fana would not appear in the fingerprint database, but Caitlin and Johnny Wright might, if they had been here. "Soon we will have our answer," Dawit said.

"Whether or not we want to hear it," Teferi muttered.

Dawit checked the viewer in his palm, which was still black. Nothing from the cameras.

"Your Spiders move like snails," Mahmoud muttered.

An insect-like chirp in Dawit's earpiece signaled that a Spider was transmitting. Half of his viewer lit up; the other side was still black. Spider 1 was inside the house, positioned on a wall. Dawit enlarged the image: He saw a crowd of law enforcement officers wearing hooded biohazard suits. The living room was cluttered, but there was no sign of struggle.

"Hot suits," Dawit said. "They're treating it like a contamination."

"How very odd," Teferi said.

The mortals' voices were too faint to hear. Dawit adjusted his volume.

"*. . . looks like they've all bled out through their mouths, noses, ears and eyes, but we're not seeing any obvious injuries . . *" Dawit toggled, and the Spider leaped to the opposite wall. From there, Dawit had a better view of the hallway. Officers were studying the wall while a technician swabbed for samples. Dawit could see large letters written on the wall, but the Spider's angle didn't allow him to make them out. The Spider sped to a higher perch, and words came into view: AND BLOOD TOUCHETH BLOOD.

Dawit's heart skipped. More than a hundred years had passed, and none at all. When Teferi and Mahmoud leaned over to see the image, Teferi gave a heavy sigh.

"Sanctus Cruor hiding behind Scripture," Dawit said. "Just as before."

Teferi's voice trembled. "They may have Fana and Caitlin, Dawit."

"I've told you as much," Mahmoud said, untroubled.

Dawit glared. "And I'm to blindly trust the word of the man who is the most likely to have sent them here?"

Mahmoud *tsked* with a small smile. "Is that your voice I hear, or your wife's?"

For an instant, rage turned Dawit's vision white. But this was no time to quarrel. "Are we bound to a common cause?" Dawit said. "Tell me the truth, Brother."

"It is now as it was then, Dawit," Mahmoud said. "Sanctus Cruor's influence is worse than we feared. Just as our colony was endangered if Ethiopia fell to Italy . . . if you are not safe, we are not safe." He met Dawit's eyes. "Our common enemy makes us friends again, Dawit."

HE IS SINCERE, DAWIT. I DETECT NO LIES, Teferi said.

Another chirp in Dawit's ear, and Spider 2 was finally broadcasting. Dawit saw a long room with a row of cots. Like a dormitory. Or a prison.

"It's a safe house," Dawit said. "Fana and Caitlin may have had haven here."

"Perhaps Sanctus Cruor was waiting for them," Mahmoud said, his voice quiet.

Teferi held his temples, shaking his head. To him, his descendant was as dear as a child.

Spider 2 showed three investigators in hot suits kneeling on the floor, collecting samples the camera's angle didn't show. Another turned on a bathroom light. Dawit toggled to see more, but the camera didn't move. Dammit! And Teka was not here to repair it.

"... *kill the lights so we can look for blood traces* ..." a woman's voice said from Spider 2.

Spider 1 chirped. The camera was now on the ceiling of a bedroom. The walls were covered with bright pictures and drawings. A boy lay facedown on the floor, ringed by enough blood to have drowned him. True to form, Sanctus Cruor had no qualms about killing children.

"They were surprised overnight," Dawit said. "Perhaps . . . taken."

Teferi made a grieved sound. Sanctus Cruor might have taken the mortals to gain influence over Fana. Even if Caitlin had not died on Floral Street, she was surely dead by now; and her death would not have been gentle. Dawit squeezed Teferi's shoulder.

"Fingerprint results are up," Teferi said in a flat tone, his attention on his computer. "I just saw the name Mitchell Rolfson. He was Caitlin's teacher. She spoke fondly of him."

A succession of identification card photos appeared on Teferi's screen, accompanied by thumbprints. ROLFSON, NATHANIEL. A boy who looked twelve.

GRAYS-ROLFSON, SHEILA. A full-faced woman with a cheerful smile.

WRIGHT, JOHN JAMAL. A boy. Dawit remembered meeting his father once.

O'NEAL, CAITLIN. A blonde-haired teenager time had changed beyond recognition.

"Yes, I knew she was here," Teferi whispered. "I felt her."

UNKNOWN, said the red type beside the next fingerprint. No photo.

Another print came up: UNKNOWN. A third. Then, a fourth.

Fana, Dawit thought. Strangers to the mandatory national identification system were either phantoms, like Fana, or people who weren't from the United States. The passport fingerprinting system was mired in international red tape, so mostly citizens and convicts had their fingerprints in the FBI files.

"There were three of them," Dawit said. "At least."

"That was careless, leaving fingerprints," Mahmoud said.

"Sanctus Cruor is arrogant," Dawit said.

Teferi's eyes widened as he switched screens, scrolling through other data files from the mobile lab. "Something very irregular," Teferi said. He peered more closely. "These corpses will not be autopsied by FBI forensics. They're bringing in outsiders."

"Who?" Dawit said.

Teferi squinted. "That isn't clear. But this is listed as a joint investigation between the FBI, the Drug Enforcement Agency and . . . the Department of Homeland Security."

They need only add the Vatican, and it could be 1896 again. But when had Homeland Security involved itself in Glow? His colony's DEA contacts had never mentioned that alliance. Had Sanctus Cruor crafted a lie to enlist unwitting government aid in their search for the Blood? Dawit suddenly wished that Justin's memory had not been destroyed. In crisis, they had no one to spare.

I WILL NEVER FORGIVE THE HURRY TO THROW JUSTIN AWAY, Teferi said, intruding into Dawit's thoughts.

Spider 2 chirped. The camera was in Dark mode because the lights were off, so all light on the image was exaggerated. The monitor showed an investigator squatting in a tiny bathroom. She spoke up loudly: "*Blood on the bathroom floor . . .*"

Sanctus Cruor would consider it sacrilege to leave behind even a drop of Living Blood, so Dawit wasn't concerned about the blood on the wall. The blood in the bathroom was different. Was it from one of the dead? Or could it be Fana's?

"Burn their computers," Dawit said.

"Already done," Teferi said.

From his computer, Teferi could send a pulse to disable any computer it was linked to, destroying functions and files to prevent investigators from analyzing the blood sample immediately. But Teferi was free to view any information he had already stolen.

". . . *the MCAV is down!*" a man's voice shouted, joining a sudden chorus.

"We'll leave this to Berhanu," Dawit said. Berhanu would be in Casa Grande in little more than an hour, and there was no one Dawit trusted more to clean up whatever mess had been left behind in this house. Berhanu and his Brothers would study the crime scene and destroy the blood samples, no matter what it took.

But their mission here would not go quietly, Dawit knew. Any mission involving so many armed investigators could end with a Life Brother's capture, and capture was not an option. The mortal blood spilled during a rescue mission might trigger the public uproar they had always feared. Their problems would compound exponentially.

"I can stay," Mahmoud offered. "I'll see that the work here is done discreetly."

Mahmoud excelled at stealth work. He practically vanished into walls.

"No. We must look for Fana," Dawit said. "Is there a trail, Teferi?"

Teferi blinked. "Perhaps. They might have gone . . . south."

Mexico. Of course.

"We face a job for an army, and we are only a few . . . ," Teferi sighed, switching between computer fields to read the stolen records. He gave a start. "The fingerprints we saw aren't new: They were posted nearly two hours ago to the national FBI field offices. I see heightened activity in Jacksonville and Atlanta."

Garrick Wright lived in Tallahassee, two hours west of Jacksonville, five hours south of Atlanta. Dawit looked at his watch: eleven-fifteen. The Wright family might already be in custody. Berhanu had always said that no outsider should have set foot on their grounds.

"Are your families provided for?" Mahmoud said.

Teferi looked crestfallen. "We must send them to Lalibela."

Dawit's oldest friend spoke Dawit's mind before he could open his mouth.

"No," Mahmoud said gently. "It is far too late for that."

Twenty-two

You heard me," the man said.

Garrick Wright blinked. His eyes were still trying to take in the sight of the armed strangers behind his front door and the shambles in his living room. He had been at Publix for less than an hour, and he didn't recognize his home. Tahira's purse was on the floor, its contents spilled. The only thing still right was the smell of Tahira's chicken stewing in the kitchen.

A man across the room was wearing an armor suit of Kevlar, and he had an assault rifle trained on Garrick. Four other men had assault rifles slung across their shoulders, hands ready to draw their sidearms. Someone took the heavy paper grocery bags from Garrick's arms. He barely noticed. The stranger who had opened his door had a 9mm, but Garrick only stared at Tahira's spilled purse. He saw her pale orange lipstick, her favorite, in a case the color of a pearl.

"No, I don't think I did hear," Garrick said, blinking again. His mind was a blank sheet. "Where's my wife?"

The man with the 9mm had a gold badge hanging from his neck. His red-blond hair was a short military fuzz, and he had a long scar across his forehead that looked like he'd been in a knife fight. He spoke with condescending deliberation. "We have your wife in custody. Your wife is a Jordanian national. She is going on a terror list, and you will never see her again, if you don't tell me everything you know about Glow." He blew a large bubble, then sucked the air out, leaving the limp gum intact. "Did you hear me that time?"

Garrick felt a pain in his chest. Any other day, he would have been worried about a heart attack. Johnny must have something to do with this. "What's happened?" Garrick said.

"Mr. Wright, let me explain something," the man said. "You just applied for an exit visa to go to Jordan. The State Department has confirmed that your wife's father had terrorist ties. We know you. We know your family."

In college, Tahira's father had joined a religious organization run by a Saudi man who'd become a terrorist decades later. Tahira's father had only known the man six months, but the ancient affiliation had dogged him until he'd died. Tahira's family had been on the U.S. government's no entry list since Johnny was ten, after the business in Iraq had started everything. Until now, the problem had only created a morass of bureaucracy every time they'd wanted to plan a family visit, and Tahira had never been allowed to take citizenship. Now Garrick understood the true price.

The man with the 9mm took off his sunglasses. His irises were nearly colorless. "Given all that . . . Do you understand that my country is at war, and I don't have the luxury of politeness?"

Garrick felt his life sinking away from him. He never should have trusted Lucas.

"I need my lawyer," Garrick said.

The man's eyes went cold. "I hope you're too smart to fuck with me today, Professor."

"Please let me see my wife," Garrick said. He was begging the man.

The man gestured inside. "Let's sit down and see if I can find her for you."

The men and women crowding his living room wore jackets of many affiliations. Most notable to Garrick were the initials DEA and FBI. The man blowing bubbles wasn't wearing a jacket to identify his branch, but Garrick knew he was DHS. Sometimes people disappeared after DHS interviews; anyone who watched the news knew that. He had written a half dozen letters to Congress to complain. The disappearances. The prisons no one could find. Those letters were probably in his file, too.

One of the agents, whose dress was shirt-and-tie FBI, held a

sheaf of papers with newspaper clippings. Garrick recognized his
own name and photo from a year-old copy of the *Tallahassee Dem-
ocrat*. An editorial. "Lies behind the War!" screamed the headline.
He'd hounded the newspaper with editorials since his retirement.

Was Tahira lost to them already?

"I won't ask nicely again," the DHS agent said. "Sit down."

Garrick took the first seat he could find, at the edge of the piano
bench. He had never sat at the bench before. The piano was Tahira's.

The agent blew a bubble, sucked it dead. "Your son, John Jamal
Wright, is wanted for questioning in a triple homicide."

Although he was closer to tears, Garrick couldn't help laughing,
a reflex. "What?"

"Is that funny to you?"

It was hard to meet the agent's eyes. "My son wouldn't kill anybody."

"The victims were Glow dealers," the DHS agent said. He picked up
a box of files Garrick recognized from his bedroom—his Glow archives.
Holy Lord, this looks bad, Garrick realized. His throat burned.

"So it's not funny now?"

"No," Garrick said. He couldn't bring himself to say *sir,* although
he knew he should.

The agent leaned over Garrick, the old intimidation tactic that
made men feel small. Garrick saw through it, but that insight didn't
help. "John was at a safe house in Arizona, and now the people who
ran it are dead. John's fingerprints are all over our crime scene."

This person *John* must be someone else, Garrick thought. *Dear
Lord, please don't let Johnny have been anywhere near there. And if he
was, Lord—please let him be all right.*

The DHS agent went on. "We know John's a good kid. No
record, good grades. He wasn't alone at the house, and maybe he's
no killer."

"He's not. My son wants to be a doctor."

"That right?" The DHS agent's icy eyes were unimpressed. "Then
he probably doesn't have anything to do with funding terrorists with
drug money, or introducing bioweapons into our country through
the drug trade. For your sake, let's hope not. But John can help lead
us to those people. So if you do the right thing today, you can expect

your wife Tameka—or whatever her fucking name is—to be home before the falafels get cold."

Garrick glanced at the photo of his family framed on the piano—him, Tahira and Johnny posing at the Sears store at Governor's Square Mall. Johnny's fifteenth birthday. Garrick ached to escape into that old captured moment.

Garrick had warned Johnny. He had *told* Johnny that prisons were the new Jim Crow. If Johnny made it through whatever had happened to him, a prison would knock the wrongheadedness out of him. At least he would have visitors. And basic rights. God only knew what might happen to Tahira, or where she would be sent.

"I'll talk to you," Garrick said. "Please just let her go."

"Where is John now?"

Garrick shook his head. "I wish I knew." Johnny's roommate had finally called last night to ask where Johnny was. "He's not at school. I was planning on calling the police."

"Your son is missing . . . and you were *planning* to call the police?" the agent said, incredulous. "How long has John been dealing Glow?"

"I don't . . . know if . . . ," Garrick said began. The DHS agent's bicep tensed so suddenly that Garrick was sure he was about to hit him. "But there's a girl," Garrick went on quickly. "Caitlin O'Neal. If Johnny's doing that, it's because of her."

A crowd gathered around the piano bench. Perspiration soaked Garrick's armpits and thighs. The DHS agent spoke calmly, his jaw pounding his gum. "Tell us more about Caitlin O'Neal."

"She's . . . a friend of Johnny's. They both went to Berkeley. But she dropped out."

"Where is she now?"

"I don't know."

The agent's features sharpened. "What *do* you know, Professor? Think fast."

"There's a . . . compound, like a commune." A half dozen pairs of unblinking eyes told Garrick that he was about to tell them exactly what they wanted to hear. "It's in the Pacific Northwest. Maybe . . . midway between Portland and Seattle. The Five corridor."

Notebooks scribbled fiercely. An agent near the kitchen talked hurriedly on his radio.

"Be more specific," the agent said.

"Two hours north of Portland, maybe. It's in the woods. Hundreds of acres. That's where John met Caitlin and her family. A friend of mine invited me out. Dr. Lucas Shepard. He said . . . he'd found a miracle."

The room went so quiet that it was as if Garrick had been able to hear the thundering of all their hearts.

Garrick took a deep breath. His lungs were stone, unyielding.

Was he doing the right thing? Garrick didn't care. It was the only thing.

"Tuesday night, I got a call . . ."

Twenty-three

The twin concrete towers of the casino stood as if to defy the ornate white piety of the Moorish-styled Spanish mission that shared the reservation's arid land; sin and salvation competing for souls. *The perfect place to look for a car,* Caitlin thought. Anyone inside a casino was begging to get robbed.

Charlie was waiting in the casino parking lot, his arms folded across his chest as he sat astride his idling black Kawasaki. He took an unlighted cigarette from his mouth and offered it to her. He was quick with his lighter; courtly. No wonder Fana liked him so much.

"Thanks," Caitlin said. "Fana thought we'd lost you at the exit."

Charlie smiled. "No one's getting rid of me that fast."

Halfway full, the parking lot had a glistening array of cars. Most were clustered near the modernistic casino's entrance, but a few were parked farther out, isolated. Caitlin walked beside Charlie at a casual pace as they scouted. Charlie was such a comforting presence, the way Maritza had made her feel. A fellow soldier. She had been as relieved as Fana when Charlie's motorcycle had drifted into her rearview mirror when they'd pulled off Highway 19. If Charlie had been gone, she would have had to make it to Mexico on her own, and she wasn't sure she could.

She needed Charlie to help her keep the Railroad alive.

The PT Cruiser and its tag number had been announced on the

radio a half hour ago on a Homeland Security bulletin, as if they were terrorists. The police had probably seen them drive away on a traffic camera, so it was a miracle they hadn't been stopped on the highway. At least three highway patrol cars had passed them, each one making Caitlin's heart hammer until she'd thought she would faint. But Fana had come through; the police had never slowed.

Caitlin had parked where the casino's lot was most crowded, leaving Johnny and Fana in the car, and she didn't dare leave them long. They were like children, especially Johnny. Johnny's whining was getting on Caitlin's nerves.

A 1990s gray Toyota RAV4, parked by itself on the far side, caught Caitlin's eye. Maybe the driver had played all night, losing track of time.

"That one," Caitlin said.

"You read my mind, *chica*," Charlie said. He grinned, walking with a carefree bounce.

The RAV's driver's door wouldn't open when Caitlin tugged on it, but the passenger side opened for Charlie. He let her in, and Caitlin took the driver's seat. She wished she'd had her body puller to drill into the steering column; instead, she would have to try a dummy key. Caitlin flipped through her key ring, looking for the Toyota's red ring. Filed keys didn't work on newer models, but sometimes they did on ancient ones.

Caitlin took a deep breath. "Wish me luck."

"You won't need luck," Charlie said.

He was right. The car turned over right away, sweet as a baby. The radio blared a plaintive trumpet from Tejano music. Caitlin turned the volume down, flipping to the AM news station she had been listening to while she'd driven.

". . . this shocking story that is still developing," the male news-caster's somber voice said. "A Casa Grande family of three has been killed—a minister, her husband and their fourteen-year-old son. This case involves the illegal drug Glow, with federal authorities reporting possible terrorist connections. The alert level for all of Arizona is High. The Department of Homeland Security has issued a bulletin for a white PT Cruiser they believe is being driven by the suspects. California SXT555. The suspect's names in this gruesome triple murder are Caitlin Gloria O'Neal, age twenty-one, and John Jamal Wright, age nineteen. For photos of the suspects, check out News 1180 on the Web . . ."

Caitlin was so shocked to hear her name on the radio that she couldn't move.

"Fuck," she whispered, her eyes filling with tears. Her cover was blown. Mom and Casey might have heard her name all the way in South Africa, if it was on CNN.

"You're underground for good now, *mia bambina*," Charlie said.

Caitlin looked at Charlie and blinked, distracted by his eyes. His dark eyelashes were so long and plush that they looked feminine. His face was nearly as smooth as a woman's, too. Caitlin couldn't remember what Charlie had just said. Had he been speaking Italian?

"We have to get to Mexico," Caitlin said. It was the only thing on her mind.

"And we will," Charlie said. "But first, one small thing . . ."

Charlie leaned close, and his lips hovered near hers. Caitlin felt a strong instinct to pull back, but Charlie's warm, flowing breath seemed familiar. His face felt smooth to her fingertips, smelling of vanilla and honey. *Maritza*. Charlie captured Maritza, somehow. Maritza's breath, stolen from her and now returned, was dizzying. Caitlin felt faint, melting away from herself. Becoming. She leaned forward to kiss Charlie, but he pulled away before their lips touched.

"I need to know I can trust you, Caitlin," Charlie said.

Caitlin couldn't see through the tears clouding her eyes. She trembled. "I just want to keep Fana safe," she said. Even if she was forgetting herself, she could never forget that.

"Then we want the same thing," Charlie said. "Like we said, it's up to us."

Something cold touched Caitlin's right hand. She looked down and saw that Charlie was offering her the shiny .38 he had found at the Rolfsons' house, or claimed he had.

"Take it," he said.

Caitlin clung to the gun with both hands. "Why?" she whispered.

Charlie touched her lips lightly with Maritza's lips, his fingers grazing her with Maritza's featherlike touch. "You're going to help me, *mia bambina,*" he said.

"Oh, God. Oh, *shit.*"

Johnny was in the front seat, hunched over the radio dial. Fana was afraid he might pull out the clump of hair trapped between his fingers, or hyperventilate from breathing so fast. His thoughts were rioting inside the headache she'd had since Tucson. Fana considered a massage to quiet his thoughts, but she forced herself to resist. She tried to block him out instead.

"Johnny, calm down," she said, struggling against her impulse to silence him.

"They're saying I'm a terrorist!" he said. "Look at what Caitlin's gotten us into!"

Fana leaned her head back against her seat. *Trance. Trance out.*

Johnny turned to face her, leaning across his headrest. "I'm gonna' get away from here, call my dad and get a lawyer. You have to come, too. I can't leave you with her."

"Caitlin needs me," Fana mumbled. She felt herself drifting.

"*Listen to me,*" he said, nearly a roar. His eyes were red. "Do you have an ID card?"

Fana hesitated, then shook her head. Her parents had been careful to keep her out of official records. She'd never gotten a national ID card despite the new law five years ago, after Salt Lake City. Her passport, which she'd forgotten to bring with her, didn't bear her real name.

Johnny reached over to grab her shoulders. "That means they don't know your fingerprints! They don't know your name. You can walk away. You can hide in the woods with your family. Forget about going to Mexico with Caitlin!"

Fana felt a tremor, and she knew she couldn't argue. Her trip had been doomed before it had begun, from the instant she'd run into Aunt Alex. Fana never should have left her that way.

Johnny went on. "I don't know Caitlin anymore, and I don't trust Charlie. He gives me a bad feeling. As soon as I met that guy, a whole house full of people turned up dead."

"That wasn't Charlie's fault." She wished Johnny knew what Charlie had been through.

"I don't know if it was his fault or not," Johnny said. "When a day starts off this messed up, you change the company you're keeping." As Johnny ran his fingers through his hair, his breathing slowed. "I have a credit card. It's in my dad's name. We can find a phone. I can cut my hair, make it easier to hide."

Johnny sounded more reasonable with every breath. Fana knew Johnny had only stayed this long because of her. She could use her gifts to keep people from noticing him, the way she had shrouded them from police on the highway. But as long as Caitlin believed the Life Brothers were their enemy, Caitlin couldn't be trusted to devise their plans. And if the Underground Railroad had been compromised, the breach might have reached Mexico.

Johnny grasped Fana's hand. His heartbeat pulsed through his damp, warm palms. "Fana, I know I'm fucked," he whispered, his eyes fevered. "But you have a chance. Please let me help you out of this. I'll never forgive myself if I leave you, but we have to go *now*."

Fana clung hard to his hand. "Help me find something sharp."

Johnny's eyes dimmed, confused. "Why?"

Fana dropped Johnny's hand and rooted around the backseat's floor for a tool. She found candy bar wrappers. An ice scraper. Scattered coins. She kept a soda can aside; her receptacle. "I have to leave blood for her. Hurry."

"Leave her . . . blood?"

Johnny's mind clouded with confusion as he stared at Fana, and then knowledge dawned on him. Childlike amazement replaced the fear in his eyes. *Dammit.* Not only had she just broken her colony's cardinal rule but she'd also paralyzed him. Would she have to try to make him forget later? Fana gave Johnny the most gentle massage she could, barely brushing his mind. *We have to hurry,* she whispered to his unconscious.

Johnny blinked, freed from his awe. He flung open the glove compartment, throwing aside papers and CDs. He pulled out a small pocket knife with a Boy Scout insignia.

"Yes!" Fana said. "Give it to me."

Johnny gazed at the tiny knife in his palm, not moving again. As if he were made of stone. Exasperated, Fana probed toward his mind again, trying to whisper. She couldn't find him. He was right in front of her, but her mind couldn't feel a trace of Johnny Wright, as if he was as strong as Teka and had masked himself completely. Was she blocking her own gifts somehow because she knew she was abusing them?

A car engine gunned, and Fana looked out the rear window. Caitlin drove behind the PT Cruiser in a small gray SUV, and Charlie pulled up alongside her on his motorcycle. Charlie wasn't gone, after all! At least Caitlin wouldn't be alone.

Fana reached over and grabbed the knife from Johnny's hand, shoving it into her back pocket. "We'll get out of this," Fana whispered to Johnny. "Don't worry."

Charlie knocked on her window, and Fana opened her door for him. Charlie kneeled to gaze at her at eye level, his face only two inches from hers. "You okay, *negra*?" Charlie said.

Now it was Fana who felt paralyzed. Her heart pounded as she gazed at the boy whose allure surprised her with its intensity. Charlie's eyes were hard to blink away from. The idea of leaving him felt tragic.

"I can't . . . go with you," Fana said.

Charlie's jaw flexed in anger. He glanced at Johnny, who was hanging his head. "Why?" Charlie said. "Because he said so?"

Caitlin's window came down. "We have to *go*," she hissed to Fana. "Come on!"

Charlie touched Fana's face, and she rested her chin against his strong fingertips. "Does he think he'll call his parents and make everything fine?" Charlie said. "These are feds after us. They already have his parents. I'm sorry to tell you, Fana, but they probably have yours, too. If they catch us, they'll send us to dungeons where no one will see us again."

Charlie didn't know about the firefence. He didn't know about the Life Brothers' weapons. But he might be right about one thing: The police probably had questioned Johnny's parents by now, and Johnny's father had visited the colony. Even if Mr. Wright didn't know exactly where it was, he knew enough. Homeland Security might send an army to Washington.

"I have to warn my family," Fana said.

"*Sí*," Charlie said, nodding. "And you can. In less than an hour. From *México*."

"The Railroad has a sat phone in Nogales," Caitlin called. "Fana, please hurry."

Fana looked at Johnny, whose back was turned. The radio clamored Johnny's name.

"What you think, Johnny?" Charlie said. "Convinced yet?"

Johnny stared at the windshield. "Mexico it is," he said in a dead voice.

Why had Johnny given up so easily? Fana probed Johnny again, and this time no invisibility blocked her. Johnny's anger churned loud and clear. Johnny thought she had betrayed him, and now he felt trapped. *I won't let anything happen to you, Johnny,* she whispered to him in the hidden recesses he might uncover only when he slept.

Charlie smiled at Fana. "I'll ditch my bike and ride in the car. Would that be better?"

Fana hadn't thought anything could make this day feel better, but she wanted Charlie closer to them. She didn't want to keep looking out for him, wondering if he was in danger. Teka had taught her that Khaldun had stayed with the Life Brothers for more than five hundred years, postponing his Rising, because he had given them the Living Blood, so he considered them his responsibility. Caitlin, Johnny and Charlie were *her* responsibility.

Fana nodded. "Yeah," she said. "Ride with us. That's much better."

"Johnny, go get in the car," Charlie said. "Sit up front. I'll be in back with Fana."

Fana expected Johnny to complain about Charlie telling him what to do, but Johnny opened his car door and climbed out without a word.

Fana tried to catch his eyes to apologize, but Johnny refused to look her way.

At first, Johnny thought it was a stroke. Or a nervous breakdown.

He had been holding a pocketknife in his hands, and suddenly he hadn't been able to move. When he'd tried to give the knife to

Fana, his arm had ignored him. When he'd tried to turn his head, his neck had felt like stone, bent as if in prayer. Panicked, he'd tried to blink; his eyes had stayed open, burning.

What the FUCK?

Johnny tried not to panic, racing through a medical checklist: Paralysis. Racing heartbeat. Had he had a stroke? After a day like today, it was possible. Nervous breakdown? Why not? He'd heard his name on the radio as a suspected terrorist. Caitlin had been accusing him of zoning all day, as if it was possible to overreact to a slaughter.

Johnny had seen Fana's hand swipe the knife away from him. She'd said something to him, but he hadn't been able to hear her over the blood rushing in his ears as his heart had thrashed.

A loud motor had revved had behind their car. *It's over. Police. Too late.*

Johnny had almost been relieved. At least someone would send him to a doctor.

Johnny had felt his head turning toward the window, as if he'd been watching himself sleepwalk. He'd seen the gray hood of an unfamiliar car behind them, and Caitlin sitting in the driver's seat. He'd wished he'd been able to get away before Caitlin had gotten back, but it would have been better to face Caitlin than the Department of Homeland Security. She would find help for him.

Then, Johnny had seen Charlie climb off his motorcycle, or someone who'd *seemed* to be Charlie. He'd been dressed like Charlie, in jeans and a biker jacket. He'd had Charlie's white-toothed smile. Charlie's curly tangle of dark hair. He'd even walked like him; an easy, cocksure jaunt.

But his face had been covered by a thick swarm of bees. Only his smile had shown through.

If Johnny hadn't been frozen in place, he would have trembled to his bones. Johnny had been able to make himself blink, and Charlie's face had looked normal again. Charlie had winked at Johnny, puckering his lips in a mock kiss. Then he'd leaned over and knocked on Fana's window.

Don't let him in Don't let him in Don't let him in Don't let him in Don't let him in Don't

Johnny had heard Fana's door open behind him. "You okay, *negra*?" Charlie said.

While Charlie had talked to Fana in a soothing tone, another version of Charlie's voice had crashed into Johnny's head. Unlike the voice talking to Fana, the voice in his head was in a bad mood:

THE WITNESS WRITES THAT ONLY HE WHO IS WORTHY SHALL WALK BESIDE THE CHOSEN. YOU ARE WEAK, AND THEREFORE NOT A WORTHY DISCIPLE. THROUGH SUFFER-ING, YOU WILL BE CLEANSED AND LEARN OBEDIENCE.

Distantly, Johnny had heard Charlie's spoken voice sounding as gentle as a priest's as he'd told Fana that her parents were probably in custody. Johnny had experienced the eerie sensation of Fana's voice in his head in Berkeley, but he'd thought he had imagined it. Had he imagined it again? *What's happening to me?*

Only one thing had kept Johnny's mind from drowning in confusion: He'd remembered the awe-inspiring white Spanish church they had passed while Caitlin had looked for a place to dump the car, almost a vision of Heaven. The memory of the church had felt like God's message to him in the shadows, and his thoughts had miraculously cleared.

His father's mother, Nana, was a country woman who went to church every day, and her closed-door beliefs went back to slavery and beyond. Nana threw salt and red clay dust to ward off spirits, and she'd told Johnny a story about a man she'd known in childhood who'd walked the streets possessed by the devil for forty-eight hours straight. In Jordan, *Jaddah* Jamilah complained about evil jinns, devils called *shayatiin*. She blamed the Most Evil, Iblis, for the wars. Far from his mother's homeland, Johnny had been raised in his father's AME church. Praise God from Whom All Blessings Flow. Johnny had sung in the choir since he was five. In high school, he'd seen himself in a dream standing at the altar in vestments of white, and he'd believed he was being called to preach. His friends and teachers had always said so. Even Omari had told him he should be a preacher. But he had fought.

He wanted to have a normal college life. Get kegged. Get laid.

As if God could wait. As if Good and Evil had not survived after the Bible's scribes had died. As if Evil did not walk beside him wearing the face of a man. As if the King of Lies slept.

"What do you think, Johnny?" he'd heard Charlie say, a disembodied voice in his brain's fog. "Convinced yet?"

"Mexico it is," Johnny had heard himself say, a stranger's words in his mouth. A new horror.

help me help me help me help me Lord

But no help came.

Johnny was opening his car door. Standing. Walking. Johnny screamed and wept inside, and he understood how Jesus must have felt, nailed helpless on the cross. Forsaken. Opening the door to the new car, Johnny's body paid him no mind. His body climbed inside to sit beside Caitlin. He heard his name on the radio again, with the announcer emphasizing his middle name, *Jamal*. The car's frigid air conditioner blasted across his face.

Johnny felt Caitlin's hand on his knee, and his heart surged with hope. He fought to pull his lips apart, to breathe out a puff of air. To whisper Caitlin's name.

Don't go with him. He's not who you think he is.

"Don't look so fuck-eyed," Caitlin said to him. He could only see her face in his peripheral vision; a thin smile twisted her lips. "We're almost there."

As the car carrying him pulled away with a lurch, Johnny Wright could only pray.

Twenty-four

Fana's teacher was losing his composure. Jessica could see it in the constant drifting of Teka's eyes, in the way he rubbed his temples as he stood over Alex's bed. She had never seen him so worried. What if Teka was falling apart too?

Dawit had called to tell her about the dead bodies in Casa Grande, and he had cooed comforts while Jessica had sat in her bathroom, hidden, and cried softly to his image on the video phone. Those tears had been long overdue, but she'd had to cut them short. The names of Caitlin O'Neal and Johnny Wright had already surfaced in the national news. Caitlin and Johnny hadn't been caught yet, but the full force of the United States government and media was on their heels.

Naive zealotry had gotten that poor family killed. How many others would follow?

You need each other now, Fana. Please take care of yourself and your friends.

Jessica could think of a dizzying array of mistakes she had made in only forty-eight hours. She wanted to scream for letting Lucas call Garrick Wright on his sat phone Tuesday night. *Yeah, right. The damage was done as soon as you invited Garrick and those others here.*

Today's trouble had started ten years ago, at her own insistence. In all, seven outsiders had come. She, Lucas and Alex had created a list of health care providers and journalists they had believed could be partners with her and the Life Brothers to distribute blood. How could God want them to do anything else with His gift to mankind? Jesus healed the sick, and so should they. *But Satan has followed us step for step.*

How had she ever thought she could follow this calling and bring her loved ones too?

Bea sat at the table stirring instant grits Jessica had made her, comfort food, but Bea wasn't eating. Conserving her strength, Bea had hardly spoken since morning. She'd stopped protesting against the oxygen tubes in her nose, because she said the air underground was too thin. The tubes and Bea's forlorn eyes made her look like a disaster victim, like the images that still haunted Jessica from Hurricane Katrina and the Salt Lake City bombs.

"How are you, Mom?" Jessica said.

"Tired, baby. Tired."

"Maybe you should go back to bed."

Slowly, Bea only shook her head. "Alex might wake up. I can't help watching for it."

Alex still lay in her bed as if she were in a deep sleep, gaining nutrients from an IV Jessica had found in her medical supplies. She'd had to insert the IV herself, because Lucas wasn't in much better shape himself. Not yet, anyway.

Teka rubbed his temple again while he pressed one hand against Alex's forehead.

"Are you all right?" Jessica said.

"A headache," Teka said, without his usual smile.

Jessica had never known Teka to have a headache.

"My first in nearly three hundred years," Teka answered her thought. "It's . . ." He looked bewildered, another unusual expression for him. "It is strange."

Jessica's heart jumped. Teka would not use that word lightly. "Strange how?"

"It is as if Fana is trying to reach me, as she did last night. The presence feels like Fana, and yet . . ." He shook his head, troubled. "It does not. Now, a headache. Very unusual."

Jessica sighed. *Don't fall apart on me, Teka,* she thought, hoping he could hear.

I ASSURE YOU I WILL DO MY BEST, JESSICA.

Dawit still had trouble interpreting thoughts she tried to send him consciously, but Teka could pick out her relevant thoughts like marbles in a field of grass. It felt like taking a bath with someone, or swimming together. No wonder the Life Brothers cared for each other so much: They lived in each other's minds!

Does your headache mean something has happened to Fana?

IT NEED NOT.

Is it anything like Fana's headaches when she's in a city?

VERY MUCH SO.

Could you become debilitated?

I DO NOT ANTICIPATE IT, BUT ALL THINGS ARE POSSIBLE.

Jessica felt dizzied by the rapid exchange, and Teka's admission made her heart shudder.

If something happened to Teka, she and the others would be in trouble. Already, the Duharts had come close to getting killed last night—the whole family, even the babies! Nita still refused to open her door or talk to her. The problems with the Duharts wouldn't go away.

"What brought on your last headache, Teka?" she said.

"I had an audience with Khaldun, and I was overwhelmed when he first shared his thoughts with me. Khaldun's presence is large."

Khaldun! Yes, Jessica knew what it felt like to be swallowed by Khaldun's presence. When Jessica had visited Khaldun's chamber in Lalibela, the leader of the immortals had planted knowledge in her, showing her things Fana had done. Through Khaldun, Jessica had seen her daughter casually kill a soldier at the airport in Rome. Fana had killed the man under Jessica's nose, but without Khaldun, Jessica never would have known. Jessica had been frightened of Khaldun at the time, and resentful of the burden he'd placed on the child he had called Chosen. Today, she would drop to her knees in gratitude if Khaldun appeared.

"Is Khaldun trying to reach you?" Jessica said. "To help Fana?"

"How I would welcome him!" Teka said. "But I think not."

Jessica hadn't realized how high her hope had risen until Teka dashed it.

"What about Alex?" Jessica said. Anxiousness slashed her throat.

The panic she'd stuffed away all day yesterday was clawing its way out. The longer Alex lay unconscious, the easier it became to imagine that her sister might be gone.

Teka shook his head, rubbing his temple again. "Alex is unchanged."

"I still don't understand," Jessica said. "Is it brain damage?"

Teka seemed tired, speaking slowly. "Physically, her brain is unharmed, functioning as usual. Fana has placed her in a transcendent state, a high form of what Khaldun called the Rising. Only years of meditation would achieve a state this deep. Khaldun himself lived this way much of the time. But it is usually self-induced. As you see, Fana's gift was great enough to impose it on another. It is a wondrous catastrophe."

Jessica's head swam. "It sounds like . . . death."

"Death would be the highest form. In that instance, the mind rises, but the body dies."

"I would say that when our bodies die, our spirits rise," Jessica said.

"Our words are different, Jessica, but our meaning is much the same."

Bea cleared her throat from across the table. "'Whosoever *believeth* in Him should not perish, but have Everlasting Life . . . ,'" she said in a whisper, quoting John 3:16. Bea complained that the Life Brothers gave her ulcers, the way they worshiped Fana when they should be following Christ. "You don't have sense enough to know where your own blood is from."

"When you Rise, madame, all will be clear to you," Teka said.

"Amen," Bea said, nodding. "That's the first thing you've said that makes sense all day."

There was a polite knock on the door.

"Blessed Mother?" Fasilidas called gently from outside. "Teka has visitors."

Before Jessica could answer, Jima, Yonas, Melaku and Kelile came in, and her room was suddenly crowded. Eight Life Brothers remained in the colony—these Council members and two other sentries like Fasilidas. The rest were out searching for Fana.

Those remaining behind had changed into street clothes, preparing to be seen by outsiders. Jessica knew that the slim batons they carried on their belts were related to the firefence, using a similar energy field to act as both information-gathering tool and weapon. Teka had shown her the device in a display case once, but she had never seen them worn before last night, when the Brothers had come to evacuate her from the Big House.

None of the men glanced Jessica's way as they crowded near Teka. From their grim expressions and long gazes, they were engaged in private conversation within their silence.

"I need to hear you, please," Jessica said. "Any new developments affect all of us."

The three glared at her impatiently, but Teka nodded. "We are discourteous," Teka said.

Kelile scowled. "Shall we consult Teferi's women and boys too?" he said with sarcasm.

Melaku addressed Teka. "Their search is confined to woods southeast of us, so far, but their helicopters will reach us soon. Our window for escape is small."

"The firefence will fool their helicopters," Teka said. "Our structures won't be seen."

"But for how long?" Melaku said. "Relocation is the only sure course."

"Nothing is sure," Teka said. "Access to our plane may be restricted."

"You sound fearful, Melaku," Jima said. "The firefence will slay any comers."

"And thereby stoke their hysteria," Teka said quietly. "Why should we kill when we can simply elude them? Shall we kill dozens? Hundreds? Would you have war declared on us?"

"Perhaps, Teacher, you are last to know," Jima said. "War already has been declared."

When Lucas opened his eyes, he saw Cal Duhart standing over his bed.

"Well, you didn't have to drive so goddamn fast," Lucas said. His voice was hoarse.

"You didn't have to jump in my goddamn way," Cal snapped back.

As Lucas's vision brightened, Cal's bloodshot eyes reminded Lucas of bad times in Tallahassee, before Cal quit drinking. "Did they hurt you?" Lucas said, propping himself up on his elbows. The room spun, and his arms tried to buckle. He almost fell back flat on his bed.

Cal's lips pursed with an untold story, but he shook his head. Cal laid a gentle hand across Lucas's back, helping him support his own weight. "Don't sit up. I ain't company."

Lucas was relieved to sink back to his pillow. Cal was right; no need to put on a heroic display. Lucas's body felt like a foreign object, unwieldy and numb. He knew it was after noon, but it felt like midnight. Jessica had come by to check on him that morning, and she'd told him he should feel fine in a few hours. But he didn't.

His body was wrung with the memory of pain, like an amputee. And Lucas's stomach raged with hunger. Jared had tried to feed him every time he'd opened his eyes, but Lucas had kept drifting out of consciousness, too weary to eat. The cold was almost as bad, sometimes worse. Jared said their unit was eighty degrees and counting, but the room felt frigid.

After last night, you should be in ICU. Didn't take you long to get spoiled rotten.

"How do you feel?" Cal said, watching Lucas carefully.

"Better than you look." Cal's hair and clothes were disheveled. Lucas doubted that Cal or Nita had slept all night.

"Then I guess that makes us even, Doc." Cal blinked with glassy eyes. Lucas had never seen Cal so close to tears.

"I'm sorry." They both said it at once, but Lucas pushed on first: "I was sure you'd get your fool self killed—"

"Nita's here too," Cal said suddenly, as if he'd just remembered. He motioned behind him, and Nita came to his side. She was still wearing yesterday's clothes. She tried to smile at Lucas, but her smile nearly fractured.

"'Morning, Lucas," she said.

From habit, Lucas tried to prop himself up again, but Cal's hand was planted on his chest, holding him still. Lucas grunted and gave up. "I'm so sorry about last night, Nita," he said.

"I know," Nita said and patted his hand. "None of us wanted that."

"Hank's here too." Cal turned to look over his shoulder. "Come on over and say hi to Uncle Luke, Hank."

Lucas caught a glimpse of Hank near the quarters door, his GamePort headpiece hanging around his neck. Hank lingered near Jared, who was frying an egg on the stove. Lucas felt a wave of hunger so severe that he thought he might faint.

Jared gave Hank a nudge, and Hank shuffled toward the bed, reluctant and wide-eyed.

"Go on, Hank," Jared said. "He won't bite."

Hank came to the bed, but his eyes dropped away from Lucas's.

"Sorry you had to see that last night, Hank," Lucas said. "But I'm fine."

"Can I . . . look?" Hank said, gazing toward Lucas's midsection.

Cal and Nita started to protest, but Lucas waved at them to be quiet. "No, it's all right. I'm pretty damn curious myself."

Lucas pulled away the sheet and heavy blanket, shivering when he lifted his shirt. Three faces stared with shining, awestruck eyes.

"Holy shit," Hank said. Cal might have backhanded Hank for that language in front of his mother any other day, but Cal didn't move. Like his son and wife, he only blinked and stared.

"You should have seen him last night," Jared said from the stove. "Black and blue."

Lucas raised his head as much as he had the strength for, gazing down his chest toward his stomach. He couldn't see any marks or bruises, except for the scar he'd had across his chest since his bicycle crashed through a fence when he was ten. Last night's bloody sheet still lay crumpled in the corner, but Lucas's body wore no signs of its trauma.

"Well, I'll be damned," Lucas said.

Hank grinned. "What would happen if you exploded into a million pieces?"

"Let's just hope to God I never find out," Lucas said.

Cal glanced at the wall clock, uneasy. He webbed his fingers to comb away hair from his ears. "I'm glad you're alive and kicking, Doc, but this isn't a social visit."

Hank's grin faded, and he stepped away from the bed. Nita took Cal's pale, freckled hand and clung hard, raising their linked hands to her bosom. Her eyes were mournful.

"What's going on?" Lucas said.

"We need help," Cal said.

"Are they treating you badly?" Lucas said.

Cal glared. "Is that a fucking joke?"

Jared excused himself past the Duharts to bring Lucas a sandwich on a plate. "Sorry," Jared said to Cal. "Protein helps him heal."

Lucas was grateful for the diversion. If the Duharts were about to ask him to help them escape, he wasn't ready. His mouth sank into the sandwich, and he nearly tore off half of it in one bite. The eggs were hot enough to scald his tongue, but he didn't care. Lucas chewed fast and swallowed. "Where are the twins?" Lucas said, his mouth still half full.

"With Abena," Nita said. "Just for a few minutes, so we could talk."

"Let's talk, then," Lucas said. "What happened while I was out?"

Cal and Nita glanced at each other, fortifying each other with their eyes. Nita held Hank close with her free arm, as if to protect him.

Cal took a deep breath. "We've decided to go through with it, Doc," he said.

"Go through with what?"

This time, Nita spoke. "What they did to Justin. The . . . memory wash."

"We want to get it over with," Cal said. "We're leaving today. Right now."

Lucas's throat sealed itself, and suddenly the smell of the food made him sick to his stomach. Lucas studied their faces. Their eyes were set with resolve, even Hank's.

"Jesus," Lucas said. For several seconds, he couldn't shake a coherent thought loose. "What they did to O'Neal was a *punishment*. You thought it was cruel."

"Not if it means we can get the hell out of here," Cal said.

Lucas glanced at Hank, whose face was still pudgy with baby fat. Hank was only fourteen! A memory wash would wipe away his life.

With an effort that made his arms tremble, Lucas propped himself against the wall. He couldn't lie down for this conversation. The Duharts were so scared that they weren't thinking straight; it was a perfect storm of irrationality.

"Cal ... Nita ... can we talk about this with Hank out of the room?"

Cal shook his head. "Hank was gonna' help me shoot my way out of here last night," he said. "If he's man enough for that, he's man enough to have his own say."

Hank nodded. "I've already decided, Uncle Luke."

"Cal, I know Teka knocked you out last night," Lucas said. "Maybe you're still recovering. You can't expect your mind to just snap back—"

"Don't piss me off, Doc." Cal gritted his teeth. He hovered above Lucas, lowering his voice. "You've missed a few news bulletins. The Department of Homeland Security's looking for them. Terrorist talk. The Africans are suited up like they're going to war."

"We weren't sure before, especially about Hank ... ," Nita said, her voice cracking. "But we are now. Help us get out while we can, Lucas. Please."

When his sight started to dim, Lucas stuffed the rest of his sandwich into his mouth. He didn't taste anything. He was near fainting. He could barely follow Cal and Nita.

"... they got Justin on a plane home," Nita was saying. "That's all we want. They can send us to our house in Antigua—"

"Anywhere but here," Cal said. "We've all got ID cards and passports. We should be able to travel, if we leave right fucking now."

"We'll figure out the rest," Nita said. "We'll be all right, Lucas."

Lucas raised his hand, trying to shake his head clear. "Just ... slow down."

The door to the unit slammed, and they all turned around, startled. Lucas thought Yonas or one of the immortals had entered without permission, but instead, Jared was gone. Of course. He'd gone to find Jessica. The plan wouldn't have a prayer without her.

"Doc, every minute lost gives them more excuse to hold us," Cal said. "There's some kind of High Alert in the works on the I-10 corridor. Checkpoints."

"What happened?" Lucas said.

"Speaking as a monkey, I'm out of the loop," Cal said, a bitter glint in his eye. "But it sounds like somebody tipped them off. I'm betting it's got to do with Caitlin and Fana."

"Then they'll make sure we're all taken somewhere safe, Cal," Lucas said. "They've kept themselves hidden for more than five hundred years."

All civility fell away from Cal's voice. "You'll either help us or you won't."

"Fine. Right," Lucas said. "But there's got to be another way. Let's stop and . . . think."

Cal lifted Lucas's shirt again and pressed his hand against Lucas's abdomen, prodding. "Lucas, my rig rammed into you at a good twenty miles per hour, maybe more. Probably broke half your ribs and did God-knows-what to your insides. You flew in the air like a rag doll and ended up hugging a tree. But now you're as good as new."

Lucas nodded. "That's right, Cal. And you'll have my blood whenever you need it. I'll convince Jessica to let all of you undergo a Ceremony to have your own. That's a vow."

Cal blinked, moved. "And it's a mighty generous offer, Doc."

Nita was shaking her head. "No," she said. Her voice skated at the edge of a sob. "Lucas, I was a history major. The history books are nothing but records of the punishment inflicted on places where riches are found. Salt. Gold. Cotton. Diamonds. Oil. What you're walking around with in your veins is all that and more. It's a blessing. But—"

"We can't afford it," Cal said. He sighed, rubbing his son's close-cropped hair.

"They took *twenty years* from Justin," Lucas said. "What about that price? You don't want to remember your time with your children? You want to throw away how you watched Hank grow up from diapers? You want to deny your own son his childhood memories?"

Cal's eyes burned into him. "We've known each other a long time, Doc Shepard. Maybe we haven't always seen eye to eye on politics and race, all that. Remember how you used to always say you grew up in a different Georgia than me? Look me in the eye and tell me you don't understand a man wanting his family to be free."

Cal was right: Lucas couldn't hold his friend's gaze. He would do the same thing for his family, and Cal knew it.

There was a knock. The door cracked open, and Jared stuck his head in.

"Uncle Cal?" Jared said. "I've got Aunt Jessica out here. And . . . Teka."

Cal looked wild-eyed, and he seemed to shrink. The sudden shift in Cal's body language told Lucas how invaded Cal felt after last night's mental manipulation. Cal stared at the table. "These are your people, Doc," Cal said quietly. "Say what you need to say."

"Just watch your temper, Cal. Promise me."

"Promise," Cal said, although his teeth were glued tight.

"I'll get you all out of here," Lucas said and waved his son inside. If he blew it again, Cal and his family might not survive.

Nita accepted an apologetic, tearful hug from Jessica but quickly gestured for Jessica to sit at the table. Jessica and Nita had grown apart over the years, and it showed. Nita no longer trusted her. Teka looked distracted, but he sat too.

Jessica gazed at Lucas with horror as he explained what the Duharts were willing to do to be released. After he finished, the room was silent for a long time.

Cal sat strangling a cloth napkin while he fought his temper and his nerves. Jared stood over the table, transfixed. Teka listened with his eyes closed, a million miles away.

"An extraordinary request," Teka said finally, his eyes still closed. His face showed no emotion. "And extraordinarily ill-timed. The effort alone . . ."

Blood crept into Cal's face in splotchy red spots. Lucas knew that Cal would rather punch Teka through a wall than engage in polite debate about his family's future.

Lucas's voice cleared. "Then let them walk away free and clear, without restrictions. Like they tried to do last night."

Jessica gave a long, pained sigh, shaking her head. She squeezed Nita's hand. "When Fana comes back, I'll get you out on your terms," she said. "I just need time."

"*When* Fana comes back?" Cal said, finally breaking in. "Don't you mean *if*?"

"Jess, it's too late," Nita said. Politely, she slipped her hand away from Jessica's. "No more promises. If we give up the memories, how can you say no?"

"How can I sit by and watch friends do that?" Jessica said.

Cal laughed grimly. "There's plenty you sit by and watch, Jess. *Plenty*."

Lucas swung his legs over the side of the bed. "They have a right to go, and we don't have a right to stop them. When we agreed to stay here, none of us knew all the facts."

When Teka looked squarely at him, Lucas felt a chill, a sensation of being physically touched. "This crisis has grown much bigger than the handful of people in this room," Teka said. "And certainly bigger than the whims of three mortals."

You mean three monkeys, Lucas couldn't help thinking.

Suddenly, Teka's voice filled Lucas's head: *I CAN ALLEVIATE THEIR FEAR.*

The effect of hearing Teka's voice so clearly while Teka only stared silently from across the room was so disorienting that Lucas shook his head hard. Jessica gave Teka a discreet glance, then she looked at Lucas. She had heard Teka's voice, too.

Lucas shook his head. "If it's worth saying, say it in front of them," he told Teka.

A wince of irritation passed across Teka's lips. Teka turned to Cal. "I offer you peace of mind until Fana's return," he said. "I will soften your mood. Without your fear to hamper you—"

Cal suddenly let out a yell, and he lunged from his chair, wrapping his arm around Teka's neck. Cal's weight threw Teka's pinewood chair backward, and it cracked beneath them on the floor. The bump toppled a drinking glass, which broke inches behind them.

"Cal, no!" Lucas yelled. From where he sat, he couldn't tell if Cal had snapped the Life Brother's neck in half.

"*Stop it!*" Jessica said, leaping to her feet.

Cal's arm swung, and he punched Teka's face as he choked him. One punch. Two.

"Don't you fuck with me, you sonofabitch!" Cal said through a spray of spittle. He punched Teka a third time; the blow was hard. Teka groaned.

All sound seemed to vanish as Lucas lurched to standing. He grabbed Cal before he could hit Teka again, but Lucas couldn't unwind Cal's arm from Teka's neck without help from Jared. Cal was still panting and cursing when they pulled him near the bed, and Cal might have yanked free of them if his burly son hadn't come and hugged him around the waist. Cal bucked with such fervor that he was a challenge even for three.

"Dad, quit it!" Hank said.

Cal finally stopped fighting and hung limply. He was exhausted from his outburst, breathing in harsh gasps. "What's wrong, ass-hole?" Cal taunted Teka. "Didn't see that coming?"

Teka lay on the floor, holding his throat, his bottom lip split and bleeding. Droplets of blood stained his white tunic, near the complex pattern embroidered on his collar to signify his station as the Highest Teacher. Jessica knelt beside Teka, offering her arm to help him stand.

"Forgive him, Teka," Jessica said, her head inclined almost in a bow. "He's very upset."

Lucas had known the Life Brothers would come, but the sound of the door slamming open against the wall still made his heart drop. Fasilidas and Yonas ran into the room with batons pointed like guns, and for a grim millisecond Lucas expected to witness a slaughter like the one he had seen at Jessica's clinic in Botswana.

The Life Brothers' faces were angrier than the faces of the white gunmen. Those had only been mercenaries carrying out their work; the Life Brothers were enraged. Fasilidas's bright, youthful smile was gone, and a glint in Yonas's eye made Lucas wonder how they had ever mistaken him for a docile caretaker.

Cal was ready for them, swaying from side to side, his eyes ready to fight to the death. Lucas prayed that Hank wasn't about to see his father killed.

"Teka, he's under duress," Lucas said. "That won't happen again."

Fasilidas and Yonas had their eyes on Cal, but they each grabbed

Teka's arms to lift him up. When no one spoke, Lucas realized that the Life Brothers were communicating silently.

"*Get out of this room,*" a gravelly voice said, but Lucas couldn't tell which of the men had spoken. A blink later, he realized that the voice had been a woman's.

Jessica's fists were clenched at her sides, elbows locked as she glared at Fasilidas. Lucas's heartbeat rattled in his eardrums as he waited to find out if the Life Brothers were willing to defer to his sister-in-law, or if they only pretended to.

Fasilidas bowed, looking mortified. "Blessed Mother—"

"*Never* enter my quarters without my permission, Fasilidas," Jessica said. "How *dare* you! Now leave us." Her voice was an earthquake.

Their eyes still on Cal, neither immortal moved.

Teka delicately wiped blood from his lip with the back of his wrist. Finally, he nodded to the men. "Leave us," he said. Teka probably said much more, but he didn't share it aloud.

Without a word, Fasilidas and Yonas gave final bows and closed the door quietly behind them. Lucas was so relieved that he nearly swooned. He staggered to an empty chair.

"That was beyond foolish," Teka said to Cal. He went to the sink and turned on a stream of water to rinse blood from his hand. "My Brothers are incensed."

Lucas pounded the table. "Let them go, Teka. If you don't, Cal will have to answer for this."

"All of us answer for what we do," Teka said, sounding noncommittal. He turned off the water and shook his hands dry.

"Fana would want us to let them go," Jessica said.

"Fana is yet a child," Teka said.

"Fana would never keep prisoners," Jessica said. "She ran away to protest the imprisonment of Caitlin and Justin O'Neal. You know Fana's heart, Teka. She wants our blood used to help humankind, not to hold families against their will. This is a perversion of her ideals."

Teka walked back to the table and sat beside Lucas. "They should leave the boy."

This time, Nita stepped toward Teka, flinging her arms for emphasis. "Oh, *hell* no! We're not leaving anybody."

"She's damned right about that," Cal said.

"I'm going with them," Hank said, his voice unwavering.

Teka turned his laserlike gaze to Hank. "You are at a tender age to forget so much."

"I'm not scared," Hank said. "If I forget stuff, I'll learn it again."

"Experiences and learning are not the same thing, Hank," Teka said. "The things we learn are like streams through our conscious mind. Experiences are the ocean within us. They shape our perceptions in ways we cannot predict. You will be the most changed."

"Then let him go, but leave him his memories," Nita said, a mother's plea. "Only him."

Teka closed his eyes again. "That," he said, "I cannot do."

Again, silence sank across the room. Nita bit her lip, her face shining with rage and tears. When Teka opened his eyes next, he was looking at Cal. "Your position is now so precarious with my Brothers that it would be inhumane to keep you here. I will wash your memories, preserving what I can. You will not remember the healing or the Blood. After the memory wash, Yonas will drive you to town. You will have no awareness until you wake on a bus on your way to SeaTac airport. Unless you are detained, you will fly to Antigua."

"You can do that?" Nita said, sounding like a young girl seeing Santa Claus. Breathless.

"I will do my best," Teka said. "I will leave as much as I am able. Especially for the boy."

"Jared?" Lucas heard himself say, and Jared's eyes darted to his as if Lucas had spied on his thoughts. Lucas felt his heart crumbling, but he went on. "What about you?"

Jared shook his head, firm. "No, Dad. I'm staying. This is my family."

Thank you, God, Lucas thought, all the while despising his selfishness.

"We'll wire money as soon as we can," Jessica told Nita. "But you won't know—"

"There is no time for these sentimentalities," Teka snapped. "I must begin."

Jessica hugged Nita. The women cried together, eyes closed, swaying in a silent dance.

Lucas brought himself to his feet again as Cal walked toward him. Lucas had never seen so many expressions woven on one man's face: Relief. Joy. Terror. Grief.

When Lucas had first committed himself to the colony, the Life Brothers had insisted that he cut off contact with his old friends and colleagues. Jessica and Alex had made the same sacrifice. He had been stunned when Cal and Nita had said they would move to Washington to be near him, and even more stunned when Dawit had convinced the Life Brothers to agree. For fourteen years, they had been each other's family, eating their meals together, godparents to each other's children. Before that, they'd been neighbors on Okeepechee Road.

Without Cal, Jared would have been dead today, and Lucas might never have found the blood. Cal had given him the magazine article that had led him to Botswana, when Jared's illness had made them all feel desperate enough to believe in miracles.

"You'll be fine," Lucas said, assuring himself as much as Cal. "Jess and I saw the footage of Justin O'Neal at the airport. He seemed fine afterward. Just a little confused."

Cal nodded, grateful for a hopeful image. "Hope to Heaven I'm doing the right thing, especially for Hank. We just can't live like this. Not another day."

"I'm sorry, Cal." Lucas's words were too weak for the occasion. What could he say to a man he had cost so much? "I wish I'd known. . . ."

"Don't be sorry," Cal said. "Teka may take away most of it, but"— he patted his chest, above his heart—"we'll always know, Doc."

Lucas Shepard hugged his best friend goodbye.

Their colony really was at war, he realized. But it had nothing to do with the Department of Homeland Security. Their war was between those who had the Living Blood, and those who didn't. Mortal and immortal. Just like the oil wars in the desert, their war would be a long one.

The Duharts were the first casualties, but Lucas knew they would not be the last.

Twenty-five

The white Spanish Mission–style church looks like a palace atop the hill, encircled by dead, craggy trees. The sky's clouds are thick, aflame with twinkles of green lightning. The skies are preparing for a hurricane. In the bell tower, two bronze bells toll in cacophony, swinging in opposite directions. Roaring winds devour their sour music.

Townspeople flee the thrashing rains, but the doors to the church are locked. A man and woman lean out of the dome's window, only their silhouettes visible in the Shadows as they gaze down at the people below. The townspeople surge to a throng. Many of them hold small children above their heads, begging for shelter. Others are thin and frail, reeking of illness.

In the church dome, the man and woman open their arms to welcome the storm, which drenches the townspeople. Their upturned faces are pelted with raindrops.

The rain is the color of blood.

Fana woke, locking a gasp in her throat as the car rocked on a bump in the road.

She expected to find herself riding in the Orbit with her parents, Gramma Bea, Aunt Alex and Uncle Lucas, surrounded by evergreens. But that was childish wishful thinking. Instead, Caitlin and Johnny sat in the front seat of a strange car while the radio screamed hysteria.

Caitlin had left the highway. Now they were in a nearly deserted warehouse district.

Had Fana dozed off while she'd been meditating? She'd been trying to reach Teka to tell him what she had learned, since it might be too late by the time she had access to a secure phone. Sometimes her teacher felt so physically close to her that he could have been in the car with them.

"Was I sleeping?" Fana said.

The radio was loud, burying Fana's words. Neither of her friends turned around; they only gazed ahead through the dust-spattered windshield.

A warm, soothing arm tightened around Fana's shoulder. "Shhhh. It's all right, *negra*."

Charlie's scent plied Fana's nostrils; his skin mimicked honey in every way, from its coloring to its smell. Charlie's smile greeted her, and his eyes that promised peace.

Charlie had found a straw cowboy hat painted with a snakeskin pattern in the car, and it fit him. The sight of him quelled some of her misery. Fana rested her head on Charlie's shoulder, and his soft slope of muscles met her cheek. She heard the whisper of his heart beating inches from her ear. He wore an old trace of cologne, but his skin smelled perfect by itself.

"How long was I out?" she said.

"Not twenty minutes," he said, stroking her hair. "I didn't have the heart to wake you."

Fana settled against him, nestling, and he lay back to make a bed for her. The backseat with Charlie felt like her cocoon. Fana wished the world could vanish and let her rest. She was exhausted from the day, but this wasn't the time to sleep.

"Where are we?" Fana said.

"Nogales," Charlie said. "On the Arizona side. Near the border."

Fana could just make out the blue numerals on the car's dashboard: 1:15. Was that all? One day felt like five or six, and it was only halfway done.

Fana raised her voice, hoping Johnny would hear her. "You OK, Johnny?" she said. She resisted the urge to probe him. She had abused her gifts too much already.

Johnny shrugged, not turning around. "Fine," he said, barely audible over the radio.

Caitlin laughed, startling Fana. Caitlin didn't laugh often anymore. "Those assholes thought they'd catch us with those check-points!" Caitlin said. "Huh, Charlie?"

Charlie grinned. "Nobody's catching us today."

The man on the radio was talking nonsense about a link between Glow and bio-terrorism. His voice was full of authority. Fana hadn't realized how easy it was to make lies sound plausible.

"Can you turn that off, please?" Fana said.

A flick of Caitlin's wrist, and the car was silent. A loud, low-pitched horn sounded outside, and suddenly a cargo train with brown cars sped alongside them, in the opposite direction. Fana stared out at the passing train until its countermotion made her dizzy. The *chunk-chunk* sound of the train's wheels charging across the tracks made her anxious, as if the train was an omen. Was she going the wrong way?

She had dreamed while she'd slept. Something about a church, but not like any she knew.

"Caitlin, where are we going?" she said.

"Close your eyes and count to ten," Caitlin said. As if it was all a game.

Charlie suddenly held her cheeks and kissed her lips. His mouth jolted her skin with tiny ripples. "I've been dying to do that for the past twenty miles," he said, and kissed her again.

Fana felt self-conscious with Caitlin and Johnny so close, but then she realized how silly a worry that was. Anything might happen today. Why should she deny herself her first kisses?

When Charlie turned his hip toward her, she felt his urgent, hidden arousal against her stomach, which fluttered a nervous response. She had seen nude men in movies and photographs, some of them aroused, but nothing captured the raw potency of what she felt buried in Charlie's jeans. If they had been alone, her hand might have ventured there to sate her curiosity.

Instead, Fana touched the warm nape of Charlie's neck and basked in his mouth and tongue, lingering, cleaving herself to him everywhere their skin wanted to touch.

Caitlin was so pleased with herself that it was hard to suppress a smile.

She'd always had a good memory, committing names and tele-phone numbers so she wouldn't leave a trail, but today her mem-ory was *perfect*. She had visited Nogales only once, but every street sign and building felt as familiar as her home neighborhood. She avoided Highway 19 and International Street, since there were sure to be checkpoints near the border. Instead of panicking every time a police car or white border patrol van came into sight, she nearly laughed. She could walk up to a cop and kick him in the nuts, and just maybe she would.

She had Charlie on her side.

Every time she'd glanced at Charlie in the mirror during the drive from the casino, she'd learned something new and fascinat-ing about him. Charlie wasn't his real name, for instance. He hadn't revealed his name to her yet, but he would if she proved herself. And Charlie wasn't Puerto Rican, as he'd told Fana: He was an Italian, born in Tuscany. His face looked younger than hers, but he was as old as Dad. At least fifty.

For the first time since Caitlin O'Neal had known Fana, *she* was the one who knew things. *She* was the one who could hear what was unspoken and see what was hidden. Charlie had given Caitlin that, asking so little in return. Charlie only wanted to take Fana far from the reach of authorities who would imprison her and abuse her blood. They both wanted to keep Fana safe.

Nelson Avenue. They were close!

Caitlin slowed. The squat concrete building was sandwiched between large warehouses, with lettering painted in red on the dark-ened windowpane: *Clinica de Esperanza*. Clinic of Hope. Beneath that, a list of services: *VIH/SIDA Pruebas y Medicinas. Maternidad.* The small parking lot outside was empty, and Caitlin felt a pang of sadness from her old self.

Maritza had worked here two summers ago. The Nogales clinic had cleaned out at least fifty HIV and AIDS patients, under the supervision of Dr. Raul Puerta. But even without help from Char-lie, Caitlin could see that the clinic was closed. Dr. Puerta and his staff were gone, in hiding. No one had been cured in Nogales since Maritza's death.

Caitlin hoped the tunnel was still here.

Caitlin pulled the car around to the rear of the building, out of sight. She heard glass crunch beneath the tires. Luckily, they didn't need the car now.

In the mirror, Caitlin saw Charlie kissing Fana, and she studied them, transfixed. Then Caitlin saw her own eyes in the mirror, and she felt her mind wriggle. Her elation dissipated.

Instead, cold terror pooled across Caitlin's heart.

What's happening to me?

As the car inched to a stop, Caitlin O'Neal felt her mind quietly dying.

He was gone.

From the first instant Johnny had realized he hadn't been able to move on his own, he had been aware of a sensation like an immovable weight sitting on him, holding him still—Charlie's weight, crushing him. But the weight was lifting.

Johnny shifted his eyes right, then left. He blinked once. Twice. His chest heaved as he breathed faster, gaining control of his lungs.

Oh God please please please please help me.

Sensation returned, slowly. Johnny concentrated until his head hurt, and his index finger rose. Johnny's heart thundered to life. He might have a small chance! Everything in him cried out to run, but he couldn't. Not yet. He *might* have the strength to open his car door, but he knew that as soon as Charlie saw him move, he would be a prisoner again. *What,* then?

The Lord is my shepherd I shall not want He leadeth me beside the still waters.

Johnny glanced toward Caitlin. She was gripping the steering wheel with both hands, staring at the rearview mirror with unblinking eyes. Charlie had Caitlin too; Johnny could see it in her face, slack with confusion. Charlie had her in a different way, but Caitlin was Charlie's now.

A tear slipped from Johnny's eye.

Johnny almost sobbed, feeling hopeless, when he saw a metallic gleam from the back of Caitlin's waistband. A gun! It was partially concealed under her shirt, but the butt lay not a foot from him. Johnny wriggled his fingers, one by one. He remembered the vision of Charlie's face covered in bees, and he had never been more sure of anything.

Please Lord give me the strength Please Lord let it fire.

A warming sensation shot up and down each of Johnny's arms, as if in response.

Johnny flung himself toward Caitlin. His motion was clumsy and uncontrolled, so he fell against her with more force than he'd intended, knocking her forward against the steering wheel. His left arm splayed awkwardly behind him, but his right arm reached out toward the gun. The gun didn't come free from Caitlin with his first tug, but he pulled again, and he had it!

Johnny's shock that his plan had worked nearly froze him in place.

"*Hey*—," Caitlin said. But her reflexes were slow.

Charlie and Fana were so absorbed in each other that neither of them moved, as if a bubble separated them from the world.

Johnny was afraid he would drop the gun; his palm shook so much that he could barely keep it in his hand. Still, he pointed squarely at the cowboy hat slanted across the back of Charlie's head. Johnny tried to command his trembling finger on the trigger, and he felt it tighten.

"Fana, *move!*" Johnny shouted from numb lips.

Fana shifted suddenly, her face clear of Charlie, and her eyes went wide.

Johnny squeezed the trigger. His ears rang with an explosion and the sound of shattering glass. Fana screamed.

Even before Johnny saw Charlie's head intact and untouched, he knew his chance was gone. His body was lost to him again, submersed and useless in numbing cold. Johnny watched his own arm with horror as it swung back toward Caitlin, aiming the gun at her head instead.

"*Stop* it!" Fana screamed.

Caitlin grabbed his wrist with both hands, and her strength seemed superhuman only because he felt so weak. But he wasn't weak. Somehow, the barrel trembled toward her face.

Charlie reached toward him from the backseat while Caitlin wrestled with Johnny, still clasping his wrist, and Johnny could no longer tell where his limbs ended and theirs began. He only realized where the gun was when he felt the cold nozzle against his side, right below his ribs.

Thank God it's not Caitlin—

Johnny didn't finish his thought before the explosion.

His body's numbness gave way to searing, incomprehensible pain. Fire tore at his insides. Johnny's mouth was locked tight, mute, but his mind screamed.

WHAT TOOK YOU SO LONG? Charlie's voice said. *YOU KEPT ME WAITING.*

Then, Charlie took mercy on him.

Johnny Wright's mind sank into blessed darkness.

"Shit, shit, shit. What the *fuck*?" Caitlin stared at her bloodied hands, shaking with sobs. She dropped the gun to the floor.

Fana would have been certain she was dreaming except for the painful throbbing in her ears and the smell of blood and gunpowder. Fana covered her mouth, feeling sick to her stomach as her mind danced in a frenzy. How had this happened?

Charlie opened his car door and jumped out. He ran to Johnny's door and pulled it open. Johnny nearly fell out before Charlie caught him with a grunt.

"Is he dead?" Caitlin said, red-faced. "*Shit*! I d-didn't mean t-to . . ."

Charlie checked Johnny's pulse, and relief washed over his face. "He's just passed out," Charlie said. "Come on! We've got to take him and get ghost."

The backseat was covered with glass from Johnny's wild shot, which had broken the window. Fana noticed a new, singed hole in back of Johnny's seat. A matching hole had left a trail of cottony stuffing only inches from Fana's leg. The bullet had passed through Johnny and barely missed her. The ringing stopped as Fana's eardrums healed, but sulfur stung her nose.

Dammit. Fana knew she would have sensed such a violent impulse from Johnny if she hadn't been fooling around. This was her fault! Again.

But she would make it right.

Fana nearly tripped over her feet as she scrambled out of the car. Already, she could hear a distant siren, coming fast. She glanced at the buildings around them to see if anyone was watching. Just an alley and loading bays for warehouses. No one in sight.

Charlie hoisted Johnny over his shoulder like a fireman. Johnny flopped, limp, smearing Charlie's clothes with blood. Blood painted Johnny's seat.

"It's bad," Fana said. She could feel Johnny's heart struggling. He was bleeding to death.

"Bad enough," Charlie said. "*Vamos.*"

A glance told Fana that the scuffed white rear door to the clinic was locked, and she didn't sense anyone inside who could let them in. She whirled around to look for Caitlin, whose legs dangled out of the door like a child's.

"Caitlin, *hurry!*" Fana said. She ran to Caitlin and held her hands.

Caitlin looked up, startled, and shook her head, her lips shivering. "F-Fana . . . I'm so sorry . . . ," she said. "I d-don't know why I sh-shot him . . ."

"It was an accident," Fana said. Because their situation was so dire, Fana tickled Caitlin's mind with a quick massage.

And something felt . . . wrong.

Just like the temporary blockage Fana had felt when she'd tried to probe Johnny at the casino, Caitlin's mind did not yield as usual. Caitlin's fear and horror clamored, but part of Caitlin seemed hidden. Masked. Part of Caitlin did not seem afraid or horrified at all, more like a detached observer. Worse. A deeply hidden part of Caitlin seemed to be smiling.

Fana gazed deeply into her friend's eyes, as if they could show what her inner world did not. Caitlin's eyes were red from tears. She looked weary and broken.

It's your own mind blocking you, so you won't hurt her like Aunt Alex. Stop zoning.

"Do you have a key to this place?" Fana asked her.

Sniffing and wiping her face, Caitlin nodded.

Fana tugged on Caitlin's hands to bring her to her feet. "You got us this far, Caitlin. You can make it. Johnny needs us."

Charlie was waiting for them at the rear door, staggering under Johnny's weight. Caitlin fumbled with her keys, nearly dropping them. The siren was closer, maybe only a couple of blocks away. Fana tried to mentally pick the lock the way she had broken the McDonald's security camera, but her mind flailed with confusion. She didn't have a clue how to begin.

Caitlin could open the door. It was more important to shake the police.

Fana closed her eyes. With the help of the siren, for the first time in memory she could *clearly* see a remote object without a mental struggle: A white Santa Cruz County sheriff's car was approaching, driven by one officer. A male. Fana knew him, suddenly: Sgt. José Calderón. Fifteen years of experience. A father, a son, a brother. The closer he drove, the more intimately her thoughts merged with his. Fana could taste the coffee and onions from his lunch.

POWPOW

Using her memory of the gunshots, Fana re-created the sound inside Calderón's head. She misdirected him a dozen blocks farther, hoping the distraction was enough. Adrenaline surged through him; Fana felt his excitement prickle across her skin. Her heart sped with his. Her mind overflowed with jargon as Calderón picked up his radio, reporting what he had heard.

The siren wailed past, toward Fana's phantom gunshots.

"*Fana!*" Charlie called, pulling her back to herself.

The door was open, and Charlie and Caitlin were already inside the darkened clinic. Fana followed them, slamming the door. She could barely see the windowless storeroom, which was crammed with boxes of supplies.

"Let's get to the tunnel," Charlie panted.

"No, not yet," Fana said. "I have to look at Johnny."

"You're the boss," Caitlin said. The door she opened led to a narrow hall. Light.

The examination room was a few feet beyond the doorway, lighted by a window. The room was bare except for an exam table and an empty supply cabinet with open doors. Charlie lowered Johnny to the frayed cushion on the table while Fana held Johnny steady so he wouldn't roll to the floor. He lay on his side, almost fetal.

Johnny's T-shirt was soaked with blood, worse in back than in front. Fana lifted the fabric from Johnny's abdomen, wiping away blood so she could see his injury. A neat hole spurted out thin streams of blood where the bullet had passed, below his ribs. The exit wound was a mess: The bullet had punctured vital organs, or ruptured an artery. She didn't know enough about physiology to trust her mental gifts to heal him. If she guessed wrong, she might make it worse.

She would have to give him some of her blood.

"Shit, what can we do?" Charlie said.

"I know a little about medicine," she said. "My aunt and uncle are doctors. I'll try."

"What do you need?" Anxious perspiration gleamed on Charlie's face.

Fana needed Caitlin, but her friend was sitting on the floor against the wall, hugging her knees, staring at nothing. Caitlin's paralysis was as scary as Johnny's injury. Zoning.

Fana sighed. She hated to lie, but she needed privacy. "Sterile bandages. Alcohol."

"There's gotta' be some in back."

"Be careful," Fana said. "The police might see the car and come looking."

"I'm always careful." Charlie kissed her forehead, the way her father kissed her mother.

Fana pulled the tiny knife from her back pocket and stretched out her forearm beside Johnny's bleeding wound. She glanced at the doorway to make sure Charlie was gone, then she jabbed the blade into her skin. After the initial flash of pain, Fana felt the familiar tingling that signaled that her skin was already repairing itself. She never bled much, or long.

But it was enough. Fana rubbed her skin against Johnny's, pressing her wound to his, mingling their blood. She could change his blood when his heart stopped if she used the Ceremony, but that was too risky. She couldn't wait for him to die. Besides, Fana had never performed the Ceremony before. What if it didn't work? Instead of waking up as an immortal, Johnny might just die.

Blood healed by itself, Ceremony or not. Her blood wouldn't protect Johnny from his next injury or illness, but maybe it would be enough to heal the damage to his organs. Teka had told her that her blood was more powerful than anyone else's. She hoped her Teacher was right.

Fana gazed at Johnny's face, which looked untroubled in sleep. She pressed her palm against his warm forehead. He was handsome too, she realized. His face shined with promise.

"Magic show's over," Caitlin said in a monotone, startling her.

Caitlin now stood behind her, clear-eyed and alert. Caitlin took Fana's hand and lifted it away from Johnny, almost as if she'd been jealous about the way she'd been touching him.

"Welcome back," Fana said. Caitlin only grunted behind her.

Fana peered closely at Johnny's injury. The blood had already stopped its rhythmic spurting, and the wound seemed to be congealing at the edges. She had to lean close to see, but the clots were there. Her blood was strengthening Johnny's, speeding his healing. Fana smiled.

"It's working," Fana said, relieved.

Caitlin didn't answer. When Fana turned around, her friend was gone.

Instead, Charlie stood in the doorway with an old wheelchair loaded with medical supplies, his cowboy hat askew. "What's working?" he said.

Fana pursed her lips. "Praying," she said. Mostly, it wasn't even a lie.

Charlie had brought gauze, tape and topical antibiotics. He helped Fana disinfect Johnny's wounds with cotton swabs, and he wrapped his midsection in bandages. Charlie was strong, and he secured the bandages tightly, as careful as a doctor. They worked quickly. Even now, Fana was aware of her arm pressed against Charlie's. Yearning burned from her skin, and she was sure she felt rising heat from his; their bodies were always in a separate communication.

"The people waiting for us can get a doctor," Charlie said.

Caitlin had never mentioned that anyone would be waiting for them.

"Another safe house," Charlie said, seeing her puzzlement. "A church."

Usually, the mention of a church didn't make Fana shiver. But it did, this time. "I just had a dream about a church," she said.

Charlie smiled. "Then it's destiny."

Charlie hoisted Johnny up again, and Fana helped him sit Johnny in the wheelchair, where Johnny's limbs dangled. His head hung forward, limp. Fana noticed that her T-shirt was dotted with Johnny's blood. There had been blood in her dream, too.

Something isn't right. The certainty was so vivid that Fana did not follow Charlie into the hall as he pushed Johnny in the wheelchair.

"Caitlin said there was a secure phone here," she called after him. "Where is it?"

"Not here," Charlie said over his shoulder. "Nogales on the Mexican side."

Fana sighed. Right. She had forgotten that the neighboring cities shared a name, even if a newly fortified fence separated their people.

Leaning against the doorway of the bathroom, Caitlin waited with a flashlight across the hall. Caitlin smiled when she saw Fana, but her smile was warped by a glitter in her eyes.

"Someone is still tracking us," Fana said. "I feel it. Someone . . ." She glanced around the empty clinic, which looked like it had been hurriedly cleared. Stray papers littered the floor. There was no one else inside, yet she could feel eyes watching her. "Someone close."

Caitlin only shrugged, still smiling. What was *wrong* with her?

"More reason to hurry, no?" Charlie said.

Caitlin stepped aside with a sweep of her arm, inviting Fana to the bathroom. "Welcome to the rabbit hole," Caitlin said, sounding playful again.

The tunnel was in the bathroom floor.

Caitlin pushed aside a woven rug and lifted a thick square of the bathroom tile's panels, revealing a dark, yawning hole in the floor. The hole was narrow, not even three feet by three feet. It looked like something the Life Brothers would have built, except that all of the colony's shelter entrances were in the woods.

Her mother, Gramma Bea and Aunt Alex were underground too, in the shelters. The knowledge came to Fana easily, peeling ignorance away as if she had known all along. *They know danger is close,* she realized. She was relieved and felt her anxiety's binds loosening.

"How long is the tunnel?" Fana said.

"Almost a mile," Caitlin said. "The Railroad's greatest accomplishment. Smugglers built part of it, and we did the rest. Took almost a year." Pride shook her voice. "This tunnel was originally for smuggling illegal drugs. Then they figured out there was bigger business in prescription meds. Lots of retirees in Arizona."

Fana walked to the edge of the tunnel and stared. Two shiny handgrips led down, but beyond them she saw only the deep pitch of the descent.

Shadows waited beneath her feet.

Twenty-six

Fana shuddered, claustrophobic. The tunnel was narrow, with barely enough room for Charlie to push Johnny's wheelchair. In his cowboy hat, Charlie was so tall that he had to duck.

The rough walls were fortified with plywood, but they were mostly soil and rocks, flaking away when she brushed too close. Lightbulbs were strung overhead the length of the tunnel, spaced just within sight of each other, more for reassurance than vision. They needed their flashlights to light the way.

Charlie had said it would only be about a mile, but the walk seemed endless. Fana was close to choking on the thick smell of raw sewage all around them, coating her hair and skin. She would have nightmares about this smell, just as each new horror of this day would follow her dreams. She would stink for days, but the smell would wash away. What about the rest? The tunnel brought back memories Fana thought she had shed.

Circuitous darkness. A long-haired man with a gun. *Mahmoud.* A wall of bees.

I was afraid, and the bees did what I couldn't do.

Fana had seen the wall of bees in her nightmares, but she hadn't realized how the image fit into her past until now: She and her mother had been fleeing the Lalibela colony the first time she'd met Dad and his people. A man with a gun, Mahmoud, had chased them into a tunnel. Then bees had come, blocking the tunnel in a swarm. The bees had protected her, Mom, Dad and Teferi.

My bees.

No. Not hers. *The Shadows'. Whatever controlled the bees had their own wishes, and they enjoyed my fear. They still remember me.* The Shadows wanted to ply her with sweet talk and imaginary treats, like when she was three. If she lost control and fed the Shadows, Fana didn't know what she would become. Teka had warned her.

Charlie grunted. The tunnel floor was rough and uneven. Charlie kicked aside an empty beer bottle, and the glass rattled against the wall as it spun, echoing.

Johnny was still unconscious in the chair. Fana had to hold him so he wouldn't fall.

But Johnny's heartbeat was stronger all the time. Fana trained herself to listen for it, and she enjoyed the reassuring *thump-thump* beneath her thoughts, a pleasant drumbeat to pace her walking. Johnny would be fine. She had saved him. That was the first good news all day.

Caitlin's thoughts were a quiet burr. Caitlin's anxiety level had dipped to almost nothing once they were in the tunnel. Fana probed once to make sure Caitlin was all right, and she found a calm hum.

That's it. No more probing. Will you ever learn?

"Almost there," Charlie said.

The wheelchair hit a bump, and Johnny shifted, his arm falling loose. Fana caught Johnny's arm and nestled it across his chest. "You keep saying that."

Charlie chuckled. "I mean it this time. Not even a hundred yards."

Fana peered ahead, but she saw only the pathetic glow of the next lightbulb.

"Are you sure?" Fana said.

"Trust me." Charlie's words were almost a plea.

Fana did trust him. Why not? Charlie hadn't zoned once today, which was amazing. *Especially for a mortal.* If Caitlin heard that thought, she would accuse Fana of bigotry, but Fana knew it was harder for mortals to keep their equilibrium. For mortals, death was much more than an inconvenience. Yet Charlie was as fearless as a Life Brother.

"Thank you for getting Johnny down here," Fana said.

Charlie looked at her over his shoulder, grinning. "Hey, if you care about him so much, he's *mi familia*. Is he your boyfriend?"

Fana couldn't believe it, but she was smiling. Again.

"No," she said. "He's not my boyfriend. I don't have one."

Hearing herself, Fana winced. Did she sound like she expected Charlie to be her boyfriend just because he had kissed her? Someone as rootless as Charlie probably had girls waiting in a dozen cities. Even without probing, she could feel his past sexual experiences simmering in his memories. *It's not like he expects you to be the mother of his children.*

"Good to know," Charlie said, grinning. "In case you're the mother of my children."

It was like speaking in thoughts to Teka! Fana peered into the darkness to try to see Charlie's profile better, longing to find his eyes. Only his radiant smile was visible, but his smile was enough. They were making each other smile. Today. Now. They were a miracle.

Aunt Alex and Uncle Lucas had met during a time of strife, and it had woven them together at the roots. And Mom had told her that the first thing she'd loved about Dad had been the way he'd seemed to know her already. Mom's love for Dad had been born instantly: She'd found it in his eyes. His smile. Mom had buried those feeling about Dad for a long while, but the impression was always there.

That was the happy part of Mom's memory, before it had been turned upside down. Dad insisted that he hadn't delved into thought perception until Teka had helped him a few years ago, so he hadn't heard Mom's thoughts on that first date. But Mom wasn't sure; maybe he'd cheated with his mind, whether accidentally or on purpose. And then there had been the lies.

Would Charlie feel betrayed like Mom one day, too?

Fana itched to return to the treasures in Charlie's head. To see his mother's face. To see him when he was ten. How long would it be before she could tell him about her blood? Or about the hurricane? Could she ever?

Suddenly, Fana's stomach ached, sharp pain. Fana's mind and body always suffered in concert. She would not lie to Charlie the way Dad had lied to Mom. She would not pretend.

"I'm not the mother of your children," Fana said. "Sorry."

"We should ask Caitlin," Charlie said.

"I know the truth," Caitlin said in a singsong. The perkiness in Caitlin's voice surprised Fana, since Caitlin's walk was so slow and listless. "There are no two others in the world, nor in the history of the world, better matched than you."

It was too dark to see Caitlin's face clearly. Although Caitlin didn't sound sarcastic, Fana suddenly felt angry. "Johnny just got shot, and we're fugitives. Maybe this isn't the time to talk like we're thirteen years old." Caitlin would have said that, if Caitlin had been acting like Caitlin.

"We're not talking like children, Fana," Charlie said. "What's more adult than admitting that we don't know anything about tomorrow? I've put away childish things. That's why I kissed you, Fana. That's why I want to kiss you again. And again." She could barely hear him even in the silence of the tunnel. He had a hypnotist's voice, tickling her skin. Charlie sighed. "I don't always tell the truth—I have my vices—but I don't do anything unless I mean it. My kisses are words, not just kisses. My kisses are a promise."

A poet, Fana thought. Teka was the only other poet she knew, but his poems couldn't be translated into words. Charlie's poetry was meant to be spoken aloud.

"When do you lie?" Fana said. It would be foolish not to ask.

"Only when the truth would be misunderstood," he said.

Amen, Fana thought. "There are things I can't tell you," she said. "Things about myself."

Charlie's smile faded. "Me, too."

"I can't stay with you if my family needs me."

This time, Charlie didn't answer right away. He paused a moment, slowing his walk.

"I could go with you," he said. "To help your family."

"No," Fana said. "You can't."

Charlie looked at her over his shoulder again, and in the glow as they passed beneath the sole overhead light, she saw a wounded gleam in his eye. She had hurt him already. Charlie looked away from her.

"I see . . . ," Charlie said. "At home, they depend only on you."

Charlie's casual intimacy startled her again.

"Are you a telepath?" she said. She had never met a mortal with the ability, but, then again, she hadn't met many mortals. Teka credited the Blood for the gift, but he might be wrong.

Charlie chuckled. "A mind reader? Maybe I am. Or . . . maybe I'm the strongest one in my family, too, and everyone I know has relied on me since I was young. So . . . I know that burden."

Fana couldn't remember a day without burden. Teka's expectations were the biggest burden, next to her mother's fear. Children weren't supposed to start out stronger than their parents, and Mom had always been bracing for her next storm. But now Fana knew that Mom had been right to be wary, no matter how much it hurt them both.

"How do you know me so well?" Fana said. Her heart pounded, but not with the sickening dread she had felt since waking in the Rolfsons' house. Instead, she felt wonder; maybe for the first time since she was three. "We just met."

"I don't know you yet, Fana," Charlie said, "but my soul does. As soon as I saw you."

Fana's chest floated, a starburst. Then, quiet tears came, invisible in the tunnel's darkness. Her stomach ached in rhythm with her tears.

Why had she chosen such a horrible day to fall in love?

I will never hurt you, dear Fana. Li amerò per sempre. *I cherish your every breath.*

Each moment Michel spent with Fana, he loved her more. Papa had told him that Fana's presence would feel like no other, that no forgettable tryst could compare to his predetermined mate. But how could he have guessed how quickly, and how deeply, she would move him?

She was unlike anyone he had ever known! Selfless. Merciful. Humble. Fana's beliefs were misguided because of her ignorance, but she was remarkably unspoiled for one with the Blood. Would he have been as gentle-hearted as she if he had been born in her place?

He wanted her to know him. His desire to merge his thoughts and memories with Fana's was so strong that his skin felt hot, just as his loins had burned for her while they'd kissed in the car. With

Fana's kisses, he sank into a state of bliss, forgetting himself. Remembering himself.

He knew Fana's heart. He remembered Papa keeping him locked away for weeks at a time, hidden from human contact after he'd accidentally killed his nanny during a toddler's rage. He surely would have killed his parents, too, if not for their Blood. He knew what it was like to be feared by one's parents. He knew a child's horror at unintended killing. Michel had been little more than a prisoner when he was young, just like his mother.

But such was the burden of powerful children. Hadn't as much been written about Jesus? The Infancy Gospel of Thomas claimed that when Jesus was a boy, he'd killed his Greek teacher in a rage over his alphabet lesson. Shriveled a playmate into a withered husk. Terrorized his village. Papa gave little credibility to Thomas and the other Apocrypha—only the Letter of the Witness carried the Blood as proof of its validity—but as a boy, Michel had been thrilled to learn that even his blessed ancestor might have traversed the valleys of terror before he'd ascended to spread Joy.

So it would be with him and Fana. Together, he and Fana could cleanse the world with only their thoughts: The false prophets. Unbelievers. Adulterers. Thieves. Gluttons. *Let he who stands over the Blood take every worldly measure to wrest the Blood from the hands of the wicked.* Once wickedness was flushed from the world, the killing would end—and the killers would become the saviors. After the Cleansing, only the true worshipers would remain, and the Witness's prophecy would be realized.

The world, at last, would be ready for the Blood. Death would touch mankind no more.

Michel's heart shook his body as he realized how close he walked to the New Days.

"You see?" Michel said to Fana, his voice unsteady. "The light is just ahead of us now."

The tunnel was so suffused with light that he could finally see Fana's face. Her tears.

"Please don't cry, *negra*," he said. "We're safe now. We're home."

"Home?" Fana said, then she shook her head. She missed her

family. She was desperate to reach Teka, her teacher. Thoughts flowed from Fana toward Teka, and for an instant, Michel could see her teacher in meditation: Teka looked like a boy, as he did. The Blood had come to him when he was young.

But Fana had no more use for Teka. *He* would be Fana's teacher now, both in mind and body. Teka's plodding methods had retarded poor Fana's development. Teka had steered her *away* from the very source Michel had discovered in his dreams when he was young, the source that would empower her the fastest. But Fana would learn. She was only frightened now.

"This is home for now, Fana," Caitlin said suddenly. "Home is wherever you can rest."

Caitlin was a brilliant conduit! Her grief and rage over her murdered lover and her father's fate made her so vulnerable that he did not have to steer her often. Sometimes Caitlin spoke his mind as well as he did. Caitlin and Johnny were useful, or he would have left them dead at the house in Arizona, too.

But Johnny was more work. He had no deep losses to lay his soul bare. His life had been too sheltered for such easy manipulation. Michel had not intended to give Johnny so much freedom while he'd kissed Fana in the car—in truth, Johnny's sudden lunge for the gun had surprised him—but the shooting had worked in Michel's favor, just as he had expected it would.

Through Johnny's suffering, Michel had demonstrated his compassion. Loyalty. Love. And he had allowed Fana to touch Johnny with the Blood despite his unworthiness. One day, Fana would understand what a generous gift he had offered them both.

How soon could he reveal himself to her without fear that he would be reviled? Was Papa right to believe that Fana would be joined to him permanently once she lay in his bed? Would Fana bond to him like no woman had ever bonded to her mate? If that was true, Michel could reveal himself tonight.

Suddenly, Fana gasped. The sound of her fear stabbed him.

Michel reached for the gun in his jeans. "What is it?" he said, but he knew: Fana had sensed Romero and Bocelli waiting for them at the mouth of the tunnel.

Foolish oversight! Romero and Bocelli had been granted the Blood to better serve him, but they had not learned the nuances of the mind. After decades of training, even Papa was often clumsy at telepathy; otherwise, Fana's father never would have spied on his thoughts in Seattle. He must remember to cloak them all, or Fana would know too much before he was ready. A glimpse into the minds of Romero and Bocelli would be more than enough to drive Fana away.

Fana clung to his hand atop the wheelchair he steered. She pressed close to him, and he nearly drowned in her lovely scent. Her proximity made him light-headed.

"Someone's here," Fana said.

"Monks from the church," he said. "The safe house. They're waiting for us."

"Maritza knew them," Caitlin said, unprompted.

True enough, Michel thought. Romero and Bocelli had killed Maritza, after all.

Growing sunlight beckoned from the end of the tunnel. Here, the debris was more visible; food wrappers, bottles, diapers, empty prescription bottles. In the new light, graffiti spray-painted on the tunnel walls from travelers was clear. GIVE ME YOUR SICK, one message read. As if a passing traveler already knew what awaited.

Movement ahead. Bocelli was waving to him with a flashlight. Michel's two servants ran toward them, breathless and overjoyed.

Romero and Bocelli wore frayed brown monk's robes. Unlike the doorkeepers' at the church, they kept their guns concealed. None of them were Catholic, certainly, but Papa imitated the Catholic church because he enjoyed its taste for pomp and costumes. Catholics were no less ignorant than the rest, but they looked more pious in their grand vestments.

Romero was dark-haired and handsome, with an actor's face. Bocelli was not so lucky; he was wiry and sharp-featured, with a misshapen nose. Almost insectile. Bocelli might have frightened Fana, but Romero's attractiveness made him look kind. Neither was a true monk, but Bocelli was more akin to one. Bocelli accepted his uglier duties only grudgingly, but Romero enjoyed his violent deeds.

Without Sanctus Cruor, Romero would have been a sociopath without purpose. Sometimes Michel wondered if that could be said of Papa, too.

"Welcome, dear son!" Romero said and kissed his cheeks. If not for Fana's presence, Romero would have fallen to his knees to greet the Most High. "We were worried about you."

Their eyes rested on Fana, who was shielding her face from the sunlight.

Do not be so impolite to Fana, Michel chided them. *Greet her, but do not touch her. I alone may touch her.* Romero and Bocelli obeyed, giving Fana their warmest smiles and words of welcome in counterfeit Mexican accents. Slowly, they urged a smile from her lips. Michel was relieved, but he would be much happier when cloaking his servants was no longer necessary.

"What's happened to this poor child?" said Bocelli, examining Johnny. In the light, they could see how much Johnny's blood soaked his shirt. Bocelli's softheartedness made his inquiry convincing. Romero might have choked on those words.

"He was shot," Michel said.

Romero turned on his heels, beckoning with two fingers. "Then, come. You three climb out first. We'll carry the boy."

"Be careful," Fana said. "He's lost a lot of blood."

"Of course," Bocelli said. "*Está bien, señorita.* We have a doctor at the church."

A sturdy ladder awaited, and a ten-foot climb to the surface. Unlike the tunnel opening in Arizona, the opening in Mexico was outdoors. Romero and Bocelli had pushed aside the Dumpster that concealed the manhole from the street.

Climbing out, Michel found himself in the alleyway. The smell of garbage awaited, but it was a vast improvement over the tunnel. It grieved Michel that his charade had forced Fana into such an unpleasant passage. He reached for Fana behind him, guiding her up. Next, Caitlin.

The mud-painted white van waited only a few steps from the tunnel. Still clasping Fana's warm palm, Michel led her to the van and slid open the rear door. The van had been baking in the sun, so the interior was hot and musty. But in the New Days, Fana would travel like a queen!

Fana sat down in the far corner of the seat, hugging herself, eyes squinting. The nattering thoughts of the city's population were hurting her head. Michel had had the same problem as a boy. That was only one of many things he would teach her to control.

"What about the phone?" Fana said, her voice small. "You said there's a sat phone."

Her eyes were so wide and anxious that Michel hated to deny her. But he must.

"Brother Tómas!" Michel called toward the tunnel. "Where's the telephone?"

Tell her you do not have it, Michel directed his servants.

Romero's head popped out of the manhole. "*Lo siento,* my son. It is at the church."

Fana's face seemed to break into pieces. The sight of her tears nearly made Michel cry, too.

"*Shhhhh,*" he said, sliding beside her. "You'll talk to your family, Fana. I promise."

Fana's head sank against his chest. Papa had advised him to gain her trust, but the ruse was breaking Michel's heart. Caitlin took the seat behind them. She leaned forward, gently massaging Fana's shoulders.

"Soon, hon," he whispered to her through Caitlin's mouth. "This will all be over soon."

Romero and Bocelli worked quickly. In less than five minutes, Johnny lay in the seat beside Caitlin while she held him in place. The engine rattled when it started, but the vehicle sped away with ease, turning onto the street from the alley.

Nogales, as always, was a city of contradictions—part tourist haven, part barrio. Sunny-faced Americans crowded narrow stone streets lined with colorfully painted shops, bargaining for baskets, rugs, beads, pottery and other pieces of the nation's culture to appoint their homes while homeless brown-skinned children begged around them. Cafés and money changers abounded on the main streets, alongside the requisite strip clubs and brothels.

But pharmacies ruled the streets of Nogales. In every direction, Michel saw signs painted in red, blue, green and yellow to catch shoppers' eyes, advertising the Viagra, Flonase, Lipitor, Albuterol, Retin A, Vioxx and countless other medications that Americans were addicted to. Smugglers used the tunnels, but tourists drove over the border in herds, searching for relief from their symptoms, real or imaginary. Fleeing home for better prices.

No matter. After the Cleansing, illness would be only a memory. Those who remained would be the healthiest people in the history of the world.

Gentle Fana gazed out her window with eyes made pitiless by her own grief as she stifled her sobs. She hardly noticed the seekers mingling on the streets around her, deaf to their ailments and fears. In this instant, she thought only of home.

So be it, Michel decided. He could not permit Fana to leave or try to call home.

But he would bring his bride's family to her.

Twenty-seven

Dawit saw the blood smeared on the car's passenger side door as soon as he peeked around the corner of the clinic on Nelson Avenue. The gray Toyota RAV4 parked behind the building wasn't the same make and model and as the one being trumpeted on police radios nationwide, but Dawit knew the car. Fana had been here. He could almost see her plaintive eyes staring at him from the glimmering ball of sunlight in the car's passenger window.

Police had cordoned off an area of Nelson Avenue farther west, investigating a report of gunshots that had sent local law enforcement into a frenzy, but Teferi had insisted that they stop at the darkened Clinica de Esperanza instead. Again, Teferi's gift had proven true.

Dawit froze, ducking back against the wall. He clasped Teferi's arm tightly to halt his eager progress. Mahmoud fell to a crouch beside them, his gun ready. Long before either of them had learned any grasp of telepathy, he and Mahmoud had known the unspoken language of warriors who faced battles as one.

I see their car, Dawit told Teferi. Teferi gasped and tried to pull toward the car, but Dawit held him: *Are we alone?*

Teferi blinked rapidly, then squeezed his eyes closed. Teferi's gifts had led them here from Casa Grande, so patience with Teferi was always rewarded.

I SENSE NO ONE. FANA'S PRESENCE IS FRESH. PERHAPS NOT AN HOUR.

Still, an hour was an eternity. Dawit sighed. *I warn you—there is blood.*

Teferi nodded with vacant, unhappy eyes, prepared for Caitlin's death.

"Warn us if anyone approaches," Dawit told Teferi.

Mahmoud ran ahead, quick as a cheetah, and Dawit followed cautiously. He could not rely on Teferi's gifts entirely; even Teka could be surprised.

Closer inspection revealed a broken window—from a gunshot, Dawit guessed—and enough blood in the front passenger seat for a fatal wound. The blood was drying, so it was not Fana's. When Teferi saw the volume of blood puddled on the vehicle's upholstered seat, his face went slack with sadness. In the backseat, evidence of another gunshot through the fabric.

"One of them is lost," Mahmoud said.

"How many were there, Teferi?" Dawit said.

"I would say . . . four," Teferi said. "Fana, certainly. Caitlin. Johnny Wright, we can assume. I do not know the fourth."

Dawit examined the broken window. No corresponding entry point. "The gun was fired inside the car," he said. "The fourth is their captor. Perhaps . . . he lost his patience."

Dawit imagined Fana huddled inside, frightened. As hard as he and Jessica had worked to shield Fana from violence, his daughter's psyche had been stained yet again. When he and Jessica had had that last personal audience with Khaldun in Lalibela, Khaldun had warned them of dire consequences if Fana was traumatized. Now, this. Dawit's rage made his fingers tremble.

"The trail ends here," Teferi said. "They might be inside."

Dawit's heart stirred with combined joy and dread. "She could be masking now."

Dawit was not one to pray, but he came the closest he could remember to prayer as he left the bloodied vehicle: *Let us find her. Let us bring her to safety and spare her from Sanctus Cruor.* If they lost Fana's trail now, they might not find her for years, just as it had taken Sanctus Cruor years to find Fana. After years in that sect's hands, he would no longer recognize his child.

There were bloody fingerprints on the door and droplets on the ground beside it. One near-silent *Pffffffft* from Mahmoud's air pistol blew a neat hole where the doorknob had been, and mangled metal clattered to the asphalt. The door fell open. In a careful V formation a few strides apart, they searched the storeroom that awaited.

More blood on the floor, a trail, but no one was in the room. Dawit tried to flick on a light switch, but it didn't work. No electricity. This clinic might have had visitors today, but no one else had walked here for weeks or months. The clinic smelled forsaken.

The clinic was small—only the rear storeroom, a bathroom, tiny examination rooms and the front lobby, which had the receptionist's cubicle and six folding chairs in disarray, one overturned. The clinic was a shambles, but no corpses had been left behind.

"Here," Mahmoud said, pointing to the floor. "More blood."

The dribbling trail of blood led to a smallish examination room, also nearly empty. Upon second glance, Dawit noticed a pile of bloodied bandages discarded on the sink. Fresh.

Teferi scoured the room with him. "Perhaps the fourth isn't a captor," he said, hope ringing in his voice. "One of them was injured, and they stopped here for treatment."

More smudges of blood on the examination table. Dawit's insides went cold.

Fana might have exposed herself, sharing her blood!

This examination room would have to be carefully cleaned, he realized. Even if Fana hadn't been bleeding, traces of her blood might lie in this room. Dawit reached into his leather hip pouch for the bottle of clear, acidic blood-cleaning solvent he and his Brothers had created to mask the presence of their Blood's living cells. He would have to clean the car, too. But could they risk the delay?

"I'll wipe this room down," Dawit said. "Try to learn where they went."

As soon as he said it, he knew: Nogales was a border town. This clinic might have once been a safe house on the Underground Railroad, along the route to Mexico.

"A tunnel!" they realized in unison.

A careful study of the floor and empty storage cabinet in the examination room found no sign of a tunnel entrance, so Teferi and Mahmoud searched the rest of the clinic. Dawit pulled out his lighter and set the bandages in the sink afire. Armed with his solvent and clean bandages for wiping, he sprayed the sink and counters. Next, the floor.

Perspiration dripped into Dawit's eyes as he rushed to complete his work in the room's hot, stale air. If a tunnel was found, he would have no time to clean the car and the hall. He could only hope that Fana hadn't bled anywhere else.

And wasn't it fruitless to try to erase their traces from the world? They would be known, just as they had feared. Just as the Lalibela Council had always warned.

"Here!" Teferi's muffled voice shouted from the hall, excited. "I've found it!"

Still on his knees, Dawit looked through the doorway to see Teferi crouching in the bathroom. Teferi's fingers pried at the floor, and suddenly a block of tiles lifted in his hands. Teferi looked up toward Dawit, grinning wide.

Dawit leaped to his feet and ran into the hall. "There may still be time—"

Dawit never finished his sentence. A stranger's voice bellowed from the direction of the storeroom. "*Police! Drop your weapon! Do it NOW!*"

The room reeled. A thousand curses flew through Dawit's mind. Teferi, his face framed in the doorway, looked crushed.

I AM SORRY, DAWIT.

A shaft of sunlight signaled that someone else had entered through the rear door behind them. Static and chatter from a police radio.

At least Mahmoud was not in sight. Dawit raised his hands. His gun fell to the floor.

Dawit turned slowly and saw the intruder, another deputy in a cowboy hat. The deputy was middle-aged and overweight, with a paunch that threatened to rock him from his feet. Unless Teferi could influence him quickly, Dawit realized that this man would not live long.

The deputy seemed to know it, too. Even with a two-handed

gun stance, his barrel was unsteady. He might never have drawn his weapon before today. His thoughts bubbled faintly to Dawit's hearing: *OHSHITOHSHITOHSHITOHSHIT*

"Leave us," Dawit told him quietly. "We are too many. You cannot subdue us."

For an instant, the deputy's eyes widened, as if he was willing to consider Dawit's advice. Then his face flushed from sunburned brown to bright red. "*SHUT UP!*" he shouted, gesturing toward Teferi. "You too! Both of you on the ground—facedown! *DO IT!*"

Releasing the gun with one hand, he fumbled for his lapel radio. He never reached it.

The familiar *Pfffffft* marked his final words. A compact hole appeared in his chest. The deputy didn't make a sound; he only fell like a tree, face-first, to the floor. Mahmoud.

Dawit dove for his gun an instant before he saw a motion from a hidden corner of the storeroom behind the fallen deputy. Dawit squeezed his silent trigger three times. The wall chipped away as a dispatcher's voice clamored, *"Repeat. What's your 20?"*

A deputy's cowboy hat skittered across the storeroom floor. The second deputy's leg twitched wildly in the doorway, and Dawit heard panicked gasping for breath. A death rattle.

"How many?" Mahmoud called to Teferi, charging forward.

Teferi shook his head. "I th-think . . . only two. I didn't hear them. I . . . I'm s-sorry."

There was silence except for the radios. With Mahmoud flanking him, Dawit crept over the first deputy's splayed corpse toward the storeroom.

There, his heart fell.

A girl in a deputy's uniform lay on her back atop a crushed cardboard box, clasping her throat with both hands while blood spurted between her fingers. Two other holes passed straight through her Kevlar vest. Air pistols never missed except if the shooter was out of range; the guns tracked heartbeats. The girl's inferior weapon lay forgotten at her side, never fired.

Dawit gazed at her, aghast.

The girl wore her hair in thin, short-cropped braids, like a

Hamar maiden in Ethiopia. She might be in her twenties, but she had the round, unblemished face of a child. When he stood over her, the girl's wide, petrified eyes flooded with tears.

"P-p-puh . . . ," she sputtered, unable to find language to beg for her life.

Dawit's mouth fell numb. He raised his gun and shot her in the heart, ending her pain with one last body spasm. What choice did he have? He might have given his Blood to this stranger and even tried to invoke the Ceremony, but at what consequence?

He could not save them all. He had told Jessica as much when she'd first begun her mission.

Mahmoud crept past Dawit to the rear door, peeking outside. "Just one car!" Mahmoud said. "They must have arrived right behind us. So far, it's only these two."

Hot moisture on Dawit's cheeks told him that he had shed tears. In the hundreds of mortals he had slain, he could not remember ever killing a woman. Not in this way. He had smothered Rosalie, his dear child, to release her from the prison of her infirm, aged body, and he had killed poor Kira accidentally, hoping to share his Blood with her. But he had never killed a female adversary, a stranger embarking upon adulthood. She was hardly older than Fana.

JACKSON, IMANI, her name tag read. She wore a wedding ring. Was she a mother?

Dawit expected Mahmoud to mock his tears, but his Brother squeezed his shoulder. "So comely, and now she is wasted," Mahmoud said quietly. "You see? This is what comes of it. We cannot live in harmony with mortals. Khaldun was wise to tell us so."

COME, Teferi's voice pleaded. *WE MUST FOLLOW FANA IN THE TUNNEL BEFORE OTHERS COME. ENOUGH INNOCENTS HAVE DIED ON OUR BEHALF TODAY.*

In the bathroom, Teferi had already climbed midway down the tunnel; he was visible only from the waist up. Teferi inclined his head, an apology. "I am to blame," he said. "I should have sensed their arrival. I was too eager to find the girls."

"No," Dawit said. "The blame does not rest with you, Teferi. Sanctus Cruor killed these two as surely as the others."

If Sanctus Cruor was indeed a sect of immortals, no matter. Any men could die, even men with the Living Blood. Incineration. Exsanguination. If he must, he would invent a method. No matter what it cost him, Dawit vowed, Sanctus Cruor would be destroyed.

This time, for eternity.

THE NEW DAYS

". . . And so a man and woman, mates immortal born,
will create an eternal union at the advent of the
New Days. And all of mankind shall know them as the
bringers of the Blood . . ."
—*Letter of the Witness*
  Chapter 4, verse 6

The Devil can cite Scripture for his purpose.
—William Shakespeare, *The Merchant of Venice*

Twenty-eight

Mom?

If not for Fana's voice, so vivid that she could be sitting next to her, Jessica never would have realized she was sleeping.

Jessica hadn't wanted to sit down—her mother's condition worried her, and she was waiting for confirmation that the Duharts had reached SeaTac safely—but she hadn't been able to keep standing. Her blood gave her as much energy as a twenty-year-old, but she still hadn't slept in two and a half days. To keep herself awake, she focused on the beeping cardiac monitor Lucas had attached to her mother's wrist, like an oversized watch. And the dripping water in the sink.

Somehow, through it all, she was sleeping anyway.

"*MOM?*" Fana's voice said again, a thunderclap. "*RUN.*"

Jessica gasped, her eyes flying open. She leaped to her feet and looked around the room, bleary-eyed. Her mother was sitting across the table from her with a startled expression, and Alex lay in the bed. No Fana.

Then Jessica realized that Bea's heart monitor was beeping in a frenzy. *A heart attack?* Jessica clutched her mother's arm, her own heartbeat racing the monitor's flurry.

"Mom?" she said. "Just relax. I'll c-call for Lucas—"

"Baby . . . didn't you hear that?" Bea whispered with the breath her lungs hoarded from the oxygen tubes. Bea pulled her arm away from Jessica.

"Hear what?"

"That *voice*, Jessica."

Jessica's head cleared. She was almost afraid to say her daughter's name, but the alertness in her mother's eyes gave her hope. "Fana?"

Bea nodded at Jessica, her eyes wider, spilling tears.

Jessica felt gooseflesh across her arms. "I thought—"

"I heard her . . . too . . . clear as day," Bea said. Her fingers trembled as she raised her hand, pointing. "From there."

Alex's bed.

Jessica's heart tumbled as she gazed at Alex's stock-still lump under the blanket. It didn't make sense, but rationality was irrelevant when it came to Fana. Long ago, when Jessica had battled the faceless thing that had stolen her child's mind for a time, an invisible force had made her hallucinate that poor Kira had come back to life to taunt her. Was that happening again? Had the force Khaldun called the Shadows followed her, parroting Fana's voice?

That nameless thing was the closest she had ever walked to Satan. Jessica was sure of it.

Jessica stepped toward Alex's bed. Bea pulled herself up from the table and held Jessica's arm, leaning on her for support. Bea's shallow, hurried breaths fluttered in Jessica's ear.

Alex's eyes were open for the first time since Fana had disappeared. Staring at the ceiling.

Bea gasped. "Alexis?" she said, overjoyed. It had been Alex's voice all along!

Jessica clasped Alex's hand and pulled it beneath her chin. "Alex? We're here!"

But Alex didn't blink. Her lips had fallen slightly apart, but Alex didn't move now, except to breathe. Gently, Jessica shook her shoulder. Alex was still in a trance; Jessica could see that even without Teka's guidance.

"She's not back with us, Mom," Jessica said gently.

"She *is*." Bea sat at the edge of Alex's bed and stroked her daughter's forehead the way she had when they'd been children. "She sounded . . . like Fana. She called out . . . and she said to run. You . . . heard her."

Jessica blinked, staring into her sister's unseeing eyes. She moved closer, until there was only an inch between them. Did she see Alex in those eyes, or was it Fana? With everything her daughter was capable of, why should it surprise her that Fana could speak through Alex's mouth?

"Fana?" Jessica whispered to Alex's ear. "Is that you? We heard you. Talk to us, sweetheart. Please tell us where you are. Tell us if you're all right."

Alex's lips trembled suddenly, and air forced its way from her throat. "*Run . . .*"

The voice was weaker, but it was Fana. As if she'd been trapped inside Alex's body.

"Stay with her, Mom. Teka needs to hear this."

Jessica ran to the intercoms built into her corner desk—a row of lighted buttons linked to individual underground quarters, as well as the Council House, Big House and other buildings aboveground. The buttons were assigned numbers, not names, so Jessica had to try to remember which was Teka's. For maddening seconds, she drew a blank. Sleep deprivation, she realized.

The wild beeping of Bea's cardiac monitor was a distraction; not only was it racing but it was also erratic. Even good excitement was bad for her mother's heart today. And Bea's labored breathing terrified Jessica; her mother sounded almost as if she was drowning.

Teka's is Three. Jessica pressed the white-lighted button but didn't hear the gentle bell tone that preceded responses. She heard only the speaker's empty static, unanswered.

Jessica pushed the button again, leaning close to the pin-sized microphone. "Teka? I need you right away. Fana is communicating through Alex! We hear her voice."

Bea fought to speak. "Call that . . . boy . . . outside the door. He'll . . . get him."

"Mom, please don't talk. Save your breath," Jessica said. Bea's suggestion to send her guardian, Fasilidas, for Teka was a good one, but first she hit the button to reach Lucas. Bea was her new priority, even above the miracle from Alex's lips.

Silence again. The buttons weren't working. A technical breakdown *now*?

"*Dammit,*" Jessica said, running to her door. Her wrist snapped painfully when she tried to turn the doorknob. Her door was locked, from the *outside.* She hadn't realized that someone else could lock her door—or that anyone would dare.

Jessica pounded on the metallic door, angry. "Fasilidas! Open this door *right now*!" The doors were heavy and flame-proof, meant for protection, but now her quarters were a cage.

When there was no sound, Jessica felt afraid in her own home for the first time since she and Dawit had established their colony. The full depth of the drastic measure the Duharts had taken to escape washed over her in a flood, and Jessica's knees wavered as she remembered Fana's message: *Run.* Something had happened. Had Sanctus Cruor found them? Or government agents tipped off by Garrick Wright?

"What's . . . wrong?" Bea said.

"Nothing I can't take care of," Jessica said.

Jessica grabbed the sat phone from the table and dialed Dawit's number, her fingers jittery on the keypad. *Please pick up, David,* she thought.

SYSTEM BUSY, the satellite's message said in the black viewer.

Damn damn damn.

Jessica felt her mother's eyes on her, so she kept her face as calm as she could. Jessica's lessons from meditation came to her: *Calm. Patience.* Thankfully, panic receded. She looped the strap of the phone's black carrying case over her shoulder, planning to try Dawit again when she had a chance. Even if she could reach him, what could he do for her from so far away?

Jessica noticed perspiration on Bea's forehead, and how Bea's fingers fanned across her breastbone, a sign that she was in pain. Were Bea's lips slightly bluish? To try to relieve Bea's breathing, Jessica carefully adjusted the oxygen machine's output.

"Mom, are you having an angina attack?" she said.

Reluctantly, Bea nodded. She hated to admit to pain, thinking of it as weakness. She had suffered from painful chest pains for years, even before her heart attack. Grandpa's side of the family was dogged by heart problems; most of them died by their sixties.

Jessica unfastened the top buttons of her mother's blouse. Alex always tried to cool Bea's skin during her attacks, so Jessica pulled off the kimono Bea was wearing over her clothes. Bea's thin skin clung to her collarbone, as fragile as a bird's bones. In the robe's pocket, Jessica found the bottles of aspirin and nitroglycerine her mother always carried with her.

"Take an aspirin," Jessica said, although she knew Bea wouldn't want to.

Bea shook her head. "Bothers . . . my stomach," she said. "Give me . . . nitro. I'm fine."

Ignoring her, Jessica opened the aspirin bottle and pressed a tablet into Bea's palm. "Chew this first," she said. "Then nitro."

Bea gave her an evil eye, but she slid the pill into her mouth. When she bit into it, she made a sour face. "Give me . . . water."

"Chew the aspirin. The nitro goes under your tongue. You know they work faster that way. Then you'll get water, Mom." Jessica had no time for her usual polite pleading.

Once Jessica was satisfied that Bea was taking her medications, she reached under the table and pulled out the gun case, unlatching it. Jessica dug out the gun her husband had taught her to shoot.

When Bea saw the gun, her face went sallow. She pursed her lips, hard.

"Mom, I don't want to scare you, but you need to listen to me," Jessica said slowly. "Our door is locked. I'm going to shoot it open, and then I have to see what's going on. I need you to stay where you are and listen to every word Fana says. No matter how long I'm gone, do not move. I have to be able to find you again in a hurry. Please don't argue with me."

Bea's bottom lip trembled. The pain in her eyes told Jessica that Bea wished she was the one on her feet, ready to defend her children. Bea opened her mouth, seeking more oxygen than the tubes could give her. Bea's whisper was heartbroken. "I thought this was . . . the right thing."

Somehow, Jessica smiled for her mother. She pressed her palm firmly to Bea's clammy face. "It *was* the right thing, Mom. This is just a test. I'll come back when I know something."

Bea smiled back at her, trading assurances. "It'll be . . . all right. You're in . . . God's hands."

"Amen, Mom. You taught me and Alex that a long time ago. We'll be fine."

Jessica went to the door to bang again. Suddenly she was sweating too, swimming in nerves. "Hello?" she called out. "Is anyone out there?"

Silence again.

Jessica took a deep breath. "*Stand clear!*" she shouted. "I have a gun!"

There was no traditional safety on Dawit's gun; the Life Brothers never drew these weapons unless they were ready to fire. But Jessica had to be careful not to engage the gun's heartbeat targeting mode, which would seek out the first beating heart in range. She felt for the slider on the underside of the butt, making sure it was forward, in manual. *OK,* she thought. *OK.*

"Stand clear!" she yelled out again. After listening for scurrying feet but hearing only her heart's throbbing, Jessica stepped back five yards. She pulled the trigger.

The gun was silent, but the splintering metal exploded, and she jumped. The doorknob flew against the wall in the kitchenette, shattering the microwave door. Jessica fired a second time, this time at the dead bolt.

Two large, jagged holes in the door. The guns were powerful enough to pierce walls.

Behind her, Bea was breathing faster. "You OK, Mom?" Jessica said, not looking back. She kept her eyes on the door, just in case someone ran in.

"I'm . . . fine."

"Take slow, deep breaths. I'll be right back."

With each step she took away from Bea, Jessica realized that she might never see her mother alive again. The idea made her legs heavy. But Jessica couldn't make herself look back, even if one glance was her good-bye.

The door swung open into the hall, but it stuck in place after six inches.

Jessica pushed, and it still didn't give. She had room to stick her head out.

Fasilidas lay on the floor outside of her door, not moving. His odd black wet suit was slick across his back. Blood. For two seconds, Jessica could only stare. She thought her eyes were fooling her. *He's a telepath, and someone still got to him. What the hell can YOU do?*

Jessica wanted to pull her head back into her quarters, slam what was left of her door shut, and barricade herself inside with Alex and Bea. But she couldn't. She was responsible for more people than just Alex and Bea.

She had to find out if the Duharts had made it safely home. She had to check on Lucas, Jared, Abena, Sharmila and the boys. Lucas had the protection of the Living Blood, but he didn't have a gun, and she doubted that Teferi's wives did either. She was all they had.

Breathing fast, Jessica pounded her hip against the door to force it open wider so she could slip through. Fasilidas's baton lay on the floor, just beyond his motionless hand; she scooped up the two-pound device, clipping it to her belt loop. She wasn't as familiar with the baton—the row of three small buttons had been the subject of a very short lesson long ago—but she would figure it out if she had to. It emitted an energy field, like an invisible laser.

Instinct made Jessica press the crook of her elbow tightly against her nose as she held her breath, running toward Lucas's room. Was there gas? Was that how the sentries had been disabled before they'd sensed an attacker?

Twenty yards from her, toward Lucas's quarters, another body lay on the floor. Yonas was down, too. A gleaming red hole sat above the bridge of Yonas's nose, a third eye. He had been shot. He and Fasilidas weren't truly dead, but they were dead enough.

And Lucas's door was wide open. Jessica felt her heart crack. *Oh, God.*

"Lucas?" Jessica whispered, peeking into her brother-in-law's quarters. "Jared?"

The room was empty. A pot of coffee, two mugs and a sandwich on a plate sat on the table, as if Lucas and Jared had been interrupted during a meal. Quickly, Jessica searched the only hiding places—under the beds, inside the small closet. No one was here.

Panic and grief shredded Jessica. If something had happened to

Fana's cousin, Fana would be devastated! This time, the empty tunnel and its guardian corpses felt so ominous that Jessica had to fight to breathe, like her mother. The underground shelter looked like a glorified tomb.

By the time she reached Abena's silent quarters, Jessica knew that Teferi's wives and children were gone, too. Toys were strewn on the floor, abandoned next to small suitcases lined up by the door. Bowls of food sat on the table. They had been eating, too. *But what happened to them?*

Could Lucas have somehow orchestrated an escape, taking the others with him? The idea lightened Jessica's heart, but she couldn't imagine how. Lucas was no fighter, and neither was Jared. Besides, Fasilidas and Yonas had had too great an advantage: Yonas was a practiced telepath too, and would have known the plot as soon as it was born.

It had to be Sanctus Cruor. Other immortals. She couldn't believe any government agency could have found them so quickly, or overtaken the colony with such ease. No wonder Fana had burrowed her way into Alex's body, warning her to run!

One last open door remained: Teka's. *Please be there, Teka. Please be deep in meditation, oblivious to what's happened. I need you.*

But Teka's sparsely furnished quarters were empty, too. For the first time since she'd found Fasilidas crumpled outside of her door, Jessica felt helpless tears sting her eyes.

SYSTEM BUSY, her phone insisted again when she tried.

The lights at the east end of the tunnel were more dim, nearly dark. Her legs pumped as fast as she could make them move as she forgot her cautious pace and ran toward the last room, the communications center. Maybe she could find a working phone! She had to tell Dawit.

The comm center door was open, too, but Jessica trembled with despair when she came within six feet of it: A Life Brother named Kelile lay unconscious in the doorway, facedown, his fingers spread as if he had fallen clawing the floor. A trail of blood snaked from Kelile's head, pooling around the baton still in his hand. A sob swelled in Jessica's throat.

Inside, the comm room was the scene of a massacre. The Life Brothers had been meeting when they'd been surprised: Two more were slumped over the small round conference table, still in their seats. The room smelled like blood. Jessica's stomach curdled, trying to empty itself.

"My apologies, Jessica," a quiet voice said. "I hoped to spare you such a startling sight."

Jessica knew the calm voice before she gazed toward the rear of the room, where the communications console sat, but her mind rejected the knowledge. She had to *see* him.

Even when she saw, she didn't want to believe. Her mind spun, searching for an answer.

A dolphin's smile. That was the phrase that came to Jessica's head when she saw Teka sitting in the console's leather office chair, his hands folded in his lap. Smiling peacefully.

Unlike the other Life Brothers, Teka was wearing his traditional white tunic, still sprinkled with the blood from Cal's attack. Or was it someone else's blood?

"Whuh . . ." Her first attempt to speak was fruitless. Her mouth was confused, too. "What's going on, Teka?"

Even now, if he had the right explanation, Jessica longed to run to Teka and embrace him. He had survived! But Teka's smile kept her rooted in place. He was no longer her friend, even if she didn't understand why. *Shoot him,* her mind advised with cool, detached logic.

Teka's smile vanished.

"First," he said, "you'll need to put down that gun."

Jessica's arm slammed the gun to the table with such force that she crushed her own fingers. Jessica screamed. Her pinky pulsed with such a flare of hot pain that she was sure she'd broken it, but her scream was from terror, not pain. She had lost dominion over her own body! Raw helplessness swamped her, a horror matched only by the horror of watching her daughter die.

Teka rose slowly to his feet. Jessica tried to run away from him, but although she could feel the clothes on her skin and the floor beneath her feet, her body ignored her mind's pleas. She couldn't retreat from Teka any more than she could control the quivering of her bones.

Teka stood in front of her, only two inches taller, with a teenager's smooth face. One slow tear crawled from his left eye, the only part of him she recognized. He stood so close to her that their noses nearly touched.

I AM SO SORRY, DEAR JESSICA. I DID NOT MEAN TO CAUSE YOU PAIN.

That single tear, and the tenderness of Teka's voice in her head, gave Jessica hope. "Teka . . . ," she said, relieved to discover that she could still speak. "It's all right. Just let me go. Whatever's happened—"

"We must have a moment of honesty between us," Teka said. "We must unburden ourselves from what we have kept hidden."

Teka gently rested his palm on Jessica's shoulder. Slowly, his hand journeyed down her arm, until his warm hand passed the fabric of her T-shirt and cupped her skin in a lingering caress that made her flesh recoil. Fresh panic gripped her, primal. Teka's forearm brushed against her chest, across her breast. Almost accidentally.

Teka rested his chin on her shoulder, his mouth near her ear. "I know," Teka breathed. "Often, you have looked at me and seen all of Dawit's lost potential. But for his life's sorrows, and his own excesses, Dawit might have been as gentle as my twin. Your heart never allowed the thoughts to surface, but I know your needs better than you, Jessica. You prefer me to Dawit."

Tears scalded Jessica's face.

"Truth is painful," Teka said, nodding. He stroked her fingers, and suddenly the throbbing pain from her injury was gone. Erased. "I, too, have felt pain. I followed my Teacher's path so closely that I never heeded the call of my heart. My loins. How often have I wished that I, like Dawit, had disobeyed Khaldun to follow the heady currents of my heart? Then you would be mine—and Fana might be my own child."

Another tear joined the first on Teka's cheek. Gently, he squeezed her fingers.

"*Take your fucking hand off of me,*" Jessica said through gritted teeth.

Teka's eyebrows shot up. His smile was stuck in place, but his eyes glimmered. He pulled his hand away, taking a single step back, and Jessica trembled with relief.

"Such coarseness does not suit the Blessed Mother, Jessica."

Jessica didn't have time to spew the obscenities churning in her mind, but she was glad he could hear each one. "What have you done, Teka?"

PLEASE DO NOT BELIEVE I COULD EVER BETRAY YOU.

"Where are Lucas and Jared?" she said. "And the children?"

Teka walked away. He took his seat at the console and turned his back to her, typing on the computer as if he had forgotten her.

"Where are they?" Jessica shouted. "You *will* answer me!"

"Ah . . . You are a queen even when you are a captive."

THEY ARE SAFE, JESSICA. I WILL NOT HARM THEM UNLESS I AM FORCED.

Teka seemed to have been transformed into two people. The voice she heard in her head sounded so much more like the Teka she knew!

Please, Teka, she begged him, trying to offer her thoughts. *Tell me what's happened.*

I AM SO SORRY FOR ALL I HAVE DONE—AND YET WILL DO.

Has Sanctus Cruor done something to you?

PLEASE DO NOT COMPEL ME TO SILENCE YOU, JESSICA.

Desperation clouded Jessica's thoughts, and she gave up straining to send him mental messages. "Teka, my mother needs help. It's her heart! You know how weak she is. Please let me bring Lucas to her."

This time, Teka ignored her. No soothing voice entered her head.

"There." Teka's chair whirled around, and he faced her with an unblemished smile. "Our flight has been approved. The FAA is not nearly so clever as it believes. Its computer security is rudimentary at best."

"Please let me take care of my mother, Teka," Jessica said. "She's Fana's grandmother!"

"Do not look so sad, Blessed Mother," Teka said. "You cannot see it now in your ignorance, but this is a day for rejoicing! You will meet your new son, the union that was foretold in ancient times. As the supreme wedding gift, you are to be reunited with your daughter!"

Moments before, Jessica would have been overjoyed at the prospect of seeing Fana again, no matter how troubling or mysterious the circumstances. Now, her heart languished as she wondered how she could endure admitting to her child how badly she had failed her.

Twenty-nine

Lucas berated himself as the black SUV carried him across the asphalt tarmac of the Toledo-Winlock airport, past rows of grounded prop planes. He had never trusted that SOB Teka—not since the day Teka had shown up at their colony with that empty fucking smile. He and Alex had always wondered why Jessica and Dawit treated the boyish man like a demigod, entrusting Fana to him without reservation. *What were they thinking?*

What had any of them been thinking?

Lucas's stomach ate a hole in itself every time he thought about the Duharts, but he had to face facts: He hadn't seen any sign of Cal, Nita and their kids, so they were probably dead. And he and Jessica had offered their friends to Teka on a sacrificial altar. How could they have believed Teka would send the Duharts happily off to catch a plane to freedom?

And he'd brought Jared home! Lucas heard himself moan softly. His insides tangled, doubling him over. He still felt faint, but it wasn't from last night's injuries. Had he saved Jared from illness only to lose him so senselessly now?

Jared sat like a stone beside him in the vehicle with his knees pressed tightly together, his eyes on his window. Lucas and Jared were bound together hand and foot with bands that looked like clear plastic rings but felt strong as iron.

Shackled. There was no other word for it.

Lucas felt haunted by the memory of his last night with Alex, when she'd been packing and he'd been in such denial that he'd gone upstairs to bed. Instead of helping her salvage their lives, he'd gone to sleep. Just like poor Cal said.

Almost two hours ago, Teka had slipped into their quarters like a ghost and put his gun to Jared's temple. He'd explained that if Lucas uttered a word of protest, he would shoot Jared dead. As soon as Teka had spoken, Lucas's eyesight had vanished; his world had become completely black. Lucas had let out a yell, as terrorized as a child locked in a dark closet. The sensation had lasted only two or three seconds, but Teka's demonstration had made its point.

So Lucas had kept his mouth shut. He'd done everything he'd been told. As far as he knew, Teka had not exerted any further mental manipulation. Jared was all the control Teka had needed.

It was a chilling *déjà vu*: He and Alex, then strangers, had been kidnaped from the clinic where Alex had been distributing blood in Botswana. Then, like now, they had witnessed a collection of the dead at the hands of their captors. The fallen Life Brothers in the shelter might rejuvenate in a few hours, but the bodies had terrified the shrieking children.

The Life Brother who'd met them at the vehicle, Jima, had repeated Teka's threat in more graceless language: *I require silence. If any monkey within my hearing speaks a single word, your children will die.* Obediently, Abena and Sharmila had kept silent, except for involuntary, bitter wails when Teka had taken the boys away.

Teka was driving the children separately in an SUV behind them, another control tactic. The women still sniffled and sobbed quietly in the backseat as they clung to each other and gazed desperately out the rear window to try to get a glimpse of Miruts, Natan and Debashish, their sons with Teferi. But nobody in their vehicle dared to utter a whisper.

Alex was in the vehicle behind them too, along with Bea and Jessica. Lucas and Jared had watched through their window with anxious eyes while Teka and the sole remaining Life Brother had transferred Alex, and then Bea, into the SUV from the shelter opening. Bea had looked as limp as a scarecrow as the men had lifted her, and

Lucas had been able to gauge Bea's deterioration from Jessica's face. Lucas had never seen Jessica look so abject, already in mourning.

Until then, Lucas had honestly wondered if Teka's new tough tactics had had Jessica's blessing.

But Jessica was a prisoner, too.

Alex didn't look any worse than when he'd seen her last, but their separation had felt final when the other vehicle's doors had shut them away from each other, toward what might be separate destinies. Teka's passengers were related by direct blood to either Fana or a Life Brother, and the rest of them were not. That meant that Alex and the rest of Teka's cargo might be safer.

Lucas wished that gave him solace, but it didn't. Not with his only son stuck beside him.

At the airport, the colony's shiny executive jet came into sight at the end of the runway, dwarfing the smaller planes. Jared gave him a questioning gaze, jarred by the sight of the plane. Lucas could only shake his head and shrug. *They're flying us somewhere, but I don't know where.* Gestures were his poor man's telepathy.

Lucas had traveled on the colony's Legacy 600 luxury jet often, back when his work had taken him between Washington and Accra, Gaborone, Johannesburg and Beijing. Maybe he would find a way to forgive himself one day for what hindsight told him was unforgivable stupidity; but in those days, he had been intoxicated by the sight of the world changing before his eyes.

Back then, this plane had represented euphoric hope. Now it was only a mobile prison. Long, narrow steps led from the tarmac to the cabin door, which yawned open up high.

Jima braked the vehicle under the plane's wing, and Teka pulled up alongside him. Jima climbed out without a word or a glance behind him, slamming his door.

"Oh, God, please help us . . . ," Abena whispered, her voice trembling. "Are Teka and Jima possessed by Satan? What have we done to deserve this?"

"*Shhhhh*," Sharmila said sharply. "Do as they say, woman. If you talk, they'll kill us all."

"Are the boys hurt?" Abena said. "Oh, *God . . .*" Her voice was rising, creeping toward hysteria. If she started screaming, Sharmila's prophecy might come to pass.

Lucas looked back at Abena's round, pretty face and forced his lips to smile. "They just want to take us on a trip," he said. "I've been on this plane, and it's first-class luxury all the way. The boys are fine. Just keep calm, follow directions. You'll see, darlin'."

"Cross your heart?" Jared muttered, their sacred oath from his youth.

Instead of answering, Lucas patted his son's knee, then squeezed hard. *Hope to God.*

This time, all four of them craned to see through Jared's window. The immortals rapidly carried Bea out of the SUV, then up the steep steps to the cabin. Bea's eyes were closed as she swayed in their arms; Lucas hoped she was only resting.

Time passed, and Teka and Jima returned for Alex.

Just as before, Lucas felt relieved when Alex appeared. She was still unconscious, but she was alive. Before they carried her into the plane, even through the tinted window, he could see his wife's chest moving with steady breathing. He and Jared held hands, both of them savoring the only morsel of joy in their day.

Next, Jessica emerged from the back of the vehicle, walking in a shuffle because of the restraints around her ankles. She didn't glance Lucas's way, preoccupied with helping the three boys out behind her. Through the glass, Lucas heard Jessica's assurances and the boys' crying.

"Oh my God . . . Lord Jesus, what will we do?" Abena whispered, her face pressed to the window as she squeezed beside Jared and Lucas. Her skin was hot. Fevered.

"Easy . . . ," Lucas said softly. "They're fine, Abena."

Long-legged Natan came first, looking taller than his ten years, and then the younger two. The boys had not been shackled when Teka had first taken them from their mothers, but they were tied together now. Just like Lucas and Jared, they were bound by a wrist and ankle to the one behind them, a human train. They nearly stumbled out of the SUV, their balance was so hindered.

Lucas's vision blurred as ancestral memories filmed his eyes with tears. The shackled children reminded him of a horrifying photograph he had seen of the hold of a slave ship crowded with nothing but the faces of the young, an image he'd wanted to forget as soon as it had polluted his eyes. That photograph had filled him with rage, but not as much as this.

Abena was breathing so fast that she was close to hyperventilating. Whimpers bled from her throat. Lucas held her shoulders tightly as Sharmila held her waist from behind. When Jima glanced in their direction, Lucas's body went cold.

"It's OK," Lucas whispered, desperate to soothe Abena. "They're fine. See? They're fine. *Shhhhhh*. It's OK."

Lucas didn't realize he was holding his breath until Jima looked away from them, back toward Jessica and the children. As the group ascended the metal stairs, vanishing inside the plane, Lucas wondered if this was where they would be separated for good.

This time, no one emerged.

Should they try to run? Was that their only option?

Lucas leaned forward to check the ignition, just in case the keys were still there. No keys, of course. As soon as he moved, Jima came trotting back down the steps. *If he jumps back behind that driver's seat, the only place he'll take us is a mass grave,* Lucas thought. He sat back quickly, watching Jima's approach with a chest-rattling combination of fear and hopefulness that paralyzed his higher thinking centers; he was only a beast in a cage, like any other.

Jima flung open the SUV's passenger door beside him, filling the vehicle with sunlight. Abena gasped, squirming beneath Sharmila's strong grip.

"Come out one at a time," Jima said. "You will board the plane. Move quickly."

Thank you, Lucas thought, testing a prayer as his fingers tightened around his seat's fabric. *Thank you, God.*

All the while, he knew they should be anything but grateful.

Far beneath them, the woods were burning. Her home was afire.

As the jet soared over Toledo with clamoring engines, Jessica couldn't see the Big House or the school in the sprawling acreage of green woods. But she guessed that the sudden wildfire sending smoke to chase them into the sky was neither coincidence nor accident. Besides, her heart knew: Yet another blood mission had ended in destruction.

Everything she and David had built was gone. Again.

Aren't we doing your bidding, Lord? Why are we punished so?

Jessica's eyes ached. Mercifully, the plane's ascent stole her into the clouds, and the world below yielded to white sky. But there was no reprieve from the sound of the children's frightened cries, or from her mother's dying face.

Jessica was alone in the plane's rear section with Bea, who lay on the leather sofa, her face twisted in pain. As the plane shuddered, climbing, Jessica sat on her knees on the carpeted floor beside her mother, holding Bea's clammy hand.

Teka and Jima had closed the doors to cordon off the plane's three sections: Abena, Sharmila and the children were in the first-class section closest to Teka and Jima in the cockpit—most vulnerable to an attack. Lucas, Jared and Alex were in the middle section, with Alex's seat fully reclined to make her a bed as she slept. Jessica had hardly had the chance to ask Lucas's advice before they'd been shut away from each other, the doors between cabins closed. *Watch her monitor,* was all Lucas had said before Jima had snapped him silent. But watch it for what?

Jessica didn't have to understand the monitor's staccato signals to know what impending death looked like. Bea was sweating profusely, and her struggles to breathe were torture to Jessica's ears. Bea would die on this plane unless they intervened.

Jessica's ankles were bound together with a six-inch cord between them, so she shuffled to the cabin door that separated her from the rest of the plane.

Jessica pounded on the locked door, calling out. The doors weren't metal, but they were sturdy. "Teka!" she yelled. "Fana's grandmother needs medical attention! If you care about Fana, you'll let Lucas help her!"

Silence, except for the engines.

"Teka, you'll answer to Fana if something goes wrong!" As if

Fana was Vengeance itself. Could Teka even hear her? Jessica closed her eyes. *Teka? I know you can hear my thoughts, even if you don't hear my words. Please let me save Fana's grandmother.*

Only the hum of the plane's Rolls Royce engines answered her, along with a muffled sob from little Debashish, who was inconsolable at the front of the plane even in his mother's lap.

Jessica banished her panic. She didn't have Lucas's medical expertise, but she had the Living Blood. Jessica looked at her fingernails, which were uneven but long. If she had to claw her skin until she bled, she wasn't going to sit by and do nothing while her mother died.

"Jessica." Bea's wind-soft voice.

Bea's eyes were bright, struggling to stay wide open. Her knowing gaze made Jessica remember that her mother had been the first mind reader in her life. Bea held out her unsteady hand, and Jessica stumbled toward her.

Bea squeezed Jessica's hand, her grip firm. "You remember . . . that promise . . . you made me?" An unfamiliar rasp, and that horrible gurgle underneath.

Jessica's strength melted. She shook her head so violently that her neck hurt. "No. Mom, *no!* Don't say that again now."

"You . . . look me . . . in the eye . . . and *promise,* Jessica. No . . . blood."

Childish tears fell. "*Why?* Why can we give it to everyone else—"

"Because . . . they don't know."

"They don't know *what?*"

"It's . . . stolen. And . . . besides . . . it's all right."

"*It's not all right!*" Jessica heard herself shriek. For an instant, she broke away from herself, as if she were floating on the ceiling staring down at her own face, red and knotted. Her joints shook, and she lost her balance as the plane pitched slightly sideways. She fell against Bea's chest, and her mother held her there. The monitor chattered in Jessica's ear.

"Yes . . . baby. It's . . . all right," Bea said. "I'm . . . tired. I'm ready to see . . . Kira. And . . . Randall. And . . . your daddy."

Jessica sobbed from a place so deep that the cry felt ripped from her, as if by a claw.

"Trust . . . in Him, baby," Bea said. "We can't . . . see . . . everything . . . from where we're . . . standing."

Jessica could barely hear her. Her frame shuddered with another sob.

Bea squeezed her hand again, harder. "Jessica . . . promise me. Hear?"

Jessica couldn't form any words. Instead, she nodded her head against Bea's breast. *No blood, no matter what.* The thought dug free a sob more painful than the one before.

Suddenly, like a miracle, Teka's voice boomed on the plane's loudspeaker: "Lucas? You and your son may join Fana's mother and grandmother in the rear."

Jessica sat straight up, electrified. Everything around her had been dimming down, burying her, but suddenly she could breathe again. *Thank you, Teka. Bless you. Bless you.*

I AM NO MONSTER, JESSICA. YOU MUST BELIEVE THAT.

Jessica fought against her ankle restraints to make her way to the door. "Hurry, Lucas!" she called, and an eternity of silence passed. "*Lucas!*"

The door finally clicked, unlocking. Lucas and Jared opened the door and shuffled through, still bound together. As soon as Jessica saw Lucas, she understood the delay: Lucas had retrieved the plane's large black medical kit. His eyes were clear, fixed on Bea.

"Her heart . . . ," Jessica said.

Lucas nodded curt assurance. "I'll see to her, Jess."

Jessica felt the universal relief humankind has experienced since the first shaman was summoned to a sickbed. *She'll be fine. He'll take care of her.* The fervor of her wishing squeezed her hands into tight fists. Lucas gazed at the wrist monitor's readings, then he lifted Bea's blouse to press his old-fashioned stethoscope to her chest. He trusted his ears best. Bea's shrunken breasts fell apart, nearly weightless.

"Don't see . . . all the fuss," Bea panted.

Lucas smiled, although his eyes weren't smiling when he glanced at Jessica. His alarm was plain. Lucas fumbled inside the medical kit, tossing plastic-encased bandages and creams to the floor. He was in a hurry. The kit's boxy shape reminded Jessica of paramedics trying to save Kira, a memory that tried to steal her fledgling calm. But Jessica wiped that memory away.

"Mom . . . ," Lucas said. "How's that pressure in your chest?"

"Just . . . angina," Bea said. But her features fluttered, fighting pain. "I'm . . . dizzy, though."

"Jess? Grab me a glass of water," Lucas said. His voice was so relaxed that it was ethereal. "Mom, I wish I had morphine for the pain, but these pills are beta blockers to help strengthen your heart, give it some relief. And we're gonna' throw in some aspirin for good measure."

"She had 325 milligrams an hour ago," Jessica said, before she turned toward the mini-bar.

"More won't hurt," Lucas said.

At that, Bea laughed weakly. "Aspirin? We could have . . . done that."

With the sound of Bea's laughter to buoy her, Jessica made her way back to the plane's lavish minibar, clinging to the leather seats to keep upright. Suddenly, a day that had felt doomed was changing its mood. *Thankyouthankyouthankyou.*

"Sometimes the old ways are best, Mom," Lucas said behind her.

"See, Gramma?" Jared said. "Just like you always say."

The minibar's granite counter and gold-plated faucet promised comfort and ease. Jessica grabbed the first glass she saw—a champagne flute—and the water splashed into the sink in a strong stream. God had begun all of life with nothing but a little water, after all.

She heard Bea chatting on: "Jared . . . you watch out for . . . those kids. And . . . Fana."

"I will, Gramma."

"Mom?" Lucas said. "I need you to hush a while. Just try to take deep breaths."

Bea never liked anyone trying to shush her, so at first Jessica thought the curdling wail from her mother was only indignation. When Jessica whipped her head around to tell Bea to stop arguing, she saw her mother's wide-mouthed agony instead.

Bea was in a ball. Her body rippled with a convulsion, then fell still.

The cardiac monitor, instead of beeping, was suddenly the steady hum Jessica remembered from watching *Emergency!* as a child. A flat line, like Kira in the Louisiana motel.

The glass fell from Jessica's numb fingers, cracking on the granite counter.

"She's arrested!" Lucas said.

Nonononononononononononono

When the plane pitched forward slightly, Jessica's legs nearly buckled. Her senses telescoped; all sound was buried by the plea in her mind and on her tongue. "No . . . no . . . no . . ."

Lucas and Jared pulled Bea down from the sofa, and Bea's arms flopped to the carpet. Jessica noticed that her mother's fingernails were freshly painted, a pale pink that matched her favorite Easter hat. Bea prized her vanity; she had met every stage of life on her own terms.

"CPR!" Lucas said, and Jared folded his hands across Bea's chest, pumping. Jared was biting his lower lip hard, blinking back tears. Lucas and Alex had trained Jared in CPR in high school, when he'd insisted on being a summer lifeguard in Longview. Jared's compressions were precise, so forceful that Jessica was afraid he would break every frail rib in Bea's body.

"One . . . two . . . three . . . ," Jared counted aloud.

Working awkwardly because one wrist was chained to Jared, Lucas opened another compartment of the medical kit and brought out two glistening metal pads, one in each hand. They were smaller than the devices on 1970s television, but Jessica recognized defibrillators when she saw them. Electric shock for the heart.

"Back, Jared," Lucas said, and Jared pulled his hands away.

Please Lord you took Kira but don't take Mom like this pleasepleaseplease

When Lucas pressed the pads to Bea's chest, her frame arched with the jolt, as if the pads had been magnetized. Then Bea fell back to the carpet. The monitor hummed, unchanged.

This moment had felt inevitable since the day of Bea's heart attack. No, before then: since the day of Jessica's wedding, when she and her mother had been getting dressed together, and she'd noticed how her mother's skin had been gently drooping away on her cheeks, falling loose from her arms. Bea had been slowly transforming ever since, just like David had tried to warn her: *In a very short amount of time—it will amaze you how quickly—one by one, they will be gone. They are mortals, and you are no longer one of them.*

As if the memory of David's words summoned him, Teka's voice swamped Jessica's head: *IF SHE IS TO LIVE, SHE MUST HAVE BLOOD,* Teka said, telling her what her heart already knew. *THE CEREMONY CAN SAVE HER, AND YOU WILL HAVE HER FOREVER.*

Yes. Just like David had tried to save Kira. Forever.

Lucas pressed the pads a second time, and Bea's body jittered again.

"*Dammit,*" Lucas said.

A third time. Jessica gasped when Bea's leg kicked out, a dance from the electricity that ended as soon as Lucas pulled the pads away.

"Go, Jared," Lucas said. "Keep her blood circulating."

As Jared jabbed Bea's chest with his palms, Lucas gazed up at Jessica with an expression that might have been carved in rock. Jessica knew what his face meant before Lucas produced a tiny scalpel, flashing it in the cabin's light. He pressed the blade to his bare wrist.

"Jess?" Lucas said.

Jessica fell to her knees beside Lucas. She grabbed Bea's hand. Still warm. Bea's fingers seemed to squirm inside of hers, but Jessica knew it was the illusion of her own trembling.

Lucas poked himself with the scalpel, and dark blood spurted from his skin. "Blood alone won't do it. Her heart's stopped. Do you know the Ceremony?"

Jessica nodded. David had taught her the Hebrew words, explaining the Ceremony he had invoked to save her life when her heart had died, and later to save Lucas, too. *The Blood is the vessel for Life . . . The Blood flows without end, as a river through the Valley of Death. . . .*

How many times had she tried to transport herself back to that Louisiana motel room to whisper the same words to Kira and steal her from Death?

Forgive me, Mom.

Droplets of blood fell from Lucas's wrist to Bea's face. Crimson tears.

Jessica closed her eyes, and the sudden darkness was clarifying. "No," she said. "We can't."

"*What?*" Jared said. Disbelief and rage deepened her nephew's voice to gravel. "Is there some fucking rule—"

"I promised her," Jessica said. "No blood."

Jessica felt a hand beneath her chin, so she opened her eyes. Lucas's stare filled her sight. "This is it, Jess," Lucas said. "She's gone. Do you understand?"

Jessica nodded. A fire was brewing in her lungs, but somehow she spoke. "I know," she said. She leaned over Bea and wiped the stray blood from her face, suddenly frantic for her mother to be clean of it. "I know." She tried to say it a third time, but the fire ate her words.

No matter. Gently, Jessica pushed Jared's hands aside, to stop his manic compressions. Jared resisted at first, but Lucas made a stern clucking sound, and Jared finally pulled away with an angry sigh. Then, a sob.

Jessica buttoned Bea's blouse where Lucas had loosened it, then she grabbed her mother's shoulders and gathered her into her arms. Bea seemed as light as a child. Jessica squeezed Bea's body against her, rocking. A last, warm communion. Jessica cupped the back of her mother's head, sifting through the strands of hair Bea always kept so neatly combed, textured with the Africans, Europeans, Seminoles and Cherokees who had made peace to create her.

See, Mom? Sometimes I listen. I'm not as hardheaded as you think. You see?

Jessica heard herself howl. But that was only her body, talking out its pain.

Jessica's face was washed in sunlight from the plane's window, and the open sky reminded her that they were thousands of feet above the earth. The plane's urgent ascent made sense of the day: They were ferrying Bea in her gilded chariot, just like the preachers said.

Her mother was already halfway Home.

Thirty

Outside of Nogales
Sonora province, Mexico

Fana was mired in a place beyond sadness.

The pull toward trance was so strong that Fana had to fight to keep her eyes open. The surly late-afternoon sun and a monotonous, dusty mountain road conspired with her misery. Fana swayed with each bump, rescued from trance by the creaky van's motion.

The road's uphill climb was so steep that Fana expected the van to pitch backward. Each sharp turn on the narrow road felt like taking flight from the cliff. From where she sat in the middle passenger seat of the four-row van, Fana pulled forward to try to see through the windshield. The rest of the windows were clotted with dust, but the windshield was a panorama of lush vegetation and mountains. Another time, it might have been beautiful.

With the next bump came a jolt of dread.

Something awful had happened. Something at home.

Once she'd realized she wouldn't have a telephone in the van, Fana had brought herself as close to trance as she'd dared, trying to send mental signals. She'd wanted her family to know what she knew: The shelter wouldn't be enough to protect them. She'd felt Teka for a time, but his presence had vanished as soon as it had appeared. She hadn't been able to find her mother, of course—Mom's streams were too unpracticed—but again and again, Fana had run into Aunt Alex.

Always behind the schoolhouse, frozen in surprise.

The image of Aunt Alex had been so vivid that Fana had felt

herself climb into her own fantasy, visualizing herself whispering in Aunt Alex's ear: *Mom? Run!*

But it had been too late. Home had felt like a lie, suddenly. A childhood memory, already gone.

Behind the van, the border town was still in sight below, hazy and sprawling. Without the distracting roar from Nogales, grief shredded Fana's stomach. Sharp, awful pain. She found a scarf on the seat and wrapped it over her head to try to block the window's light, which suddenly seemed too bright.

Trance. Trance out.

But she couldn't trance out today, or ever again. She had to face this day somehow. She couldn't undo the colossal mistake of running away, but she had to minimize the damage. Fana remembered one of Teka's mantras: *Your past is your shadow. It has form but no substance, except in the places you allow it to touch you.*

Shadows.

Yes. Fana could almost remember now. Once she had known she could do anything she wanted to do if she enlisted her mind. She had enjoyed that feeling, once. No struggle. Pure, naked will. Even her unborn thoughts had become manifest. Once.

Remembering made Fana's fingers tremble. She had hurt people. She had burdened lives already rife with pain, turning herself into the kind of evil humans had invented prayers against.

Fana heard a droning hum. She pressed her palm against the van window, because the sound seemed loud enough to shake the road. But she couldn't feel the humming against the window. Instead, she heard it better when she covered her ears.

The sensation was strong, and gaining strength. Like a massive machinery gearing up.

But it was no machine. Buried inside the humming, a whispered invitation: *FANA?*

Voiceless, yet distinct. Not male, not female. Definitely not Aunt Alex, Teka, or her mother. Fana shivered from the top of her scalp to the ends of her toes. *Don't listen.*

To block out the humming, Fana turned around and leaned across her seat to focus her attention on Johnny. He was still unconscious, flat on his back, strapped in with seat belts. But his wound was healing. *She* had saved Johnny.

She didn't need the Shadows again. Never.

"Never," she whispered, although she had vowed never to speak to Them again.

NO SUCH THING AS NEVER, BEE-BEE.

Gramma Bea's voice?

With a burst of concentration, Fana shut the humming sound away. As soon as the vibration stopped, her mind missed the lulling assuredness. The humming had felt like a portal into herself, leading to everything Teka had been coaxing her to bring out. And here it was, waiting. Why shouldn't she touch it?

Because you'll turn into someone else, just like Mom said. Remember the hurricane?

To keep herself away from the humming, Fana set her restless mind free throughout the van. Johnny's sleeping thoughts were calm, as if the day hadn't happened; he was dreaming himself back to his parents' dinner table. Caitlin sat beside Johnny, one elbow leaning on the car door as she gazed through the window, her thoughts riveted on the mountains. Charlie's chin rested on his chest, his cowboy hat hanging forward; he was near dozing, too. Charlie's thoughts were placid memories of his history with the Mexican monks. They made him feel safe.

But Fana didn't like the monks.

Fana turned around to study the monks' square-jawed profiles. They had none of the Rolfsons' friendly chattiness; it was as if they had appeared by obligation. And they didn't wear their feelings in their faces. Were they monks at all?

Fana tested the two monks, probing toward the front of the van.

Most High.

The peculiar phrase lighted on Fana's perception in a gentle pulse from one of the monks, startling her. Did they know who she was? How could they? Fana sat up straighter, trying to amplify her mental probe, but everything was a blurry mess, just out of her reach.

The van pitched to the side in a pothole, and Fana's gaze fell to her window.

A figure stood at the side of the road, not ten yards in front of the van. An old woman.

The woman seemed to have appeared in the bright circle of sunlight through the branches of the pine trees. Fana hadn't seen anyone just an instant before, and now suddenly she was there. The van's nose passed within six inches of her kimono.

As the van sped past, Fana caught an eye-blink's glimpse of her face. *Gramma Bea!*

Gramma Bea's face was as still as a photograph: a thin nose, sharp cheekbones and skin softly etched in patterns of wrinkles narrating stories from her life. And the kimono was hers too; black silk, with patterned roses in pink. Gramma Bea's eyes didn't just fly by—they stayed with Fana. But Gramma Bea didn't smile. Her face was sour, eyes flashing sad disapproval.

As the van sped on, Fana's neck snapped so she wouldn't lose sight of Gramma Bea. She was barely visible, as if they had traveled three times the distance they had. Gramma Bea took a lurching step, favoring her bad hip. Then she was gone; swept around the bend, hidden by trees.

Fana's face pressed against the warm glass. Her fingertips tapped on the window, her last wave stolen as she stared at the empty road behind her. Fana's heartbeat shook her body.

Was that good-bye?

Fana knew the answer and fought knowing. The pool of grief was waiting for her whenever she was ready to wade in it. Just not yet. She had a bigger imperative: What did Gramma Bea's visit mean? Gramma Bea could have brought a happier face to say good-bye.

I've made another mistake, Fana realized. Gramma Bea had come a long way to tell her so.

Fana nudged Charlie's knee and felt him snap awake, rigid.

"What's wrong?" he said, ready for a crisis.

Fana wished she could just send him her thoughts, but she would have to settle on keeping her voice low. "We have to stop. I have a bad feeling."

"What are you talking about?" Charlie said.

Caitlin sat forward to lean between them. "Fana gets feelings. No bullshit."

Fana wished Caitlin would keep her voice down. The monks' ears must be ringing by now from the urgency in their voices, but she didn't have a way to write Charlie a note.

"I don't trust these people," Fana whispered. "They're not who they say they are."

Charlie searched her eyes, matching her whisper. "How do you know?"

"Because I *know*," Fana said.

"Fana knows things," Caitlin said. This time, she gestured her hands with a flourish, as if she was dispensing fairy dust. "She saw the words *And blood toucheth blood,* like prophecy."

Caitlin was still speaking too loudly and saying too much, like she was kegged. Fana expected Charlie to laugh at them; or worse, to look at Fana with accusation. But Charlie's eyes were sober and accepting. He glanced toward the men driving their van, then he leaned closer to Fana. His scent plowed past her fevered thoughts.

"The thing is," Charlie began, his lips close to her ear, "I've known these guys a long time. So has Caitlin. They've been friends to the Railroad."

"They're not friends, Charlie. I think . . . they're pretending. Playing a role."

As she spoke, she felt more certain. Her probes might be weak, but she felt it.

Charlie didn't blink. "Then we have to kill them," he said. His eyes waited, not blinking.

Fana imagined Gramma Bea's disapproving face through the van window again, and gooseflesh crawled across her skin. "What?" Fana said. "Are you joking?"

"Hell, no," Caitlin said, hushed. "It's all or nothing, Fana."

Charlie went on: "We know somebody gave us up in Casa Grande. We survived by luck. Someone on the inside is after us. What if these guys are spies?"

"If they are," Caitlin said, "we need to kill them now, before we get wherever they're taking us. So are you *sure*, Fana? As sure as when you knew the cops were coming?"

Fana felt dizzy. When had Charlie and Caitlin become such a

united front, practically finishing each other's sentences? And since when did Caitlin casually talk about killing people?

"What about Gandhi and Dr. King?" Fana said. "The Railroad is nonviolent."

"Weren't those Mitchell Rolfson's last words?" Caitlin said with a smile that chilled Fana. Caitlin was still completely zoned.

"No killing," Fana said. "We can take the van and leave them on the road."

"That's *loca*. So they can send people to hunt us down?" Charlie said. His eyes gleamed like glass. "Those two guys are about to kill us, but we should sit on our asses?"

"I never said they were about to kill us," Fana said.

Charlie brought his lips closer to her ear. "But if you *knew* those guys wanted to kill us, you'd want us to sit and wait?" Charlie said. "Or should we defend ourselves?"

Caitlin stared, defying Fana to lie. Fana's eyes smarted. She felt another bubble of grief. Had Gramma Bea cast her that stern gaze for something she was *about* to do?

"OK," Fana said. *OK what? It's OK to kill them?* Her tongue felt thicker as her heart pounded. "But I have to be sure."

Fana probed the two monks again. This time, the cloudiness was gone, and she found a nest of repetitive and predictable thoughts. The driver, Tomás, nursed a secret, unconsummated love for a farm girl. The other, Esteban, warred with inner doubts over his faith.

These were good men. At her word, they might have died.

Charlie's hand slipped into his waistband, toward his gun. Quickly, Fana grabbed his fingers. "*No*," she said. "I was wrong."

The taller of the monks glanced back at them in his rearview mirror, then away.

Gradually, Charlie let go of the gun, but he felt like a coil beside her. He had never killed anyone before. She felt him tremble. "You're *sure*?" he said.

"I'm sure," she said. "Sorry."

"Jesus, Fana," Caitlin said. "Don't freak us out."

"Be careful what you say," Charlie said, vanishing beneath his hat's brim again. "I would do anything for you, *negra*."

Sadness. A thicky, murky pool.

A large structure appeared ahead on the dirt road, higher on the mountain. A church, not quite finished. Like the palatial San Javier del Bac Mission they had passed in Tucson, the unfinished church looked like a princess's castle in a fairy tale. Breathtaking.

But Fana hardly noticed the church. All she saw was Gramma Bea's unhappy face, her lurching, painful walk. Gramma Bea filled her being. Grief took her breath. Her chest ached.

It would be so much harder to talk to Gramma Bea now.

Because her own head was so painful, Fana flung herself into Charlie's, looking for something to cling to. She found it: Charlie had lost his *Abuela* when he was twelve, and he would understand what she was feeling, perhaps even better than she did. He might be the one to tell her what to do about the hole falling open inside of her.

"I think . . . my grandmother died," Fana said. A whisper.

But Fana said it so softly that even Charlie couldn't hear. There was no time for sharing. No time to hide in Charlie's head, violating him again.

The Shadows were nearby. Other immortals, too. Someone as strong as Teka, or even Berhanu, could hide themselves from her for a time—longer than she wanted to admit. Someone could learn her thoughts without her knowledge, if they were strong enough. Teka always said she was the most powerful immortal, but that had never rung true. How could it be?

She had to reinforce her masking, even if it made the world hazy. Fana knew from long experience that she could keep others out if she locked herself in.

And she had to do her best to mask Caitlin and Johnny, too. Caitlin's mouth was bad enough, but her thoughts were dangerous. And Johnny was unconscious, but he would wake soon; his mind stirred with fresh, miserable memories of the day.

Fana's sight faded, and colors dimmed as her mind covered itself in what felt like a gossamer wrapping. She stretched her imaginary blanket over Caitlin and Johnny, too, the way she had protected Caitlin in the woods.

But she had to be careful. The Shadows dwelled nearby, and the

Shadows liked to talk. If she listened long enough, Fana knew she might remember everything she had sworn to forget.

Maybe I need to remember. Maybe I can't protect us without extra help.

Beneath her, through her, around her, the humming was starting already.

The day had come! Michel's fingers shook in his lap.

He had read of this day when he was only four. Papa had pointed the passage out to him in the Letter of the Witness. Mates immortal born.

It is you, Michel, Papa had said. *You are Most High, the Bringer of the Blood.*

And now the time had come, a promise fulfilled. Michel closed his eyes, stilled by joy.

MICHEL? IS THAT YOU I SEE?

It sounded faint, a flea's whine, but Michel heard Papa trying to reach him. Papa was improving: They were still half a kilometer from the church. It had just come in sight.

Michel shared his exuberance: *Papa, she loves me!*

SHE WILL IN TIME.

She loves me now. Already. She loves my face. She loves my heart.

DO NOT COMPEL HER, MICHEL.

How could Papa think he would be cruel enough to abuse Fana the way Papa had abused his mother? The thought of his mother's empty head enraged Michel so much that his triumphant moment felt sullied. He wished he had ignored Papa's pitiful calls.

Let Papa see Fana's love himself, the irrefutable vision of how gloriously he had succeeded where Papa had failed. Michel had not exerted an ounce of will on Fana. He was not the monster his father was.

MICHEL?

This time, Michel didn't answer his father's probe. He took Fana's hand, and she looked up at him with those aware eyes, laced with sadness. Michel felt shaken by her grandmother's death, too. He had been so careful! Her family was intended as a gift to her, not a punishment.

But Teka was not easy to master. Even with aid from Fana's marvelous thought streams, Teka often felt farther away than he should. It had taken Michel nearly thirty minutes to find entry into Teka's meditation; Teka traveled far. And he was slippery.

But Michel had held on.

Michel might have done more for the grandmother sooner, but the logistics! Sometimes he'd had to close his eyes to maintain the fragile thread with Teka, whose loyalty to Fana was fierce. Michel hadn't been able to play nursemaid to the grandmother at the same time Teka had been piloting a jet plane. And with a second puppet as copilot? Impossible. Not without Fana's help.

He'd been lucky the plane hadn't crashed from the sky.

Have I cost you a loved one already, my darling? I promise you— never another.

He would try to honor his promise with all his might.

"Are we here?" Fana said, her doe's eyes blinking at him.

Fana could never help probing him, even unconsciously, so he flooded her with the happiness her eyes inspired in him. That made her smile.

"Yep," he said. "This is the place." *Your destiny.*

"Destiny?" she said, wrinkling her brow.

She had forgotten, and he had forgotten.

She had forgotten not to parrot his thoughts, and he had forgotten to filter. Not for long, but long enough. The more of himself he gave her, the more he longed to dive into her, shedding the fictions he had created for her inquisitive mind. He would have to be more careful.

It would be unthinkable to lose Fana's smile now.

Michel gave her Charlie's bashful grin, lapsing into Charlie's blessed simplemindedness. "I was just . . . thinking about something I read when I was a kid. How things happen the way they're supposed to. We're here because of destiny. You believe in that too?"

Fana's smile survived despite her tears. "Yes."

Even the divine needed something to believe in.

Maybe it was a sudden shower of blood from Michel's celebrating heart, but the church's size and height felt dizzying as the van circled the fountain in the courtyard's round driveway. The last two months' improvements were striking. Even the pebbles in the drive-way glistened. The west altar was draped in scaffolding, but its walls soared high. The dome, once complete, would stand in testament to its inhabitants.

Until the pilgrims came, it would be theirs alone.

Michel hadn't always intended to bring Fana's family, but why shouldn't they have their own wing? If Fana chose, she could live far from his touch or gaze. He already had her room prepared, and he would give her time if she needed it. But how long must he wait?

The van stopped, and Romero gave two short bursts on the horn. Six attendants appeared from the garden, wearing paint-spattered aprons. The attendants opened the van's doors, but they quickly stepped back to keep a distance.

No one was to touch Fana. They knew that anyone who did would lose his hands.

The sanctuary doors flew open, one doorkeeper tugging on each. Papa walked briskly down the marble steps, nearly running. He was dressed in a white *guayabara* and pressed blue jeans rather than the ceremonial robes he usually preferred. Papa had cut his hair short and dyed it an unflattering silver-blond since his escape from the morgue.

As Caitlin hopped out of the van, Stefan's grin vanished.

"Your old friend," Michel called through the van's open door. "Caitlin, you remember Father Garcia." Caitlin grinned, heartily shaking the hand of the man she had seen Fana's father kill. Caitlin's reaction, though buried, was powerful; Stefan's face jarred a memory that loosened Michel's hold on her. Michel saw her eyes go flat, and it had nothing to do with him.

Papa hugged Caitlin while he cast Michel a predictably wary look. *DO NOT BE TOO CLEVER FOR YOUR OWN GOOD, MICHEL.*

She is a simpleton, like soft clay.

AND ANOTHER IN THE VAN? HOW MANY MORE?

"Father!" Michel said, enjoying the term's double meaning as he interrupted Stefan's mental stream. "*Por favor*. Our friend was shot. We need a doctor."

While Stefan called for a stretcher, shouting at the attendants, his stream was clear and uncluttered: *WE MUST NOT ALLOW ANYONE*

WITHIN FIFTY METERS OF HER. PERHAPS MORE. SHE WILL NOT BE FOOLED LONG. DO NOT UNDERESTIMATE HER.

Papa was bold to say so much with Fana just inside the van, a grand gesture of trust in Michel's ability to keep their communications private. More and more, Papa treated him like the Most High, instead of only preaching the words.

I have the best advisor in human history, Michel told his father. *I will not fail you now.*

Michel hopped out of the van, extending his hand for Fana. She took it, clinging to his fingers, and he supported her weight as she stepped to the running board, then to the ground. As she stood in the bright light, the sun made her skin glow. Beneath her scarf, her face was a blinding wonder. Michel could keep his father's thoughts muted, but he could not hide the tear that came to Stefan's eye. Of course Papa was overwhelmed. Papa had always had a taste for Ethiopian beauty, and Fana could be his mother's sister. And Fana's power! Her presence was like braving a windy beach before a storm; intense and electrified, countless grains of swarming sands.

Stefan looked at the ground, away from Fana. "All the b-bloodshed . . . ," he said, babbling. "So many have suffered in our cause." His first words sounded like a confession.

"Father Garcia feels everyone's pain as his own," Michel said to Fana.

"Father *Arturo,* you mean," Caitlin said. "I saw him on the news."

Dumbstruck, Michel looked at Caitlin. Her thought had come from so deep a place that it had emerged unnoticed. And Papa was here to witness his sloppiness!

Stefan looked angry before he remembered to soften his brow. "The news?"

Fana's dull eyes became alert, suddenly glued to Papa's face. Michel tried to probe her, but for the first time, he met a wall. His effort to control Teka and the other immortal meant that he had no reserves to work around Fana's barriers. Papa was right: He had stretched himself too far.

Michel's heart fell. Had Fana turned against him so soon?

"A priest was killed," Fana told Stefan. "You look like him." Judging by her eyes, she wanted to say more. If only Michel could glimpse her mind again!

Stefan clasped his hands. "And now he lives forever in our Father's arms, no?" he said with a warm smile. "Please come inside. We will care for your friend."

Fana didn't smile, but she followed the direction of Stefan's outstretched arm, toward the open doors. Her thoughts were still cloaked, but hiding might only be a reflex, Michel remembered. The powerful always brace in each other's company.

Others are coming, Michel told his father as he walked behind him. Fana's mother and the others had landed at Nogales International, and they were already on their way to the church. Michel sensed Fana's father nearby, too; Dawit was coming on his own.

But he was ready for Dawit.

Stefan glanced at Michel over his shoulder, unable to hide his surprise. *OTHERS?* Once again, Papa trusted Michel to safeguard his thoughts.

We are family now, Papa. Her Blood is our Blood.

HOW MANY OTHERS?

This time, Michel did not answer. Instead, he held Fana's hand as she stepped into the unfinished sanctuary and gazed up at the beams high above them. Stefan's smile veiled disapproving eyes as he clamped his hand on Michel's shoulder, as if to amplify his thoughts.

IT WAS ARROGANT FOOLISHNESS TO BRING OTHERS. ROMERO AND BOCELLI WILL DISPOSE OF CAITLIN AND THE BOY.

Even when he sowed death, dear Papa never lost his smile.

Thirty-one

The taxi lurched to a stop at the base of an ancient oak tree on the twisting, unpaved mountain road. Dust flew up behind the battered white Jeep. If not for the tire tracks ahead of them, Dawit would have been certain that Teferi had lost Fana's mental scent long ago. They were forty minutes outside of Nogales on a road ringed by thick bands of oaks and pine.

"*Lo siento, pero no más lejos,*" the driver said earnestly, shaking his head. "I stop here."

The sky was losing its last light. Dawit surveyed the brush, expecting a gang of bandits to emerge. He and Teferi had scanned the driver's mind for good intentions at the *sitio* taxi stand near the tunnel opening in Nogales, but their probes were not infallible. The driver's name was Javier, a white-haired grandfather, and he had seemed trustworthy. He supported a large family as a *pollero* smuggling migrants across the border, and he valued his reputation as a man who kept his word.

Mahmoud was sitting directly behind the driver, so he leaned forward, tapping his gun on his side window. "*Vamos.*"

"*No, no, lo siento,*" the driver said, shaking his grizzled head. His fingers brushed the rosary beads and wooden cross swinging from his rearview mirror. "I am sorry for this. If you ride back to Nogales, I will take you to a very nice hotel, no charge. I cannot go here."

Mahmoud flicked the driver's ear with his nozzle. "Then you'll travel on foot."

The driver flinched, gazing at Mahmoud's reflection in his mirror, but he didn't dare look him in the eye. "Truly, I am sorry," the driver said. Pleading.

HE IS AFRAID OF FEDERALISTAS, Teferi said. *THE ARMY PATROLS THIS AREA.*

"Are soldiers looking for narcos out here?" Dawit asked the driver.

Mexico was in the midst of an internal war between narcos and an unpredictable federal army that was accused, at turns, of either widespread corruption or overly cruel tactics against suspected drug dealers. On any given day, it was impossible to predict which side the army was fighting for. Mexico's northern neighbor still sowed chaos far beyond its borders.

"There are soldiers here since the construction started," the driver said. "A big church."

A church! "How far?" Dawit said.

"Less than two kilometers, *señor.* You will see it soon, on a ridge. If your friends are there, you can find them. But my car is my life, *señor.*"

I HAVE AN UNEASY FEELING, DAWIT, Teferi said. *WE ARE TOO FEW.*

Dawit wished they could enlist Berhanu and the others, but they could not wait for their Brothers to arrive from Arizona. They needed the vehicle, no matter what advantages lay in going on foot. They needed transportation to take Fana to safety.

"Get out, Javier," Dawit told the driver gently.

The driver's eyes were moist. "You will leave an old man? Like a dog in the street?"

"Better than what's ahead," Dawit said. He peeled his cash from his wallet, about five thousand American dollars. "For your trouble."

As the driver snatched the money with twitching fingers, the nozzle of Mahmoud's gun was at the sun-crisped nape of his neck. "We're finished," Mahmoud said. "*Lágarte.*" Get lost.

"*Dios,*" the driver whispered, nervous. Lips pursed, he opened his creaky door while he grabbed several children's photographs pinned to the sun visor and the rosary from the mirror. Breathing fast, he stepped away from the car with his hands above his head.

Dawit climbed out of the Jeep to take the driver's place, and Mahmoud slid into the passenger seat, his gun trained on the driver.

"We'll find you on the way back," Dawit told Javier, closing his door.

Javier wrapped the rosary tightly around his palm. "I am a child of Christ, so I must warn you even though you are thieves—"

"Thieves?" Mahmoud said. "We should charge *you* to take this wreck."

Javier clung to the door handle. "They call it a church, but it is not from God," he said in Spanish, staring at Dawit with dark, earnest eyes. "El Diablo is building that church. There is much death on this road. Remember: The Aztecs sacrificed humans to Huitzilophochtli because they believed their god needed blood to live. *¿Comprende?*"

Javier looked wild-eyed. His mental streams told Dawit that he knew nothing of Sanctus Cruor or the Living Blood—he was only worried about corrupt police and drug lords destroying his nation. But Sanctus Cruor indeed fed on innocent blood.

"*Comprendo,*" Dawit said and patted his leathery hand. "Thank you for your charity."

As Javier sighed, resigned, Dawit switched gears. Dawit fished out his gun and sped off, jouncing over a large hole in the road. In the headlights, he saw a low-hanging branch ahead weighted down by moss and a massive beehive. Bees flitted against the windshield.

Dawit gazed at Javier's slouched, weary posture as he vanished in the rearview mirror, wondering how the unlucky man would fare in the dark.

"We might soon envy him," Teferi said from the backseat, his fingers clacking on his keyboard. "Sanctus Cruor might have bought half the army. And I've been looking for satellite images, but everything is shadowed. No sign of a church. It's as if this road does not exist."

Dawit's phone, too, had failed him. He had tried to call Jessica several times, and by now he was certain something was wrong.

"An ambush awaits us," Mahmoud said.

Dawit eased his foot on the accelerator until he was driving at a crawl. "We should separate," he said. "One drives on as a decoy. Two others take separate paths on foot."

"One or two may not be enough," Mahmoud said. "We must—"

WAIT! Teferi's voice screamed in Dawit's head. Dawit jammed his heel on the brakes, and the car slewed left several feet in the dusty gravel, making a half-spin.

A hailstorm fell upon them.

The sound of punching metal and shattering glass swallowed Dawit. He heard the rapid sound of automatic gunfire only later, as instinct made him crouch low, reaching for his door handle. A brief glimpse, and he saw Teferi already slumped over the dashboard. Teferi's thought stream was gone, leaving a deafening, painful silence.

The gunfire came from everywhere.

Mahmoud sprang from the Jeep in a roll, and Dawit escaped through his door. Dawit landed hard on his hip when he tumbled, and his gun flew free. No time to retrieve it! He scrambled toward cover in the trees in an evasive, erratic pattern. Bullets rained near his feet, spitting into the earth.

Tree bark scraped Dawit's palms raw as he scrambled across the forest floor, hiding behind the trunk of a fir. He saw Mahmoud bound catlike over a fallen log on the other side of the road, in characteristically fluid motion. Mahmoud was quick, as always. Dawit's heart sailed.

Two, then. Mahmoud and I will find Fana.

Dawit's thought died when the back of Mahmoud's head flew away, a bloody tail of long hair trailing behind like a kite string. Mahmoud's body went limp, and he fell.

Alone.

The tree trunks around Dawit chipped away with gunfire, and he crawled on the twig-strewn ground to seek out new cover. A swishing sound a few yards behind him made Dawit whirl around. He saw movement from the corner of his eye.

Dawit's knife flew.

A man cried out from the brush.

Dawit bounded toward the noise. He found a bare-chested, tattooed young man on the ground, wearing green army trousers and boots. Dawit's knife had pierced his breastbone to the hilt. Both of the man's hands clung to the knife, pulling. His eyes were wide with shock.

The man's hair was long, and he was unshaven. Enlisted army? Not likely.

With Teferi beside him, Dawit might have probed the dying man's thoughts quickly, but Dawit couldn't risk allowing him to live long enough to yell out again. Dawit yanked the knife free, gagging the man's scream with his palm. The terrified man tried to bite him, crazed with anguish. His muffled cry was cut short when Dawit slashed his throat.

Blessed silence. Nestled by shrubs, Dawit searched around him for the soldier's weapon, his prize. Nothing! It must have flown free when he'd fallen, hidden in foliage. Dawit cursed.

Dark green *federalista* uniforms swam through the brush from every angle. In the glare of a floodlight, he saw at least thirty, perhaps more! The commander was close enough for Dawit to feel the man's adrenaline and excitement. Army defectors impersonating soldiers, Dawit realized. He raised his head long enough to see the commander point toward him, shouting out his location.

As Dawit ducked down again, bullets taunted him. His heart thundered. He might have killed them all if he'd had an automatic weapon, but he was trapped with nowhere to run.

Gettysburg. Adwa. In five hundred years, Dawit had slain scores of men and tasted death's sleep a dozen times. But he had never found himself panting as he'd pulled off his shirt and waved it above his head, frantic for the white fabric to be seen.

Surrender. If he was felled here, eight hours' sleep or more might mean losing Fana. But he might still have a chance if he gave himself up. These troops were not immortals; they were only paid guns on Sanctus Cruor's payroll. Dawit would still have the advantage of telepathy even if he was subdued, and that might be enough.

For what seemed like an eternity, gunfire chopped the leaves around him. In the din, Dawit was deaf even to his thoughts.

"*No más!*" Dawit shouted. He could barely hear his own voice. "*Me rindo! No más!*"

Dawit closed his eyes as wood particles pelted his face. He hoped the bullets' treachery would at least be quick; Dawit loathed being shot.

Faintly, he heard the commander's voice again: An order to cease fire! One soldier's voice after another called out around him, and the volleys of gunfire slowed, replaced by the footsteps running toward him. Light flooded him.

Dawit stood slowly, his hands raised high. *"Por favor, no más!"* He soaked his voice with fearful tremors, in case he could fool them into underestimating him.

Like most soldiers, these were very young. Some barely looked old enough to shave, and their uniforms hung too big on wiry frames. Dawit tried to find their thought streams, but there were too many at once. All he heard was noise.

The commander was older and bearded, nearly as thick as Berhanu. He charged purposefully toward Dawit with his machine gun ready. Careful to keep his hands raised while he blubbered for mercy, Dawit tried to penetrate the man's thoughts.

His name is Raffi. Dawit saw a palatial church on a ridge. He almost saw a face . . .

Then, an explosion of crimson. Dawit barely saw the commander lift the buttstock before a blow across his jaw knocked Dawit from his feet. His concentration was too scattered to probe as the soldiers swarmed him, binding his arms and legs with ropes.

Six soldiers began dragging him back to the road. Dawit lifted his neck high to keep the ground from abrading him, but even so his face was poked by twigs and brush.

"No tengo drogas . . . ," Dawit said, although he knew these soldiers weren't looking for drugs. "I don't have any drugs! I'm an American t-tourist. My friends and I were lost!"

"Silencio," the commander said and kicked him in the stomach.

Dawit had trained his body to absorb such a basic blow, so he exaggerated his groan of pain. He blinked rapidly, feigning light-headedness. Better to be quiet, he decided. As long as he was conscious, he might learn something about Fana. *And even if I'm rendered useless, Teferi and Mahmoud will find her when they wake.*

But as Dawit blinked dust from his eyes to watch the soldiers rushing around him, he felt his heart go still. Two soldiers were dragging Teferi from the Jeep. The commander snapped his fingers, ordering another group to retrieve Mahmoud.

"*Tráigame los cadáveres,*" the commander said, motioning. He wanted the bodies!

Dawit breathed faster as he watched the soldiers dump Teferi and Mahmoud beside him, close enough to smell their blood. Even knowing they would wake, grief stabbed Dawit when he saw Mahmoud's lifeless eyes staring at him. The soldiers threw blankets across the bodies and lashed them with ropes as if they, too, were prisoners. As if they knew!

Dawit's heart tumbled. He closed his eyes, searching for mental clues about his fate. The commander's thought stream was fragile, but Dawit held on with all of the concentration Teka had taught him. Sensation melted away as he slipped more deeply into the stream. All noise, gone. Only images: The church. A courtyard. Two monks with unfamiliar faces. Money changing hands. *Tráigame los cadáveres.*

The monks had asked for the corpses! The soldiers didn't know about the Living Blood, but the monks did. Not only was Sanctus Cruor close but they also expected to capture immortals. Someone had known they would be coming.

Suddenly the thought stream was gone as the commander walked away, barking orders to at least two dozen soldiers gathered around him. Two Humvees drove up from the direction of the church, and more young soldiers jumped out. Someone straddled Dawit and tied a sour-tasting, grimy rag over his mouth, pulling it tight. A gag.

Was he about to be executed?

Dawit's heartbeat seemed to shake the ground. It had been five hundred years since Dawit remembered what it felt like to fear death. Possible catastrophes always awaited Life Brothers—especially the specter of being buried alive. He and Mahmoud had once *wished* for death after drowning at sea, stranded in the open water, their bodies racked by dehydration as they'd been stalked by predators for days. At the time, it had seemed worse than death.

But now, Dawit knew the difference.

Sanctus Cruor could dispose of them permanently: Burial. Mutilation. Incineration. Perhaps his time had come at last. The idea awed him as much as it filled him with dread, with one thought tormenting him above all: *Like this?* The day felt like a fever dream.

He heard scuffling feet, and several soldiers grabbed Dawit's legs and armpits, then dumped him in the bed of a Humvee. Dawit's face skidded against the metal floor. He tasted blood from a split lip, but he was grateful for consciousness.

The commander must want him alive, for now.

Teferi and Mahmoud were dumped beside him. Six of the soldiers climbed in to ride with them, robbing him of the hope of an escape, even if the ropes' knots weren't so expertly tied. For the first time since the day his first daughter died, Dawit felt breath-stealing fear.

The Humvee began its bumpy journey.

The uneven mental streams Dawit picked up from the soldiers near him were useless. These were lawless mercenaries whose lives were a chaotic jumble of insults and poverty. Their commander, Raffi, was like a father to them. Soccer. Women. Movies. Their thoughts and conversations were maddeningly trivial, made nearly incoherent by the cocktail of mind-numbing drugs in their bloodstreams. Drugs helped them kill without conscience.

One boy who looked sixteen saw Dawit gazing at him and spit in his face. The others followed, and the vehicle exploded with laughter. The sixteen-year-old produced a pistol, and the soldiers dared each other to shoot him in the head, passing the firearm back and forth, pointing it.

Dawit stared into the gun's barrel without blinking. They respected their commander too much to displease him; Dawit knew that without help from their mental streams. His stare unnerved them so much that their laughter turned to dead silence.

After ten minutes, the Humvee's brakes groaned, and it lumbered to a stop. Dawit saw a glimpse of the church through the dusty rear window—an ivory-colored palace. The beauty made Dawit's eyes ache. He had never understood the grand power of holy edifices until that instant, when he needed hope. The part of him that still clung to hope of finding Fana soared, freed.

Dawit almost felt at peace.

Then he heard a woman's fear-stripped voice somewhere outside, only a few yards away.

"Please let us go," she was begging someone in English. "They're just children. Please."

He couldn't mistake the voice that had been imprinted on his soul since the day they'd met.

Jessica was *here*?

Peace was replaced by searing rage, his chest swelling as if to burst. Dawit fought to call out his wife's name, wriggling against his ropes until his muscles were raw.

Jessica had never seen a church with a dungeon.

Outside, the stately church promised sanctuary, but inside, the labyrinthine underground walkways felt like ancient Roman catacombs for the dead, as if all of them were being buried. The lack of windows told Jessica they must be underground.

The large, bare room where they had been locked had uneven stone-brick walls and a solid oak door that looked at least six inches thick. Teka closed the door behind them, still their captor. The room had three twin beds with bare mattresses; Alex lay in one, and Bea in another, draped beneath a bedspread Teka had brought. Jessica couldn't bear to leave her mother on the unpolished stone floor, even if her bed would be badly needed later.

Misery swamped Jessica, from the migraine headache that made her squint against the room's feeble light to the stabbing pain she felt beneath her rib cage, the punishment of grief. The room's dankness and the smell of paint and chemicals made her throat constrict. The children coughed between whimpers, huddled on the floor in a corner with Sharmila and Abena.

Jessica's bladder ached, but she didn't dare ask for a bathroom. Teka had offered her a private room, but she'd refused to separate from the others. The men who had met them at the church, dressed as monks, chilled her to the bone. They were killers; she could see that in their eyes. Soulless. Jessica had felt enraged since she'd realized Teka was kidnapping them, but the sight of men flaunting Christian costumes, hiding their evil inside a mimicry of God's house, sparked a different kind of anger. Rage was eating away everything she recognized about herself.

Jessica could not remember ever wanting to kill anyone, but she did now. Teka. Jima. The monks. She wanted to kill them so badly that her joints shook.

Only Jessica's active imagination calmed her: She closed her eyes and saw her mother safe and alive, standing over the kitchen stove stirring a pot of mustard greens. The image seemed real enough to touch; Jessica could almost smell the steam from the pot, scented with peanut butter and green onions. Bea was fine, at home waiting for her. That promise kept Jessica on her feet.

Jessica felt a warm palm around hers. "How you holding up, Jess?" Lucas.

Jessica squeezed, holding on. Lies cost too much, so she told the truth. "I'm not. You?"

"Been better," Lucas said.

Jared huddled beside him, his face ashen, eyes red. Jared's shoulders were hunched, hands shoved deep in his pockets, his lips pursed inward. In shock.

"I'm sorry," Jessica and Lucas said simultaneously.

"I did everything I could . . . ," Lucas said in a haunted voice. "I just wish—"

Jessica shook her head. "It's my fault," she said. "Everything. I d-didn't know . . ."

No words were big enough. Instead, she, Lucas and Jared fell against each other, arms across each other's shoulders. Miraculously, there were no sobs between them. They only swayed together, absorbing each other's tremors.

Jessica hadn't realized she would have to prepare her heart to lose another child. Despite her daydreams, her mother was gone. Dawit was unreachable. There was nothing left to cling to except each other—and how long would they have even that?

A loud sound from the door made them jump. Someone was turning a key in the lock.

They stepped away from the door. Jessica couldn't guess what horror lay next.

Jared's fists clenched as he pulled away. "I won't let them touch the children," he said.

None of us will, Jessica thought. *Not this time.*

When the door opened, Jessica blinked twice. Three times. Refusing to believe her eyes.

Dawit stood alone in the doorway, shirtless. Could that be him, only fifteen yards away?

Light shone from Dawit's face. "Jess!" His voice cleared her confusion.

As the door slammed behind him, the lock clicking tight, Dawit ran toward her. Her quaking legs ran to meet him, with Lucas and Jared on her heels, shouting with relieved joy.

Jessica and Dawit hugged each other so tightly that they nearly lost their balance, swinging in a circle that took Jessica's feet off the ground. So much blood rushed to her ears that she could barely hear him. She tried to talk, but she could only sob.

"It's all right, Jess," he said, stroking her hair. "I'm here, *mi vida.* I'm here with you."

Her mouth fell against his, as if she needed to taste him as proof. He kissed her with sad fervor; long enough to last. Jessica touched Dawit's face, still afraid to believe. He was bruised, with a bloody lip, but his scent was a homecoming.

"T-Teka . . . ," Jessica said.

"Teka could not have done this," Dawit said. "I've probed him, and he's not himself. Jima either. Someone used them to bring you here—someone powerful. It's Sanctus Cruor."

Someone who could control Teka? Jessica's thoughts fogged over. How could that be? The only being she imagined with that kind of power was Khaldun, or maybe Fana. One day.

Sharmila, Abena and the boys flocked to Dawit. The boys shrieked as if it were Christmas morning, all of them grinning and scurrying to climb on Dawit's back. Dawit sank to his knees to hug the boys, ruffling their hair and kissing their tear-stained cheeks.

"Where's Papa? Where's Papa?" they asked in a chorus.

Sharmila and Abena hung back, wide-eyed, watching Dawit's face for news about Teferi. When Dawit hesitated before looking toward the anxious women, Jessica knew something was wrong. The spark of joy sloughed from his eyes.

"We were separated," Dawit said. "I don't know where Teferi is."

Abena *tsssked* her teeth, muttering. Sharmila clapped her hands to her cheeks and stared at Dawit with a hollow-eyed gape, shaking her head. Dawit stood up to put one arm around each of them, and their foreheads rested together. From the grief in Dawit's set jaw, Jessica wondered if they would ever see Teferi again.

"Is everyone else all right?" Dawit said.

Jessica couldn't give language to what had happened. Instead, Lucas leaned close to Dawit, nodding toward the bedspread. "Bea didn't make it."

The simplicity was a wonder. Jessica never would have thought of those words.

Dawit looked at Jessica, appalled. He blinked tears as he reached for her hands. "Oh, Jess . . . ," he said. His bloody lip trembled. "Oh, baby . . ."

No. No. No. Jessica shook her head, feeling her brain sink into numbness. *Mom's at home in the kitchen. I can smell the greens cooking. I can—*

Dawit took Jessica's unsteady hands and pulled her to him. He wrapped himself around her, stroking her back, her arms, her face, her shoulders. He stroked her as if she were afire and his caress could smother the flames. Finally, she had somewhere she could lay her sobs to rest.

"I'm sorry I wasn't there," Dawit said. "I'm sorry."

"You had to look for Fana," Jessica said, keeping her eyes away from the lump in the bedspread that used to be her mother. "David . . . do you have any idea where she is?"

Dawit grinned, his bright teeth an unexpected promise.

"Teferi led us here," he said. "I think Fana may be right here at the church, Jess. She's very close. Can't you almost feel her?"

Jessica's next sobs came from a different place entirely. She swooned with relief.

Yes, Fana, she thought. *I can feel you, always. Be strong, sweetheart.*

We have faith in you.

Thirty-two

Caitlin O'Neal couldn't stop thinking about Father Garcia.

Father Garcia made everything fall out of place. Caitlin's brain had been lost from her, but Father Garcia sliced through her haze because her memory of him was acute. She remembered crying for him, screaming as she'd watched him die.

His name was a lie. That was the first thing. And if Father Garcia's name was a lie, there were other lies too. She was surrounded by lies. Sometimes Caitlin heard lies spilling from her own mouth. And if she wasn't doing her own talking, then who was talking for her?

"No, Fana," she heard herself say, her voice distant and distorted, a shout from the other end of a tunnel. "Neither one of us needs a babysitter. This room's fine for me and Johnny. I'll keep an eye on him. You go with Charlie."

Caitlin blinked, jarred, as too-bright colors assaulted her eyes. In the brilliance, she saw Fana standing a foot in front of her, wrapped in a white terry-cloth robe over her clothes, ready to take a shower. When the bright colors stopped swimming, Caitlin realized that she and Fana were standing inside the doorway of an elegantly furnished bedroom. Johnny was just visible out of the corner of her eye, lying asleep on one of the beds behind her. An IV dripped into his arm.

Caitlin didn't remember a doctor visiting Johnny.

Fana looked exasperated. "You really think it's a good idea to split up?" she said.

No! The idea was horrifying. *Please please don't leave us, Fana.*

Instead, Caitlin's mouth said, "I wouldn't have suggested it if I didn't think it was a good idea." Her tone was sarcastic and ugly. Hearing herself, Caitlin wanted to cry.

Fana looked annoyed, eyes flashing. Just when Caitlin needed Fana close to her, the distance between them was unfathomable. She might as well be dead already.

"But we still don't know who we can trust, Caitlin."

"Will you please grow the hell up? I need to sit and think—alone."

Is that the way I talk to her? Caitlin was mortified by the lies from her mouth. *His* lies.

She must have conjured him. As soon as Caitlin thought about him, he appeared behind Fana in the doorway in a fluid sliding motion, as if his feet didn't touch the ground. As he slipped his hands to Fana's shoulders, Caitlin felt a flash of insight the way unusual thoughts and ideas came to her whenever she was near him: His name was Michel Tamirat Gallo, and he thought Fana belonged to him. Like Fana, he was immortal born.

But in most ways, Michel wasn't like Fana at all.

Caitlin wanted to pull Fana free of his touch, but she couldn't move. When his hands touched Fana, Caitlin felt his attention slip away—Fana mesmerized him—but not quite enough. Not yet. Caitlin's mouth was not her own. Without Michel's blessing, her lips were sewn shut.

"Fine," Fana said. "I'll give you some space for an hour. Then we need to make a plan."

We won't live another hour, Fana.

Romero and Bocelli would come for her long before then. They had grabbed Maritza on Alton Road, pulled her into their car, and slaughtered her in a warehouse. Their pitiless faces had been Maritza's last sight. Fana's father had never had anything to do with killing Maritza. Would that misunderstanding cost Caitlin her life too?

Romero and Bocelli were waiting in the library. A few drops of arsenic in the IV bag would take care of Johnny, but they had long, lingering plans for her. They wanted to punish her and enjoy her. Taking turns, or both at once. Afterward, they would kill her too.

Don't leave us, Fana.

Fana only swayed gently back and forth, closing her eyes as Michel kneaded her shoulders. Michel had long, lingering plans for Fana, too.

"You two behave," Caitlin heard herself say. Her voice surprised her as much as it did Michel.

Michel glared. "Mind your business," he said. He didn't sound like sweet Charlie at all.

Michel's attention snapped back to Caitlin, and she felt her own hands fly up to brush through her hair, as if she didn't have a care in the world. She heard herself humming.

"Like you said, neither of us needs a babysitter," Fana said. She flicked her tired eyes away from Caitlin, her chin upturned and defiant. *Can't she see?*

No, Fana couldn't see. Fana thought she needed Charlie's touch. She wanted an anchor to keep her from flying away. She was afraid no mortal man could want her for anything except her blood, and she was too stubborn to let Charlie go, even today.

But he isn't Charlie, Fana. It can't be love if it's a lie.

He had taught himself through the Shadows, and the Shadows were greedy. If Fana gave herself to Charlie, she would be entwined with Michel forever.

He'd killed all three of the Rolfsons with a *thought*. He had commandeered Fana's teacher—and another immortal!—from thousands of miles away. Fana had not yet learned the lessons Michel had known since he was twelve, when the Shadows had first courted his dreams.

"Take care of yourself, Caitlin," Michel said, and he leaned over to kiss Caitlin's cheeks, one after the other. Her skin quailed at his touch. "If you need us, we're right down the hall."

That was what his mouth said. But she heard different words inside the loud rumbling sound that might be humming. *THOU SHALT NOT STEAL, CAITLIN. THE WAGES OF SIN IS DEATH, REMEMBER?*

Michel gave Caitlin a final smile before taking Fana's hand and bringing it to his lips. Fana's wrist went limp in his hand.

"Get some rest," Fana said. "Hope you're feeling better when we come back."

Michel closed the door, and Fana was gone.

YOU HAVE TRIED TO PROTECT FANA, Michel said from out of her sight. *YOU AND JOHN WILL NOT SUFFER A KNIFE'S BLADE LIKE MARITZA. I PROMISE YOU.*

Michel's mercy.

Caitlin stood captive by the door with a flailing heart, listening for her killers' footsteps.

Thirty-three

The bedroom stopped Fana in midstride. It was the most beautiful room she had ever seen, even in a photograph. A bedchamber worthy of a queen.

The twenty-five-foot ceiling and Spanish chandeliers made the room look like a cathedral. Ten-foot palms in shiny, colorful ceramic pots swathed the clay-colored walls, shading the glorious tiled Moorish arch that led to the balcony. The four-poster bed, long dining table and hand-carved bookshelves were Spanish Colonial style, striking simplicity in dark, gleaming woods. Large canvasses of resplendent paintings adorned the walls. Was this a fine museum?

But museums didn't have music! A lively Afro-Cuban *son* was playing—her father's favorite music, after jazz. The chamber was filled with an earthy celebration of horns and drums. A trumpet pealed as she stepped over the threshold.

"You're letting us stay *here*?" Fana said.

"Of course, *bonita*," Father Garcia said behind her. He had been waiting for them beside the door when they'd emerged from Caitlin's room down the hall. "Please enjoy our meager hospitality. The bathroom is through that second archway, and food is waiting on the balcony."

Fana blinked. "But . . ."

"Welcome home, my child," Father Garcia said and bowed low. Just like a Life Brother.

Fana had heard mostly static when she'd tried to get through to her parents on the church's secure telephone line. She hadn't been able to connect to her father either. The kitchen phone in the Big

House had finally rung and rung, but no one had answered. She'd hoped it had meant that they had fled already, but what was wrong with Dad's phone? Uncertainty was agony.

But Johnny was healing. The portly church physician—that was how he'd introduced himself, although Fana had never heard of that title—had given Johnny a saline IV, cleaned his wound, and declared that he would be fine with a couple days' rest. No surgery necessary, he said. The doctor was familiar with Glow, so Johnny's rapid healing hadn't raised his eyebrow.

An hour to rest, at last.

Fana hoped to spend her hour washing away the grime from the tunnel and enjoying Charlie's company, but the room's paintings held her eyes hostage. Masking bled away some of her ability to perceive vivid colors, and Fana wanted to *see*. Her mind loosened, and the room jumped into sharp focus. A musician's cowbell rattled its seductive call, and Fana's heart danced.

The oil paintings, some European, some Mexican, others African, were rich, colorful tapestries laden with voice and history. Impressive sculptures were mounted on tables. Artwork crafted from aged leather or parchment were spaced between the paintings; two in glass cases looked faded enough to be hundreds of years old. Could that writing be Ethiopian Ge'ez?

Fana was about to ask when she noticed that one of the paintings was in glass, too.

As Fana stepped closer, her eyes widened. A da Vinci?

The painting was only twenty inches high, but it radiated as if it filled the wall. The portrait of the pensive Madonna and playful child looked familiar: The baby Jesus, in his mother's lap, gazed up toward a spindle that looked like a cross in his pudgy fingers, staring into his future. A breathtaking portrait of innocence. *So young, and his destiny was waiting.*

Fana heard a *swish* from the glass balcony door, and Charlie was gone. Outside, the moonlight made his skin look like polished bronze.

Charlie brought back a bowl and a fork. Fresh-cut mango! Fana had forgotten how hungry she was until her stomach growled. Charlie raised a sliver of the fruit, and Fana's teeth sank into the perfectly ripened sweetness. Fana gazed at Charlie's long, slender fingers as he stabbed another slice. Then her eyes went back to the painting.

"This reproduction is incredible," Fana said. The canvas had cracks and age lines.

"It's an original. They all are," Charlie said. "This church has many friends."

Originals! Fana's eyes traveled over the masterworks again. Priceless! She would only expect to find treasures like these in a museum, or in the Vatican itself.

A burst of color cried out from behind her, so Fana whirled around. The piece she'd seen from the corner of her eye was by Mexican artist Frida Kahlo. She recognized the artist's signature self-portrait in the middle: her unswept dark hair, pronounced single eyebrow and piercing gaze. Fana had never seen a painting by Frida except in books or online, and it was so fertile that Fana's eyes sat to feast. Lush greens, reds and browns.

Frida wore a bright red dress, cradling a nude, childlike man who clasped orange flames between his hands. A massive third eye marked the man's forehead. *He sees everything, even what he doesn't want to see.* A giant figure behind them looked like Mother Earth, made of clay or mud, nestling him with a larger, darker arm. Mother Earth's hair was ropy dreadlocks, and a droplet of milk dangled from her breast. *She looks like me!* Behind Mother Earth, in a sky that was half in light, half in shadow, floated a giant mask. A woman? *The face behind the mask is God.* God's strong arms encircled everything; one, light for day, the other, dark for night.

Fana might have painted it herself, except that *she* would have been the one with the all-seeing eye. *She* was the one who yearned to be cradled, infantlike, in a lover's arms. Just once. How long would she have to wait?

"This one's called *The Love Embrace of the Universe,*" Charlie said. "Frida's husband was another artist, Diego Rivera. She and Diego had a stormy love, but it was forever. In this painting, she's showing how she is his salvation."

Fana's head floated. When she was with Charlie, a new eye

blinked open inside of her, just like in the painting. Colors were brighter. Her ears heard better. Like the music! The Spanish-style guitar music flowing from the speakers in the wall was as magical as the painting, so crisp that she heard the guitarist's fingertips slide across the strings.

The song was heartbreaking. The lead singer was a priestess; Fana could tell from her voice's pleas that she was talking to her gods. The song sounded like death.

There had been enough death, Fana realized. She was endangering Charlie, but how could she say good-bye? The singer's wail spoke Fana's fears: With you I'll go my saintly one / Though it may cause me to die.

"That's called '*Lágrimas Negras*,'" Charlie said. "Black Tears."

"I'm fluent in Spanish," Fana said. "My parents taught me."

Charlie smiled. "That's one thing."

"One thing what?"

"One thing you've told me about yourself," he said. "I've been waiting."

Fana swallowed back the instant lie that tried to climb to her mouth. "I don't talk about myself much," she said. "But . . . that could change."

Why had she said that last part? Were false promises in her blood?

Charlie lowered his head to meet her at eye level. "Promise?" he said.

Charlie's lips were a rosy pink. "Promise," she told his lips.

Charlie's sweet breath warmed her. "Me, too," he said. "We'll tell each other everything. No matter how bad."

"What makes you think it's bad?" Fana said. Could he really see through her?

"People don't mind talking about happy things," Charlie said.

"You haven't told me anything happy."

"I love you," he said. "That's happy."

I love you I love you I love you I love you I love you I love you I love you I love you.

Those words were an incantation.

"*Te quiero también,*" Fana said. I love you, too.

Charlie's lips fell against hers, and she bathed in his flavors; clove and mango-sweetened seawater spilling inside of her. Fana drank him, and he drank her.

Suddenly, the robe on top of Fana's clothes felt sweltering. Her shoulders wriggled, and the heavy terry cloth fell to the floor. Gently, Charlie nudged the robe aside with his foot and moved closer. His skin's heat raged through his clothes. Or was the heat from her?

Charlie's palms slipped beneath her T-shirt, across her waist, and Fana's stomach flipped. Her belly shivered, calming only when she pressed herself closer to his hands. Charlie's skin was magnetic, beckoning.

"Is the door locked?" Fana said. She would hate for Father Garcia to walk in and be reminded of what he had sacrificed for his calling.

Fana felt Charlie's heart kick against her chest. A haze of desire passed across Charlie's face, tugging his lips so that he looked like he was in pain. "No one will dare," he said. "This room belongs to you now, Fana. It's yours."

Could they be safe here? It felt more possible with every throb of Charlie's heart.

"I've never . . . ," she began, and sighed. "I mean, I don't know why . . ."

Fana forgot what she wanted to say when she saw her reflection in Charlie's staring eyes. Charlie's thick, dark eyelashes made her think of the artist cradling her husband in her arms. She wanted to seek out Charlie's heartaches and pluck them away.

Fana felt her mind spilling into Charlie's. She couldn't help herself—she probed.

AND BLOOD TOUCHETH BLOOD.

I know, sweet Charlie. Those words haunt me, too.

The kiss stolen from Charlie's mind skated up and down her spine, intensifying her skin's fever. Was she masking at all? Fana didn't know. Her body's clamor drowned out everything. Fana had never felt so rooted to her flesh, and her mind was grateful to rest. Skin was *wonderful*. Exquisite distraction.

Gentle drums, a clave and a cowbell moved her hips slowly from side to side, and Charlie's hips mirrored hers. One step closer, and he kissed her. His tongue darted across her teeth, then peeked into her mouth, brushing her tongue. His flavors were endless!

Charlie nudged his hips closer, and his rigidness nestled across her stomach and pelvis, unabashed. Fana's knees nearly buckled when Charlie's mouth nibbled her neck, leaving sweet chaos. Nerves fluttered and knotted as her throat spit fire, and Charlie's tongue licked the flames. When her muscles sagged, Charlie held her so she would not fall.

A wounded cry from the music's trumpet brought tears to Fana's eyes. Grief. Pleasure.

The room was so hot it was unbearable. Fana felt herself fumbling for her T-shirt.

Again, Michel was her mirror: He snapped his shirt over his head, and his chest was bare in front of her, almost hairless, sculpted with lean muscle.

In a blink, the room went from hot to cold. No man had seen her this naked, in only jeans and her bra. Fana's arms slowly folded across her chest, blocking her skin from his sight.

Charlie's head listed, practically resting on his shoulder as he gazed at her. "How can someone so beautiful be so shy?" he said. "I'm honored you would show yourself to me."

Fana's face tingled. Was this what blushing felt like?

With one gentle hand, Charlie took her wrist and guided one arm away from her chest, then the other. Fana felt herself shrinking under his eyes, or trying to. Her heart pounded, flooding her thoughts with blood. *What am I doing?*

"Are you a virgin?" Charlie said.

Fana tried to make a joke but couldn't think of one. She only nodded, silent.

Charlie looked like he was holding his breath. "My eyes . . . are the first?"

Fana nodded.

Charlie blinked twice. "May I see?"

Fana remembered her mouth. "Yes," she said.

Charlie's hand slid across her shoulder blade. *Snap.* Her bra fell open, unbinding her breasts. The straps slipped from her arms, and the bra dropped to the floor. Almost by itself.

"I wish I was a painter," he said, blinking again. "I would immortalize you, Fana. I will."

He pulled her close to him, and his broad chest swallowed hers. Skin on skin. Shoulder on chest. Breasts pressed against fiery flesh. He held her more tightly, hugging her still. His arms were warm around her back. Their own private *Love Embrace*.

"'Bone of my bone, and flesh of my flesh.'" Charlie whispered Adam's words about Eve in her ear. "I've found you, Fana. At last."

Like the words *I love you*, a lover's hot embrace was a revelation. They stood a long time enjoying the feeling of each other; feeling the joy of each other. The drumming grew faster, or else time slowed. Three snappy rings of the cowbell commanded Fana's hips closer to Charlie's.

Fana's eyes fell closed. She had no need for them.

Careful not to move an inch from Charlie's impossibly broad chest, Fana kicked off her sneakers, one by one. Curled toes pulled off her socks. The floor was bare wood, as cool and smooth as marble. She felt a vibration beneath her feet. Humming tickled her veins, like the humming she had heard on the mountain road—but deeper now. Inside of her.

Charlie stood so still that Fana forgot he was separate from her. Charlie's fingertips fanned across her back with the clave's one-two-three rhythm. He dipped her slightly, and her hipbone nudged against his erection. His arousal fascinated her. How did longing feel to a boy? The humming vibrated up her legs, her calves. Behind her knees.

Fana moaned.

Charlie's hair brushed across her face as he leaned toward her chest. His hair was a perfume of warm, damp scalp and soap. Charlie's hand slid to her breast. When his hot mouth touched her nipple, Fana's world became all rippling sensation. Charlie sucked, a hungry babe, and Fana writhed beneath his tongue. Droplets of perspiration between her legs electrified, sending shocks up and down her body.

Fana whimpered.

Charlie's free hand traveled across her hip, toward her thigh.

Gently sliding, burrowing, he pressed his hand across the denim that separated his skin from hers. Fana squeezed her legs tight against him. Her body wanted to swallow him whole. Charlie's tongue flicked across her nipple, and a river dampened Fana's thighs.

Yes. She would give herself to him. Today. *Now.*

Fana's body and mind fell against Charlie, and he met her in the place no one except them could see. Naked. Luxuriating. Were her feet still touching the floor, or were they both floating, buoyed by the humming beneath their feet? Her toes dangled, tingling. Weightless.

Michel.

The name came first, unadorned.

Michel. Fana nudged, probing, and washed her mind in his.

The sensation was like flash-fire.

Fana's lungs howled when she gasped. She heard a *thump* as her feet landed on the floor, and she swayed. The room spun, lurched, and spun again.

A dagger must have pierced her. The pain was astonishing, like everything about him.

The songstress had warned that death was easier than heartbreak: At least she could visit the dead. Her wondrous Charlie was simply gone.

"Johnny, *wake up!*"

Someone was calling him. *Caitlin?*

Johnny blinked, stirring. A wall of light swallowed him when he opened his eyes. Whiteness, as far as he could see. Was he dead?

"*Yes,* that's it!" Caitlin sobbed. "Johnny, p-please—wake up. Oh, God . . . please . . ."

He was staring at a ceiling, he realized. From a bed. Johnny's head seemed too heavy to move, but he forced himself to look toward Caitlin's voice. Movement ignited pain in his stomach, and he gasped. Pain made him forget everything else. His vision doubled.

"Johnny, *they're coming to kill us,*" Caitlin's voice said, a hissed whisper.

Johnny blinked again, and this time he saw Caitlin standing about twenty yards from him, facing a closed door. Her back was turned to him, her arms pinned to her sides like a wooden toy soldier. Caitlin looked back toward him, straining to see over her shoulder. Her pose was odd, as if she was fighting against her own body. *Where are we?*

Caitlin's face was bright red. She must have been calling him a long time.

"J-Johnny . . . ," she said, her jaw shaking. "They're coming. T-two of them. They have guns. Close your eyes and pretend you're sleeping. They're g-gonna pump you with poison . . . You have to fight them. I c-can't move."

Unwanted memories flooded Johnny, and the room whirled. He hadn't been able to move either! Johnny remembered Charlie's grinning face, covered in bees. *The Other.* A gun. Shocking pain. Johnny's brain rejected the memories before they could fully surface. *I was shot. I should be dead. She healed me.* He felt himself slipping away, back to the calming darkness.

"Johnny, we're both gonna' die if you don't stop them," Caitlin whimpered. "P-please."

Alertness returned, sharp. Caitlin and Bea-Bea needed him.

"Where's Bea-Bea? . . ." Johnny said, his voice hoarse. His mouth felt coated with sand.

"*Shhhhhh,*" Caitlin said. "Pretend you're sleeping. They're coming. I hear them."

Johnny lay still, his eyes closed, but he was sure his heartbeat was shaking the walls. Fear and confusion tangled his mind. *Who's coming? Stop them how?* Sweat drenched Johnny's legs and arms, and his pores wept with panic.

He was breathing too fast. Anyone would know he was awake right away.

The door opened with the squeal of a tight hinge. At first, Johnny couldn't tell if the sound was real or just his waking nightmare. His breath caught in his lungs.

The voices came, two men chatting casually in Spanish. One of the men cooed at Caitlin in the doorway, and they both laughed. "*Hai dormito bene, bella?*" one said.

Not Spanish. Italian? The men chatted cheerfully, but Caitlin was so quiet that Johnny had to fight to keep his eyes closed. Was she all right? His heart knocked the base of his throat.

Johnny dared a fluttering glimpse through his eyelashes. Two monks stood near Caitlin, one in front of her and one pressed behind her, playing with her clothes. The shorter monk pulled up Caitlin's shirt and murmured something that made the other laugh. The taller monk's hairy arm snaked inside Caitlin's shirt, and he closed his eyes, biting his bottom lip with mock rapture. The sight shocked Johnny almost as much as the blood in Casa Grande; a glimpse of Hell.

Johnny remembered to close his eyes just as the shorter monk turned his way. Footsteps in his direction. The other monk grunted, and Johnny heard Caitlin's legs dragging across the floor. The bedroom door swung shut, penning them inside. Rage soured Johnny's mouth.

Footsteps, closer to him. Adrenaline turned Johnny's limbs rigid. Johnny heard Caitlin cry out across the room, a sob, but his ears were riveted to the sound of a stranger breathing above him. Johnny could smell his sweat.

The monk clucked, speaking gently, as if to soothe him. *Does he know I'm awake?*

Johnny felt the stranger's hand graze across his cheek with a stink of cigarettes. Johnny's teeth gritted tight, but he lay still. When the monk moved his hand away, Johnny couldn't help slitting his eyes open again.

The monk's deep-set eyes were focused on a hypodermic needle. He tested the needle; a spurt of clear liquid. The large golden cross that hung past the monk's waist was swinging slowly in front of Johnny's nose. Last daylight from the window made the cross gleam like fire.

Seeing God so close by changed everything.

The monk pulled Johnny's arm, stretching it out to find a vein, the needle poised above Johnny's skin. *I surrender, Lord. Show me.* Johnny felt his pulse slow.

Caitlin cried out again; this time, in pain. The monk with the hypodermic turned over his shoulder to call to his friend. "*Rallenta,* Romero!" he said. An admonition?

His companion only laughed raucously, drowning Caitlin's cries.

Teeth still gritted, Johnny swiped at the needle, snatching it away. While time crawled around him, Johnny's mind and body had never felt so quick. The man above him didn't have time to speak or turn. Johnny plunged the needle into his exposed carotid artery, and pushed the plunger. Moving so quickly made him dizzy.

The monk looked at him in openmouthed silence—part surprise, part admiration. Loose skin on his face trembled, and he sank to the floor without a sound.

Bless me as you blessed David against Goliath, Lord.

Johnny ripped the IV out of his arm, ignoring the sting.

As he sat up, dizziness rocked him, and he planted his palms on the mattress to keep from falling over. Caitlin lay across the bed on the other side of the room, her legs folded at the knees. The monk lay astride her, his hand exploring her freely while he tried to trap her face beneath his mouth. Caitlin was as still as a rag doll; all she could do was sob and try to turn her face away.

Bless me as you blessed Moses against the Pharaoh, Lord.

Johnny looked down at the dead monk at his feet. His frayed robe had fallen away, revealing a black shoulder holster. Johnny slid from the bed, his soles silent against the floor. His fingers shook, but he commanded his body to unsnap the holster and dig out the unfamiliar nickel-plated pistol. It was heavier than the gun he'd held in the car.

Bless me as you blessed the Archangel Michael against the dragon.

Johnny's knees wavered as he took one step toward the bed. Then, another. He should not be on his feet, he realized. He would faint before he could shoot.

The monk was nuzzling Caitlin's neck; or he might be biting her, from the pain wrenching her tear-streaked face. But Caitlin's face softened when she saw Johnny, her eyes wide and clear.

The gun seemed to weigh fifty pounds, but Johnny lifted it and pointed. The room slid out of focus with every heartbeat. Caitlin and the monk were side by side. He had to walk closer.

Bless me as you bless all believers against the Beast, Lord.

Johnny's last step was a stumble. His arm ached from the gun's burden, but the back of the monk's head looked close enough to touch. The monk chuckled, taunting Caitlin's ear.

Johnny pulled the trigger.

Nothing. The trigger wouldn't give. The room was silent, except for Caitlin's feigned whimpers that didn't match her eyes, begging Johnny to shoot.

His gun was jammed! Johnny heaved for air, silently. Doubt welled up, ready to bury him. The monk would see him soon. *I need you, Lord. Please don't forsake me now.*

"Safety!" Caitlin called out, the same instant Johnny remembered. "Thumb!"

The monk raised his head to look at Johnny; an easier target. Johnny's thumb found the lever and pushed. When the lever wouldn't go up, he clicked it down. Johnny felt calm to his bones even as he watched the monk's arm snap for his own gun, racing him.

The monk's hand was only halfway to his holster when they both knew he was dead.

The monk grinned like a ghoul, leering with gray teeth.

This time, Johnny Wright's gun fired six times straight.

Thirty-four

Somewhere, there might have been gunshots.

Otherwise, the room was silent, or seemed to be. Fana's ears took in no sounds.

Who are you? Fana quivered as she stared at his face, learning and unlearning. She could barely keep steady on her feet. Her teeth chattered; the room was suddenly frigid.

He was a name with no face, and a face with no name. He was a stranger, yet she knew him. She knew which soccer shirt he had worn on his fifth birthday, and the way he liked his steaks to bleed. His memories were nearly as vivid as hers; some of them more so, especially from his childhood. The new memories collided with Charlie, dominoes falling in her head.

Fana sobbed. *Why?*

Something stirred at her feet. Fana's bare foot had backed against her robe (*you showed yourself to him and let him touch you*), and the fabric moved as if a raccoon had scurried beneath it. Suddenly the robe flew up in a swoop. Fana gasped as the cloth billowed toward her, chasing her when she sidestepped it. When the fabric lighted across Fana's shoulders, she screamed and flung it off. The robe slid across the floor, limp.

COVER YOURSELF, his voice said. *IT WON'T HURT YOU.*

Fana felt silly, which only enraged her. She hated giving him the satisfaction of seeing her startled by such a simple levitation. She grabbed the robe from the floor and flung it around herself, trying to close any gap where she might give him another stolen gaze. Remnants of arousal chafed her. Fana trembled with rage at the memory of his touch.

I HATED LYING TO YOU, FANA. I'M SORRY.

His true voice was chilling in its foreignness. Standing near him felt like swimming against a current, and Fana's mind whirled. Now Fana understood how her mother had felt when they'd tried to meditate together, and Mom had said she'd felt her racing away.

He adjusted his thoughts, trying to give her clarity, to slow down for her. She felt his efforts, but he was still a blizzard. His unfiltered presence made Fana's head hurt, but she didn't block him out. Instead, she waded more deeply into him. She didn't like what she saw in his head, but it was better than not seeing.

He could kill her with a thought. And he believed he loved her. His love for her was as real as the blood on the Rolfsons' wall.

He turned away, as if to give her privacy. Fana didn't trust the shame he seemed to feel.

"You killed them." Fana spoke aloud. Her voice was shaky, but words carried more significance when they were aired out. "A whole family. A *minister*."

A HERETIC.

"A fourteen-year-old boy! There's no way to justify it. You're a murderer!"

AM I THE ONLY ONE OF US WHO HAS KILLED? He made himself sound gentle.

Fana's wrists shook. She still didn't have control of her body. She didn't think he was manipulating her limbs—she hoped she could tell—but his presence made her body forget itself. Rage was so foreign to her that it blotted out her muscles. It blotted everything.

Fana's face flamed. "I was three years old!"

YOU WERE READY TO HAVE ME KILL THOSE MONKS IN THE VAN. EVERY KILLER HAS REASONS. OUR LIVES WERE ORDAINED FOR US, NO DIFFERENT FROM THAT BABE PAINTED BY DA VINCI'S HAND.

In her fearful indignation, Fana's knees knocked together. "You're deluded! You've forgotten everything He grew up to say."

THE LETTER OF THE WITNESS SPEAKS ALL, FANA.

"Did that letter tell you to kill Maritza?" Fana said. "What else would Jesus do with this blood except give it to the sick?"

"*WREST THIS BLOOD FROM THE HANDS OF THE WICKED.*"

"*You're* the wicked! That's what you've become. Those were innocent people!"

I WOULD GRIEVE TO HARM A TRUE INNOCENT. I HATE HURTING YOU, FANA.

"Use your voice," she said. "I don't want any part of you inside of me."

His face stiffened. Her words could lash him. *Good.*

He stepped away to pick up his own shirt, quickly pulling it over his head and tucking it into his jeans. "I could have ridden you," he said. "Like a horse. I chose not to."

"So it's better to lie?"

"Isn't it?" he said.

His eyelashes made Fana's stomach cinch; she nearly vomited from mourning Charlie's memory. She turned her face away. She couldn't look at the Frida painting either. Instead, she forced her unsteady legs toward the door. She heard a lock click as soon as she got close. The air seemed to ripple as a humming sound skated past her ear.

"Let me go!" she said.

"I can't, Fana," he whispered. He took a step, as if to comfort her. But only one.

As she probed him, the humming rattled Fana's teeth. A cloud traveled from the room's eastern windows to the northern ones, slowly stealing the moonlight. The room was getting dark, casting the paintings in Shadows.

"Where's my family?" Fana said.

The blizzard in his head gave way to a blank spot. He was still withholding from her, she realized. What else was so horrible that he wouldn't want her to see?

"Show me," she said. "*Right now.*"

A kaleidoscope of images from home battered Fana. Blood. Weapons. Tears.

Gramma Bea.

Fana screamed, remembering Gramma Bea's visage on the road-side with trauma so fresh it was stamped on her face. "*I never got the chance to say good-bye!*" Fana said.

"I'm sorry, Fana."

Fana's knees gave way, and she slid to the floor. She had suspected that Gramma Bea was dead, but it was worse to know her suffering. Gramma Bea should have passed quietly in her sleep, or doing something she loved. Gramma Bea could have died well.

"*You're SICK!*" Fana shrieked from the floor.

He offered his hand, standing high above her. "Heal me, then."

The floor's vibration roiled beneath her. That same power had lifted their feet from the ground while they'd kissed, she remembered. The floating sensation had been real, not just her love-struck imagination! Had the Shadows carried her? Fana had shied away from the Shadows since her first taste, but he breathed Shadows as if they were oxygen.

They came to Fana as soon as she stopped ignoring their call, flushing her with giddiness. The humming suddenly thrilled Fana the way his fingers had thrilled her skin, scores of gentle tendrils. Fana's skin and mind crackled, charged. The humming was deafening.

Fana stared at Michel, realizing she had never hated anyone so much. As soon as the thought came to her, blood crawled from his right nostril in a teardrop.

Did I do that? A pinch of concentration, and blood trickled from his left nostril too, resting above his lip. *Am I hiding from him somehow?*

Yes. Hiding in the Shadows.

Fana imagined Michel's mind as light patterns, like the firefence she had learned to evade at home. She felt herself eluding him, too, predicting his probes. She hid inside the pathways his mind's potent stream carved in her, like riding on a lion's back.

Blood dripped to his shirt, and he stared down. "I'm bleeding." He sounded shocked.

Fana's heart thrashed with both fear and exaltation. She forced herself to her feet.

"The Cleansing starts now," Fana said. "With you."

Fana rode the Shadows' surge. His ears bled next, spurts across his neck. He winced in pain as he clapped his hands to his ears. He looked at her, confused.

"Fana . . . you would try to kill me?" he said. He sounded exactly like Charlie, because a part of him *was* Charlie, of course. How else had he created Charlie so convincingly?

He created Charlie to hurt you. He wanted Charlie to touch you.

The man with Charlie's face cried out and lurched in anguish, backing into an end table, crashing it on its side. When he spun, blood oozed from his mouth. He gazed at her, wide-eyed. Even knowing who he was, Fana couldn't stand to watch him suffer. She turned away.

"You're a quick study," he said. His throat gurgled.

"I've had practice," she said. "Remember? I killed a Life Brother when I was three. You'll lose every drop, just like him."

"But he wasn't me, Fana," he said, gasping. "I shouldn't bleed from you."

"Your mistake," Fana said. "You let me in."

He spat. Blood splattered the spotless floor.

"Re . . ." His chest heaved, his breathing became labored, and he spat again. He smiled widely, with bloodied teeth. "Remarkable. You're exquisite. Papa was right . . . "

Slowly, his smile faded. His face, streaked crimson, lost its humor. "I hope you understand, Fana . . ." He tried to straighten, bracing himself against the wall, where his palms left a collage of bloody handprints. "I can't allow this."

His arrogance was infuriating. The Shadows surged through her, and he howled.

"Don't be naive!" he shouted. He spat again. "You think because you're hiding, I can't find you? That I'm defenseless? Fana, please— don't make me hurt you. The time comes when . . . you can't stop yourself . . ."

Fana closed her eyes so she wouldn't have to watch him bleed to death. He might have Charlie's face, but his voice was not Charlie's. Between agonized groans, he vomited blood.

DON'T MAKE ME KILL YOU! he screamed, just when she had hoped he was dead. *IT WOULD BE WORSE THAN KILLING MYSELF, FANA.*

"Then kill yourself," Fana said. "My way will hurt more."

DON'T

His thoughts babbled, snuffed.

Suddenly, a vise encircled Fana's head, tightening her eyes in their sockets. While Fana was still absorbing the scope of the agony—it was new and dizzying; worse than physical pain—a water glass danced on the nightstand, then fell and broke. Paintings jumped from the walls in succession, cracking wooden frames. The floor shook violently, nearly swaying.

Earthquake. But it wasn't nature's work. *He* was causing it. Or she was. Or both.

STOP, FANA, OR I'LL HAVE TO HURT YOU. SHOW YOUR-SELF TO ME.

"I'll die before you touch me."

THAT PAIN YOU FEEL IS ONLY A TASTE. FERMATI! STOP THIS

Fana felt his probe riding with her inside the humming. He couldn't penetrate her mask to control her body, but he could find the source of his pain. He held on, fighting to turn the currents she was riding against her. His strength was a wonder.

I can't win, she realized. No wonder he had begged her to stop! If he couldn't unmask her, his only defense was deflection. The pain wasn't from him: He was only sending it back to her. Soon, she would be bleeding, if she wasn't already.

Even if she killed him, she would die too.

Don't wanna die for a while . . . I think I'll fly for a while

Reflexively, Fana tried to retreat, to separate from the Shadows. But suddenly the humming was the only thing she could hear, even as she watched furniture tumbling around her. The bowl of mango fell to the floor, breaking in silence. The humming clogged her ears.

He said she might not be able to stop. *Maybe everything out of his mouth isn't a lie.*

Nosebleeds always came first. Warm blood dripped across her lips and chin.

Fana tried to be ready, but the ripping sensations surprised her. Her insides cramped and twisted, wringing out. Her vision shifted, and the light in the room faded to dim red.

She looked at her white robe, dotted with blood. Fana's throat and cheeks burned as her veins and capillaries burst, and blood spilled out of her mouth. The salty, coppery taste drowned her tongue. Fana's heart wriggled, struggling. A mountain sat atop her chest, smothering her.

Fana's body craved the fetal position, but she staggered to stay on her feet. She looked up at him and saw the horror on his face, inside his bloody mask.

FANA PLEASE DON'T MAKE ME.

Another surge came, from nowhere and everywhere. This time, both of them screamed.

Senseless with suffering, Fana threw herself against the trembling wall, where her bare feet slipped against spatters of blood on the floor. She fell in a heap, her muscles locked. Hot blood escaping her ears snaked across her collarbone.

Michel grunted, as if he was carrying a heavy load, and he pulled himself upright. His teeth were gritted so hard that it transformed his face, expanding his jaw. His body shook violently, as if his skin could pull itself free.

As Michel stood taller, the Shadows stole everything. Fana watched his face fading above her as her eyes shut down, locking her in darkness. The Shadows' humming tried to overtake her, but her favorite music was alive in her, untouched. *Don't wanna die for a while . . .*

Fana was too racked with pain to be afraid, but she felt sad for Mom and Dad. She wished she had known she had so little time, or she would have left the woods long ago.

Fana screamed again.

All she wanted now was to stop the pain. She would put herself to sleep if she could, but her mind thrashed, useless. Michel was standing over her. She could smell him through her blood-clogged nose. She wished she could kick out at him, but her legs ignored her. *He got past my mask. He has me now. Better to be dead.*

At least she had hurt him like no one else had. At least she would die trying to bring light to the world, just as her name and Blood promised.

YOU SILLY FOOL YOU NEARLY KILLED US BOTH.

His voice came, scolding like a parent.

Fana couldn't respond, even in her head. He thought he loved her, but he couldn't possibly. If he did, he would have put her to sleep and spared her the blistering agony.

PROMISE ME YOU'LL NEVER TRY TO KILL ME AGAIN, FANA.

For an instant, Fana was too stunned to understand. Was he bargaining with her?

Her mind struggled to clear itself. Her lips wouldn't move, so she sent him a thought: *Promise you won't hurt anyone else.*

His answer came in such a roar of frustration and anger that it was incomprehensible. While his mind raged, Fana felt herself sinking away. Becoming smaller.

Stillness.

PROMISE ME, FANA, OR I CAN'T LET YOU LIVE.

Trance. Trance out.

IS IT WORTH DYING FOR? YOU WOULD ROB THE WORLD OF SO MUCH?

"I p-promise," Fana heard herself say. "Never again."

Had he formed those words, or had she? Did either of them know the difference?

The torture subsided, a sensation so startling that Fana gasped again. The shaking in the room stopped. Light and sound returned. For the first time, Fana heard the church bell tolling wildly above them to proclaim the earthquake. Fissures veined the wall above her.

Had there been gunshots? She wasn't sure.

Fana wiped her eyes, and the blood stinging her tear ducts stained her hands. She knew it wasn't possible for all of her pain to have vanished so quickly. He must be soothing it somehow, massaging her. His mind was nesting inside of her; she felt him.

He offered his palm to her. "*Stai bene, Fana?*" Michel said gently in Italian, his first language. "Are you all right?"

"Don't touch me," she said.

"I don't want you to hurt," he said.

"Too late."

He sighed and stood up straight, taking a step away. His eyes hung on her, watching. Pain cascaded over her as he stopped soothing her injuries, but only enough to make her wince and hiss. At least she was healing instead of bleeding.

Someone pounded at the door. "Fana?" a voice called. Caitlin!

Michel slid his hands into his pockets and strolled toward the door.

YOU'RE NOT THE ONLY ONE I'VE UNDERESTIMATED TODAY, FANA.

Fana's heart leaped. The gunshots had had something to do with Caitlin and Johnny!

Fana tried to lunge after Michel to grab his ankle, but she couldn't move, whether it was because of Michel's influence or her body's exhaustion. She tried to probe him again, but he was a fortress. She could never burrow inside of him now. Only his ardor had weakened his mask, and he would not make that mistake again.

More banging. "Fana?" Caitlin said. "I hear you! I'll b-break the door down!"

Fana's weary heart raced as she watched Michel walking toward the door.

"Michel!" Fana called after him.

The sound of his name straightened his spine. He turned around to look at her, waiting. Hearing his true name from her lips was a gift to his ears. Maybe he did love her.

"Don't hurt my friends," Fana said. "Or my family. Please."

His expression was lost behind the blood on his face.

Suddenly, the door flung itself open, slamming against the wall. Caitlin stood wild-eyed and disheveled in the doorway, her fist raised to pound again. In her other hand, she held a shiny pistol. As soon as Fana noticed the gun, the weapon disintegrated to gray dust, falling through her fingertips to the floor. Caitlin stared at her empty gun hand, dumbstruck.

"Michel, *please*!" Fana begged.

When Michel walked forward, Caitlin screamed and leaped back. Then she stood as still as a sculpture. Fana felt Caitlin's thoughts shrivel away like the gun.

Then Caitlin saw Fana, and the shock in Caitlin's face made Fana remember that she was covered in blood. Caitlin shrieked, and Michel seemed to vanish from her sight. Caitlin squeezed her body against the wall and ran past him, not looking back, flinging herself over Fana. They trembled together.

"Clean her up, Caitlin," Michel called quietly, walking away. "Take care of her."

While Caitlin wiped blood from Fana's face with her hands, Michel vanished through the doorway. Would Caitlin forever be under Michel's control?

"*You fucking asshole!*" Caitlin shrieked behind Michel, hugging Fana close to her.

All Caitlin. Fana was so relieved that she almost laughed. Instead, she sobbed.

"What happened?" they both said together.

They told each other their stories while Caitlin wiped away Fana's blood.

Thirty-five

His mother was sitting by the window in his father's bedchamber, staring outside, hands on her lap in a prayerful position. She was the last person Michel had expected to see today. Her head was covered in an Ethiopian silk scarf colored in gold, crimson and purple, against dark skin that made her Fana's twin. Michel brought her a new scarf for her birthday each year—remnants of her past as a village girl from the Ethiopian highlands.

Stefan was at the bar with his back to the doorway, pouring tequila. Bottles had fallen from the bar, shattering glass and liquor across the floor, but otherwise the damage was not nearly as severe as it was in Fana's chamber. Stefan didn't turn when Michel walked in, and Michel was glad to be spared the disappointment on his father's face.

"Quite a racket," Stefan said. "We felt the earth move, didn't we, Teru?"

Michel's mother didn't blink; her gaze was fixated on the window.

Stefan flung back his first shot and poured again. "You're not with your new bride, which tells me something's gone wrong—that, and the earthquake's ring of desperation. As you know, your two little clay toys made fools of Romero and Bocelli. It's too bad, Michel, you're not so gifted at cleaning up your messes."

Tragedy didn't curb Papa's criticisms.

Michel ignored his father and went to Teru. She had been sixteen when she'd met Stefan more than fifty years ago, and she looked no older than Fana now. Teru was the only woman Stefan had ever shared the Ceremony with. The others with the Blood numbered only a handful. Romero and Bocelli had earned the Blood through service, and then there were the Four Horsemen, as Papa liked to call them: one in Rome, one in Tel Aviv, one in Beijing, one in Washington, D.C. The rest of Sanctus Cruor's followers were only seekers.

Michel had never known a fellowship like Fana's. He had never even had a true mother.

Michel knelt in front of Teru. He smiled as her eyes were drawn from the window.

"Tamirat!" she said, grinning. She always called him by his middle name, her father's name. Whenever she saw him, she thought of the fat baby in her arms.

"Mother." He rested his warm forehead against hers, and his thoughts sighed.

I've missed you, Mother. As always, he heard nothing in response.

"My God, Michel, is that blood from Fana?" Stefan said. After finally turning to see Michel, he was stunned. When Michel didn't answer, Stefan's face paled. "From *you*?"

Michel wiped his face with his T-shirt, blowing blood from his stinging nose. He must look like a horror, and his mother hadn't noticed. Without wanting to, Michel glanced toward his parents' bed. The rumpled sheets made his stomach queasy.

PLEASE TELL ME WHAT HAPPENED, MICHEL, his father implored.

Michel gazed into his mother's smiling eyes. He brushed her chin with his finger.

"She loathes me," Michel said.

He allowed his father to see his memories of Fana. Stefan groaned under the memories' weight, sharing his son's pain. He paced behind him. "Michel, Michel . . ." He sounded near tears.

"No lectures now, Papa," Michel said.

"We're far beyond lectures," Stefan said. "How could you have allowed her so close to you? But we've no time to dwell on the losses. You see there is no other way now. Everything is as prophesied. Your mother is here for the wedding."

Michel closed his eyes and squeezed his mother's hands. She

squeezed back, but vaguely. Nothing held her attention long, only her mind's pleasant dreams.

"Be thankful," Stefan went on. "At least you have memories of love in Fana's eyes. You can return to those memories again and again. You can create Fana as anyone you choose."

Michel rose to his feet with an unfamiliar ache in his limbs. The remnants of Fana's attack had faded to a throbbing, but it wasn't any easier to breathe or stand straight. His father's gold-leaf-covered replica of the Letter of the Witness was mounted on a stand at the foot of the bed, so Michel flipped the parchment open at random, touching the pages he had first loved as a child. *"Wickedness is cunning, and can hide in the hearts of men."* 17:10.

Fana considered *him* the Wicked; he knew that from both her words and thoughts. Fana's beliefs were so clear, and yet so different. His mother's interpretations of the Letter had disagreed with Papa's too. Heretical. *Wickedness is cunning.*

The loathing in Fana's face seared Michel's memory. How could Papa believe he would want to savor any recollection of this day?

Slowly, Michel became aware that his father was standing beside him. Stefan gently draped the silken white gown over Michel's bare chest and bloodied clothes, capturing one arm inside the sleeve, then the next. Stefan methodically fussed over the rarely worn Sanctus Cruor vestments, straightening each crease until the soiled clothes underneath were hidden. The robe seemed too heavy to be silk alone. Had it been spun from stones?

"There will be no New Days without her beside you, Michel," Stefan said quietly. Reasonably. "The Blood brings responsibility, Most High."

His father lowered himself to his knees and took Michel's hands, bending to touch his forehead to Michel's knuckles. This was Papa's first bow to him as Most High, a moment Michel had anticipated as long as he could remember. Now, the gesture's emptiness pained him.

Michel pulled his hands from his father's grip and forced a glance toward his mother, whose eyes had found the window again. He hid his face so Papa would not see his tears.

"I want her family brought to me," Michel said. "When Romero and Bocelli recover, we'll dine together, no matter what the hour. Her people and mine."

"What do polite gestures win us now?" Stefan said. "Go back and finish it. Take her."

As if Fana had been a sport! Stefan's hunger made Michel so angry that he expected his father's nose to bleed. When Michel whirled to face Stefan, his robe flew.

"I am Most High, and Fana will be my bride," Michel said. "Our marriage was prophesied before we were born. But yours is done, Papa. I'll let you keep Mother in your bed tonight, if you're petty enough—but at dawn, her mind is hers again. I'm setting her free."

Stefan's face went chalky, then red. "F-free?" he said. "Teru is *happy* as she is. Freedom means nothing to her."

"Then that lesson is my wedding gift to my mother."

Could cruelty be blunted by kindness? Michel prayed so.

During the New Days, he might never smile again.

Thirty-six

Aunt Alex? I'm right here. Follow my voice.

Alex's brow creased and her eyelids fluttered.

For ten minutes—after the hugs, tears and reunions—Fana had sat at her aunt's bedside and tried to bring her back. Aunt Alex felt nearly as far away as Gramma Bea, caught in a between point. Fana pumped Aunt Alex's hand gently, coaxing; the mind was powerful, but an embrace could travel a long way too.

Fana closed her eyes, squeezing her aunt's hand again.

Yes, that's it. Follow me.

So, so close now . . . Aunt Alex's eyelashes flickered harder, looking for light, and Fana smiled. It should have taken her all night to find her way to Aunt Alex—she was sure of it—yet she was speeding through the maze of Aunt Alex's mind, deft and sure.

A souvenir from Michel and the Shadows. She was a quick study, as he'd said.

How else had her time with Michel changed her? Were the changes permanent?

Fana shivered, almost losing her aunt's stream, so she pushed Michel out of her mind. Mom, Dad, Uncle Lucas and Jared stood behind her, waiting over Aunt Alex's bed. Fana ignored their thoughts, but she felt their anxiety in their shifting bodies and tightly clasped hands.

Come with me, Aunt Alex. Open your eyes.

Aunt Alex's eyes flew open, wide and aware. She blinked, then squinted, raising her hand to cut the brightness. "Mom?" she whispered.

Jessica, Lucas and Jared yelled out, thrilled, but they hushed themselves when Alex cringed, covering her ears. Jessica and Lucas fought for space to hug her, one clinging to one broad shoulder, one to the other. But Aunt Alex's eyes were riveted on Fana; it was only natural that Aunt Alex's attention would gravitate toward her guide.

"I'm sorry, Aunt Alex," Fana said.

"Sorry?" Aunt Alex said, blinking again. "Fana, I was *there*. I touched her. I . . ." Aunt Alex's eyes shined like those of a toddler who didn't have the words to explain how beautiful the Christmas tree looked. "She's right there!" Aunt Alex said. "*Right there.*"

Aunt Alex repeated those words, shaking with joyful tremors. She reached for Jessica and hugged her neck. "Jess, Mom's all right."

"I know," Jessica said, crying and laughing while they hugged the life back into each other.

Fana envied their ecstacy, even if it was a wounded ecstacy. She wished she had seen her grandmother's crossing, to share in Aunt Alex's joy. Instead, she had seen Gramma Bea's troubled face by the roadside. Fana couldn't celebrate this day.

A hand slipped into Fana's. It was Johnny's.

"Hey," he said. He had a dimple even when he wasn't smiling. "I'm glad she's OK."

Fana smiled, suddenly self-conscious. Her gifts had never been known to anyone outside of the colony, except Caitlin, but Caitlin had told him. After what he'd been through, there would be no more secrets from him.

What did Johnny think of her? Fana didn't know, and she wouldn't probe Johnny to find out. She was better at probing than ever, so she would have to learn better discipline. *Starting now.*

"You're probably confused," Fana told Johnny.

"Actually . . . I'm less confused," Johnny said. "It's better than thinking I'm crazy."

"You never trusted him," Fana said. "You knew all the time."

"You're not the only one who gets hunches," Johnny said. Then he looked sheepish. "Caitlin says I fainted after I shot that guy, but just for the record, I was planning to come for you next. Gun blazing, all that."

He sounded like Charlie.

Johnny's hand was still pressed to his abdomen, against his wound. He would have died long ago without her Blood, but he was far from well. Still, when Johnny smiled, his dimple was a crater. He swung his head closer to her ear, his voice private, just for her. "I know you saved me."

Fana's hand felt lost inside Johnny's, and her skin turned to iron. The warmth and dampness of Johnny's touch made her sad. She and Johnny had friendship and history, but they were only meeting each other now.

"Caitlin loves you as a friend, but she'll never feel what you feel," Fana said. It was only fair to tell him. She didn't need to probe Caitlin to know that.

Johnny glanced toward Caitlin, who was across the room with Abena and Sharmila, talking in hushed tones while the boys slept on the bare floor. Caitlin's eyes caught theirs before she looked away. As if she could hear them.

"I know," Johnny said. "But I understand it now. Caitlin brought me to you." Johnny squeezed her hand tightly with unconscious fervor.

You mean she brought you to Glow, Fana thought, unable to silence a cynical voice in her head that wasn't quite her own. Johnny pulled her wrist toward his lips, but Fana knew it would not be a lover's kiss. She wasn't interested in any other kind today.

When Fana slipped her hand away, Johnny looked apologetic. "I'm s-sorry. I—"

She pecked Johnny's lips. "I'm still just Bea-Bea, right?" Fana said. "Lil' Sis?"

Johnny nodded. He understood, but knowing who she was made wonderment twitch his face. "I'll work on that, Fana," he said. His voice barely trembled. "I promise."

The word *promise* hurt, fresh from Michel's mouth. But Fana managed to keep her smile.

"Excuse me, son," Dawit said. His voice was a commandment.

One last shy, overwhelmed smile, and Johnny went back to Caitlin's side.

Dawit steered Fana to a darkened corner of the room. He gazed back at Jessica, who was still near Alex's bed. Her eyes checked in with

Fana every few seconds; Fana felt them on her, always watching. Mom had been watching over her so long that it was all they knew.

Dawit draped his hands across Fana's shoulders. Fana couldn't hold his stare, so she looked toward the sleeping children.

FANA? Her father's projection was clear and powerful. He was still waiting for her to tell him what had happened. Mom had tried, too.

He didn't rape me, she told him. *He could have, but it never came to that.*

Flames sparked in Dawit's eyes, and his jaw was tight. "But he hurt you."

"I hurt him, too," she said. "I struck first."

The fire in his eyes danced. "He's vulnerable, then."

"This isn't a war, Dad."

"It's the very definition of war, Fana."

Fana felt an impulse to whisper, although she knew full well that it didn't matter. A shout, a whisper and a thought were the same in his house.

"A war is a clash between two well-matched opponents," Fana said. *Otherwise, it's called a slaughter,* she finished, out of the others' hearing.

Dawit's face fought irritation and dread. *WHY WOULD WE FAIL?*

Because of him, Fana told him. *He could kill all of us with a thought. Talking freely under his roof is foolish. He's listening to everything. Assume Teka is still his ears.*

Teka believed he had been set free, but he might be wrong. Teka sat in a meditative pose in front of the door, crestfallen, as if he did not deserve to enter the room. Fana probed him—again, much faster than usual, especially considering his forty-foot distance from her—and she didn't find the telltale wall. Still . . .

WE COULD RALLY THE BROTHERHOOD, her father said. *LALIBELA, TOO.*

They're not enough. While we were building clinics, they were building armies.

Her father had always believed that distributing the Blood was more trouble than it was worth, constantly calling for precautions. He had agreed because Jessica had been so committed to the mission. He would do anything for Mom. Dad had gone against everything he'd believed in, all for love. Did he regret it now?

As if her mother knew she was thinking about her, Mom appeared suddenly, slipping her arm around Fana's shoulder. Jessica rocked with Fana, an unspoken salve for the wounds Fana had not talked about yet. She and her mother had never hugged easily, but it was easy now.

Mom leaned upward to press her mouth to Dawit's, kissing him as if she needed his oxygen to breathe. They kissed as if effort would make it last. Fana wasn't used to seeing her parents kiss, except in their memories. Her parents had been through a lot. *There are no fairy tales.* Her parents' kiss was snuffed by their worries.

"Teka wants to counsel us," Dawit said.

"We can never be sure Teka is free of him," Fana said.

"Let's go on and hear what Teka has to say," Jessica said. Her voice was so raw that it was nearly unrecognizable. "Even the devil can tell the truth sometimes."

BLESSED JESSICA, NO WORDS CAN EXPRESS MY SHAME

Before Teka spoke to the circle of concerned faces around him, he sought out Jessica in a torrent of apologies. The sorrow in his thoughts was palpable, steeping inside Jessica's anger. Jessica blinked, but her tear ducts had dried long ago. Her lost friendship with Teka was the least of what she had to mourn today.

I BETRAYED YOU. I BETRAYED FANA. I BETRAYED DAWIT.

Teka's litany went on. Jessica had been so rocked by her mother's death that she'd barely remembered her confrontation with Teka in the comm room. Teka might never have spoken his hidden thoughts without Michel's intervention, but she was sure Teka's longing was genuine.

You're wasting time, Jessica told him. *Say what you need to, or leave us the hell alone.*

Teka sighed and surveyed the people gathered around him: Fana sat between Jessica and Dawit, leaning against their knees. Jessica tried not to be alarmed, but she had never seen Fana so weary. Whatever Fana had been through had nearly torn her to pieces. Was Fana all right? Were any of them?

Jessica hoped that Teferi—and even Mahmoud, God help her—would be returned to them; but for now, they were only twelve. Lucas, Alex, Jared, Caitlin, Johnny and Teferi's family were crowded behind them. Teka's eyes lighted on Fana before he lowered them in deference.

"I can tell you something of the origins of Sanctus Cruor," Teka said, and no one blinked. "Khaldun once told me he committed a story to paper, sealing it with a drop of the Blood. It was the same story Khaldun always told, about Blood stolen from the cross. Khaldun always feared that the Blood was too powerful to be entrusted even to himself, but he wanted to see the Blood's impact on the world. He told me that his letter never reached its intended party, lost. If Sanctus Cruor is a result of his letter, they are proof of Khaldun's fears. So he sent you to Adwa, Dawit."

"But he told us nothing about his letter with the blood and the Ceremony!" Dawit said. "Why did Khaldun send us out blind?"

Teka shook his head; he didn't know.

"Because it wasn't time," Jessica said. "Fana wasn't here yet."

Fana looked up at Jessica over her shoulder, startled. The sweatshirt Jared had given Fana was too big, dwarfing her, and she looked so much smaller, so childlike. Jessica wished she could bundle Fana in her arms and carry her away like she had when she was three. Fana laid her head on Jessica's shoulder, showing a rare vulnerability. Jessica pressed her palm to Fana's cheek.

Jessica continued the story: "When Khaldun met with me and Dawit, he told us that Fana would intervene in a coming war between mortals and immortals. I never understood that—the other Life Brothers are so reclusive that I couldn't see them waging a war with mortals. I remember Khaldun telling us, 'I will not say all that I see.' Well, this is what he kept from us. *These* are the immortals Khaldun knew Fana would face. It was Sanctus Cruor."

A flash of rage ignited in Jessica as she remembered how Khaldun had used her child to conduct social experiments with the Blood. What an impossible burden for Fana!

Teka licked his lips. "As Khaldun's attendant, I knew him as well as any man could. He would not approve of Sanctus Cruor's interpretation of his Letter. But Sanctus Cruor believes the world is too full of sin. They believe they can create Paradise again. Like Eden."

"Through killing?" Jessica said.

"The Day of Judgment is prophesied in other religious books, is it not?" Teka said. "Khaldun may have used the story of the cross because he believed the future Church would safeguard its contents, protecting the Blood from greed and abuse. But that doesn't mean Khaldun's story of the cross is true. Khaldun was a storyteller foremost. He told stories however he believed they would have the most power."

"If he had future sight, he knew his words would create Sanctus Cruor," Jessica said.

"No," Dawit answered her gently. "Khaldun saw much. He did not see everything."

Teka nodded in agreement. Even now, they were quick to forgive Khaldun's chaos.

Jessica suddenly had a headache. It had once astonished her that the Life Brothers weren't convinced their blood was from Christ, but she understood better now: A single man's miracles burned less brightly when you had miraculous blood in your own veins. Even a letter from an eyewitness hadn't created Christlike behavior in Sanctus Cruor! *Do human hands destroy everything we touch?*

Johnny Wright shook his head, stunned. "It's the opposite of Christ," he whispered. "The antithesis."

Jessica shivered. Johnny was a believer, too, and she couldn't have said it better.

"It's called the Cleansing," Fana said. She cleared her throat to speak up. "Eliminating sin. The survivors get the Blood—maybe immortality, too. But Sanctus Cruor chooses who lives and who dies, and they get the glory. He wants to use my gifts to help him."

Teka went on: "I have taught Fana what I can, but aspects of her awakening are not mine to shepherd. If Fana joins with Michel in body, she would also join him in mind. She would learn her hidden reserves, as would he. Exactly what would happen, I cannot say—two beings such as these have never mated. But since Michel is already capable of slaying through mind arts, as is Fana, they would be a formidable weapon."

Jessica glanced at Fana's hollowed face: Fana understood the stakes better than they did. A chorus of outrage erupted from Jared, Johnny and Caitlin, vows that no one was going to touch Fana. Jessica glanced at Dawit for a truer assessment of their options, and he could barely look at her. *We can't stop him,* she realized. A cold knot mushroomed in her stomach.

"There's only one reason anyone in this room is alive," Fana said suddenly. "Because he thinks he loves me. That's our only weapon."

Utter silence.

Fana straightened and pulled herself away from her parents' embrace, standing tall.

"This is our situation: We love Teka as family, but we can't trust him," she said. "Why? Because Michel can influence Teka's mind without his knowledge. He can force us to hurt each other, or ourselves. That's how you got here. That's how Johnny got shot. He can do the same to me, or to any of us here. That's the hard truth, so get used to it."

A coil of fear passed through the group. Alex's face was groggy, but her eyes were rapt.

Fana took a deep breath. "Trickery isn't an option, stealth isn't an option, and neither is violence. Anyone who stands against him will die. Caitlin and Johnny only survived because Michel was preoccupied with me." Jessica saw a painful memory cross Fana's face, and her agony rocked Jessica, too. "Michel is overconfident, but he won't make that mistake again. Dozens of Life Brothers wouldn't be enough to stand up to him."

Lucas raised his hand and spoke calmly and thoughtfully, ever the scientist. "But if it's the same blood and the same circumstances of birth, why is Michel so advanced?"

"Teka teaches mind arts through a higher plane," Fana said. "The Rising. Teka's process is deep and pure, but it's slow. Michel's only teachers were his father—who is *vile*—and a force we call the Shadows. The force is real, and it's been calling to me since I was three. But there's a reason Teka was careful to steer me from the Shadows: Michel's lost inside of them now."

Was that compassion in Fana's voice?

"You can use the Shadows, too, Fana," Teka said. "It may be the only way."

Fana's eyes sparked at Teka. "Is that your advice, Teacher? Or is it Michel's?"

Teka lowered his eyes and sighed. He couldn't tell the difference himself.

Fana looked at Jessica, squarely but softly. "I felt the Shadows when I fought with Michel, and they made me stronger. But they're too dangerous. Right, Mom?"

Jessica nodded, blinking away stubborn tears. The devil never gave a gift for free. Jessica had felt the Shadows when Fana had been possessed as a young child, and she had learned enough about the invisible force. Jessica was glad she had passed on to Fana the simple lesson Bea had passed to her and Alex, the lesson from their parents before them: Follow God.

"Fana . . . ," Dawit said. "You've said only what we cannot do. What's left for us?"

"Not for *us*, Dad," Fana said. "For me."

Jessica felt her soul sway, drifting toward an unnavigable ocean. Jessica suddenly knew her daughter's heart and mind. She reeled, dreading Fana's words.

"I need to clean up and get dressed," Fana said. "Michel has invited us to dinner."

FIRST SUPPER

Beware that no one lead you astray saying

Lo here or lo there!

For the Son of Man is within you.
—Coptic Gospels, *Gospel of Mary*

Thirty-seven

One last pin, and Caitlin cinched the white cotton dress around Fana's waist, flaring out the skirt. The housekeeper who'd brought the dress to Fana's bathroom had looked terrified, so Caitlin wanted Fana to look nice for that woman's sake. Her life might depend on it.

Caitlin gazed at herself in the tall mirror's reflection: She was standing behind Fana, looking blue-skinned and fuck-eyed. But Fana was regal and tranquil in a traditional Mexican dress that hung smartly just past her knees, embroidered by a servant's hand. Thirty silk bows made Fana's hair a crown. She was a vision.

"How do I look?" Fana said.

Like Maritza, Caitlin thought. On their imaginary wedding day.

"He'll approve," Caitlin said, since she knew that was what Fana wanted to hear.

Fana smiled, but her smile was iron. "Good," she said.

Fana had spent only a short time with Michel, but already Caitlin didn't recognize her. Especially her new smile. Caitlin couldn't imagine smiling anytime soon.

"Aren't you scared, Fana?" Caitlin said.

Fana gazed at her reflection for a long time, pondering the question with vacant eyes. *Is she tranced out? Does he still have a hold over her?*

"No, I'm not scared," Fana said finally. "I don't feel anything."

"What will you say to him?"

Silence. Fana pressed her fingers against the creases on her dress, smoothing them neatly. It took Caitlin a moment to realize that Fana wasn't going to answer.

"I have some advice, if you still care what a shortie thinks," Caitlin said, although Fana was far beyond any place where she would hear anyone's advice. She didn't wait for Fana's answer. "Don't do anything crazy, like marrying this guy. That's what he wants. That's how it begins. I *know*, Fana—he was in my head, too."

For the first time, Caitlin saw a blank sheet fall across Fana's features, hiding any trace of her thoughts. Fana's entire face was her mask now.

Caitlin sighed. "I know you'll do whatever you think is right," she said. "But if I get the idea you're not really you—if I think he's playing mind games to get what he wants—don't expect me to just sit there. Or your parents. Or Johnny. We're all in this, Fana."

That broke through. Fana looked sad, even angry. "Don't you think I know that?"

"Yeah, well . . . I can't promise I'll be on my best behavior."

Fana grabbed Caitlin's upper arm with surprising strength. Fana's eyes were steely suddenly. If Caitlin hadn't just survived the fight of her life, Fana's eyes might have scared her.

"Then stay away from him," Fana said. "Don't complicate my life. This is hard enough."

"I just want to get your blood to sick people. That's all I've ever wanted, Fana."

The glint in Fana's eyes melted.

"All of this is for Glow," Fana said. "'If you get hungry, keep going.'" Maybe she was still Fana.

Caitlin wouldn't let her tears come. "'If you get tired, keep going.'"

Someone knocked quietly on the door, probably Fana's parents.

"Be careful, Fana," Caitlin whispered.

When Fana hugged her, it felt exactly like good-bye.

A giant oval mirror with fleur-de-lis etched around its gilded frame hung above the antique gold vessel sink and polished elegance of the Italian marble vanity. A feast for the eyes.

A shiny dream in the midst of Jessica's nightmare.

The Shadows smelled rancid, an odor Jessica would never forget from the night she'd huddled with an altered version of Fana while a hurricane had howled outside her mother's house. That stench was everywhere now, as if sewage lines had burst beneath the church.

Maybe it was damage from the earthquake. Or maybe not. It would be impossible to know anything for certain, at least for a while.

But Fana was lovely. That was certain, anyway.

Fana clasped Jessica's hand, her eyes ready for counsel. Fana looked ready to listen for the first time since Jessica could remember, and Jessica didn't like what she was about to say.

"Everything may not come out all right, Fana," Jessica said. "It already hasn't."

Bea's ghost seemed to walk across the room, admiring the way Fana's dress accentuated her hips. *Jessica, where is this girl's lipstick?* As if her mother's hands were guiding her, Jessica opened a drawer beneath the sink and found piles of newly purchased cosmetics. Most of the makeup was useless to Jessica, but she found a tube of lipstick. Rose-red. Mom would approve. Jessica traced Fana's lips until they were bright and costumed like the rest of her.

"He almost killed you, didn't he?" Jessica said. No one had told her plainly.

"Almost," Fana said matter-of-factly. She was deep inside her head, but not like before. She wasn't hiding; she was preparing herself. "I tried to kill him first. Like Kaleb."

No wonder there had been so much blood on Fana's clothes! Kaleb's blood had made a river in the passageway at the Lalibela Colony. That was the first time the Life Brothers had realized how easily they could die, too. Maybe Fana had helped them decide to spend their centuries doing something other than meditating and worshiping the man who'd given them the Living Blood.

"This burden isn't yours, Fana," Jessica said. "I don't care if Khaldun said it, or the man on the moon. If there's going to be a war between mortals and immortals, the whole world will cross that bridge next. Right now, we're going to get you away from him."

"I'm the only one he'll listen to," Fana said.

"He might, sweetheart, or he might not," Jessica said. "This dinner invitation is a good sign, I think. Maybe it'll inspire civility, and both sides can talk. But . . ." Jessica sighed. Her message had seemed straightforward enough when she'd rehearsed it outside of the bathroom's arched doorway. "Fana, listen to me: You may have to watch people you love die. Me. Your father. Any of us. No matter how much it hurts, don't give him a reason to kill you. Mom knew it was her time: It's not your time yet, sweetheart."

Fana blinked and nodded. All childish defiance was gone. "Because I have to prevent the Cleansing?" Fana said, searching for her purpose.

Jessica shook her head. "No. Because you're my baby girl. It's not your time."

Fana smiled, and the rosy lipstick burst to life for an instant before her smile faded.

Jessica hugged Fana, who had to lean down to meet her. The Shadows might have contaminated this church, but Fana smelled as fresh as a new morning. Their hearts beat in calm, steady concert. Had they found stillness at last? Jessica felt as if she could sit on the floor and meditate for twenty-four hours straight—all she'd have to do was remember her conversations with Bea, cataloguing everything she would miss about her mother. But there was no time for stillness here. Jessica hated to ask Fana to use her gifts now, but she had to know. "Teka says he sent the Duharts away before his breakdown . . ."

Fana nodded. "They're alive. I feel it. He's telling the truth."

Thank you, Jesus.

"Caitlin says you had a dream about this," Jessica said. "Can you see the future, Fana?"

"I see things in dreams sometimes," Fana said. "But I don't always know what they mean. And I didn't see this." Fana's eyes grew dull. Even now, she didn't like to talk about her gifts—a reminder of their differences.

Jessica laced their fingers together. It was difficult for Jessica to believe that she'd had a role in creating this amazing young woman. "You know, Fana, you may not remember, but during those years you were in trance, I used to sit and read you stories. There was a children's book about Harriet Tubman."

"Black Moses," Fana said. "I remember every book you ever read me, Mom."

Fana's gentle voice tried to assure Jessica that she had been a good mother, despite the fears inspired by the hurricane and the Shadows.

"How many people did you and Caitlin help with the Underground Railroad, Pumpkin?" Jessica said, using Bea's favorite nickname for Fana. Bea's ghost was still in the room, a part of their conversation. Fana could probably convey a message to her if they had time.

"Thousands." Fana's lip quivered with escaped emotion. "All over North America."

"And was it worth it to you? Knowing what you know now?"

Fana's smile brought a brilliant light to her face. To the room. To Jessica's heart.

"It's worth it no matter what, Mom," Fana said. "Even if we only helped one."

Yes, Jessica thought, pressing Fana's hand. *Sacrifice.*

Jessica held on as Fana's electricity churned beneath her fingertips. She would never again be afraid to touch Fana's power. She would embrace all of Fana, as long as she was able.

Jessica and her mysterious and wonderful second-born had never been different. Why had she ever thought so?

For better or worse, she and Fana were exactly alike.

Uniformed doorkeepers pulled open the doors to the dining hall, and Fana heard the unlikely sound of children singing, enhanced by a string quintet. The piping, carefree voices sang Pachelbel's Canon in D at a celebratory tempo, a cascade of angelic harmonies.

Fana's chest almost swelled, until she saw the children's faces.

The thirty elementary-age children lined up inside the doorway couldn't have looked more disheveled if they had been roused from sleep at gunpoint. The young children were sleepy, their white and blue school uniforms rumpled. It was after two o'clock in the morning!

He can't be decent even when he tries, Fana thought.

Fana felt his big, boiling presence in the room. She smiled at the children, but she made sure her mask was intact. If he wanted to see through her, she couldn't stop him—but at least he would know he wasn't invited. Fana kept her eyes straight ahead, between her parents' shoulders. She wanted to be sitting down when she first saw his face.

Fana walked two paces behind her parents into the dining hall, which looked hazy and undefined inside her mask, nearly sepia. The rest walked behind her in pairs—Uncle Lucas and Aunt Alex; Johnny and Caitlin; and Teferi and Mahmoud, who were barely strong enough to stand. The Life Brothers were fresh from waking, but both had insisted on being there. Teferi and Mahmoud leaned on each other. Fana only casually noted the irony that Mahmoud had once tried to kill her. Now Mahmoud was here to try to preserve their family.

Fana's party came unarmed except for her father's knife, but Fana felt weapons around the room: The doorkeepers. The servers. Even the cellist and a violinist were armed, she realized. Sanctus Cruor enjoyed its guns.

Part of the room was hidden behind a theater-sized curtain, still unfinished, but the visible half was gilded with sparkles and rich fabrics. The hall smelled of garlic and tomatoes, and not a hint of meat. The tables were long twins arranged across from each other, a dozen tea candles lined across each. Dawit's palm guided Fana to her seat at the center of their table, and she was glad to sit. Movement was awkward under heavy masking.

Michel was masking, too.

He was sitting directly across from her, six feet away, dressed in a silken white robe with the crest of his Order on his breast—a cross with a teardrop of blood. His eyes were carefully removed from hers as he talked to his father beside him. A beautiful black girl wearing an Ethiopian scarf sat on the other side of Michel.

Michel's mother! The eyelashes, lush like her son's, gave her away. She barely looked eighteen. She could be her twin sister, Fana realized. *No wonder he fell for me so fast.* Teru had a pleasant smile fixed to her face, but her eyes were unfocused. Fana wanted to probe her, but she didn't dare provoke Michel. She knew enough from his memories: Teru was a prisoner, trapped inside her mind.

Teru's eyes swept aimlessly across the room, landing on Fana's.

Her face didn't change, but she inclined her head half an inch. Fana nodded back, low and polite, but Teru's eyes were gone before Fana looked up again.

Fana stared at the girl-woman's high-cheeked profile, so much like hers. Michel was holding his mother's hand, she noticed, twining their fingers. *He really thinks he loves her.*

Michel's eyes stayed distant, his neck craned away from Fana as he spoke to his father, who wore a crimson robe and matching skullcap. Stefan's frigid face told her that he couldn't wait to have everyone at her table killed—and then chain her to his son's bed.

Fana's heart kicked. Her limbs drew inward as she slouched down, small. Mom squeezed her hand beneath the table in silent support. After long seconds, Fana could sit up straight again.

Michel glanced at her while she slouched, but his eyes fled with a blink when she caught him. *Good.* He couldn't help looking at her either. Maybe he was worried about her. Maybe he really was ashamed. She needed his worry and shame, or everything was lost.

Fana ventured her first words to him.

If there is any kindness in you, I need a real demonstration tonight—not just the singing voices of sleepy children. She wanted to take the chide back as soon as it flew out.

Michel's eyes slashed her, striking a blow before they drifted away again.

Fana's heart pounded. *I'm asking for mercy, Michel. Please don't make me like your mother.* This time, Michel didn't glance her way.

Mahmoud and Teferi staggered to the seats directly across from Bocelli and Romero, who now wore dark tailored suits instead of monks' robes. The dinner had been delayed so that Michel's attendants could awaken after their encounter with Johnny. The four healing immortals were weakened but angry, trading glares. Johnny and Caitlin watched Michel's attendants with nervousness, protecting each other as best they could by sitting close, staring daggers.

Dad sat beside Fana, across from Michel's father, and their history was plain on their faces, too. Dad had killed Michel's father twice before, and he wanted a chance to get it right.

Stefan sounded a small bell, and the angry silence in the room became a mandate. The children's clothes rustled as they were ushered through the doors. To bed, Fana hoped.

"*Benedetto sia il Sangue,*" Stefan said.

Everyone at Michel's table repeated the Italian words, except his mother. The language was different, but Fana recognized the words Gramma Bea had finished every mealtime grace with: *Bless the Blood.* They were strangers to each other, but Khaldun had made them cousins.

Stefan stood. With careful precision, he lowered himself to his knees, at Michel's feet. He gazed upward, arms extended in posed piety, as if he could see the sky. "And so it was written, 'One day shall be born a child of the Blood. And he will be a male child. Of all the creatures who walk, he will be the Most High.'"

Fear's claw assailed Fana. The room grew cold, draping her bare arms in gooseflesh. Fana had never read the Letter of the Witness, but Michel's memories in her head echoed Stefan's words: "And it was also written, 'He will wait fifty rains to meet his mate. And she will be known by the name of Light.'"

Fana meant "*light*" in Amharic! She had chosen that name for herself when she was three. *Even my name is in the Letter.* That thought flew into Fana's mind just as a flock of white doves was released above them, flapping toward the rafters. Specks of down floated above them.

"'And so a man and woman, mates immortal born, will create an eternal union at the advent of the New Days. And all of mankind shall know them as the bringers of the Blood.' So says the Witness . . . and so it has come to pass."

Stefan prostrated himself before Michel, eyes closed. Then Stefan stood up and raised a shot glass. "To the New Days," he said, gazing at Dawit with a sardonic gleam in his eye.

Before Fana could send him a warning, Dad was on his feet. "Our women, children and mortals should be released," Dad said. "Nothing to be said among us concerns them."

Michel kept his eyes away from Fana, but his jaw flexed hard.

Stefan smiled a bitter smile at Dawit. "Every word spoken here concerns your entire party, *mi amico,*" he said. "Don't test my hospitality."

Sit down, Dad.

Fana's private command. Reluctantly, Dawit sat.

Stefan's face warred between anger and phony civility. He sat, too. "I will speak for the Most High. Who speaks for Fana?"

"*We do,*" Jessica said. Her voice rang in the hall. "Her parents."

Contempt played on Stefan's lips as he gave Dawit a mocking gaze. "She speaks for you?"

"No more delays," Dad said. "This treatment is an outrage."

Stefan's eyes were ice. "Be glad the Most High is kinder than his father."

"Be glad your son is not so easily slain," Dawit said, and Mahmoud chuckled. Romero and Bocelli snapped warnings to Mahmoud in Italian.

"Or so easily captured," Stefan said.

"Soldiers are a great advantage to the weak," Dawit said. "With the exception of that feeble army at Adwa, as I remember."

"Adwa was a different time, African," Stefan said, teeth gritted.

"We're all tired," Jessica said, interrupting their volley. "It's late. Our family is grieving. We've tried to respect your traditions, but you have no right to keep us here. Please let us go." Mom was the best diplomat Fana knew.

MARRY ME TONIGHT, Michel said to Fana. *AND YOUR PEOPLE ARE FREE.*

Fana glanced at Michel, startled. Even now, Michel's eyes stayed away while he languidly dipped his flat bread in olive oil. His smooth face stung her with Charlie's image.

You know I can't do that, Fana said.

Michel flung the bread to his plate, annoyed. His sudden movement made her jump.

Stefan's father bickered with her parents, but Fana only heard Michel's breathing.

YOU ARE VERY CARELESS WITH YOUR LOVED ONES, FANA.

Threats are your father's language. Try to find your own.

AND BRAZEN! YOU SPEAK YOUR FATHER'S LANGUAGE TOO.

"Fana will be wed to the Most High!" Stefan said, suddenly shouting as he looked at her. "This dinner is only a gesture of goodwill. What is written is what shall be!"

Don't let him speak for you, Michel. Talk to me.

HAVEN'T I TRIED?

Look at me, Michel.

At last, his eyes rested on hers, large and brown, the color of sandalwood, swathed in his mother's thicket of black eyelashes. Fana's skin charged under his gaze, even now.

I came to offer you my terms, Michel.

He muted a condescending smile. His dismissal made her angry, but she carefully filtered anger from her thoughts before she went on: *No good would come of a marriage between us tonight. The only way you can keep me here is against my will. Is that the marriage you want?*

I WANT THE UNION THAT WAS PROPHESIED.

And I want to be a Bringer of the Blood.

THEN YOUR FEARS ARE ANSWERED IN THE LETTER.

I was three when I told my parents I wanted to change my name to Fana, which means "light." During that time my first teacher, Khaldun, visited me regularly through meditation. My parents believe his visits may have awakened my gifts prematurely.

I SAW THAT IN YOUR MEMORIES.

Khaldun wrote that letter, Michel.

WHAT WOULD THAT CHANGE?

Maybe he helped his own prophecy come true. He was guiding me.

GUIDING YOU TO ME, FANA.

Fana sighed. Was Michel right? Had she been destined to be paired with Michel hundreds of years before she was born?

Michel's face softened, and he leaned forward slightly. *I WILL NOT TOUCH YOUR MASK. MARRY ME TONIGHT, AND YOU WILL KEEP A SEPARATE CHAMBER.*

I would never adjust to something I didn't choose.

A silent server slipped beside Fana and ladled tomato soup into her bowl. Fana's gaze with Michel never broke, even as the thick-boned woman came in and out of her vision.

I WOULD WAIT FOR YOU TO FEEL AT HOME HERE.

You are not patient, Michel.

I WILL LEARN.

Bocelli and Romero joined the chorus of arguing voices at the table. Silverware clattered when Romero slapped his palm on the table.

She and Michel had worked it out just in time, Fana thought. She wasn't sure how she should feel about her decision, but she was glad a decision had come.

"Silence, please."

Fana spoke aloud for the first time. Her heart thundering, she pushed her chair back and stood to preside over her future. She raised her water glass. "Michel and I are to be married. As of tonight, we are engaged."

Michel looked stunned. *ENGAGED?* As if the word were foreign to him.

Jessica tugged Fana's elbow hard, but Fana ignored her mother's silent plea.

"We will marry at a future time," Fana said. "Mutually agreed upon."

SIX MONTHS, Michel offered.

Ten years, Fana told him gently. She would prefer to delay by twenty years, or fifty, but he would never agree. Even now, Michel sat ramrod straight, flushed with anger again.

Fana went on: "During our engagement, I will be free to live and do as I please. I will conduct my blood mission without interference from Sanctus Cruor, or Sanctus Cruor's agencies. If Sanctus Cruor hurts any parties involved in my mission, or patients who have received my blood, the engagement is called off."

Stefan barked a laugh. "This child is mad!"

Fana didn't hear the rest. Her mother whispered *no* in one ear, her father in the other.

ONE YEAR, Michel said. *NO MORE. YOUR MISSION CONFLICTS WITH THE LETTER. "WREST THIS BLOOD FROM THE HANDS OF THE WICKED."*

"My guiding principle," Fana said, ignoring Michel, "will be the words of our great teacher, Khaldun, as he wrote in the document you know as the Letter of the Witness: 'All of mankind will know them as the Bringers of the Blood.'"

Her recitation of the Letter brought silence to the room.

"Our engagement will last ten years," Fana said.

Michel shot to his feet, and the fury in his eyes made Fana's knees weak. She might be bleeding soon, or her parents, or she might feel Michel piloting her face toward his for a kiss. It took all of Fana's will to hold Michel's gaze without stammering. "At the end of that engagement, if I am in love with Michel, we will marry."

"You play dangerous games, child," Stefan said.

"It's not a game," Fana said. "Those are my terms. Now, you will release us."

All eyes were on Michel, who braced himself on closed fists on the tabletop as he leaned closer to her. Mom clung to Fana's hand as if to protect her from a blow, and Dad coiled his fingers around his knife. If Dad twitched, Michel would happily plunge the knife into his throat to punish him for hurting Stefan.

The world felt fragile, suddenly.

LOVE HAS NO SAY IN THIS, Michel said. *IF I ALLOW YOU TO WALK AWAY TONIGHT, IF I ALLOW ALL YOU ASK, YOU WILL RETURN TO MARRY ME.*

Fana avoided her parents' eyes, but she glanced toward Johnny, who looked aghast, as everyone at her table did. Johnny was a good person, as strong in his way as Michel was in his. Fana would have chosen a man more like Johnny.

I agree, she said so only Michel could hear.

THREE YEARS. Michel still believed he had room to bargain.

It's ten years, Michel. You say we will rule for eternity, but you can't wait for me a decade? This is your testament of love. If you do not love me, make me your prisoner now. But I warn you, I will destroy myself at my first chance. I can make you the happiest man who has ever lived, or the loneliest. You have seen what we can be together. The choice is yours.

Neither of them blinked. Fana's nervous heart squeezed a river through her veins.

Michel's face knitted as his red-faced father whispered harshly in his ear. But Michel's eyes never left hers, and as long as she had his eyes, she had a chance. Let him learn her face and bright lips. Let him appreciate her carefully prepared dress. Was the promise of a future enough? Michel gently made a brushing motion against his father's shoulder, pushing him away. Michel raised his water glass high, mirroring Fana's toast.

"To our engagement," Michel said. The only three words he spoke aloud.

Their glasses sang merrily when they touched, but neither Fana nor Michel smiled.

Thirty-eight

The chartered bus arrived in the courtyard in the pitch of night, hissing on air brakes. Dawit and his Brothers stood in a line to shield the others, and the quick boarding was conducted in a deathly hush. Abena and Sharmila passed Teferi's sleeping boys to him, and he laid them in their seats. Hopefully, they would wake in Nogales, at dawn.

So few lights were on inside of the massive church that it was nearly invisible.

Sanctus Cruor's believers—the priests, cooks, gardeners, painters and supplicants who were faithful because of the promise of healing and rumors of miracles—lined up at a distance to watch them go, whispering tales from the dining hall. Romero and Bocelli watched, too, from the church steps. Dawit didn't see the soldiers, but he knew everyone in sight was armed.

Dawit was glad that Stefan and Michel had not come outside. Those men's faces were hard to look at, and Dawit did not want to shatter his daughter's painfully brokered peace. Dawit had faced Stefan once outside of Adwa and once in Seattle, and either encounter might have prevented this day. The difference felt as thin as a blade of grass.

"Another day, Brother," Mahmoud said, following Dawit's eyes to the darkened church doors. Mahmoud's voice was a rasp. He was still weak from his sleep, but he squeezed Dawit's shoulder with fortifying strength. "We always have another day."

Lucas and Jared helped Alex climb the steps to the bus, and Caitlin and Johnny Wright boarded next, dazed and sleepy, but eager to go.

Caitlin's gaze at Dawit was furtive. She did not trust him yet. One day, he would apologize to her about the way he had treated her father. Dawit hoped Teka could retrieve Justin's memories as he said he could. Caitlin should decide if she still wanted her father to follow wherever their journey would take them next.

Jessica leaned against Dawit. Her eyes were red and exhausted, heartbreaking. He held her as tightly as he dared, breathing the night's spoiled air with her. When he rested his head atop hers, Jessica took his hand and held it to her breast.

They hadn't spoken about it yet. There was nothing to say.

Their days were getting longer.

Jima was waiting at Nogales International Airport with the colony's plane, but Dawit trusted no one else to fly, just as he trusted no one else to drive the bus. Jima and Teka were more practiced pilots, but he would fly the jet himself. They must get far from here, and soon.

They weren't safe in Mexico. They might not be safe anywhere.

For now, Lalibela. *Home.*

The blood mission must belong to all of them now, not only a few. The Lalibela Council had far greater resources, and they would need a mountain of money for their undertaking. The mission was expensive. Armies were expensive, too.

The New Days were coming, whatever they might be.

Fana came to the bus last, behind her friends. She had replaced her dress from dinner with her soiled jeans and Jared's too-big Oxford sweatshirt. She looked like a freshman on her way to school. How Dawit wished she had been!

But Khaldun had warned them from the beginning: Fana was not an ordinary child, and she would not have an ordinary life.

I'M SORRY, DADDY. Fana's voice whispered in his head.

Nothing to be sorry for, Princess.

Dawit smiled at her, and she smiled back with her face that, to him, had never changed.

A chorus of crickets clamored from the woods, and the moon glowed bright above them.

For an instant, it felt like an ordinary night.

• • •

No one answered at his house, so Johnny tried calling his father's cell phone next. The ringing stopped so abruptly that Johnny thought the call had been cut off, until he heard his father suck in his breath: "Johnny?"

His father said he'd gotten a 3 a.m. call from the Department of Homeland Security. He was driving to the FBI office in Jacksonville, where Johnny's mother would be released from custody. Johnny told him he was fine, promised he hadn't killed anyone, and said he would call the next time he had a chance. It wasn't enough to wring the worry from his father's voice.

"You have to trust me, Dad," Johnny said. "I've seen a miracle."

That was all he had time to say. Fana's mother had warned them to keep the calls short. Caitlin had only called Johannesburg long enough to hear her father's voice, too.

Johnny gave the satellite phone back to the tall, tired man holding his young son.

Teferi. Teka. Mahmoud. Dawit. The names would take some getting used to.

The bus lurched around a tight turn on the mountain road, and Fana's father grunted at the steering wheel. The Africans were alert at the front of the bus, watching the road through dark windows. Fana's father had said there might be soldiers in the woods. He and his friends spoke quietly to each other in their language, preparing for war.

Fana's mother was asleep with her face against the window while a boy slept with his head on her lap. She had fought sleep, refusing to lie down, but she had earned her rest. Johnny saw her sadness on her face even while she slept. Grief was hard.

Fana and her parents might live forever, but some days felt like death anyway.

God makes a way out of no way, Johnny reminded himself. "Thank you, Lord," Johnny whispered.

The back of the bus was lively with conversation. The closer Johnny walked to the voices, the faster his heart sped. His injury still ached—although not as much, as if it had been weeks old—but Johnny felt light-headed with excitement, not pain.

Lucas Shepard had found a scrap of legal paper, and he was

scrawling Xs in a makeshift map, holding it against the window. Fana's aunt and cousin were huddled in back, too, squeezed beside Caitlin as she watched them write, eyes attentive. The fervor Johnny felt growing between them was powerful enough to light the pre-dawn sky.

". . . our plan to wipe out AIDS," Doc Shepard was saying. "But we'll need a much more aggressive program. No more cherry-picking."

His wife sat beside him, nestled beneath his arm. She was tall, like her husband, and her Afro reminded Johnny of photos he had seen of Angela Davis, back in the day. A revolutionary. "We go in strong," Alex said, pointing to Xs on the map. "Chicago. Los Angeles. New York. Sierra Leone. Kenya. Tanzania."

"I can be in Dar es Salaam in two days," Jared said.

"And we rely on no one," Caitlin said, ever cautious. "Our people are on the ground."

Johnny felt his mind stretch to its limits, but it didn't break. Within his lifetime—within his hearing!—he was in the company of people planning the future of the world.

Fana sat behind them in a row by herself, eyes closed, but Johnny knew she was listening because she was nodding her head. The others looked as exuberant as a Sunday-morning choir, but Fana's face was empty. Fana licked her lips, her eyes still closed. "I'll meet with the leaders in person. The health ministers. The presidents. Once I'm in the room with them . . ."

Her voice trailed off, but she didn't have to finish. At dinner, Johnny had learned that Fana could influence anyone to do any-thing. *Did you find a way to control him the way he controlled me? Is that why he let us go?*

Johnny slid into the empty seat beside Fana. The damp, gleam-ing spots of blood on the kneecaps of her jeans reminded him of why he couldn't help staring at her; it wasn't just because her face had captured all of her parents' best features. Johnny hoped she wouldn't mind his stare.

Fana's bloody clothes made Johnny think of Him, and shiv-ers banded his bones. Johnny's throat and stomach locked, as if he would be sick. That feeling wouldn't go away soon.

"He's making plans, too," Johnny whispered to Fana, out of the others' hearing. "The Cleansing. Ten years will be here before we know it. Do you have a plan for that, Fana?"

Fana was quiet so long that Johnny thought she hadn't heard. Or that she had drifted to sleep.

"Learn," Fana said finally. "Grow."

She reached for his hand and held it, sisterly. That was all it took. Johnny believed in her.

There was something about Fana's touch.

It was exactly like sunlight.

Fana wears the artist's dress from a painting she loved at first sight: The traditional embroidered dress is bright red, flowing out into a long skirt with careful white creases, as lovely as a wedding dress. Fana sits in the center of a bed of cactuses and wide-leafed plants as green as life. From Mexico, she remembers.

The church sits high above her, behind the moon. The sky is half light, half shadow.

Michel sits next to her, uninvited. Like the man in the painting, he is nude; golden brown skin set against green. She turns away from his beckoning skin, but his face fills her vision.

"I don't want you in my dream," she says.

"Yes, you do," he says. "I felt your dream call me, so I came to say good-bye."

There is no way to know if he's telling the truth, so Fana decides to believe him. Again.

"Don't follow us," Fana says.

"I promised not to interfere," Michel says. "But of course I have to follow you."

The white Spanish Mission–style church looks like a palace atop the hill, encircled by dead, craggy trees. The sky's clouds are thick, aflame with twinkles of green lightning. The skies are preparing for a hurricane. In the bell tower, two bronze bells toll in cacophony, swinging in opposite directions. Roaring winds devour their sour music.

"Our ways are so different, Fana," he says. "How can you ever love me?"

"*One of us has to die, Michel.*"

His face clouds with the memory of their struggle. "*You promised me,*" *he said.*

"*I don't think I could kill you if I wanted to,*" *she says.* "*Even if I had fifty years to learn. But it's like the song said: 'With you I'll go my saintly one / Though it may cause me to die.' One of us has to let go of what we were. One of us has to change.*"

"*Or both of us,*" *he says, wisely.*

Townspeople flee the thrashing rains, but the doors to the church are locked. A man and woman lean out of the dome's window, only their silhouettes visible in the Shadows as they gaze down at the people below. The townspeople surge to a throng. Many of them hold small children above their heads, begging for shelter. Others are thin and frail, reeking of illness.

"*Good people are suffering,*" *she says.*

"*Yes,*" *he sighs, genuine sadness.* "*I do mourn for the Good.*"

"*They're thirsty, Michel, and we have water. We can be the Bringers of the Blood.*"

"*Yes,*" *he says, enraptured.*

"*And we know each other's minds,*" *she says.* "*We can see through each other's eyes.*"

"*Yes.*" *His whisper bathes her from head to toe.*

Fana smells Michel's breath, a scent of mango. More tart than before, but still mango.

"*Then time will tell,*" *she says.*

In the church dome, the man and woman open their arms to welcome the storm, which drenches the townspeople. Their upturned faces are pelted with raindrops.

The rain is the color of blood.

Acknowledgments

First, heartfelt thanks to the faithful readers who began this journey with *My Soul to Keep* in 1997 and followed Jessica and Dawit to *The Living Blood* in 2001. I know it took many years to revisit my immortals' story with *Blood Colony,* but I wanted to have a story worth telling. Hopefully, the wait will not be nearly as long next time.

It took a village to create this novel. I enlisted assistance from many corners; but any mistakes contained herein are the fault of the author, not my sources.

Thanks to my husband, novelist Steven Barnes, for his ready and willing wizard's mind. He always suspected there were other immortals lurking out there somewhere! He is my living proof that our predestined mates are waiting for us.

Thanks to Darryl Miller, a writer, reader and editor, whose dedicated page-by-page input was more helpful than I can put into words. I don't always listen, Darryl, but you are a lifesaver. Thanks so much!

Thanks to writer and Senior Editor Robert Vamosi, an award-winning columnist for CNet, who first mentioned the names Octavia E. Butler and Harlan Ellison to me when we were undergraduates at Northwestern University in the 1980s. Thanks for your input on near-future technology, and for your constant support since our days in CRC.

Thanks to Dr. Lee Pachter, cohead of the division of general pediatrics at the University of Connecticut School of Medicine, and lecturer on pediatrics at Harvard Medical School. He is also a pediatric researcher at the Connecticut Children's Medical Center in

Hartford, Connecticut. His research interests include multicultural health care and sociocultural influences on child health. Not only did he lend medical expertise, but he served as a sounding board on the social implications of Glow.

Also, thanks to Dawit Worku, a reader and writer from Ethiopia who, like Lee, first contacted me through email as a reader. Thank you for your input on Ethiopian culture and history, especially the Battle of Adwa. (For readers who would like to learn more about the Battle of Adwa, I also suggest the documentary *Adwa: An African Victory*, released in 1999 by director Haile Gerima. It can be hard to find, but it's worth seeing! Try www.sankofastore.com.)

I gave myself a crash course on the history of Christianity while I was writing this novel. I would especially like to acknowledge the lectures of Professor Luke Timothy Johnson of Emory University in his course Jesus and the Gospels, which is offered through The Teaching Company. I also enjoyed the lectures of Professor Bart D. Ehrman, from the University of North Carolina at Chapel Hill, in his course Lost Christianities: Christian Scriptures and the Battles over Authentication, also offered by The Teaching Company. If you love learning on many college-level subjects, visit www.TEACH12.com.

For musical inspiration, thanks to the group Conjunto Céspedes and its album *Una Sola Casa* for its beautiful version of the Cuban classic "Lágrimas Negras."

For translations, thanks to Lydia Martin, Dan Moran and Giovanni Micheletto. For advance reading, thanks to Amy Stout Moran, Trisha R. Thomas and Leslie Banks. Also, thanks to my golden circle of longtime friends: Olympia Duhart, Luchina Fisher, Kathryn Larrabee, Craig Shemin and Sharmila Roy. Thanks to Blair Underwood, Nia Hill and D'Angela Steed, for their trials and commitment on the battlefield called Hollywood. Thanks to Blanche Richardson at Marcus Books in Oakland, just because. And thanks to Harlan Ellison, for his vision, friendship and generosity of spirit.

At Atria Books and Simon & Schuster, Inc., thanks to Malaika Adero, Krishan Trotman and Judith Curr, for always believing in me and my work. It has been wonderful to have a place to call "home."

Thanks also ___ my _____ _____ ___ __ _hn Hawkins and Associates; ___ _____ _____ _ _____ of The Gotham Group in L__ A_____ ___ _____ _____

Thank__ t_ _____ ____ _ghts activist __oh_ 1 Due and Patricia Stephen_ ____ _____ f__ example in h_ow t_ create social change. And thanks ___ my sisters, Johnita Due and Lydia Due Greisz, for carrying on the fight for a better world in their own ways.

Thanks to Nicki and Jason, for reminding me every day that the future matters.

Last, I would like to thank all of my readers who will vote in 2008 and beyond. I am happy to report that I believe the actual world of 2015 need not be as trying as the world *Blood Colony* depicts . . . but much of that will be up to us.

It is long past time for universal health care in the United States. Period. Rather than believing empty rhetoric and scare tactics, I urge my readers to investigate the systems in other industrialized nations—we are the only holdout—and draw their own conclusions. Then vote for the leader who will help us all build the future we deserve.

The Living Blood is a creation of my imagination. Unlike Fana, we are not immortals. We will all age. We will all get sick one day.

Luckily, we don't have to be like Fana to change the world.

www.tananarivedue.com
TheLivingBlood@aol.com